BACK WHERE
HE STARTED

BACK WHERE
HE STARTED

✤

JAY QUINN

alyson books
NEW YORK

MANUFACTURED IN THE UNITED STATES OF AMERICA.

THIS TRADE PAPERBACK IS PUBLISHED BY ALYSON BOOKS,
P.O. BOX 1253, OLD CHELSEA STATION, NEW YORK, NEW YORK 10113-1251.
DISTRIBUTION IN THE UNITED KINGDOM BY
  TURNAROUND PUBLISHER SERVICES LTD.,
UNIT 3, OLYMPIA TRADING ESTATE, COBURG ROAD, WOOD GREEN,
LONDON N22 6TZ ENGLAND.

FIRST EDITION (HARD COVER): APRIL 2005
FIRST PAPERBACK EDITION: MARCH 2006

06 07 08 09 10 **a** 10 9 8 7 6 5 4 3 2 1

LIBRARY OF CONGRESS CATALOGING-IN-PUBLICATION DATA
  QUINN, JAY.
    BACK WHERE HE STARTED / JAY QUINN.—1ST ED.
      ISBN 1-55583-927-4; ISBN-13 978-1-55583-927-7 (PBK.)
      ISBN 1-55583-859-6; ISBN-13 978-1-55583-859-1 (HARD COVER)
      1. GAY MEN—FICTION. 2. MIDDLE-AGED MEN—FICTION.
    3. REJECTION (PSYCHOLOGY)—FICTION. I. TITLE.
    PS3567.U3445B33 2005
    813'.6—DC22   2004062272

CREDITS
JACKET PHOTOGRAPHY BY DARREN ROBB/TAXI COLLECTION/GETTY IMAGES.
COVER DESIGN BY MATT SAMS.

ACKNOWLEDGMENTS

First, I must thank my editor, Nick Street at Alyson Books. While I wrote this music, he made it sing.

For their unconditional support and laughter and for keeping me from becoming way too serious about myself: Joe Riddick; Susan Highsmith; Malinda and Michael Weiss; Harold and Mary Parks; Patsy and Hailey; Heather Carr, LCSW, FNP; and Nathaniel Keller, MD.

And, as always, my incalculable love, debt, and gratitude to Jeffrey Auchter: my heart and my home.

A portion of this work appeared in different form as the short story titled "Our Family's Things" in *Upon a Midnight Clear: Queer Christmas Tales,* edited by Greg Herren.

CHAPTER ONE,
BEING ACTS ONE AND TWO

✚

It was the Sunday after Thanksgiving and, with the kids gone, I could concentrate on my packing. There was very little left for me to pack—just kitchen stuff, for the most part. Everything the kids hadn't wanted to keep for themselves, we gave to Goodwill. Zack had already taken what he wanted. Though the breadwinner got first pick, he hadn't taken much. I supposed, at 56, Zack could be forgiven for not knowing that the 30-year-old woman he'd married would want her own things. Standing in the near-empty kitchen, I remembered my own need to start new once. *Here I am again,* I thought. *Back where I started.*

I couldn't really blame Alicia. Certainly she'd want the first child of Zack's new life (I'd say *latest* if I were unkind) to be surrounded by fresh memories—not cluttered with the slightly smudged and frayed things that carried someone else's history. And what a history it was: incontinent pets, impromptu indoor field goals, cherished planned purchases, and nonchalant hand-me-downs. Many items bore the scars of sudden teenage rages—poorly patched and mended porcelain, chipped plates, and dramatically dinged furniture.

I didn't blame her a bit. Then again, I felt a small rush of amusement wondering how long Zack would have to postpone retirement in order to buy new things for an obviously ambitious and selfish new wife. Discarded for Alicia, I had certainly enjoyed buying new things for myself to start again. I'd put most of them on Zack's credit cards before he asked me—quite nicely, really—to stop.

I rinsed out the coffee pot and loaded the maker with fresh water and freshly ground beans, just like I'd done more times than

I could count, standing in just this spot. Night fell with the full weight of late November's fatigue as I waited for Zack. It wasn't yet registering that this was probably the *real* last time, after so many dry runs over the past year.

I put another log in the fireplace in the kitchen, got a dog cookie for Beau, and watched him turn stiffly and settle on the bare floor by the fire. With a nod from me, Trey's wife Susan had put the old dog's long-loved, smelly, old rug out by the curb with the pile of other unwanted things that were too worn, dirty, or useless either to be kept or given away. I didn't even have a threadbare towel left in the house for poor ol' Beau to lie on. It didn't really matter. From tomorrow on, Beau and I would be living down at the beach in my new, neat cottage. With two bedrooms, two and a half baths, a loft, a deck, and a sun porch—even an energy-efficient gas log fireplace in the "great-room"—Beau and I would be living well, if alone. I considered the cottage my partial-ocean-view consolation prize. Still, after 22 years and three inherited children grown and happy, it was hard not to feel like Beau and I had been asked to leave the show just before the last commercial break, with nothing but Rice-A-Roni—"the San Francisco treat"—to thank us for our time.

I found my cigarettes on the counter along with the new red plastic lighter I'd bought on the way back from the beach. I thumped one from the pack and lit it with all the panache of a smoking veteran. Immediately I remembered how much I'd missed the habit. It had been seven years since my last cigarette, but I figured I deserved the little pleasures in life. Bitterness could kill you quicker than anything else, and I had decided not to be bitter.

I heard Zack's car in the drive, the purring motor clicked off with German efficiency, and the door closed with a satisfied, solid thump. Beau lifted his head, thumped his tail, and looked eagerly to the door through rheumy old eyes. I wished I could say my heart didn't leap anymore at the familiar sounds of Zack's homecoming, but I was bad as Beau. It was hard not to feel like he'd put us both out to fend for ourselves or find a new master. While I considered that, Zack came in large and filled the room, crowding out my thoughts along with the last echo of the sheer happiness I'd always felt at his homecomings.

"Hey-o, Beau! Who's a good boy?"

Beau struggled to stand, but his bad hip wouldn't let him. He rose on his front legs and whined. Zack took off his coat, laid it on a chair, and knelt to shake the old dog's ears and receive his wet tongue on his cheeks. Zack looked up at me and smiled.

"Would you like some coffee? There's fresh..." I offered.

I saw the quick struggle in Zack's eyes. There was somewhere else he wanted and needed to be, but I knew he wanted to end this well. He'd never really been mean. There wasn't any meanness in him. He had just heard his life rushing ahead to its conclusion without him and grabbed onto something that made him feel young and manly and strong. "I can't stay long," he warned.

"No probs," I offered in return. "I'll get it. There's only Styrofoam cups left, I hope that's okay."

Zack stood and nodded. I felt him watching me, but as I poured the coffee, creamed it, sugared it, and stirred it just the way he liked, he said nothing. Taking the cup, he looked at the fire and said, "Is this wise?"

I sat at the table under his gaze and picked up my cigarette from the ashtray. "I still have a little packing to do, not much. Just my pots and pans. Susan and Trey wanted the everyday dishes and glasses. They're coming back in the morning with a friend's truck to get the kitchen table and chairs. You know our Susan: It was a last-minute decision."

Zack laughed and shook his head. His daughter-in-law's sentimentality was always a cipher to him.

"Andrea and David took the china and the old KitchenAid mixer," I reported. "Schooner wanted the blender and most of the other stuff. Anyway, I'll make sure the fire's out before I leave."

"You should spend the night. It's too far for you to drive after dark."

"Can't. There's not a blanket, pillow, mattress, or sheet left in the house after three trips to Goodwill in Schooner's truck. The kids took what they needed and we've put the rest out for a trash pickup."

"Did you remember to call to schedule it?"

I just smiled and nodded. Even with everything nearly said and done, Zack still got a smile off me. I'd lived with the man most of my adult life and he still thought I was the dumb, gullible 26-year-old I was when I met him. I dropped my spent cigarette into an empty beer can the kids had left from supper.

"When did you start smoking again?" he asked.

"Last week...Sunday, actually. I stopped on the way home from Mass and got a carton at the grocery store."

Zack shook his head. "A carton. When you make up your mind, you never gone at anything half-assed." He chuckled and looked around. "The kids were like locusts. I thought there'd be more left, even after they took the big pieces to Goodwill."

"There were plenty of small things," I said. "I only took the Karr paintings." Zack and I had accumulated several oil paintings and oil pastels by a particular artist down at the beach over the years. Most of them were small, but there was a fairly good-size portrait of the kids on the beach we had Karr do one year. Trey was 16, Andrea 13, and Schooner was 12 when some weekend guest took the picture we had Karr paint it from.

Funny, I couldn't even remember who took it. I only recall I was bound and determined to have a painting done from it. Those were the years when I read *Veranda* and *Southern Accents,* which were littered with pages of ads for artists who specialized in portraiture for the young scions of proper southern homes. As improper as our family was, I was absolutely committed to providing the kids with all the traditions and accoutrements that their daddy's money and my aspirations could give them.

"Chris, you shouldn't have let the kids have everything. You can't eat off those paintings."

"It's okay," I said. "I've had a good time picking up some great stuff cheap on eBay and at Target. I have everything I need, and Wade Lee has been keeping an eye out for a few pieces of furniture for me in some places up in Norfolk."

"What did you get on eBay? I hope to hell you haven't run through your settlement. I tried to give you enough for some security. I didn't mean for you to go hog wild spending money you don't have on interior decorating. If Wade Lee is looking for stuff in Norfolk, I can image he's looking for antiques, knowing him."

Zack looked tired, a little out of patience, and a little overwhelmed. He'd gone out of his way to make sure I got what he felt I deserved. God knows, he didn't have to give me anything at all.

"Don't worry. I haven't gone crazy. I just want to start fresh and new. Not to be bitchy at this point, but you understand that, I'm sure."

Zack nodded, then said, "I just want *you* to understand, once this goddamn barn of a house closes, I'm going to pay off the beach place and I'm putting the rest of your share in the annuity I set up for you. That's it, Chris, there won't be any more from me. Have you found a job yet?"

I looked in the fire, then very carefully got another cigarette out of my pack and lit it. Stalling until my fit of temper passed, I wanted to scream, *No, I haven't gotten a job! A 48-year-old faggot who's spent the best part of his life raising another man's young 'uns and washing another man's clothes and dishes and sheets and towels and running to the dry cleaners and cleaning up dog shit and waiting on the furnace repair man doesn't have a job skill in hell that anybody'd pay anything for!*

Beau raised his head and looked at me from the hearth as if he could hear the shouting in my mind. He shuddered like he expected a scolding of his own.

"I'm very much aware of our arrangement and my own responsibilities, Zack." I said as my temper cooled. "I don't think there's any more of that we need to discuss."

Zack sighed. Either he was too tired to fight or he was impressed with my equanimity. "Well, I'm going to take a last look around. Do you want to go with me?"

I couldn't look at him just then, so I just shook my head. I knew in a minute I'd be okay. I'd made it so far without being a bitch. I could make it through 20 more minutes.

Zack scraped his chair on the hardwood floor as he pushed back from the table. *God,* I thought, *after all these years, you'd think there'd be grooves in the old oak boards underneath his chair.* That was a sound I would never have to hear again, and I was glad. I was fucking delighted.

After Zack left the kitchen, I poured out his coffee and reheated mine. If I was focused, I could pack up all the past Christmas-gifted All-Clad, piss out the fire, load Beau into my Expedition, and haul ass. My leaving this house was long overdue. If Zack needed a long last look to torment himself, that was okay by me. But I had spent days, weeks, months saying good-bye to the life this old house had sheltered. I was beginning to feel if I didn't get out soon, I would somehow fade into the walls to become a creaky but unmenacing ghost that the new owners would have to contend with.

The floorboards upstairs betrayed Zack's presence in each of the rooms. I heard the upstairs commode flush while I shoved lids and cooking utensils into a box. I'd have to go back upstairs myself to take the lid off the toilet tank, and pull up and reset that fucking flapper thing so the water wouldn't run for days. I got so caught up fussing over my old resentments and freshly scabbed hurts that I didn't notice Zack in the doorway between the dining room and the kitchen.

"I guess that's it," he said, startling me. I turned to see him looking at me with what I didn't want to believe was remorse in his eyes. I still loved him enough not to feel good about that.

"You'll have the attorney FedEx the papers for me to sign for the closing, right?" I asked.

Zack nodded and looked around the kitchen. I thought, *Please God, don't let him say anything sentimental. I'll not be able to hold on to myself anymore if he does.*

"Aren't you taking the Christmas ornaments?" he asked.

For a moment, I was confused. The Christmas ornaments? I was sure I'd heard the kids arguing about them earlier that afternoon. "Oh, Christ, don't tell me…"

"They're in the attic, still," Zack said.

He looked like he was going to lose it himself, and I couldn't stand that. Not now. That bridge was cinders and smoke. "Are there any of them you'd like?" I asked.

Zack left the doorway and walked to his chair, carefully stepping over Beau. "Do whatever you want to with them," he said as he pulled on his coat.

"Zack, I thought I heard the kids arguing over them. I had no idea they were still up there."

"Well, I suppose the kids will want them, they were our family's."

I nodded. It was up to me to settle it. But then, it always had been me to settle such things. "I'll take care of it, Zack, I promise."

Zack rattled his keys in his pocket, then pulled them out and laid them on the kitchen table before stooping to rub Beau's ears.

"Bye-bye ol' boy. Bye ol' boy dog." Beau tried to stand. Zack reached across the table for my hand, took it, and squeezed it. "Bye-bye, ol' domestic partner," he said without looking at me.

I moved toward him, and as I did, he let go of my hand and picked up his keys. Without another word Zack made it to, and through, the kitchen door. Beau finally managed to stand and he tried to follow Zack. But when he got to the doorway I caught his collar and held him half in and half out of the cold, watching Zack as he left for the last time.

Beau and I stood in the chilly air long after the BMW's taillights had disappeared. Beau finally looked up at me reproachfully. "In or out," his eyes said. "Pick one." I let go of his collar and he returned to his bare spot by the fireplace and settled down heavily. At a sudden loss, I closed the door against the cold behind me and followed Beau back into the warmth of the kitchen. I had lost my momentum for leaving. I dumped the dregs of my last cup of coffee, now suddenly grown cold, into the sink and made myself another fresh cup. I wanted nothing more than to sit awhile longer in what had been the center of my home and my family. After being so adamant about not accompanying Zack on his sentimental journey through the house, now I didn't want to leave my kitchen. What lay down the road was only a sketch of a life, an idea. Even bare, the kitchen held the complete work of what I considered the best years of my life.

I sat at the table facing the fire and reached again for my ashtray and cigarettes. Over the past 22 years, I'd probably logged more time in that seat than in any other spot in my life. I'd listened to Zack's dreams there. I'd nursed the kid's hurts there, as well as my own. Now, Zack's dreams had pulled him away and the kids were gone. Only my hurts remained. I decided to tend them there for just a little while longer, just a few more minutes, before it was time to get up, face the music, and move on.

Given the choice, I doubted I'd ever have moved on. My life with Zack and the kids was far more secure and comfortable than anything I'd ever believed I'd get or deserved. The first part of my life, I lived with my mother in a housing project in Goldsboro, North Carolina. Fairview Homes wasn't bad, not like Lincoln

Homes across town. The apartments were well kept, and as best she could, my mother saw to it we were too. She was what they called a "grass widow" back then. All that meant was she'd been divorced—or more truthfully, that my father had run off. I never really knew if she'd even married my father; she didn't exactly relish talking about him, and she gave me only the barest explanations of my advent and our abandonment. I only knew I'd come along very late in her life. She was past 40 when I was born.

My mother was good to me, but strict. She had the perpetually pinched look of someone who was trying hard just to get by. She offered her effort up to heaven as the old-style Catholics did in the face of nearly insurmountable odds. We were the kind of people who walked to Mass and sat in the back of the church. We couldn't be proud, but we could be determined.

Disappointment was baked into the bricks of Fairview Homes. The hot fact of it seeped from the walls into my mother's spirit. The words *white trash* were whispered in our hearts, but my mother never said them aloud. I was forbidden to say them myself. But if we weren't white trash, we were close enough to it to smell it in the funk of leftover collard greens, to hear it in the rattle of empty Old Milwaukee cans, and to see it in bitter recriminations that simmered all around us.

I was just another barefoot towhead in an out-grown T-shirt in that place. You might be poor, but you could be clean, my mother taught me. "Soap's cheap and water's free," she'd say. But survival when I was a kid wasn't cheap and love was never free. I always had the sense my mother had loved one time late and well, but what came of it was loneliness and a brat to raise. I was *her* brat, at least, and she raised me without a sentimental eye and few expectations.

Her world-weariness never took up in me. I grew up sentimental and nurtured in myself the expectations you're handed simply by being born human. I never wanted anything more than to feel secure, and if I was never entirely self-sufficient, at least I was always confident there'd be someone, somewhere down the line I could love and trust.

I first thought I'd found that when I was 14 and Jimmy Worley from down the block talked me into coming over after school. We listened to James Taylor's album *Sweet Baby James* for a while before he got around to asking me to suck his dick on his mama's sofa before she got home from work. Afterward, we walked over to Woolworth's in the Sunrise Shopping Center and he lifted the James Taylor album for me. He looked like James Taylor on that album cover. He had Taylor's slightly crazy eyes and hard good looks as he walked out of the store with the album stuffed up under his shirt, against his warm belly. The upper corners of the album cover stuck out sharply over his lean 16-year-old ribs. No one stopped him, least of all me, after that.

For about a year, he followed me home a couple of times a week and I let him put his dick in me. After he'd gone—quick after coming—I'd play that album, over and over on Mama's long console stereo-television. *Sweet Baby James* had its own meaning for me. I stayed out of the trouble Jimmy got in because I was home mooning over him while he went from fucking me and stealing shit from department stores to fucking me and stealing cars. He was long gone by the time my mother made her last installment payment on that stereo-TV console to Sears.

The next year I joined Jimmy at the high school, and he dropped me quick when I got called a faggot not long after I first walked through the high school's clanging doors. He'd still stop by, easy and tough, with another shoplifted LP. He'd let me kiss him, and sometimes he kissed me back, but mostly he'd just screw me, long and slow. That stolen time lasted all the way through one side of a ripped-off album.

It never occurred to me that Jimmy was ripping me off—stealing a piece of me to savor in secret. I thought his vagabond attention was enough for a long time; it just didn't occur to me I might deserve better. Which isn't to say I didn't miss his fucking and his stingy but sincere tenderness. But I didn't care. I never fretted over his erratic comings and goings. For a little while he was mine and I belonged to somebody.

Jimmy got a thin-lined black tattoo on his wrist that said C.T. at the same time he got L-O-V-E tattooed on one set of fingers and H-A-T-E on the other. He whispered he was going to give me a "Sweet Baby James" tattoo on my lower back, just above the rise of my jeans. Jimmy said he had the black ink mixed with shampoo, the needle burned and ready. He said he wanted anybody else—forever—to know who had my sweet ass first. It never happened, but I was happy just to know he wanted to etch his name into my skin to claim me. No other man had claimed me, and I knew all about getting by on *enough*.

Jimmy got busted by the end of my sophomore year and I lost him to a youth farm mid-state. I became a little bit more like the kids in Fairview Homes—the desperation and habit of settling for less leached in as I learned all about disappointment and loss. For the first time I worried about making my mama's mistakes: me, a lonesome white-trash faggot, listening to the Allman Brothers and waiting for a future that had already come and gone when the screen door slammed behind Jimmy Worley for good.

My mother wanted me to join the service straight out of high school. In a kind of knowing, which wasn't really knowing at all, she told me I'd do good in the navy. God knows, if I'd joined the navy, I probably wouldn't have been so eager to be with Zack, and to take on raising his kids. Maybe I wouldn't have been left sitting in an empty house, with an uncertain future. But that's not what happened.

One thing Fairview Homes and my mother taught me was that being at the bottom leaves you nowhere to go but up. To get past the emptiness left by Jimmy Worley's departure, I studied. I studied the lessons in school with the same attentiveness I gave Jimmy Worley's lean body. I worked my tattooless ass off in school. While Mama planned on my leaving her house for basic training, I planned to escape to whatever college would have me. I got in at Wake Tech.

My mother died, or just plain quit living, a week shy of high school graduation. Since I was going to college, I got her Social Security survivor benefits. It wasn't much, but it was something I could count on.

Mama, God rest her soul, taught me how to live on little, and Jimmy Worley taught me how to make friends with my expectations, and that knowledge got me through Wake Tech with an associate's degree in business. School dropped me about four years from where Zack picked me up.

I got a job as a bookkeeper and errand boy with a guy who had four hair salons in Raleigh. I did payroll, ordered supplies, and shuttled around to all the salons to pick up deposits, stock hair color and bleach, and bullshit with the stylists. I'd never been around so many gay people before in my life and I was having a blast. Hair burners are party people, and I was ready for a little partying and a lot more fucking. Being blond with a nice ass—and new meat besides—I got all the partying and pecker I could stand.

After a lifetime of living tight and walking the straight and narrow, I was finally earning good money and finding my place in a clique of bright, fun people. Fairview Homes was a long way behind me, and I knew better than to fall in love. I had a thing for bad boys, but I was a roughneck myself in ways the sweet boys—the kind that wanted to settle down—could smell the danger and kept away. Oh, I had a good time, but I was a tattoo on only one man's arm, and I intended to keep it that way. Then I met Zack.

At the time—"back in the day," as the saying goes—Raleigh's main gay club was the Capital Corral, better known as CC's. Every Friday and Saturday night the place was so thick with faggots, all you could do was enter the front door and merge with the flow of bodies that circled the club between the two main bars. I'd shout out and get pulled into one group or another before rejoining the crowd as it endlessly circled. One Saturday night, I caught the eye of this tall preppy guy who was standing alone with his back pressed up against the bar. He looked back and held my gaze. On my second turn past him he held up a fresh bottle of Bud, and I pushed my way toward him. When I reached him, he smiled and offered me the beer.

Taking the bottle, I yelled thanks twice, but he couldn't hear me over the music. He smiled and turned slightly, to make room for me against his chest. When I stepped closer, he put one arm around the small of my back and pulled me to him. I looked up at him and smiled. He clinked my bottle with his own in a toast and drank. I watched him swallow, and his thick neck was one of the sexiest things I'd ever seen.

We were finally able to exchange names and agree that neither of us wanted to dance. I was perfectly content with his arm still holding me around the waist and his fingertips brushing my abdomen softly—but steadily enough to keep me aroused and interested.

Zack, back then, was a taller version of what his son Schooner would become: thick and solid as a rock. Black-haired and blue-eyed, he looked the perfect Raleigh frat boy, born and bred. Good manners but a bad thirst for liquor; good fuck, bad news. But I wasn't a debutante and I had no use for the country club. He had on a pink button-down oxford cloth shirt, and a pair of blue jeans that he wore loose around the hips, no belt, and honest-to-God boat shoes. Zack put his chin on top of my head briefly, then leaned down to my ear level to ask, "Do you live in Raleigh?"

I nodded.

"I think I'd really like to get to know you away from this. Are you ready to leave?"

Forward white trash that I was, I slipped my hand between his legs and squeezed the promising bulge in his jeans. Impressed, I looked up at him and grinned.

Zack grinned back but gently removed my hand and brought it up to rest on his chest. "Do you have a place?"

I nodded, and when I did, he lifted my hand and nibbled on the tip of my thumb.

All that seems funny now, 22 years later—as I sit in what became our kitchen and in a matter of hours wouldn't be ours anymore. Technically, it hadn't been ours for months, but that was beside the point; I couldn't remember the other details of that night. There had to have been the usual chitchat on the way to the parking lot. I'm sure there was more tense chatter as he followed me up the steps to my small apartment. I'm sure I offered him a joint and I'm sure he declined it. We must have shucked our clothes, and I must have longed for his body (first) and his heart (second). These memories must be lodged somewhere in the back of my heart. I must have sensed something true in what his tall form promised. I staked my heart and my life on that truth for a long time.

Watching the fire, as Beau repositioned himself under the table to rest his head on my foot, I did clearly recall waking to see Zack in my apartment's kitchen, standing naked through the door of my bedroom. He gripped the top of a chair and stared out into the moon's brightness. It glowed on his face, shoulders, and torso. I wanted him back in my bed. Standing there washed in moonlight, he looked handsome, but also lonesome, lost, and vulnerable. I felt a surge of tenderness, which I hadn't allowed myself to feel since I'd last dreamed of Jimmy Worley. I wanted Zack, period, and was dead set and determined to get him.

Zack and I always got together at my place, never his, and always at odd hours. He'd stop by on his way home from work or on late Sunday afternoons, and we'd meet for an occasional dinner in the middle of the week. When I asked why, he was evasive, if not downright hostile. I think he was testing me in ways that I couldn't have understood. I blithely offered information about myself that put checks and minuses in columns I had no way of knowing about.

While I didn't know what mattered to Zack, Zack mattered to me. The truth was, after a few months, I was only seeing him. It was simple: There was only Zack in my mind, and he played me so skillfully to get me to that point, I never considered what might be ahead. I just thought he was just consumed with his career, as most yuppies were back then.

Then, one Thursday night, in the slow weaving tangle of limbs after sex, he asked me if I'd like to come to his place for dinner the next night. I raised myself off his chest and onto my elbow to see his face. "Did I hear you right?"

"Absolutely," he replied. "I'll leave you the address and directions when I leave."

"So, you're not married?"

A shadow passed across his face, but he willed it away before I could get a read on his reaction.

Zack reached up and ran his hand through my hair, looking me in the eye all the while. Then he said: "No. I'm not married. But Chris..."

"What?"

"I'm wondering if you want to be."

Taken aback, I settled down against his chest and listened to the deep thud of his heart. It was beating faster than I was used to hearing. I realized he was nervous. I ran my hand down his side and squeezed his waist. "Zack, I want that more than anything, but..."

Zack took his hand from the small of my back and placed it gently over my mouth. "Shhh, not right now." He turned easily from under me to over me and placed me beneath the full weight of his long torso and legs. He took my arms, raised them over my head, and held them there with a tight grip on my wrists as he arched his back to lift his shoulders and look down at my face. "Right now, I want to be with you. I want to fuck you, Chris. No questions, not now." He pressed my legs apart with his knees and shifted to mount me. The thick weight of his dick dragged across my belly and lifted free of me as he reared up onto his knees and let go of my wrists.

"Zack—"

"Shhh, please, don't talk now," he said.

I didn't. If there wasn't a convincing argument or a promise in what followed, I didn't care. I kept silent and watched his face as he fucked me with a rigid determination. It was more than my mind could comprehend and more than my body could tolerate. I cried as I came, but without a sound. That time, in answer to his orgasm's strangled cry, I had only tears that Zack kissed away tenderly in our afterglow.

I was similarly speechless when I found myself at Zack's house the next day. *This* house. The one I was now leaving for good.

I knew where Historic Oakwood was; I'd driven through it on the Christmas tours with my hairdresser buddies. It was a lovely neighborhood in South Raleigh filled with Queen Anne, Italianate, and late-Victorian homes. Prosperous yuppies were beginning to move in and gentrify the area. But none of my crowd could do more than dream about getting a place there despite their deeper appreciation for the architectural styles and residential history. We crowded into the faded neighborhoods around Five Points and the apartment complexes in North Raleigh. There was no hope for anything this grand in any of our paychecks or futures.

From the little amount of personal information Zack had murmured, at my prodding, after sex or during a rushed dinner out, I'd learned he was in advertising—an account executive, and a pretty successful one. Still, I had no idea he was doing well enough as to live in Historic Oakwood.

The address and directions Zack had given me lead to an imposing, freshly painted Italianate house with grand high and narrow windows. The house seemed to have a light on in every room. Climbing the front steps, I heard small shrieks and a child's crying.

I figured I had gotten lost, but I rang the doorbell, figuring I could ask directions of the family who lived there.

Zack answered the door in a towel, carrying a naked, chubby baby boy who had a tiny fistful of the hair on Zack's left pec. Peeking from behind him were a small boy and a smaller girl, both in pajamas.

"If you don't want to leave right now, please come in," Zack said anxiously.

"They're yours?" I asked.

"Obviously."

"And you're not married?"

"Widower."

"Goddamn it," I said. Suddenly I understood why we got together, ate out, and made love at such bizarre times.

Zack's face fell. I couldn't take that, and I realized just then that I'd gone and fallen in love with the bastard. Historic Oakwood damn sure wasn't Fairview Homes, but here he was, saddled with some real problems—three of them. In a millisecond I knew I could handle it. I knew how to take whatever I got and make the best of it—and squalling young 'uns with dirty diapers weren't anything I'd not seen before. I smiled, shook my head, and said, "Well, I'm going to come in and meet the family, I guess."

Zack grinned like I'd given him the world and stepped back into the foyer. I followed him into the sparsely furnished front parlor. Motioning for me to sit down, he apologized for not being dressed. "I got home late and Miz Keesha had only just got the kids' dinner finished and gotten them dressed for bed. Then Schooner here," he said, nodding toward the baby boy in his arms, "needed a fresh diaper, so I decided to take him into the shower with me to clean him up, and we just got out when you rang the doorbell. Kids, why don't you tell Chris who you are."

The little boy came to stand right in front of me and said, "My name is Trey, because I'm a turd."

I looked from his blue eyes up to his father's and said, "Excuse me?"

"Zachary David Ronan the Third," Zack explained. "Shake hands Trey."

The little fellow stuck out his paw manfully, and I took it gently in my grasp. With a surprisingly tight grip Trey squeezed my fingers. "What your name is?"

I heard Zack mutter, "Goddamn Keesha." Louder, he said, "What *is* your name?"

"I told him—Trey," the boy said matter-of-factly.

"My name is Chris," I said. "Chris Thayer."

He shook my hand as best he could and said, "Pleased to meet you Chris Taylor."

I gave him a grin and tossed a wink to his daddy. "And who's this pretty little girl, Zack?" It was obviously the wrong thing to say. The girl shrank behind her father.

Zack reached behind him to urge her back.

"Her name is Ahn-dray-or," Trey explained.

"Andrea, don't you want to meet Chris?" Zack asked. Surprisingly, the little girl moved forward to stand next to her brother. Then she looked me in the eye and said, "My mommy is dead." Then she became bashful once more and hung her head.

"Come here, sweetness." I knelt and she stepped forward, shy as a fawn, and allowed me to lift her into my arms. "There's a good girl."

Looking up, she said, "Are you a stranger? I'm not allowed to let strangers touch me."

I looked at Zack for help.

"Chris is Daddy's good friend, Andrea. Chris isn't a stranger."

Andrea looked at me skeptically.

I heard Zack once again mutter "Goddamnit." I looked up in time to see him attempt to hold down an arch of urine jetting up from between the infant's legs. Andrea giggled. Trey looked at me and said, "Schoonoh pees wa-a-ay too goddamn much."

I laughed until the kids did, and Zack, dripping, finally joined in.

Around that time Kodak was running an ad that appeared in every magazine that littered the waiting area of every hair salon my work took me to. The ad's photo showed a large shirtless man tenderly holding a naked infant. I was living in my own Kodak moment.

Something in me broke and gave way. Fairview Homes and its hard lessons lay crumbled to dust. I longed for this man, this home and these children with the secret vast empty spaces that up to that moment had nurtured only wistfulness.

"Give me Schoonoh," I said to please Trey, "and go get cleaned up. Me and the kids will watch TV until you get finished, right guys?"

In the 10 minutes that followed, I learned much from the kids. Far more, in fact, than their father had trusted me with to that point. I learned that their Mommy was real depressed so she ate a lot of pills so she could go see Jesus, but she wasn't going to hell because Miz Keesha said she wasn't. I learned that Daddy worked way too hard and the kids and the house were breaking his back. I learned that Granddaddy was a bastard and Grandmama drank too much gin to be much help to anybody.

I learned that I could fall in love with a little boy's speech impediment, with a girl who could speak only the truth, and with a baby who was ready to pee again in less than 10 minutes.

In the kitchen of that house, 22 years later and older, I could pinpoint the minute when the second act of my life began.

Beau whined and attempted to stand, which was difficult at the best of times—extremely so, when he was under the table. I had no idea what time it was; the clocks were gone and the one on the coffeemaker blinked 12:00 steadily. I downed the last of my coffee and got down on my hands and knees to join Beau under the table to help him stand. He must have been dying to go outside. The poor old boy hadn't had a pee break in hours. In fact, he'd missed his dinnertime. I couldn't believe I'd let him go hungry.

When we were both up and out from under the table, I grabbed an old sweater of Zack's I had worn for years, pulled it over my head, and urged Beau out into the backyard. I walked down the steps to the abandoned tree swing and sat, grateful for the cold air outside the fire-warmed kitchen. Wood smoke hung in the still, chilly air, and I rocked a little as Beau snuffled along his usual route between the camellia, susanqua, and ligustrum that hedged the backyard.

Looking up, I saw there was only light in the kitchen and the upper hall. I dreaded going up into the attic for the Christmas things. For a moment I considered leaving and just walking away from them as Zack had done. But I wouldn't. They weren't his or mine anymore—they were really the children's. I'd make it right;

that's what Zack expected. That's what I'd done always, and I wasn't going to stop now.

No, not now. Not now that I was at the absolute end of Chris Thayer, act two. If I could admit it was when I met the kids that act two of my life began, I could admit I was at the end of the act.

There was no equivocation about that point. I'd always loved the song by Rickie Lee Jones where the refrain was the plaintive question "Is this the real end?" The real end began late one Saturday afternoon in February. Schooner was home from school and spent most of the afternoon in the family room with his dad watching ACC basketball. I was mostly finished with the work of cooking a real Italian dinner: simmering spareribs and stew-cut beef chunks in red sauce to make gravy, which I would serve with ziti, ricotta cheese on the side, green peas made with mushrooms and bread crumbs, and a Caprese salad. Andrea and her husband David were coming over to eat, and Trey and Susan promised to be by, at least for dessert—tiramisu, homemade.

At some point, Schooner fell asleep on the sofa and his dad slipped out. With dinner mostly done, I had a little time to turn my attention to Azar Nafisi's *Reading Lolita in Tehran*, which had me enthralled. I looked up from my book and saw him pass by on his way upstairs, but he didn't spare a glance into the kitchen. I was so absorbed in Nafisi's story, I didn't give Zack's trip upstairs another thought.

"I need to run to the store, do you need anything?"

I looked up from my book to a sleepy-eyed Schooner, pulling me into the Raleigh of the moment from postrevolutionary Tehran.

Momentarily disoriented, I thought a moment, then said, "You might pick up a couple of bottles of wine for dinner. Do you need some money." I automatically stood to reach in my jeans pocket.

"I always need money according to Dad," Schooner said with mock peevishness. I handed him a 20 and he gave me a grin.

"Why do you wear that ridiculous reindeer sweater of Dad's?" he asked. "It swallows you. You look about 10 years old."

"Why do you wear that 10-year-old baseball cap?" I countered. "You look like a refugee from middle school. Your dad's sweater makes me feel happy—kind of like a grown-up blankee. Does your baseball cap make you feel happy?"

Schooner shrugged. "Never once thought about it. It fits my head. What kind of wine do you want? It can't be anything too nice for 20 bucks."

I peeled off another 20 and handed it to him. "You decide. Just make it red and make sure you have enough change for whatever you need and gas money."

Schooner gave me a quick hug on his way to the door and paused long enough to kiss the top of my head.

"Aren't you going to put on a coat?" I asked.

"No, *Mom*." Of the three kids, Schooner was the only one who acknowledged any gender dissonance in being reared and cared for by a man. Trey and Andrea called me Chris. Schooner called me "Mom" whenever he was affectionate, happy, or irritated, which accounted for most of his emotional range. "Truck's warm, store's warm. What am I going to do, get pneumonia suddenly in the driveway or the parking lot?"

I waved him off and turned to the stove. "Just go."

"Got it," he said. Then, "Chris?"

I looked to the back door from the stove. Schooner stood on the porch, grinning.

"Thanks," he said.

I heard something clunky and heavy bang the walls along with Zack's footfalls on the stairs. I waved to Schooner and he took off. Before his truck was out of the driveway, Zack came into the kitchen with his suitcase. He passed me without a word, but I heard him mutter, "I thought the little fucker would never get out of here."

Turning back from the door, Zack's face was ruddy with exertion or high emotion or both. He had grown more florid, solid, and heavy as he moved staunchly into middle age, and while he certainly wasn't fat, he was 40 pounds heavier than he'd been when I met him. I was scared he was on his way to an angioplasty, but he claimed his heart was fine, goddamnit, whenever I urged him to walk with me or join the gym I went to in the fight against my own middle-aged spread.

"What's all this about Schooner? What has he said to get on your nerves so bad? And what's up with the suitcase?"

Zack shot me a look of pure frustration, then said, "Schooner is a spoiled brat, mainly because you persist in treating him like he's still a teenager. The sooner he gets out of college and gets on with his goddamn life without my help will be the soonest he stops getting on my nerves." With that, he picked up the suitcase and pushed out the back door.

I left the stove to stand at the window over the kitchen sink and watch him stride to his new car, open the trunk, and shove the suitcase inside. Hesitating for a moment and looking toward the house, he saw me at the window watching him and turned his back to me. He slammed the trunk lid down with one hand, shoved his hands in his pants pockets, and stomped down the drive, toward the street, and out of my sight.

It was at moments like that that I regretted quitting smoking. I took some deep breaths, inhaling and exhaling slowly as I turned back to the stove to stir the red sauce that didn't need stirring. Growing calmer, I remembered Zack was under almost constant pressure at the agency. Though he had been a partner for years, the pressure-cooker atmosphere and completely insane client demands were enough to keep him constantly frustrated and short-fused. In addition to that, his business still had not recovered from the 9/11 recession.

Zack had been short with me and at an emotional arm's length for months. In all of the business ups and downs over the years he had never been so far away, but I never complained. We lived well, mainly because of his hard work. I had been quietly suggesting for months that we downsize our lives. Schooner would be graduating from East Carolina University in the spring; the house was finally in a state after years of nearly constant renovation and repair that would allow us to put it on the market and get top dollar for it.

I wanted to cash out, maybe buy a small condo in Raleigh where we could live part of the week and a beach place where we could semi-retire. With FedEx, phones, faxes, and e-mail, Zack could continue to be as involved in the business as he needed to be and still slow down some. I thought that had been the whole point of Alicia Stiles.

As far as I was concerned, Alicia Stiles was a spider in a Donna Karan suit and Manolo Blahniks, but I generously and freely admitted she was very good at what she did. Zack had urged the other partners to buy out her very successful public relations and advertising boutique. Since they had, she had proven to be a rain-maker, bringing in new clients despite the slack-assed economy.

I was only involved in any of this tangentially. I'd learned long before not to mix too much of my opinion into Zack's business affairs. Early on, Zack had made it abundantly clear that my associate's degree in business from Wake Tech and my years doing payroll for the king of the hair burners didn't translate into an understanding of the advertising business. So I kept my mouth shut and kept the house accounts in fine order. That was my job; it was unstated, but clearly implied, that was also was my place.

I had kept that place running in fine order so we could eventually move on to a life that was less stressful for Zack. And, selfishly, I just wanted to spend more time with him. As the kids grew older and moved out, I took the time I'd devoted to shuttling them between confirmation classes and soccer and every other frickin' thing they were wrapped up in, and spent it on making myself into more of what I had always wanted to be. Someone smart, someone accomplished, well read, and urbane—that's how I saw myself. I had spent a long time mentally scrubbing the dirt from Fairview Homes from my heart and from behind my ears. I wanted Zack to find me interesting and bright as the years began to dull other aspects of our lives.

I kept myself together physically, I exercised, and while I could still spare a few pounds, I was still blond and fairly attractive, or so I hoped. Zack liked me to look younger than I'd become, and always complimented me when I bought a few new things at the Gap or Abercrombie & Fitch and walked around looking like a hoyden boy. I wasn't pretentious; the Gap suited me, and Abercrombie seemed to turn Zack on.

Or it used to. Somewhere down the line Zack stopped reaching out for me, with a hard-on a cat couldn't scratch. Claiming his back was suffering on our too-soft mattress, he had even taken to sleeping in the guest room. It was nothing I was concerned about—stress had taken its toll on our love life for brief intervals in the past. I missed him physically, but I loved him in a way and with an understanding that only deepened over time. That kept me from pressing the point. There was forever to wait for, and forever seemed to come quicker with every passing season.

I heard the back door close and the screen door bang shut behind it. Zack stood just inside the kitchen and folded his arms across his chest. "Sit down, Chris. We need to talk about something."

Wishing for a cigarette, I pulled my chair from under the kitchen table, sat, and closed my book. Zack moved from the back door to stand across from me and leaned against the kitchen sink with his arms still folded across his chest. "Zack, if this is about Schooner—"

"Fuck Schooner," he said angrily. "For once this has nothing to do with your *baby*. Did you ever once stop to think this could be about something between you and me?"

Hurt, I glanced at the pots on the stove, then looked down at the cover of the bright young women in head scarves on the cover of Azar Nafisi's book.

"Look at me Chris," Zack said as he moved from the sink to sit directly across the table from me. I looked up in time to see a flash of resignation replace determination in his face. He sighed.

"Chris, there's no easy way to say what I have to say…no way to make it easy, so I'm going to just spill my guts, okay?"

I reached across the table to take his hand, but he pulled out of reach. "Is it…your health?"

Zack shook his head and laughed a short, bitter laugh. "You really would try to talk me into a heart attack or worse if I stayed here wouldn't you?"

"What do you mean, *stay here*?"

"I mean I'm leaving, Chris. Today. Right now."

Stunned, I could only look at him and wait for what came next.

"You know for some time now, we've been growing apart. With Schooner nearly finished with school, I need to move on." He hesitated and looked out the window over the sink. "There's someone else, a young woman. I'm taking the chance to start over, Chris. I hope you'll be happy for me. We're going to be married shortly."

Reeling, I felt a thousand unwelcome sensations come rushing back at me as I retreated mentally from Zack. Sitting just across the table from me, he seemed a million miles away, and suddenly I was back at Fairview Homes. I smelled the hot bricks; the stinking leftovers; the stale oat-y smell of old beer bottles and felt their broken glass under my bare feet. "Who?" I asked quietly. "Am I allowed to know who this woman is?"

Zack didn't take his gaze from the window. "It's Alicia. Alicia Stiles."

"The cunt!" I spat. "I suppose this was her way to consolidate the buyout, huh?"

"I don't think that's really fair, Chris."

"Fair? Fair to who? Alicia?"

"No, well...not fair to us both."

"In what way am I not being fair to you?" I growled. My growing anger was threatening to boil over.

"I can't believe you'd cast me as someone who'd use marriage to consolidate a business relationship," Zack said.

A dawning realization stole into my anger, and I struck back. "Isn't that exactly what you'd do? Isn't that exactly what you've done? Unless..."

"Unless what?"

"Unless next you're really going to cut my heart out and tell me that you never really wanted me in the first place. That you made love to me to keep me as...as...you know, your housekeeper?"

"Chris! Chris stop it!" Zack said. "Why would I say that to you? Why would I hurt you that way? How can you even begin to believe such a thing after all these years?"

"Then *what*? I don't understand. Isn't this something we can just fix? How long can this affair last, Zack?"

Zack finally looked at me. "She's nearly three months' pregnant, Chris. It's all about doing the right thing."

"No doubt. How noble. I know you love me. I know you do, Zack. Please."

Zack sighed but didn't take his eyes off mine. "I *did* love you, Chris."

The internal struggle between the projects brat I had been and the polished, urbane man I'd hoped to become began to swing in the guttersnipe's favor. I was ready to take the fight into a nastier realm. "You *did* love me? What made you stop loving me? After I put up with your little indiscretions over the years...hell, I knew you were a bisexual when I came onboard—you had the kids to prove it. Why the fuck did you have to sign on for another woman...another fucking *kid,* at 56? You'll never get me to believe she didn't have something to do with this, some kind of scam. The fucking bitch. I can't believe you'd fall for this, Zack." Then, a dying gasp from the hurt child I kept locked away for so many years raised his towhead and stomped his dirty feet: "Why can't she just raise the kid herself? Even if it is yours, she's tough enough to make it on her own. Why does she get you? Why do you care?"

Zack took all this stoically, then leaned closer to me. Gently he said, "Chris, you of all people should understand, considering—"

With that, all my pretenses were destroyed. I became the white trash I'd grown up around, screaming under a yellow porch light in the bitter darkness of the Fairview Homes. "Considering *what*? Considering I grew up in a fucking housing project? Considering my mama had to work like a dog to keep a roof over our head just to do *that* good? That pushy bitch Alicia has to be pulling in six figures. You tell me she can't raise a young 'un on that? Why should I care about her or her fucking brat?"

Zack said simply, calmly, "I thought you'd understand, considering you grew up some man's bastard."

That hit me like a punch in the gut. I was stunned into silence.

"I love her, Chris."

"What does your love mean? What are you going to do if she kills herself—bring your little bastard back for me to raise?"

Zack reached across the table and slapped me hard across the mouth. In 22 years' worth of adult give-and-take, he'd never touched me in anger. Now this. The slap cut my lower lip on my upper front teeth. I wiped my mouth with the back of my hand and sat staring at the smear of blood there.

"Once and always white trash, aren't you? You had to go there," Zack said. "You begged for that."

I didn't answer him. I thought about how many times I'd been told you can't get above your raising. No matter how much you watch your grammar, how many intelligent books you absorb or pretty thoughts you have. You can never get away from getting smacked across the mouth and put back in your place. But I rebelled against the notion. I sucked blood from my lip and closed my eyes, marshaling in my silence all the good things I believed I was now, all the good things I wanted to be.

Calmly I said, "No, Zack, if I really was white trash, I'd stick an ice pick in you right now, or cut you with a straight razor. And I could too. God knows, I could. But that's really beside the point isn't it?" I stood and walked behind Zack to the sink to wash my hand and mouth. He sat at the table behind me with his head in his hands.

I looked out the window at the bare trees tearing at the wintry gray sky like long sharp claws. "It's okay, Zack. You'd better go now."

He stood and gently put his hands on my shoulders. "I'd take it back if I could, Chris."

"So would I, Zack. But what's done is done."

"This doesn't have to be hurtful, you know. We don't have to rip each other apart." He sounded hopeful, not contrite. He never relished a confrontation—he always had preferred to sulk in silence and make me miserable with my inability to know what would make him feel better. I pitied him at those times. He disgusted me. More than anything just then, I wanted him gone. Then immediately regretted that desire.

I turned to face him and gave him as much of a smile as my split lip would allow. "I honestly don't know how you can say that with a straight face, Zack. But I do think we just got through the worst of it. There's very little we could say to each other that would hurt more."

Zack gently wrapped his arms around me and pulled me close. I let him, fully aware it might be the last time I would feel his touch and praying to God it wouldn't be. I managed to ask the unthinkable, after so many years: "So, I guess that's it. Am I out on the street? When do you expect me to be out?"

Zack briefly rested his chin on top of my head, then held me away at arm's length: "22 years together, all that time spent with me looking after you, loving you, and you're back in the projects before you even give me a chance? Do you think I'd stop caring about you, looking out for you, now?"

"But you have," I said. "Oh Jesus, but you have."

Zack released his grasp on my shoulders, gently squeezed my upper arms, and let me go. He reached into his back pocket, took out his wallet, and pulled out a business card. Handing it to me, he said, "This is an attorney I've been working with. Even though we're not legally married, we *are* tied up in a lot of ways we'll need to dissolve or restructure. You'll be cared for as long as you live. He's expecting your call."

"Just like that? That's it?" I asked incredulously.

Zack went toward the door. "Call him tomorrow, Chris. Don't put it off."

"Zack—"

"You'll find I've been as generous as I can afford to be."

"Zack—"

"Just go see the attorney, for God's sake. Don't turn this into a soap opera any worse than it is. Jesus, Chris! You're ripping my fucking heart out!"

"Zack—"

"What? What, goddamnit!"

"Have you told the kids?"

Zack stopped, his shoulders slumped, and he ran his hand over his face tiredly. At last, he said, "No. I'm leaving that up to you. I'm trusting you to give it to them so they don't despise me any worse than they're going to when they get a load of that busted lip of yours. God*damn* it, Chris. How did it go so far that quickly?"

"Wait…to hell with my lip. Let me get this straight. You're delegating responsibility for your kids' reactions over this…this divorce, to *me*?"

"Oh hell yeah. It's up to you."

"God no, Zack, please! I'm just being fair. We put them into this together, shouldn't we get out of it together for their sake?"

"You're better with the feelings crap. The 'kiss it and make it better' stuff. They're used to all that mom shit coming from you."

"That's cold. I can't believe you, Zack."

Zack laughed. "Why the hell not, Chris? They're *your* fucking kids. I gave them to you a long time ago. You'll figure it out."

Just then, Beau came out from under the table where he'd been hiding and whined at Zack. For Zack, it was the last straw.

"And take care of my damn dog too. I gotta get out of here." With that, he was out the door and down the steps. Halfway to his car, Schooner pulled up in the driveway. Sternly Zack stood with one arm outstretched, simply motioning for him to back out and stay out. When Schooner was safely in the street, he got in his car and left.

I stooped to stroke and comfort Beau. As I stood to get his leash, Schooner strode in the back door. "Jesus! Where the fuck is

Dad tearing off to in such a goddamn hurry?"

Snapping the leash to Beau's collar, I looked up at Schooner and said, "Straight to hell, I hope."

"Hey! What's wrong with your lip, it's bleeding!"

"Schooner, do me two favors, okay? First, set the table in the dining room. Your beloved siblings and their spouses will be here soon, and I need your help. Second, don't ask me about my mouth, please."

"Can I come with you to walk Beau?"

"No, Schooner, please. I need some fresh air."

"Did that bastard hit you? I'll fucking kill him!"

"Schooner, don't call your dad a bastard. Just please, for God's sake, give me a little space right now. I'm big enough to fight my own battles. Just set the table for me and open the wine." With that, I nudged Beau out the door and followed him.

"He *did* hit you, didn't he! I'll cut his—"

I closed the door and cut Schooner off before he could work up a good head of steam.

Three times around the block, I collected my thoughts and walked in the cold wind and dying Saturday light. Finally, I put my own fear aside and rehearsed how to tell my kids the news.

After awkward greetings and a confused dinner, I told them all, carefully as I could, over tiramisu and the last of the wine. I always sopped their bad spills and skinned knees with a little sugar, but never any saccharine. I made no plays for sympathy and tried to put their father in the best light I could, considering he wasn't there to defend himself against his own decisions and my obviously painful lip.

Zack was right. They were my kids, and they made me proud. My in-laws—or "out-laws," as we teasingly called ourselves when we were together—made me proud as well. Trey was concerned about my financial future—solemn, hard-thinking, realistic banker that he was. Andrea, in her second year of practice as a licensed clinical social worker, had much to say about spousal abuse and threatened to drag me kicking and screaming to the hospital, primarily to have my lip sewn up and also to encourage me to file a police report against her father. With the help of her sweet husband David, we convinced her that was a little extreme. Schooner radiated a dangerous anger that kept him quiet. When pushed, he did-n't talk; he acted. It was Schooner who slipped away to call the kids' pediatrician, to talk him into paying a house call to take care of a "very personal matter."

I was abashed when Dr. Ericsson showed up with a black bag to stitch up my lip that refused to quit bleeding, but I was glad he did. My kids trusted him to keep all this to himself. God only knew what secrets they had told him over the years, but I didn't have a clue. His practice included many upper middle-class families; most likely, he was no stranger to sewing up many dirty little secrets. Wise and patient, the good doctor was a calming influence for all the kids and me. By the time he left, they were all ready to take this sudden family drama home to sort out on their own. All but Schooner—he would not be dissuaded from staying at the house that night and not returning to his apartment in Greenville.

In the calm that comes both before and after any kind of storm, Schooner wordlessly helped me clear away the dishes and clean up the kitchen. After I was done wiping off the counters with a wet dishrag and he was out with Beau, I sat down at the kitchen table, heavily. Dr. Ericsson had given me a shot "to ease the pain," but I thought it was also intended to keep me calm and ensure that Schooner wouldn't fur-ther disturb his Saturday night. Relaxed and woozy, I felt secure at home in my kitchen despite the hot flashes of anger and hurt that lin-gered like heat lightning flashing after a deluge.

I dragged my copy of *Reading Lolita in Tehran* from where it had rested unmolested since Zack had asked me to sit before he proceeded to dismantle our lives, and tried to pick up the thread of the story to distract myself. Still, I couldn't distract myself from the ache of a deeper kind of pain that crept around the edges of the shot's warm fog. In a way, I'd always known this day would come. As good a fuck as I could be, as good a mom as I could play, I was-n't a woman. If that was what Zack really needed, it didn't have anything to do with me. I had nothing to be ashamed of and three grown kids to be pretty proud of. I decided to feel pretty good about myself just then. I talked myself into believing I didn't have any hurts I couldn't handle. As far as the future was concerned, if it didn't turn out to include Zack, it might include somebody else, or it might just be me. I really didn't care.

Schooner and Beau returned, each of them shaking off the cold. The familiar sounds of sneakers and dog's claws on the old wood floors made me smile—then wince from the pain of my newly stitched lip.

"Are you okay, Mom?" Schooner asked.

"Baby, sit down." I said as I patted the chair at a spot next to me.

Schooner eased himself into the chair and gave me a look of real concern.

"You're going to have to stop calling me Mom. If nothing else, today's…uh, news, has reminded me I'm a man and made me see you as a man too. I appreciate you taking charge of the situation and calling Dr. Ericsson. I never would have done that myself."

"S'okay." Schooner said. "No big deal. I *know* you would have never done it yourself, and that fucker was bleeding all during dinner. It was disgusting."

I reached across the small space between us and took his hand. He responded by turning my hand so he could hold it in his instead. His grasp was warm and strong and I was grateful for it.

He squeezed my hand and tugged at it until I looked at him and smiled. Quietly he said, "I don't understand why you're making me stop calling you Mom."

"It's time isn't it, Schooner? You're grown, and I'm…I'm…"

"You're what?"

"It looks as if I'm not going to be with your father anymore. I'm just going to be Chris Thayer. Single man. Single middle-aged gay man."

"But that has nothing to do with me and Trey and Andrea," Schooner said. "Fuck Dad. He's nothing but a checkbook to me. Besides the money, what did he ever do to be there for me? All my life, since I was a baby, I'd look up and it was you that was there. If you aren't a mom, if you aren't my mom anymore, where does that leave me?"

I was stunned by the depth of his feelings. I had no answer for him. The fact of his father's leaving was just beginning to register with me; I hadn't fully grasped how it would affect the kids. I struggled to say something, but I had nothing to say.

Schooner pulled me toward him and wrapped his arms around me awkwardly. "Chris…I know you're a guy and everything. But to me, you're more than that. You're the only warm…you're…you're my *mom*, goddamn it. I don't know how else to say that." He gently pushed me away so he could look at my face.

His worried scowl was both endearing and heartrending. At this point, I was grateful and proud to call him my kid, and not for one minute did I regret having spent most of my adult life raising him to this point. "It's okay, sugar. Other than 'my baby,' I don't what else to call you either. You can call me whatever you want."

"It's settled then?" he asked.

I nodded and he let me go.

"Did I really pee on him the first time you came here?"

"Yep, you peed on me too, not 10 minutes later."

Schooner snickered. "Equal opportunity pisser, huh?"

"Schooner, you're the best gift your father ever gave me. It was an awesome amount of trust, considering how difficult he knew it was going to be on all of us."

"I took a lot of beatings because of it."

I couldn't look at him; I looked down at my book instead. "I figured you did. Are you ever sorry? Do you wish it had been easier for you?"

Schooner took and squeezed my hand again, then stood up and tugged me to my feet along with him. "Nope. You're the mom I got, Chris. I wouldn't trade you for anybody or do anything different. I don't blame you."

"Don't blame your dad either, okay?"

"I don't want to talk about him anymore. I want to just watch some TV and chill. Can we sleep on the sofas in the family room, you know…a good old-timey indoor campout and watch *Saturday Night Live*? I'll make popcorn!"

"The thought of salt on this lip is enough to make me throw up, but make yourself some, okay?"

"When I see that bast…when I see Dad, he'll be lucky if I don't beat the shit of him for that."

I smiled to let him know I appreciated his self-correction. "Schooner, your dad and I said some pretty hurtful things to each other, and I pushed him pretty hard. A busted lip is no big thing. I'm pretty sure he's doing a good enough job of beating himself up for the whole deal. He's not a bastard—he's just a sad, scared middle-aged man chasing what's left of his dreams. Give him a break."

Schooner shrugged and said, "You're going way too easy on him. But, I'll be civil if you say so. I'm only doing it for you, okay?

"Promise?"

"Spit-swear." He spat into his palm and held it out.

"I'll pass," I said, good-naturedly.

"Okay," he said cheerfully. "Why don't you go in the family room and turn on the TV. Get comfortable. I could bring you some tiramisu—"

"I'm pretty messed up from the shot and a really long day, baby."

"It's okay, Mom. I'll cover you up if you fall asleep, okay?"

That's how we left it, Schooner and I. In the days, weeks, and months that followed, Trey and Andrea showed me in their own ways that their attitudes and hearts echoed Schooner's absolute commitment to me. When push came to shove, their Dad could push me aside in favor of a whole new life, but nothing could shove the kids from my side.

Those were deep memories to swim up and out of. Beau was huddled at my feet, and I felt the chill of tears on my cheeks as they dried in the cold wind. Sitting in the backyard swing, I regarded my kitchen and my past. My back ached from the effort of clearing out, but I knew what I'd borne on it, and felt some satisfaction along with the ache.

I stood and stretched—I still had Christmas ornaments and pots and pans to haul out and load into the Expedition. And I had Beau to feed.

"Want a hamburger, boy?" I asked my tired old dog. "Want us to stop and get Beau a Hardee burger on the way home? Does my Beau-dog want a Bojangles chicken biscuit on the way home?"

Beau struggled and stood, tail wagging happily despite his cold, aching joints. I could kick myself for getting lost in the past and causing the old dog pain. It was time to get him warm, fed, and home.

There—I'd said it. *Home,* which obviously didn't mean the house I'd shucked like a husk and left standing mostly dark and empty in front of me. It was time. This was the real end of Chris Thayer, act two. It was time to clear the hell out and head home to the beach. Hello Emerald Isle. Hello Chris Thayer, act three.

CHAPTER TWO,
ADVENT

✦

There wasn't a stick of furniture in the beach house. My cabinets were full of pots, pans, small appliances, dishes, and flatware, but the beach house itself was empty until my new things could be delivered. My sole remaining friend from the days when I ran with the savvy salon crowd was Wade Lee Roylston. He'd moved to Norfolk and eventually became an interior designer. Thanks to him, my new life would be furnished sparely with some well-chosen but pricey contemporary pieces and a few antiques. After a couple of nights of surprisingly good sleep bundled on the living room floor, the day arrived when I was to welcome the trappings of my new life.

I got up early, made coffee, and surveyed the beach house with fresh eyes. Until I left the house in Raleigh, I'd only been there twice before: once alone and once with Wade Lee.

I'd come alone the first time at the urging of Trey after I'd spoken with Evan Strickland, the attorney Zack had sent me to in order to gently extract me out of his life. While all across the nation that winter the great debate over gay marriage raged, I went through the ugly process of dissolving a de facto one. Twenty-two years of making a very real marriage—despite its illegality—out of bits and pieces of dreams and obligations took only an hour to dismantle.

Evan Strickland was solicitous when he explained that Zack had released me from the various powers of attorney that we'd signed to protect ourselves and the kids against any unforeseen calamity and subsequent legal hurdles. Without them—and explicit instructions in Zack's will—the kids and I would have been in a legal and financial quagmire had anything happened to him. With the stroke of a pen, Zack had taken away all the meager lawful entitlements and responsibilities he'd signed over to me years before. Of course, the kids were grown, so there was no worry about their custody. But, I realized, with Zack's dissolution of my powers of attorney, my documents were still signed over to him to act for me if I was non compos mentis.

It took almost no thought to ask the attorney to transfer all my powers of attorney to Trey. I knew Trey would take care of me and my wishes. It was easy to transfer all my erstwhile trust in Zack to my oldest son. If I were in a coma, I trusted him to pull the plug, for instance, with some remorse. I resentfully doubted Zack would bat an eye at that point.

Anticipating my next questions, Evan gently explained, unnecessarily, that under the present laws I had no claim against Zack for any compensation for our years together. He quickly went on to tell me that Zack was not unfeeling. He recognized our mutual support of each other over the years and had made certain provisions for me, which I could have if I agreed to sign a legal document that guaranteed I would take no immediate or future legal action against him for any or all of his assets.

Bitterly, I realized that by signing that document I would help Zack, who hoped to avoid a North Carolina version of the drama aging twinks had caused the estates of Liberace and Rock Hudson. Zack was scared I wouldn't wait until he was dead, and he was worried about the headlines my legal battle would inspire: AD EXEC IN GAY DIVORCE COURT. This proved either he didn't know me at all or Alicia had demanded it. I swallowed hard and asked what those provisions were. My surprise must have been obvious; I had no idea Zack was well-off enough to give me the settlement he did.

The attorney told me Zack was prepared to hand over the proceeds of the sale of the Oakwood house, which was paid off. With part of the proceeds, he encouraged me to buy another, smaller place, and he'd have the rest placed in an annuity he'd set up for me. How much the annuity would amount to ultimately would depend on what sort of place I bought for myself. In addition to that, Zack had been contributing to an IRA for me for years that I had never been aware of. Of course, any further contributions to that would cease immediately. Separate from the sale of the house, he would pay off my Expedition, transfer the title to my name, and pay the car's insurance for one year.

I signed the "no-sue" contract with no further urging from Evan, which left the next obvious question: Where the hell was I going to go? The upkeep on the house in Oakwood was tremendous. I knew exactly what it cost; I had managed that end of the check-writing for years. Still, that house was the only home I had.

"I see the sense of this, Evan," I said. "But I have no idea of where to look or where to go." He looked a bit uncomfortable for the moment, as if I had given him way more information than he needed. Then he grew thoughtful and concerned.

"Do you intend to stay in Raleigh?" he asked.

"I have no idea. I have no family, other than the one we just tore up. I've spent my entire adult life here. I'd like to stay near the kids, but they're all living their own lives now. I certainly don't like the thought of bumping into that bitch of Zack's in the grocery store."

Evan allowed himself to laugh at that, which endeared him to me immediately. "I can understand that, Chris," he said. He stood, signaling me that the meeting was over. "Tell you what, with your permission, Zack's authorized me to oversee putting the house on the market. I'll take care of the details of the sale for you, that way you'll save the realtor's fees. I imagine it won't take more than a weekend open house to get a qualified buyer to meet or exceed our price. The best thing that could happen is a nice little bidding war. Why don't you think it over for a few days and give me a call?"

As I stood, a thought hit me. "Will I have enough money to buy a beach place?"

Evan gave me a cautious nod, then he told me what he thought the Oakwood house would bring. I had to sit back down.

"Really, do you think it's worth that much?" I asked incredulously.

"I think I'm being somewhat conservative, actually," he replied with a smile.

Resting my elbows on the arms of the leather chair in front of his desk, I put my face in my hands and rubbed my eyes. I was both overwhelmed by Zack's generosity and by the opportunities it presented me. In truth, my prospects were excellent. The chance that

I'd end back up in a housing project would be eliminated if I were conservative. I would, however, have to get a job. Both the annuity principal and the IRA would be locked up for years to come—17 years, to be exact. I would have to be 65 before I could begin to draw from them. Suddenly I realized after a lifetime of fear, I didn't have to be afraid. In fact, I could do well, if I were smart about managing my sudden windfall.

"Chris, I'm sorry. I have another appointment," Evan said, breaking my reverie. "Think about it and give me a call in a week."

I stood, awkwardly shook his hand, and thanked him as if he were the author of my future well-being, not Zack.

Once I got home I considered calling Zack to express my gratitude. Instead, I told myself I had my pride first of all and always, and I didn't want to sound like a grateful beggar. I had *earned* what he'd allowed me in the end. If you took into account 22 years of what child care and a personal assistant would have cost, it was at least a break-even situation for him. With that realization, I didn't call Zack—I called Trey.

In my mind, it wasn't hard to see the solemn five-year-old I'd met more than two decades ago in the man he grew up to become. With an MBA and a successful new career as an investment banker, he really wasn't much different from the little boy I'd taken to the bank to make deposits in his savings account when he was 10. He'd always been shrewd with his money.

It took a moment to get through to him, but after a mildly irritating wait with Muzak in my ear, he answered his office phone by saying, "I suppose you've seen Evan Strickland."

"Yes, buddy and hello to you too," I replied.

"I'm sorry Chris. I'm in a meeting right now. But I'd like to stop by on the way home. Could you please call Susan and tell her I'll be late?"

"Of course."

"Six then?"

"Thanks, Trey."

"Don't buy anything before I get there, okay?"

"I'm rich aren't I?" I said with a happy laugh.

"No. You're not. Believe me, Chris. Bye now." And he was gone.

I called Susan and told her Trey'd be late and why. After we talked about her concerns for me and I'd asked about how things stood with Trey and his father, she rang off as well. They were eagerly engaged in careers that I couldn't begin to fathom. When I was their age I was embarking on a career of mommyhood. While I never thought it'd pay out in spades, I didn't regret not having the socially engaged world they lived and moved in.

In the two hours before Trey arrived, the thought of moving to the beach grew steadily more attractive. Though I was basically a loner, and Zack always drew pretty harsh lines dividing his personal life from his business and social life, I learned quite a bit about Raleigh society from our various small circles of friends. Many first wives migrated to the beach or the mountains after their divorces. I had often wondered why—now I understood. When I told Evan Strickland I didn't want to bump into Alicia Stiles-Ronan in the grocery store, I knew I'd joined the first (or second) wives club.

But it was more than that. Like a hamster in a Habitrail, my life made its way through a warren of streets and destinations that had grown beyond familiar over the years. While it was comfortable to be greeted by name in the bookstore, the dry cleaners, and the post office, my route between them was also totally limned with references to a life I'd suddenly outgrown. Every street I wound along called to mind all the treats and tricks of a life that wasn't mine anymore.

The beach was vastly different in that regard. Though since the kids were small Zack had always taken us to the beach for a week during the summer, those memories were sustaining, not deadening. For me, the beach was always summery and shining with good memories. There was no accretion of life's day-to-day worries and concerns along the coast road and in its small towns, souvenir and surf shops, motels, and distinct neighborhoods.

As my library of books and future dreams grew, as my hair grayed under the carefully blonded streaks over the years, I saw myself as someone who would end up on the beach as he grew old. In my carefully nurtured reveries of retiring there with Zack, I'd still always pictured myself alone in a cinematic long shot, walking near the surf with seagulls circling overhead in the early morning light. It was an idealized picture I'd stolen from a lifetime's worth of TV commercials for everything from painkillers to track shoes, no doubt. Yet, it was something I'd been working toward for years. I'd bought into a Kodak moment when I made the split-second determination to take on Zack and the kids. Moving to the beach at this point in my life was a Kodak moment all my own.

Sitting in my kitchen in the Oakwood House, waiting for Trey, I thought a move to the beach would be the best thing for me. It was a pleasant picture I was seeing in my imagination. Surprisingly, it was a picture Trey saw for me as well. He came into the kitchen from the back door as I was lost in my sandy reverie and gave me a quick hug before he slumped into his place at the kitchen table.

"Long day?" I asked.

"You have no idea. Do you have any scotch?"

"That bad, huh?" I got up to get the bottle out of the pantry.

Trey rubbed his eyes, then looked up at me and smiled. "Nope. Just that long."

I poured him a generous slug over some ice and poured some bourbon for myself as well. I settled the drinks before us and sat again at the table.

Trey sipped at his drink appreciatively, then looked at me warmly. "I'm happy to hear you're pleased with Dad's settlement offer."

"How much of it do you know about?"

Trey sighed. "All of it. I didn't want you to know beforehand, but Dad had been in to see me before he told you he was leaving."

Feeling somewhat betrayed, I just looked at him, hurt and somewhat stunned.

"Don't be mad at me Chris. He came to me professionally. I've been managing some of his money since I got my job. He made a little rain for me that really helped when I was starting out. Bringing in new clients is part of what I do. Who else is going to trust a snot-nosed kid with a brand-new MBA? In the bank's eyes, a family investment in your potential, well...it's pretty much expected when you're new."

I touched my split lip unconsciously and looked at him. "You knew. All that drama Saturday night, and you knew. No wonder all you could talk about was the money."

Trey shook his head and had a fuller taste of his drink. "It's how I love, Chris. Ask Susan. It's who I am. For me, looking after my

loved ones is all about making sure they're taken care of financially." Trey gave me a penetrating look across the table. "You understand what I'm telling you, right, Chris?"

In light of what he'd just said, I understood completely. With all
due respect to Zack, it didn't take much thinking for me to understand my unexpected security had much more to do with Trey than
it did with his father. While Zack had never been stingy, he'd never
been exactly generous either. I was sure Trey had run the numbers
for his father and showed him the benefits of taking care of me in
the way he had. Ultimately, Zack was probably much less afraid I'd
make news by suing him than he was afraid I'd irreparably dent his
bank account. Trey had looked out for my best interests and still
gotten the numbers to come out right. I bet that had pissed Alicia
off. I nodded and looked down at the table. My kids. Thank God
for my kids. "I understand, baby." I said. "Thanks for getting his
numbers to come out right."

"Chris, it was more than that. I was looking out for you—
please understand that."

"I'm sorry, Trey. That was more what I was getting at. I know
you took care of me."

Trey nodded in return, finished his drink, then held out his
glass, rattling the ice against its sides, to wordlessly demand a refill.
I knew where he picked up *that* habit. *Behold the new head of the
family.* I took his glass, stood, and made him another.

He watched me as I turned back to the table and put the glass
of scotch down in front of him before reclaiming my seat. I was
sure he wasn't even aware of what he was doing—he always had
the imperious understanding that he was next in line to the throne.
In fact, I'd encouraged him in that direction by reminding him that,
as the eldest son, he had a responsibility to the younger ones.

"Chris, you are not rich," Trey said. "But you can be comfortably off if you listen to me. You *are* going to have to get a job to
make that happen. First, you have to get out from under this barn of
a house and find yourself something smaller and easier to keep up."

I looked up at him, and nodded to let him know that was what
I was doing. Shorter than any of my kids, I'd been looking up to
them since they were in their teens. Now I had to look up to them
out of respect. From this time forward, Trey would be the acting

head of the family—and that was a bit disconcerting. It was like the Irish mafia. I decided I had to tell him what was really on my mind. "What would you say if I told you I wanted to move to the beach...find a small cottage, and move away to start over?"

Trey looked at me sadly. "Well, I'd say I don't want you so far away. But if I wasn't being selfish, I'd tell you it wouldn't be a bad idea."

"Thanks for that—the first part especially—but can you tell me why you think it wouldn't be a bad idea?"

"Well, you'd be away from...well, you know. Then too, beach real estate is a good investment. After getting such a chunk as you'll get from the sale of this place, you're going to need to reinvest in another home eventually to keep from having to pay capital gains taxes. Even if we reinvest in your annuity—which I'm managing by the way—there are still eventual tax liabilities to consider that we can offset if you own a home. Then there's the long-term investment potential. A beach house is going to bring you a far greater and more stable return than anything else we could put your money in right now."

"What about hurricanes?" I asked.

"Hurricanes are the insurance companies' problem. As long as you don't worry too much about the possibility you might have to rebuild at some point."

I was silent for a minute, taking it all in. "So, simply put, you don't think it's a bad idea?" I finally asked.

Trey grinned. "No, I think it's a great idea. I actually have a place in mind for you to look at if you're interested."

It was my turn to grin. "I'm all ears."

"I have a client who needs to...well, let's just say he needs to reallocate some of his assets. He's almost finished building a beach place down at Emerald Isle. It's not huge, but it's certainly big enough for you and Beau—"

"And you and Susan, and Andrea and David, and Schooner—big enough for you all to visit?"

"Well, probably not all at the same time, not comfortably anyway. But Chris, it's brand-new, not even finished at this point. The roof's on and the interior rooms are roughed in. Your maintenance should be minimal because they're building it with all these new kinds of weather-resistant materials. I wanted to buy it for Susan and me, but I can't quite swing it just now. You could drive down and take a look at it if you want."

"Sure. I'd like that a lot."

Trey nodded and finished his drink in one long swallow. "I'll set it up. Meanwhile, hold off on pulling Evan Strickland's trigger. It looks like interest rates are going to stay low and I can get you a bridge loan to cover you until this house sells, if you decide you want to buy the beach place. But you have to give it time to get built out. I think this place'll go quick, and we can't leave you without a place to live."

He stood, and I stood along with him. "Thanks, Trey. For everything."

Trey stepped around the table and opened his arms, "C'mere, Chris, and give me a hug. You don't have anything to worry about. I'll see to it you're okay."

I stepped into his hug and felt his arms close around me. I wondered how I'd managed to grow such strong, tall boys. I didn't do anything but put out the feed and holler "c'mon," as far as I was concerned, Nonetheless, Trey and Schooner were both strong enough to bother themselves carrying me. I was a little overwhelmed. After returning his hug, I looked up at him once more and said, "I'm glad to hear you don't mind looking after me. As of today you have my powers of attorney and the right to pull the plug when I'm pitiful and drooling."

Trey hugged me tighter briefly, then let me go. He crossed himself quickly, stepped away, and picked up his coat. "God forbid I have to deal with that anytime soon."

"From your mouth to God's ears," I said.

He pulled on his coat and gave me a small, bashful glance. Without looking at me, he said, "I want you to know how much I appreciate you trusting me, Chris."

I walked to the kitchen door and held it open for him. "Just remember," I said, "you never get grown to your mama."

Trey stood still in the kitchen. "I think Dad's a total asshole, Chris. Seriously."

"Well, thanks for that, baby. But I'll tell you just like I told your brother: Cut him some slack. He's just a pitiful, aging man trying to outrun the inevitable. That's how I see it. But I don't begrudge him his foolishness, thanks to you kids."

Trey nodded and moved past me, awkwardly touching my cheek as he passed. With a sure-footed step down the back steps, he was gone. With no little bit of excitement over the prospect of a beach house, I went back into the warmth of my kitchen and my drink.

Within a week, I was walking through the same rooms I wandered now. Then they were only a sketch of space rendered in two-by-fours and rough-cut plywood holes awaiting windows. Now the ceilings were covered in beadboard, and the walls stood solidly between this room and that awaiting my new furniture coming that day. I smiled at the emptiness, imagining the colors and textures that would make the echoing coldness come alive—make it a home.

Probably more than anyone else, Wade Lee would be happy to see the place now. He'd driven down to meet me after the last hurricane of the season to make sure the place wasn't damaged and to measure and dream about what the place could become.

Buying the house before it was completed allowed me to pick finishes, floor treatments, appliances, fixtures, trim work, and cabinets. For once, I'd have all the built-in bookcases I'd ever wanted. Trey had come up with a budget for me after he conservatively considered what the house in Oakwood would bring. Wade Lee helped keep me on course, though I had a few splurges before I hit the outer limits of Zack's guilt and he cut me off of his credit cards. No first wife ever had a better time putting together the box to hold a new life and assembling the things to put in it.

Excited finally to have the gray days between February and Thanksgiving's end behind me, I got busy. While waiting on the furniture delivery truck, I vacuumed my new Oriental rug, carefully avoiding Beau, who slept near the middle, farting and making tiny movements with his big grizzled nose as if he could sniff a duck on the wing. Chesapeake Bay retrievers are supposed to be ill-tempered, but Beau was always a good-natured dog. In any case, he was 14, and I didn't even think he could hear the vacuum. His life had changed so much over the past few years; I thought he was past ignoring the differences. I really believed he just preferred to sleep and dream.

I often wondered what Beau dreamt of. Did he relive the days when the kids were young and ran him all over hell's half acre chasing balls and sticks and even sofa cushions until I worried he would have a heart attack? Did he dream of Schooner? Whom he slept with until Schooner left for college? Did he dream of a piece of meat or a biscuit that I'd secretly stashed for him away from the kids' ravenous hunger? Did he dream of his own old place: on the far-left cushion on the sofa in the den?

I turned off the vacuum and stashed it in the empty new hall closet. I closed my eyes before I turned back to the great room. Then I opened them to take in the acres of antique Oriental rug I'd splurged on. I'd wanted one like it for years before I saw this one in the rug store in Norfolk. It was the weekend Zack married Alicia. I'd left the house and Beau to the kids and drove up to visit Wade Lee.

Wade wasn't any help that day—there was no keeping me from splurging on things for the beach house. He'd always had more money than sense, and when I'd walked away and gone back to the rug four times, he told me if I didn't buy it for myself, he was going to. At just that moment I began to see where I was going and to appreciate everything I could do while I was getting there. For the first time in my life I could make a life exclusively for myself—I could furnish it to my taste and to the limits of the money I had access to. It was an incredibly satisfying feeling.

I opened my eyes and took in the wonderful blue, yellow, coral, and ochre of my great big rug. The wintry sun flooded through the uncovered windows and filled the large empty room. I almost wished the furniture I'd picked out so carefully and ordered so many weeks ago wasn't coming at all. When I met Zack I didn't have much. Now, looking at the intricately knotted pattern border of the rug's blue field, I felt almost as light and free as I did back then. It seemed magical surrounding my sleeping, dreaming old dog. Empty of crowding furniture, the room was as immense as the future, full of promise and possibility.

A wave of optimism welled up inside me. Everything was going to be all right. The phone rang loud from the kitchen side of the great room, and I practically sprinted to catch it. I was breathless when I picked up the receiver.

"Chris, are you okay?" my eldest asked.

"Trey! Yes, I'm great. I should know better than to really run to get the phone. How are you?"

"Really busy, Chris. I'm between meetings, but I got a message you called."

"I won't keep you," I said. "I just needed to let you know I have all of the Christmas ornaments. I thought you and Susan might like some of them for your own tree."

There was a long pause while this mundane business found a niche in Trey's complicated organizational thinking. I pictured him weighing his emotional obligation to me against the sentimental value of all the Hallmark ornaments he loved, then again against meetings and potential schedule conflicts. "Sure Chris, that's really nice of you to think of us. I'll have Susan call you and we'll set up a time to visit and pick them up. I want to get a mental picture of you situated in your new place, in any event."

"Great. That's super, you know…whenever."

"Chris? I really have to go, but are you really okay?"

"I'm fine and happy, Trey. I'm waiting on my new furniture to be delivered and Beau's sleeping in the sun. We're great." I hoped Trey didn't think I sounded depressed. God forbid I should come off as needy when I didn't feel that way at all.

"That's a load off my mind, Chris. Pat the ol' boy for me. You take care."

"You too, bye."

"Bye." Trey was off and gone. I wondered if he honestly heard a word I said. With the heavy weight off his shoulders of getting me out of the old house and into the new one, he'd necessarily moved on to other things. Knowing him like I did and imagining the demands on his attention, I supposed he'd have a spontaneous recall of the entire conversation about the middle of next January.

I had also left messages for Andrea and Schooner. I thought they might like having some of the old ornaments, even if they just kept them stored away in boxes. Andrea had always been very much into themed occasions and decorations; I fully expected her to have a Christmas tree with peacock feathers and gilded bird's nests. Of course, Andrea needed to do things her own way. She always had. Not having a mommy in the literal sense of the word always put her at odds with me, which left her to intuit how to do girl things in her own idiosyncratic fashion. In her grown-up patterns of domesticity I saw strong echoes of how I ran the house when the kids were growing up, but I took great pains not to tell her so.

I opened the drawer to the left of my new Viking range (another expensive sop to my damaged ego, encouraged by Wade Lee's solicitude and paid for by Zack's guilt money), where I'd placed my wire whisk, my stainless steel ladles and strainers, my wooden spoons and spatulas, my carving set, my manual can opener, and my corkscrew. In Andrea's kitchen you'd find the same assortment of crap in the left-hand drawer by her stove. I'd never been a fan of cutesy tchotchkes, and Andrea's kitchen counters were littered with them, but when it came to a certain kind of junky organization, I'd made my mark.

Schooner was the one I most wanted to hear from. He loved the cheesy, tinkly, fragile glass ornaments—especially the tiny blown-glass bells that we always hung from the tips of the tree branches and the hulking mercury glass ornaments of the later, prosperous years.

Andrea and Trey were each sturdy enough in their own ways. It was Schooner I worried about, in the collision of his father's blind will to reinvent his life with the way the kids saw their dad, me, and themselves. In the frantic redrawing of boundaries, Schooner had pulled away from all of us. Alternately distant and tender, Schooner blew in and blew out of our last Thanksgiving in the old house with a mysterious agenda and unspoken obligations elsewhere. He had never been a secretive kid, but I had the distinct impression he wanted to be as far from us as possible to avoid our questions and clingy expressions of concern. It's hard for some boys to become men. They have to wean themselves from the source of nurture with a relentless, set-jaw determination that really is pitiful. I could understand that—being male myself—but it was especially poignant when I saw that inclination in my baby.

I heard air brakes outside and saw the truck outside idling—the driver was looking for the house number on the pilings holding up the house. Stepping over Beau, I opened the French doors onto the deck and stepped out to wave to the delivery guys.

"You don't want your new house to look like Pottery Barn, circa summer 2003," Wade Lee had said on another refugee trip I made up to Norfolk to outrun the emptiness Zack's departure had left me with. Watching the delivery guys uncrate and bring up the clean, tailored new furniture Wade talked me into buying, I was glad I had listened to him.

I had the guys set the sleek new armchairs and a low, coral lacquered table by the fireplace. I tugged the sections of a leather mango-colored Roche Bobois sofa into position myself while they set up the red Italian contemporary bed in my room. I pulled the new wicker chairs for the sunroom in front of their bank of windows while the crew brought up a new teak sideboard and tucked it behind the hair-raisingly expensive sofa. With the new guest bed set up properly and the round pedestal table assembled by the bookshelves, the new stuff was all in place.

I was mentally arranging the antique dining table and yellow-ochre leather Cassina cab chairs Wade Lee was holding for me when the driver presented me with the delivery slip to sign. After I scribbled my name awkwardly and slipped him a generous tip, he said, "Buddy, you might want to keep an eye on your dog. He don't look so good."

Through all the commotion and comings and goings of the delivery men, Beau hadn't moved. He lay on his side, with his legs pointed stiffly away from his body. His breath labored his sides, and his paws were trembling. Alarmed, I handed the delivery guy his clipboard and walked around my new furniture to Beau's side and knelt down.

"Beau? Beau-baby? Are you okay?"

My old dog opened his eyes and looked at me. A little bit of blood-flecked foam had gathered at the corner of his mouth. He tried to raise his head and made a sound that was more of a mew than anything like his usually rumbling greetings. I put a hand under his head and lifted gently. There was no help from him in the movement—his big old head rested heavily in my hand. I looked up at the delivery guy and said, "Can you help me get him to my truck?"

I couldn't recall ever seeing one on the beach road, but I remembered seeing a vet's office across the bridge on the mainland. Making my way there, I cooed to and comforted Beau as best I could from the driver's seat. He was a good boy. He never whimpered or cried once. Halfway to the bridge, I spotted the sign for a

vet's office in a strip shopping center and nearly rolled the
Expedition when I braked hard and took a sharp right into the
parking lot.

I must have been pretty wild-eyed, because the receptionist took
one look at me coming in the door and called out "Dr. Heath!" A
moment later, the man himself strode through a swinging door
behind her, accompanied by a younger man I automatically assumed
to be the doctor's assistant. I didn't really have time to notice the doctor except to note he was male, fairly tall, and kind of rawboned.
The young man with him only took one look at his rangy, ropy self
to know he was trouble—trouble for me, anyway. Even in the midst
of my panic, I thought *Jimmy Worley* and tried to avoid his eyes.

"It's my dog," I said on the verge of panic. "I've got him out in
the truck. I think he's dying."

The doctor followed me out to the parking lot, let me get the
back hatch open, and promptly climbed in and sat down by Beau's
head. He gently stroked Beau's shoulder and flank, then opened his
eye to check his pupils. Putting on his stethoscope, he flashed a
glance at me as he placed the end of the instrument on Beau's side.
He looked up at me searchingly and motioned for me to sit opposite him as he took off his stethoscope.

"What's his name," he asked softly.

"Beau," I said as I gently smoothed back Beau's ear.

"I'm Dr. Aubrey Heath, but most people just call me Heath."

It was starting to dawn on me that I was really losing Beau, but
I pushed the thought of it away. I said, "My name's Chris Thayer."

"Well, Mr. Thayer—"

"Chris. It's Chris," I said.

"Chris, I'm sorry. Beau's gone."

"Tough break," the younger man commented. I didn't realize
he'd followed us to the truck. "But he looks old for a Chessie."

I just looked at him, astonished at his heartlessness.

"Steve knows Chesapeakes—he breeds them," Heath explained
gently.

"My name's Steve Willis," the young man said. "I'm real sorry
about your dog."

I looked at him and nodded, warmed slightly by his sincere tone
after his initial tough comment.

"I got a bitch ready to find puppies about New Year's. You let Heath know if you want me to keep you one. You know, if you're ready by then," he said, and stuck out his hand. I took it and felt his callused palm give me a quick, tough squeeze. He said, "Well, I'd better get on the road." He let go of my hand and nodded brusquely. "Heath."

"See ya then, Steve," Heath said

As he walked away, I said impulsively, "I'll be in touch."

Without looking back, Steve raised his hand and strode across the parking lot to a truck I took to be his. The truck was jacked up for four-wheel driving and spattered with mud.

I looked back at Heath searchingly.

"Steve's a good guy," he said. "Don't mind him being abrupt. He really meant well, it's just how he is."

I nodded and looked back down at Beau. I felt so disloyal even thinking about this Steve guy's offer of a new puppy with Beau not even cold.

"I can take care of Beau for you now if you'd like, Chris."

Heath's warm voice was scarce more than I could take at the moment. I felt the tears come and I choked back a sob.

"Would you like a moment to say good-bye now?" he said.

I looked at him gratefully.

"I'm not trying to be crude, but Beau's going to start to leak a little soon. His muscles are relaxed. I just want you to be aware— it won't be long—so you're not surprised, okay?"

I nodded.

"I'm going to step back inside and get a towel for Beau, okay? When I come back, I'll have someone help me get him inside for you and you can let me know what you'd like to do then. Sound good?"

I tried my best to smile at him, but my tears couldn't wait. "Why is it so hard?" I demanded of the man. "Why is this so god-damned hard?"

"It ain't never easy. Believe me." Heath patted my shoulder and left.

I lifted Beau's old head and slipped my weight across the gate of the Expedition to cradle it in my lap. I stroked his muzzle, apologizing for bringing him so far from home. It was so far for both of us to come just for him to die. I cried for both of us. I cried until Heath came and took Beau away.

"So, have you grieved?" Andrea demanded.

"Well, yeah. I mean, I cried when I got home," I lied, eyeing Wade Lee as he placed wingback chairs covered in a white denim at opposite ends of the marvelously patina'd mahogany Regency dining table he'd brought up, along with a 25-foot U-Haul load of things he'd selected and things I'd bought. "Hold on, Andrea…Wade, aren't wingbacks a little much?"

"Not considering how much time you spend sitting at your kitchen table. And face it, honey, this may scream 'formal,' but it's really whispering 'kitchen.' "

"Chris, who's that?" Andrea asked.

"It's Wade. He's brought down some stuff I picked up in Norfolk to go in my new house."

"Oh. Well, that'll be worth a trip down to the beach just to see how he's tarted up the place. Anyway, have you *really* grieved?"

"Andrea, what do you want me to tell you? Of course I grieved. Beau was always really my dog. Despite what all you kids might claim, I fed, walked, and watered him. I'll miss him a lot."

"Chris, it's okay to let the loss of Beau take on more significance than you might think appropriate. You should let Beau's death be a means to grieve for all that's happened to you—to our family—in the past year."

I rolled my eyes at Wade Lee. "Hon, I understand that. Really, it's Schooner who seems to have taken your advice. He liked to fell out crying when I told him over the phone last night. It took me quite awhile to let him get it all out of his system."

"Besides that, how is my baby brother?" Andrea asked. "He didn't seem himself at Thanksgiving. I mean, I really expected him to be a little more emotionally available, considering how sad it was for all of us to be together one last time in the old house."

"He's fine—final exams are this week. He's promised to come down to the beach for a few days after he's finished. So, Andrea, would you like any of the old family Christmas ornaments? I thought you and David might like some, just for your kids some-day, even if they're not what you'd really like. I mean, what would go well with your overall Christmas design—"

"Chris, I really can't deal with Christmas just now. I don't even think we're going to decorate. I just have too many unresolved feelings surrounding the breakup of our family. Our things scattered to the four winds. Beau dying. It's all really too much."

"Andrea, I respect your feelings and everything. But sweetheart, you must learn not to be so fragile. Our family hasn't broken up. We've just shifted. We've adjusted ourselves to accommodate someone your father loves very much—even a new baby."

"I don't see how you can be so emotionally accommodating, Chris," Andrea replied. I could hear her microwave come on and the tense slam of cutlery hitting her kitchen counter. "I don't know if I can ever forgive the old goat."

It was as if she were still 13 years old. "He's still your father Andrea, and I'll not listen to you talk about him that way," I reminded her who was the mom and who was getting to be Miss Fussy-Pants. "I don't see myself as emotionally accommodating, I'm just a grown-up. I can't begrudge the man a happy life—"

"Even at your own expense?" Andrea demanded. I was getting tired of the whole conversation. Wade Lee was unrolling a particularly beautiful frayed silk prayer rug that fit wonderfully in the space between my serving island and the new table.

"Andrea, my own girl-baby, I love you. You've grown into a very wise and mature young woman in so many ways. But just now, I don't want to talk about all this anymore. I'm grieved out. I want to get on with it, okay?"

"I want to come see you. I miss you," Andrea said softly. "No matter where you are, that'll always be home, Chris."

"Thanks, sweetheart."

"Let me speak to David and we'll see when we can get down, okay?"

"That would be lovely. Give David a hug for me, okay?"

"Okay, Chris. I love you."

"I love you too." Filing Andrea's neurosis away for further pondering at a later time, I hung up the phone and gave my attention to my friend.

Wade Lee gazed critically at the rug on the floor and moved it a foot farther away from the table. "What do you think?"

"I think that's probably one of my favorite things I bought for the house," I said.

"I agree. Now, let's have a nice, large bourbon before we start unpacking the blue and white. I need some inspiration to find a place for those huge temple jars and all that damn Blue Willow crap you bought on eBay."

"You love Blue Willow and don't lie and say you don't," I replied.

"I got rid of all mine years ago, thank you very much. I'm all about Vieux Paris gold-plated porcelain at the moment."

"No shit?" I said as I walked barefoot across the soft, worn rug on my way to the cabinet for glasses and the refrigerator for ice.

"You'll see for yourself if you come up for Christmas."

I found the bourbon still in a box in the pantry. There was dust on the bottle and the seal had never been broken. I hadn't even thought of a drink in the whole week since I moved in. I poured a generous slug over the ice in both glasses.

"What do you think?" Wade asked as he reached for his drink and gestured toward the large blue-and-white temple jars. They were sitting side by side on the teak-stained hardwood floor under the sideboard behind the sofa.

After I pondered the tableau for a moment, I said, "I think if you give two faggots enough money perfection *will* be achieved. Accessories will complement and taste will triumph over all adversity and heartbreak."

"Except for the internalized homophobia, that sounds like a toast to me baby," Wade said as he clinked his glass against mine. "Now, drop your suddenly slimmer ass down by the fire and tell me all about this hunky vet."

"Do you really think my ass is smaller?" I asked.

"Tragedy is a diet that can't be beat, sweetheart. You look like you've fallen off quite a bit." Wade looked at me critically as he sank into a club chair by the fire.

"Thanks!" I said. I was definitely cheered.

"Seriously, Chris. You need to get back into the life. You're too young to lock yourself up in this house alone. You're looking great for your age. You'd do well on the computer-dating scene. You could even use a current picture."

"Wade, get real. I don't even have a computer. Besides, you aren't cruising on the Web are you? I mean, isn't that an invitation to get beat up or robbed or worse?"

Wade Lee chuckled. "No more than picking up a trick in some bar and taking him home. You used to be pretty good at that. As I recall, that's how you met Zack."

"Yeah, you're right. But there's a big difference between seeing the guy in the flesh—getting some kind of read on him in person—rather than just hooking up in a chat room."

"How would you know?" Wade asked pointedly. "You don't even have a computer."

"Well, I'm not illiterate. I know what goes on in those chat rooms."

Wade Lee finished his drink and reached across to put his glass down on the low table between us. Giving me a dark, conspiratorial look, he said, "I could tell you some pretty hot stories."

"Would you like another? I've got to get my cigarettes if this is going to turn into an episode of *Sex and the City*."

He nodded and said, "Who said anything about the city? I've hooked up on this very beach. It's how people meet for sex these days. To hell with going to a club."

"Okay slut, tell me all about it." I downed my own drink and stood a bit unsteadily to fetch us both a refill.

"Oh you get the usual trolls, and the usual tubby guys who say they have swimmer's build. More like a heifer's build. I swear to God, you can tell how long someone's been in the life by the length of their teats these days."

I lit a cigarette and searched the kitchen for an ashtray. "Andrew Holleran wrote not too long ago that the nipples are the sexual odometer of a guy's body."

Wade snorted. "I read that. If that's the case, I've tricked with guys who are on their second hundred thousand miles. Same chassis. Teats long as my little finger."

"No you didn't say that!" I laughed, finding an ashtray and pouring new drinks.

"Oh hell yeah, girlfriend. Rusty gray chassis at that!" Wade Lee hooted from the living room.

I managed to balance the drinks and the ashtray and rejoin him by the fire, but I spilled a bit of the bourbon as I set the glasses down on the table.

"Damn son, didn't I teach you better than to serve a cocktail without a cocktail napkin?" Wade Lee said. "You aren't living in a barn full of those young 'uns of yours. You have nice things now."

"Forget about it, tell me a hot story. I don't want to hear about those nasty Richmond society queens with their 54-inch waists or 55-year-olds with 30-inch waists. Tell me about someone real and hot."

"I will not forget about it! Do you have any idea what alcohol will do to this lacquer finish? March your little ass back into the kitchen and bring me a napkin if you want the sleaze."

I did as I was told and also fetched with my pack of cigarettes and the bottle of bourbon to sit on another napkin between us. "Okay, bitch. Tell me about someone who fulfilled a fantasy *off*line."

Wade tutted over my paper napkins, then said, "I got on Man4ManSexNOW when I was here on an installation a couple of months ago. I hooked up with this construction twink—nice body. Of course, he wanted me to fuck him."

"Of course," I said smugly.

"He had the Ford logo tattooed across the small of his back," Wade Lee said archly.

"No fuckin' way. Did I ever tell you I almost got a tattoo across the small of my back once?"

"Many times. That juvenile delinquent you did in high school, right?"

"You know all my stories," I said affectionately.

"Well, you don't have that many. Now, do you want to hear about my Atlantic Beach hottie or not?"

"Okay, go ahead. He had a Ford logo tattoo?"

"Uh-huh, yes he did. Let me tell you. He was built Ford tough."

"Hot."

"Oh hell yeah, came on a dime and was ready for another road test not 10 minutes later. I had to tell the young 'un to give me a chance to catch my breath. This is a nineteen hundred *fifty-two* model here. Can you honestly imagine what that Ford tattoo is gonna look like when he's my age. It turns my stomach."

"Did he talk?" I asked.

"What do you mean did he talk?"

"I mean, did you, like, have some sort of conversation?"

Wade Lee broke out laughing. "Chris, he didn't come to my hotel room to discuss Proust or the war in Iraq. If he'd tried, I'd have done my best to stick my dick in his mouth."

"You are a common whore, you know that Wade Lee?"

"No, I'm really not. I'm just a realist in the new millennium, baby. I'm too old for a lover and I'm too set in my ways to get married. I just want a hot fuck and the sound of a car backing out of my driveway when it's all finished."

"No you don't." I said.

"Yes, I do. That *is* what I want. Your problem is you're an unreconstructed romantic. Well, you can dry up thinking like that at your age. Your pussy will dry-rot for sure."

"Let's leave my pussy out of this," I suggested.

Wade Lee topped off his drink from the bottle and gave me a half-serious look over the rim of his glass as he lifted it. "Your pussy is going to get left out, make no mistake. You Catholics, I'll never figure you out. What was it Woody Allen said in that movie? He wanted to mate for life like pigeons and Catholics. You're divorced now, baby. You better get online, and see what there is to see. Who knows, you might find true love. I'm not saying it won't happen, but you'll sure have a few nice hits in and amongst the misses."

I took his halfhearted toast, but I filed away his advice before I drank to it.

"Now, tell me again about the hunky vet and the hot *dog*-man," Wade Lee prompted. "One of them looked primed to help you get over your grief, *okay*?" he said, and settled deeper into his seat to wait for my answer.

There was nothing really to tell about Steve Willis or the good vet, Dr. Heath. I hadn't seen Steve Willis since the day Beau died, but I had seen Heath since. He had been very nice about Beau, handling his cremation. I didn't grieve all over Heath as Wade Lee hopefully projected and Andrea seemed to expect me to. Actually, I didn't really fall apart for several days. However, Heath was around for the aftermath of my stunning realization of loss.

One morning about a week after Beau died, I got up, threw on a sweatshirt and some jeans, started coffee and—continuing my morning routine—retrieved his leash from the hook I'd put by the door from the kitchen to the deck. I almost whistled for him; then I remembered. I was blindsided by sorrow that I'd glossed over by hanging art, putting away dishes and glasses, linens and new towels, and general house junk.

I knew as long as I kept moving I could keep ahead of the pain, so I just tightened my grasp on Beau's leash, closed the door, and took off barefoot down the street to the beach. The morning was sunny and windless. The sand wasn't even chilly, despite the early hour and the time of year. Because the ocean takes a long time to heat up and cool down, the days were still temperate—even warm—three weeks before Christmas.

I took off blindly along the beach without a destination in mind. There was no one out, and I wondered how stupid I must look as I walked along with a leash in my hand and no dog in sight. It all hit me then—all my senseless, compulsive, conspicuous consumption. I'd decorated and accessorized a house to hold only me: a vain, aging man, alone and discarded. There was no family coming to appreciate the thick towels. There were no helpless sighs of relaxation as someone sank comfortably into one of the generous chairs beside the softly hissing, companionable fire. Everything I'd done in the beach house was carefully calculated to welcome a brood, and there was none coming.

I'd never been given much to introspection; I'd always tried to live in the moment and give no time for regret. But that morning on the beach, I stared dead into a grown man's life, which I had discarded to be a mommy. What had made me so willing to abandon my own career—my own self—to a man and his motherless brood? What was I anyway?

My new home—my new life—was all self-delusion, ashes, and dust. The new furniture's upholstery gave off unmistakable whiffs of formaldehyde. Musky, cloying smells prescient of death rose from the old Oriental rugs. The new oven smelled of gas and subliminally called up crematory dread. The beach stank of a hapless gull, dead and torn apart by God knows what scuttling creatures.

My world was positively rank in the harsh morning light.

My head filled with mucus and my eyes stingily gave up a tear apiece, both immediately drying, chilly on my cheeks. I wiped their itchy tracks away roughly on the fabric covering my shoulders. It was the childish gesture of a once happily oblivious little boy shoved down by the schoolyard bully.

It was all so stupid and self-pitying, I knew it. I laughed at the dark mood to help it pass. I didn't want it to be a dark cloud over my entire day. I knew little goals got me through each day and even moment by moment. There was a pier up ahead and I struck out for it, hoping for some coffee and a small sense of satisfaction having reached it.

There was a grill overlooking the beach inside the pier house. It was decorated with shiny tinsel garland overhead and plastic poinsettias in bud vases on each table. An old jukebox was wedged in one corner. The cook turned around and nodded at me, gesturing generally at the empty tables. The place smelled good with richly drifting scents of greasy eggs and sausage and toast and fresh coffee.

I wasn't aware of anyone in the place other than the cook until I heard a warm voice say "Good morning, Chris." I had stopped beside a booth by the window where Heath sat smoking a cigarette. There was a half-eaten plate of toast, a fried egg, and a grits-smeared empty breakfast plate before him, flanked by a fresh cup of black coffee. Heath eyed the empty leash in my hand and my red face and bleary eyes without any judgment or comment. He stuck out his hand for me to shake. When I took it, his grasp urged me down into the seat across the table.

"How's it going?" he asked.

"Not too bad," I answered. Instead of looking skeptical, Heath nodded and gestured toward a plastic carafe in the clutter on the table.

"Coffee?" he asked.

There was an empty cup and a napkin-wrapped bit of tableware in front of me. I nodded gratefully and he filled my cup. I reached into the pocket of my sweatshirt and pulled out a pack of cigarettes and my lighter.

"Nasty habit," Heath said as he thumped a length of ash off his own cigarette and pushed the ashtray to the space between us.

"Takes a while to get used to it, doesn't it?"

Following his eyes, I looked at the leash I'd absentmindedly set on the table. I lit a cigarette and nodded while I doctored my coffee. "Fourteen years, I had ol' Beau."

"Let me guess. A puppy for the kids and he pretty much became yours, didn't he?

I took a sip of the coffee and felt its warmth spread to the chilly hollow where I figured my heart sat. The coffee made me feel better. "Something like that," I said.

Heath nodded and looked at me steadily. "None of my business, but how'd you come to be out wandering on this godforsaken beach barefooted on a December morning?"

Heath had chapped lips, and smile lines radiating in fans from the corners of his warm hazel eyes. His hair would have been reddish at one time; now it was a ruddy brown, bleached gold on the ends and streaked through with coarse silver. Not a handsome man, but not a bad-looking one either, and near my age, if not dead on it. He patiently waited for me to respond.

"End of one life, start of a new one. What can I say? Look over in that jukebox and you'll find a dozen songs that'll play just like it."

Heath grinned. "That's an interesting way to put it."

"How about you, Dr. Heath? What are you doing eating breakfast all by yourself in the Dine-A-Shore Grill?"

"I wouldn't say the answer is as pretty as a song, but you got the general idea. Want anything to eat?"

I let his evasion go; I was just happy for the company. "No, thanks. I haven't been too hungry lately."

"A full mind and an empty stomach don't make good company."

I smiled and looked down at my coffee cup. Apart from Wade Lee, I couldn't tell you how many years it had been since I had a conversation alone with another man. After I became a full-time mommy I let my hairdresser friends slip away into their own dramas and accomplishments. None of them seemed relevant to a life outside of the clubs. My life was then spent watching *Sesame Street* videos instead of ones from Falcon or Catalina. I didn't have many friends other than the ones that came with Zack. And, ever the loner, I always felt shy and ill at ease with them. I always had felt acutely awkward ever since I was a kid back in Fairview Homes; the feelings were made worse when I was a conspicuous faggot in high school. My growing social aplomb from my early days in Raleigh became stunted when I isolated myself with my kids. Somewhere through the years, I had forgotten what it was like to carry on a sociable, adult conversation with any degree of ease.

"Are you thinking of getting another Chesapeake?" Heath asked.

"I don't know yet, but I'd better make up my mind soon if I'm going to carry around a leash, otherwise people are going to think I'm crazy as hell."

"I think you should take Steve Willis up on his offer of a puppy. He's a good breeder. He's mostly concerned with dogs he trains to seriously hunt, but he always culls out a few he thinks would have a better temperament as pets. Be the best thing for you. I've found dog people aren't ever really happy without a dog."

I smiled at that. Relieved, I realized my sense of humor and simple conversational skills were all coming back to me. "I'm seriously considering getting in contact with Steve, if you'll let me know how. Right now I could use the distraction of a puppy. There's a couple of great things you can say for dogs: They're good listeners and they hardly ever lie."

"That reminds me of this joke Steve told me," Heath said as he put out one cigarette and lit another. "There was this guy walking down the street and he sees this sign in a man's yard that says: 'Talking Dog for Sale—Ten Dollars.'" He paused to check my reaction, and I nodded and sat back against the booth's back and waited for him to continue.

"So the man asks the guy, 'You really got a talking dog?' The guy tells him, yeah, the dog's out in the backyard if he wants to talk to him. So the man goes around to the back of the guy's house and there's this dog lying under a tree—no kind of special dog, just a 'sooner.' You know what I mean, right?"

"Yeah, just as soon one kind as another," I said as I put out my own cigarette, which had burned down to one long cylindrical ash. "Go ahead."

"Well, the man asks the dog can he really talk. The dog says, 'Yeah,' so the man asks him what's his story. Okay? So anyway, the dog goes on and on talking about how he'd learned foreign languages and worked for the CIA as a spy listening in on casual meetings of foreign officials, but he got tired of traveling and moved on back home, took a job working security at the airport, got this bitch pregnant, and ended up settling down. Now he's retired and happy just to hang out. The old boy thanks him for his story and the dog tells him to take it easy.

"The man goes back to the guy's front door and knocks. When the guy comes out on the porch, he asks him why he's selling the dog so cheap. The guy looks at him and says: ' 'Cause he's a damn liar. That dog ain't done none of them things.' "

I laughed until I choked.

CHAPTER THREE,
CHRISTMAS

✛

The sounds were familiar, even in the fog at the edge of sleep. My body remembered and responded despite my confusion. Aware of a strong erection, I stretched and turned to burrow into warm flesh on the other side of the bed only to find the cold expanse of unrumpled, empty sheets. Alone, I listened intently to pinpoint the source of the sounds and could just make out the muffled sounds of sighs, intakes of breath, swallowed cries, and distant rhythmic squeaks. My erection subsided when I realized where the sounds of lovemaking were coming from and who was making them.

My bedside clock read 6:15, and I briefly abandoned my considerable consternation in not having read all the signs correctly in my even stronger need to pee. Still, I remained quiet and waiting in my bed, not wanting to intrude or hinder a certain growing set of sounds that would soon end in releases of breath and sighs I shouldn't be hearing. I turned to face the window and watched as the cold dawn was warmed by streaks of orange and pink against the fading gray sky out over the ocean. I thought of nothing, but let my body recall Zack's imprint.

When I heard the guest shower come on I got up to go to my own bathroom. After I peed and ran my electric razor over my face, I got dressed and straightened my bed covers quickly. I wanted to have the coffee started before I had to face Schooner and his friend Frank. I couldn't help but smirk a little, but I knew I'd better have it wiped off my face before Schooner saw me.

From the counter bar between the kitchen and living room, I pointed the remote thingy at the fireplace, pushed the ON button, and was immediately rewarded with a cheery fire. I made coffee, searched the freezer for a bag of frozen biscuits, and put a half dozen in the oven. I placed three napkins, knives, and breakfast plates on the table along with some butter, jam, and fresh tangerines before I settled at the head of the table in one of the wingback chairs Wade Lee had rightly predicted I'd come to love.

From my vantage point I could survey the fireplace over the sideboard backing the sofa, my shelves stuffed with books, and the paintings on the walls. Hung prominently over the fireplace's mantel was the portrait of the kids on the beach. Without my glasses, their actual faces were a blur, but I could see them clearly in my mind's eye. Trey looked directly forward, engaging the viewer with a winning, lopsided grin. Andrea smiled shyly, her face resting against her brother's bare side, held close by his sheltering arm over her shoulders. Schooner stood a few steps apart, gripping a tremendous whelk shell, staring guardedly at the viewer as if at any moment he might strike out against a probing question or an unwelcome advance into his personal space.

I should have known then, but I didn't. There were a thousand signals I must have picked up on and discarded in the hurly-burly of raising him. I regretted missing all the ways I could have made his life easier—allowing him more latitude on some things, fewer social expectations, more space to open up. I should have known, but I didn't.

Now, Schooner's apparent sexual attractions surprised me. But then his father had always been sexually reflexive according to his own needs and wants. *God*, I thought. *The apple never falls too far from the tree.*

"Good morning," Schooner said, breaking into my reverie. Compact and muscular, he'd become a wrestler, while his brother had excelled at swimming and his sister at basketball. Zack demanded all the kids be jocks (whether they wanted to or not), and made me their chauffeur to practices, meets, and away games nearly from the time they could walk all the way through high school.

The image of sturdy little Schooner determinedly pitting himself against another blocklike bit of boy came unbidden to my mind. There was a grim determination laying thinly over a deeper anger when he was in a meet. God only knows what kind of hell he and his brother and sister got over me. I wondered now how much of that anger my boy had channeled into his sport. I still saw that scrappy boy, in his wet, curling hair, his face now flushed from his shower. He squared his shoulders obstinately, tightening the fabric of his too-small T-shirt across his chest as if he knew what was passing across my face. "Hell-lllo-o-o, Chri-i-is..."

"Sorry, baby. You caught me being really happy you're here," I said.

"I'm glad," he replied as he walked into the kitchen, shaking his head like a young lion, "...because I claim the loft."

"Well, you'll have to clean it out first. Right now, it's full of empty boxes and boxes I haven't even unpacked yet."

"No problem. I'll start with the Christmas decorations first thing," he said as he opened the refrigerator and took out a gallon of milk. "Where do you want the tree?"

I looked back across the wide expanse of the great room and up to the highest peak of the ceiling by the open side of the loft. The only place for the monster tree he and Frank had dragged up to the deck last night was at the end of the bookshelves, by the hall leading to the bedrooms. "How about...Schooner, get a glass, for God's sake."

Schooner grinned as he stopped drinking from the milk jug and replaced its plastic cap. "By the hall, right?"

I stood, went back into the kitchen, and squeezed the nape of his neck hard on my way to the counter. It was like a rock. "Does Frank like coffee?" I asked. Schooner grinned and nodded. I threw him an oven mitt and said, "Take the biscuits out and put them on that plate."

Schooner busied himself with that task while I poured us each a mug of coffee. I had heard the shower go off, and I knew Frank would make an appearance soon. "I like Frank, Schooner. He's welcome to visit with you whenever you come here."

"Not 'here,' *home*," he said as he picked up the hot biscuits one by one and dropped them onto the plate. He blew on his fingertips and looked at me with a grin. I couldn't recall ever seeing his usually grave, pugnacious face so constantly brightly lit with happiness.

"Schooner..." I cautiously began.

"Yeah?"

"Don't hurt him if you can possibly help it."

Schooner looked at me sharply. A bit of temper flared in his eyes and faded as one realization became another. "I'm not Dad, Chris. Do you understand?"

I broke his gaze and looked out the window. "Schooner, I know, it's just that—"

"Chris, don't worry about it, okay?" He said it gently, both to both assure and warn me to leave the subject alone.

I looked back at him. *Jesus*, I thought, *I love this young 'un so much.*

"I'm your kid in more ways than you think," he said.

"I know, baby. I know."

"Don't call me *baby*," he said as he picked up a mug of coffee in one hand and a plate in the other and proceeded to the table, shoulders squared defiantly. I watched as he took the chair closest to my wingback and sat down. He had always held himself apart, but never really too far from me.

I caught Frank in the corner of my eye. He was hesitating before coming all the way to take a place at the table. I had no idea what or how much he heard—I just hoped he understood. "Good morning, Frank. Sit anywhere you want, I've got your coffee right here," I said on my way back to the table.

He looked a little sheepish as his eyes swept the seats at the table and he glanced back at me. I smiled at him encouragingly. I was relieved when he sat down next to Schooner.

Frank wasn't a bad-looking kid; he just wasn't what I'd have pictured for Schooner if I'd figured out he wanted a boyfriend. Sandy-haired and freckled as a mutt puppy, Frank was wiry and alert-looking. He did have a terrific pair of green eyes that wandered around the room, taking in everything and picking up on details. I figured the boy didn't miss a trick.

"Your house is very nice. Isn't that Baker furniture?" he asked.

"You've got a good eye, kiddo. The chairs by the fire are Baker. How do you know about Baker furniture? Are you majoring in interior design?"

Schooner laughed and reached for a tangerine. "He's a parks and recreation major, same as me."

Frank looked relieved at Schooner's save and glanced at me to see if I was taunting him in an oblique way. I wanted so much to tell him to just relax. I wanted to let him know there were no problems with his relationship with my son, as far as I was concerned.

"C'mon Frank, tell him," Schooner said. "How many guys can tell the difference between furniture that comes from Baker and furniture that's just cheap crap?"

Shyly Frank said, "I've worked every summer since I was 14 for my mom. She sells Baker stuff."

Schooner looked at me pointedly. "She does a lot more than sell furniture," he said. "His mom is Kelly Hennessey...you know, she's always in *Southern Accents* and magazines like that."

Oh yeah—I knew his mom, or rather, I knew her work. She was like a god to Wade Lee and other designers who subscribed to the "eclectic casual low-country muted tones of green and gold" design dictum. Frank looked frankly embarrassed, the poor kid. I wanted so much to put him at ease, but I wasn't doing a very good job of it. "Then you must have seen places a lot nicer than this," I ventured, "but I thank you for the compliment."

Frank blushed under his freckles, but gave me a shy smile before he looked down at his plate.

"Here, Frank," I said, passing him the plate of biscuits. "You're going to need some fuel if you're going to help Schooner decorate that ridiculous tree. Schooner, what in hell made you get one so huge?"

Schooner stuffed the rest of his tangerine in his mouth and reached to take the plate of biscuits from Frank. "It needs to be big for all the ornaments," he said with his mouth full. He chewed, swallowed, and looked eagerly at Frank, "I can't wait for you to see all of our family's things...they're all so—"

"Christmas-y," I interjected. "They're all over the map—everything from the kids' homemade stuff to those fragile German tinkly things to Department 57 mercury glass. We've always been big on enthusiasm but not consistency."

"Same as at my house," Frank offered. "The little German pieces we call 'pantoozlers,' like from the Grinch?"

"Hey, that's what *I* call them, right Mom?"

Frank looked at me nervously. Exasperated by so much tiptoeing, I gave up. "That's right, Schooner. That's exactly what you call them." Then, gently: "Frank, please relax. I know our family is a little bizarre, and you must feel a little nervous meeting me for the first time, but I suspect you know Schooner pretty intimately, so welcome aboard, okay?"

Schooner groaned. "Chris, I cannot believe you said that. *Welcome aboard?* Goddamn, how lame."

I gave Schooner a pointed look, and said, "Well, somebody was rocking that boat before they got up this morning."

Frank turned beet-red under his freckles. Schooner just started laughing. Both relieved and delighted by Frank's reaction, I joined right in.

"Jesus, is there anything your family doesn't talk about?" Frank muttered to Schooner.

Schooner put a proprietary arm over Frank's shoulders and leaned back in his chair. "Not much, buddy. Not much."

"Frank, we've kinda had to learn to roll with the punches and laugh at ourselves. I didn't mean to shock you," I said.

Frank looked me square in the eye for the first time since he got to my house. "No, I should apologize to you," he said. "I had no idea we made so much noise. I'm embarrassed and I feel like I was disrespectful to you in your own house. I'm sorry."

I smiled, delighted by his manners and his accent. He spoke with the soft, drawn-out vowels of the South Carolina low country.

Schooner rolled his eyes and tightened his possessive hug around Frank's shoulder.

"Frank," I said, "you're a very well-brought-up Charleston boy and I appreciate your good manners. But you've walked smack into a family of rowdy Irish Catholic rednecks. Save your embarrassment and apologies and just relax. Nothing is off-limits here, though I would prefer you keep some of your rowdiness behind closed doors, okay?"

Frank nodded and offered me a grin that lit up his face in a charmingly elfin way. "If it's okay then, since Schooner embarrassed me, can I ask you a question that's going to embarrass him?"

"Shoot," I said. Schooner dropped his arm warily from Frank's shoulders and rested it on the back of his chair.

"How did Schooner really get his name?"

"I asked his father that same question when he was a baby. You understand our story, right?"

Frank nodded and tilted his head toward Schooner. "You know Schooner—I've managed to get some of it from him, but he plays around so much, I'm not sure what's Schooner and what's…you know."

"Well, I came along just after his mom passed away. He was only a baby then. The truth of the name bit is: Schooner was an accident. His father had been mooning over this actual schooner and just about had all of the plans in place to buy it and take the family to cruise around the Caribbean for a year. Then, Schooner's mom got pregnant and those plans went down the drain. He bought a house instead, to be practical. He insisted the baby be named 'Schooner.'"

"I think he's been pissed at me for screwing up his year at sea ever since," Schooner said with as much conviction as humor.

"I'm Catholic too—'Francis Shawn,'" Frank said. "How did you get a priest to christen him 'Schooner'?"

"Well, he wasn't christened 'Schooner.' A hundred bucks bought the difference between his baptismal and birth certificates. His father said it was the best money he ever gave the church. He's christened 'Michael Patrick,' but on his birth certificate, his name is 'Schooner Michael Ronan.' There you have it."

"I told you that, exactly," Schooner said petulantly.

Frank gave him a small private smile.

"Frank, you must be someone pretty special if he gave you the real story. I don't think he's ever done that before. You should hear some of the amazing things he's told people about his name."

Frank's color heightened again, and Schooner lifted his arm from the back of his chair to grab him in a gentle headlock. Giving me a significant look, he kissed the top of Frank's sandy-colored head. It made me very happy. Deciding I'd taken the line of conversation as far as it needed to go at this point, I said: "So now I've fed you guys. When are you going to get busy getting a Christmas tree *all* up in *here*?"

"Mom thinks it's cool to talk all ghetto. He's addicted to *Comic View* on BET. Please forgive him," Schooner said to Frank. "Isn't the gender thing enough for you?" he said to me. "Do you have to be *black* too?"

I held my fingers in a gangster style, hunched my shoulders, and worked my neck in my best approximation of a rapper. "I'm all about the hip-hop," I said.

"Little bitch fucking thinks he's 50 Cent," Schooner laughed.

"I'm looking for a 50 Cent Christmas album as we speak," I said. Frank couldn't control his manners anymore. He burst out laughing. I smiled so hard my cheeks hurt. I wanted to make Frank relax and feel welcome, and I didn't mind appearing absurd in the process. Wasn't that how parents always looked to their children's friends: earnest, quirky, and embarrassingly absurd? I glanced at Schooner and was rewarded with happiness writ large across his face. He winked at me and I winked back.

"Let me drop you off," Heath said as we left the Dine-A-Shore Grill. I'd gotten in the habit of walking down to the pier for breakfast each morning. I wouldn't admit it, but I was enjoying Heath's easy company. He made me laugh like I hadn't laughed in a long time. We'd talked over eggs, grits, and coffee almost every day since I'd stumbled into the diner with a dogless leash nearly three weeks before.

Even as little as I went out otherwise, I seemed to run into Heath everywhere. I'd began to look for his blue F-150 on the beach road as I drove to the grocery store or the post office. I didn't know how he got any vet-doctoring done, considering how often our paths crossed.

I'd asked Heath if he had kids, but he never gave me a direct answer. There were a great many things I never got a direct answer from Heath about, even after he'd easily managed to get me to spill my guts about being a queer dad and an ex-wife, so to speak. There always seemed to be a personal barrier with him that I hit and respected, so it surprised me when Heath offered to drop me off at my place after breakfast one day.

"Sure, that'd be great, if you don't mind," I told him. The morning was raw now, not four days from Christmas.

"No problem. I'd like to see where you live. It's always good to have a place to go with the person."

I didn't have anything to say about that. To tell the truth, I was a little concerned about how my house might look to him. I wasn't a snob by any means, but I also didn't want to alienate anybody with all my pricey furniture, antiques, Persian rugs, and oil paint-ings. To me they were just things, but even Frank—God love him—recognized Baker furniture and was a little intimidated at first.

Heath followed my directions and we were at the house within 10 minutes of leaving the pier. My 25-minute morning walk took no time at all in a truck. When we pulled into the drive Heath shut off the engine and opened his door without hesitating. I followed him up the steps to the deck and let us in.

Schooner's tree dominated the great room, making it appear less empty and large than it did without it. Heath didn't say a word but strode in as if he'd been coming by for years. The painting over the fireplace caught his eye, and he moved closer to see it.

"Good-looking kids. This is a Karr, isn't it?"

"Thanks. And yes, it is a Karr. Everything you see on the walls is. I've been a big fan of his for a long time."

"So have I," Heath said as he walked slowly around the walls to look at each oil and pastel in turn. Finally he turned to me and smiled. "I have nearly as many as you do."

"Cool," I said. I was relieved in a way I couldn't explain.

"Karr has had a succession of springer spaniels and I've always looked after them," Heath said. "Karr's also often got more paint-ings than cash. So…"

I nodded.

"Nice place, Chris."

"Consolation prize and guilt money," I said.

"You could have done a lot worse. Believe me, I know."

"What *is* your story, Heath? I don't mean to put it so bluntly, but you've never been really forthcoming about yourself. I feel kind of exposed."

"You show me yours and I'll show you mine, right?"

"Something like that."

Heath reached in his jacket pocket for his cigarettes and looked at me questioningly. I sat down on a side chair at the table and motioned for him to sit in the wingback opposite the one I usually sat in. As he sat, I pushed the ashtray between us and fished in my pockets for a cigarette. Heath lit his own and then lit mine.

"I'm from money," he began. "Being the only son, there were a lot of the usual expectations of me as I grew up, went to college. My father was a surgeon, I'm a vet. You begin to see where things start to break down, right?" Heath flicked the ash off his cigarette by flicking the bottom of the filter with his thumbnail. When he caught my eye, I nodded.

"I went into practice near Greensboro with a close friend from vet school. I got married, he didn't. I woke up one morning and decided I didn't want to be married anymore, but I did want to take our partnership a lot further. He was willing, for a while. Years, actually. It all ended rather badly and I'd burned all my bridges. I moved down here to start again." Heath ended his story there and looked me in the eye, waiting.

"It's funny, isn't it?" I said. "People have been coming to this stretch of sand and live oak for over 300 years to start again."

Heath didn't chuckle—he just held my gaze intently. "So..." he said.

"So..." I answered.

"So, you want to have lunch?"

I supposed the UPS man was used to seeing people in various states of surprised undress, but I bet he never had a naked middle-aged man accept a delivery from behind a half-opened door and ask him to put the box down and nudge it in the house with his foot. Then again, he probably had.

I didn't really care. I was absolutely *nekkid* and loving every minute of it. My body was humming like a tuning fork. Stroked, grasped, kissed, and licked, I felt more alive than I had in years. Had sex always been this way, back in the day? Back then my body was sleek and aerodynamic, built for speed. This fine morning, two days before Christmas, my body felt like a cushy sedan with a lush suspension—a Cadillac of a body driven for hours over long stretches on a straightaway, handling sudden curves by accelerating into them and taking the bumpy patches with sighs of ease. I liked being handled by somebody eager for a long, sustained ride, who wasn't just taking me out for a Sunday trip to church and back. That, I decided, was the difference between screwing somebody for the first time and married sex.

I glanced at the box—it was from Zack's agency—and I decided

I'd ignore it. I needed two glasses of orange juice with just enough vodka to give it a twang, and I needed to get my nekkid ass back in bed. This was just a pit stop after all.

But by the time I made the two drinks even my plushious-ness— hell yes! Plush and luscious was how I felt that sunny morning. Even my plushious mood couldn't distract my curiosity about what was in the box. So I left the glasses of spiked juice on the counter, took a steak knife from the wooden block, and went to retrieve the box from the floor by the door.

It was heavy, but it had a weird center of gravity. Something slid inside as I picked it up and carried it to the kitchen table. I went at the clear tape sealing the seams like a pro, slicing through them neatly. Folding back the flaps of the box, I saw what was inside: a ham. Not even a Smithfield ham, but one of the cheap ones. This was what Zack's company sent the employees. Management got a Smithfield ham, underlings and retirees got some cheap-ass off brand.

I started laughing. If I hadn't just spent a stupendous afternoon getting fucked senseless, my self-esteem would have been beat near 'bout to death by that off-brand ham. But in my current state of mind, the ham was just a ham and would be really tasty in a couple of days.

"What's so funny?" Heath called from my bedroom down the hall. Leaving the ham in its box on the table, I picked up the glasses of juice and started back to bed. Halfway there I felt my dick swing and marveled at the weight of my balls. It had been a long time since I thought of my dick as anything other than something to piss through and my balls as anything other than something that got uncomfortably creased in my boxer shorts. Looking down, I saw the whole package bouncing merrily below the slight curve of my belly. *Welcome back, boys,* I thought. *God bless us every one.*

December 24th dawned cold and lonesome. Heath was on his way to Greensboro to visit his sisters, but he said he'd be back by my house around lunchtime on Christmas. There were animal patients and boarders that needed to be checked on. As there were no real patients—only boarders—Heath had promised his assistant that if she covered the feed-up and walking on Christmas Eve, he'd be back in time to do the same chores on Christmas morning. I offered to spell them both as I didn't really have any responsibilities or plans, but Heath declined graciously.

I'd always taken Beau's vets for granted over the years. Heath's difficult dad would have been pleased, I thought, by his fierce commitment to his four-legged patients. I was so sentimental about my own dog that I couldn't even watch stories on animal abuse on the evening news, even though I could abide stories of human murder, abuse, and inhumanity with near immunity.

"Well, I wouldn't go that far," Heath had said when I told him this. "But, I do feel a great responsibility to dogs and cats. Hell, even horses and cows. Human beings took on that concern when we made them so utterly dependent on us."

That resonated very deeply with me. Heath didn't seem to be the kind of person who would discard anyone, animal or human, in favor of a prettier breed or a self-serving need. He wasn't the kind of person to send a cheap ham to the person who raised his kids, in other words.

To get some of the salt out, I set the ham Zack had his office send me to bubbling along merrily in the biggest stock pot I had. After I let it cool a bit, I'd score the tough outer skin and put it in the oven, bathed in bourbon and brown sugar to bake.

I jumped feetfirst into the Christmas spirit the moment I got up. After my morning walk on the beach—which proved to be exhilarating, not depressing, this Christmas Eve morning—I strode up the stairs to the deck, let myself into the cottage, and got busy. I had the tree on, the fireplace on, and the Temptations' Christmas CD playing loud. For no reason other than it was what I always did, I was cooking: peeling potatoes for potato salad, chopping onions and celery for oyster dressing, preheating the oven to bake a pound cake and pecan pies. I was really enjoying the home comfort of habit. I had not heard one word of holiday plans from any of the kids or their spouses, but that didn't really matter. If the food didn't get eaten, I had a near-empty freezer and a long winter ahead.

The phone's ringing caught me by surprise. I picked it up with one hand and tried to reach the volume control on the CD player in the kitchen with the other.

"Hello! Hold on a minute, I've got to turn down the music," I shouted into the phone. I got the Temptations down to a dull roar and picked up the phone again, fully expecting it to be Wade Lee. "Sorry, what's up?"

"Hello Chris, Merry Christmas," a familiar voice said.

"Well, I'll be damned! Merry Christmas to you, Zack." I was surprised, but not really.

"It sounds like you've got quite a party going on there."

"Actually, it's just me, but I'm wide open. Got that ham you sent me cooking right now."

"Yeah? Well...that's great."

"Thanks, Zack. I mean it, I do appreciate the ham. It was thoughtful of you to keep me on the list."

"You're certainly welcome, but that's not why I called."

I realized Zack had no idea I was even on the list.

"I wanted to let you know Alicia and I are having the usual Christmas party tonight, if you'd like to drop by...if you're in town."

"That's great, Zack. But I plan on staying right here. Except for going to Mass, I'm not going anywhere."

"Oh. Well, I thought you might like to see the kids. We're going to open gifts here tonight."

"Oh man, Alicia must be going nuts with the last-minute details. Christmas Eve parties are a lot of work."

"So you don't mind?"

My first thought was *Bastard,* but I said, "Absolutely not, Zack. The kids are all grown and have busy lives. It's probably much more convenient for them to spend time with you and Alicia tonight and have some time to themselves tomorrow. I'll see them sooner or later before Old Christmas."

Old Christmas was January sixth—Epiphany. I had made it a part of the kid's holiday tradition while they were growing up. It was primarily a religious event, but I did hold back one gift apiece to give them on the day tradition said the three wise men arrived to see the baby Jesus. In exchange for the last of their gifts, the kids gave me leftover Christmas cards that I made them each fill with personal promises as a present for the infant Christ.

Over the years I'd collected a lot of cards. I had the box out on the table and planned to string them up around the dining room windows as a sort of garland, like I always did. I loved reading the progression of promises, which ranged from Schooner's crayoned scrawl of his name to Trey's "This year I promise not to fart on Schooner while he's sleeping," Andrea's "I promise not to chew my fingernails" and "I promise not to become a big slut like Mary Katherine Henderson," and Schooner's thoroughly ambiguous "I promise not to smoke any more cheap bud" from last year.

Zack pulled me back from that recollection. "Have you spoken with any of them?"

"No, not for a couple of weeks, but Schooner has claimed my loft."

Zack chuckled at that and said, "Don't let him get too comfortable—he might never leave."

I bit my tongue to keep from saying he shouldn't be so hard on Schooner. Zack had always considered Schooner's casual *je ne sais quoi* as sheer laziness. Instead, I just said, "No problem there."

After an uncomfortable bit of silence, Zack said, "I want you to know how much I appreciate your...*maturity*...over the past year, Chris."

"Ah, sweetheart, I'm really not a child that's surprised you by being well behaved. You've never really gotten that have you? I raised your children into pretty wonderful adults and you've done well by me in return, Zack. I think I didn't do too badly with you, considering I really became just a housekeeper you acquired for nursery duty and the odd blow job now and again."

"Chris, that's not fair. You don't honestly—"

"No, wait. Let me finish. I really don't want to get into this. Can you just believe me when I tell you everything's okay between us, Zack? I'm actually very happy and proud of the life we made together. Now, I'm doing great, really Zack. I'm situated and happy. Okay?"

"Would it matter to you if I said I miss you?"

I let that stand just long enough to try to summon some good feelings from a lifetime of memories. It wasn't difficult, but God*damn* it, why did he always have to be the one walking away with a concession? I took another uncomfortable few seconds to collect myself.

"Chris—"

"No, Zack. I appreciate the thought, but there's no looking

back. What really matters is I genuinely wish you a Merry Christmas and a very happy New Year. We both deserve to follow up last year with a great new one, don't you think?"

I waited for what seemed an eternity before Zack said, "Take care of yourself, Chris."

"You too, baby. You too."

There's a Christmas CD I listen to only on Christmas morning. That was pretty much the only time I had to myself all day—usually between 6 to 6:30. The kids and Zack were often still and asleep until then. We seldom got home from Midnight Mass and into bed before 2 A.M. I'd get up in the chilly house, stir up the fireplaces in the living room and in the kitchen, and play the CD while I made coffee.

This year I woke up at my usual time and wandered alone into the chilly expanse of my new beach house and started my push-button fireplace. I turned on the lights that covered the embarrassingly large tree and started the CD just after I turned on the coffee.

I leaned against the sink and watched the dawn begin to brighten my partial ocean view with streaks of pink lacing the few clouds to a cold blue sky. The second song on the CD was a beautiful soprano singing "Procession from a Ceremony of Carols, Opus 28" with only the accompaniment of a piano. In reality, the song must have been recorded in some old, cold conservatory. The notes of the piano and the woman's voice were so pure in what sounded like a vast space. It was hard to imagine the song being committed to tape in a contemporary studio.

In my mind's eye I saw the pianist—a trim, spare man and the singer—a large woman dressed in a white choir robe with a navy-blue chasuble. They came, just the two of them, to a very plain, empty old church, with bright, early-morning light streaming in through large, clear windows. It is cold in the church, and the piano's notes and the woman's clear voice are achingly beautiful in the brittle air. They have come to this sacred place to offer the gift of this song to the Christ child. Not the effigy of an infant in a crib before the altar, but rather the living presence of promise newly arrived with the pure morning light.

Whatever else ever came my way on Christmas—poorly

wrapped handmade doodads carefully presented by small chubby hands or glittering boxes containing expensive things and offered with an anxious smile—it was always that song on that CD that captured the spirit of the day to me. Its austere beauty was a tonic against all the excess—religious and secular—of the season.

Like most families, mine reveled in the holiday spirit, but being practicing Catholics offered an additional dimension to the season. I especially liked going to church during Advent, with the church decorated and the sense of coming wonder tugging at the edges of my life I reserved for religion.

With Christmas morning actually begun in church the night before, I watched the pageant of the dawn with a continuing awe. I said my poorly prepared prayer of thanks and wonder and praise alone on Christmas morning. As the sun peeked over the horizon, I finished my prayer, crossed myself, and smiled.

Then, ever human and always flawed, I drank coffee spiked with Kahlua and ate cold sliced ham and potato salad off a Blue Willow plate I'd looted off eBay. I eventually moved from the kitchen table to a chair by the fire and from coffee and Kahlua to eggnog and bourbon. Feeling pleasantly potted and half asleep, I was startled by a rap on the French doors off the deck.

All I had on was a pair of flannel boxer shorts and a T-shirt from the Dine-A-Shore Grill and Pier, but I marched over to quiet the knocking that was becoming pounding. I opened the door and was nearly knocked down by Trey, who held up a bottle of champagne and a carton of orange juice. His wife Susan followed behind him a little unsteadily; one of her fingers gripped Trey's back belt loop and carried two more bottles of champagne in her other hand. Behind her came Andrea and David carrying presents, and after them Schooner followed with his hands awkwardly balancing more presents of varying sizes.

Trey and Susan claimed never to have gone to bed, but Andrea claimed they had slept in David's car on the way to the beach. I got swept up in the organization of coats and presents and champagne popping. I was more than a little overwhelmed, but I was also hugely happy.

"Look at my nontraditional household of upper middle-class white people doing Christmas," Andrea proclaimed, raising her glass of orange juice as Trey slopped champagne into it.

"Don't deconstruct my holiday you postmodernist, overanalyzing bitch," Schooner said as he handed me a glass of champagne.

"Kiss my ass, you little sawed-off Republican twerp," Andrea shot back.

"Are there no workhouses? Are there no prisons?" David intoned evilly, putting his arm around Andrea and kissing her neck.

"Mister Scrooge, would there were not," Susan said, pinching David's ass.

"Knock it off, all of you," Trey ordered. "Chris, a toast?"

I nodded and waited as Trey swung around to take in his siblings, wife, and brother-in-law. When he was satisfied they were all settled and paying attention, he lifted his sloppy glass and said, "To being home for Christmas."

"And to the best, smartest, and most beautiful kids in the world," I answered. And we all swallowed our toast, quiet for once and all happy. My family had truly returned to me.

"I'm hungry," someone said.

"I'm fucking starved."

"Where are the plates, Chris?"

"The house is beautiful, Chris!"

"I want to open presents."

"Not until I take a leak. Chris, where's the bathroom?"

"You thought we weren't coming, didn't you?"

"Schoo-ner, stop eating out of the bowl, how crude can you get?"

"No, wait. For God's sake, don't show her."

"Damn, it's hot in here. Open them French doors."

"There has got to be some potato salad, right?"

"Fuck that, where's the pie?"

"Chris, please don't tell me you forgot to make pecan pie."

"Schooner, you forgot the biggest present, run downstairs and get it."

"What am I, your fucking slave, Trey?"

"Jesus, Mary, and Joseph! The mouth on you on a Christmas morning."

"Are you drunk?"

"A little. Are you?"

"A little."

The afternoon sun was westering and the day had warmed the sand so it was nice under my bare feet. Heath and I walked along the beach toward the pier.

"Does your family always drink so much?"

I shrugged. "They're Irish, almost full-blooded. Their father's mother was a drunk and their mother...well, let's just say she had her own problems. I think that gives them some caution, but alcohol was never a big deal with their father, so it's never been a big deal with me. They can handle it."

We walked a few minutes in silence. As we neared the pier Heath said, "My father was a drunk. A social drunk, but a drunk nonetheless. It makes me think about it, you know?"

"Yeah, I know. But you're part of that Protestant country club world. Baptists are like cats: You know they're out raising hell, but you can't ever catch them at it. We Catholics are more out in the open."

Heath laughed and stopped. "Are you ready to turn around yet? I need to be getting back to start getting some dogs and cats taken care of for the evening."

"Sure," I said. "Let's turn around."

We turned back toward the wintry sun. The island lay east to west with the beach along its southern exposure, and the cool colored sun still washed our faces with warmth.

"How long do you think they'll all sleep?" Heath asked.

"For a while longer. I imagine they'll be waking soon, hungry and facing a long drive back to Raleigh."

"Traffic shouldn't be too bad for them. The highway back from Greensboro was nearly deserted this morning."

"So, what do you think of my kids?"

"They're a handful, for sure."

We walked along for another silent minute or two. Terns and gulls scooted out of our way, unperturbed and peaceful.

"The sun is really nice, isn't it?" I said to break the spell.

"It's a beautiful Christmas Day," he replied.

"One thing I wanted to ask you..."

"Shoot."

"Where's my puppy?"

"Excuse me?"

"Where's my Chesapeake puppy...that's the way I saw today ending."

"You're a bit of a princess, aren't you?"

"You have no idea," I said with a grin.

"I suppose I could get you a Chesapeake. Do you think you're ready?"

"Dog people aren't ever really happy without a dog. A good man told me that once not long ago."

"I know that man. Maybe it's time to give Steve Willis a call. His girl-dog's litter came earlier than we expected. They're 10 days old now."

"What's the story on that guy?" I asked.

"Steve? Oh, he's been here long enough to be a local. His folks moved to Salter Path when he was about 12 years old. He's real 'old school' as the kids say these days."

"What do you mean?"

"Well, he had a scholarship to the Naval Academy, but he gave it up to be a water man. He crews on a head boat during the summer—black marlin fishing mostly—and spends most of his off-season hunting and fishing the sound. If you want oysters, he's the go-to guy. If you want to pay a hunting guide, he's the best. People who'd shoot you for trespassing let Steve hunt their land."

"And he raises Chesapeake Bay retrievers."

"He's got a pretty good reputation as a breeder and trainer. You'd be amazed at what some people pay for one of the Chessies he's gun-trained."

"Then I suppose he'd be out of my price range for a pet."

"Not necessarily. I think he likes you or he wouldn't have offered one to you."

"How could he like me? He only met me that one time."

"Oh...well...Chris, he's really low-key, but he's one of us," Heath said, giving me a significant look.

"No way," I said dismissively.

Heath laughed. "Don't be fooled by the rough exterior."

"So, how do you happen to—"

"He and I had a thing a few years back."

"Oh, I see. Well, if he likes me, I'm sort of busy right now."

We walked on in silence, nearing the dune we'd have to cross to return to my place. Heath still didn't answer. Finally I said, "*Am* I busy right now?"

Heath sighed and stopped. "Look, Chris...you've just gotten out of a long-term situation. We're enjoying each other's company, but..."

Heath's back was to the sun and I was standing in his shadow. I felt the unmistakable chill of being out of the sun. While I was dis-appointed—maybe even hurt a little—I was also glad to have to face the limits of my own expectations. I really didn't want to give Heath the impression that I was looking for more than I was right then. As much as he'd wanted to gently set me straight, I felt the need to respond as strongly.

"Look, Heath," I said. "You don't need to say anything more. I feel the same way—it's all too soon. I'm really enjoying your com-pany right now. You should know for sure that I'm enjoying you in bed. But I don't mean to give you the impression that I'm looking to get married again."

Heath looked down at me and then away again, nervously. "Don't be offended, Chris."

I laughed. People had always thought I was on the defensive when I was only trying to be honest. It was the goddamn un-Botoxed wrinkles at the edges of my eyes and the deep line between my brows. "I'm not scowling at you, Heath. I've got my worry lines going because I'm trying to let you know I'm being serious."

Heath looked back at me, and I gave him an open, sincere grin.

"I'm glad, Chris. I didn't want to hurt you," he said.

I thought a moment and tried to think of what to say to the man. I was genuinely puzzled; I didn't think I'd said or done any-thing to communicate I wanted more out of him than someone to talk to and to have some seriously good sex with. "Heath, look. I'll freely admit I'm more than in touch with my feminine side, but if I've given you the impression I wanted to turn back into a wife and have us become an old married couple, I apologize. That's not who I want to be anymore."

I tried to not laugh when I saw the deep relief wash over the man's face. "No apology necessary, but that's good to hear. Still, if you change your mind, you should know I'm not interested in any-thing other than what we have now."

"Really?"

"Yeah, sir. Really."

"Why's that?"

"Well…Chris I'm not the marrying kind these days. And I think you might need to see a man about a dog."

I was puzzled. That expression usually meant someone needed to go to the bathroom. I supposed he meant I needed a puppy to lavish my domestic instincts upon. Heath gave a low chuckle and turned toward the dune to head up to my house. Walking to catch up with him, I said, "I have no idea what you're talking about."

From the crest of the dune's rise, he stretched out his hand to help me up the last steep steps of the way. "I think you'll find out, sooner or later."

After I said good-bye to Heath in the drive, I climbed the stairs to the porch to find Andrea alone sitting in a deck chair looking out toward the sea. She seemed content as she reached for my hand and guided me to the chair next to her. "I've started coffee," she said, "it'll be ready soon."

I sat and said, "I think we'll need a gallon. Speaking for myself, I'm still sort of drunk. I don't like the thought of you guys driving home after drinking so much."

Andrea squeezed my hand but didn't let it go. She scooted forward in her chair and turned a bit to see my face. "We're Ronans. You shouldn't be too concerned." Then, "Nice man, your Dr. Heath."

"Thanks for that. He is a nice man, but he's hardly mine."

"Well, you certainly seemed chummy. I was wondering if I was going to have to deal with a new daddy, sheesh."

I laughed gently at that, but I met and held her gaze. "Well, we're enjoying each other's company, but I'm not ready to even think of jumping into anything long-term."

Andrea tried to grin, but her natural state of anxiety took over. "I hope you're being safe."

I let go of her hand, then patted it reassuringly. "Darlin' daughter, I hope you don't think you need to give your nontraditional-parent sex ed lessons."

Worriedly, Andrea said, "AIDS is spreading wildly among retirement home residents. HIV infection in the elderly is a very troubling situation, Chris."

Andrea could go from endearing to irritating with clocklike dependability. I sincerely hoped she'd switch back to endearing, quickly. "First, Andrea, I'm not elderly *or* retirement-aged. As your father reminds me every chance he gets. Second, while I appreciate your realizing I still have the capacity for a sex life, it's really none of your business, okay?"

Undaunted, Andrea said, "Will you promise me you'll be safe?" Andrea demanded it as she'd adamantly required my promises when she was younger. In some deep and abiding way her abandonment issues, birthed in her third year by her mother's death, had wounded her subconscious beyond repair. She had always insisted on assurances no one could live up to. Privately I wondered how David managed to live with her.

"I promise, Andrea," I said with a sigh. "I've just begun an exciting new phase of my life—just for myself, do you understand? I'm not going to jeopardize it by compromising my health for anyone. Okay?"

Temporarily satisfied, she gave an unguarded sigh of relief and stood. "I'm going to bring us out some coffee, okay?"

I nodded gratefully. "No liquor in it please. I've had enough of the Irish for a while."

She winked at me, and I watched her walk back into the house quietly. Having lived in such a stir for so many years, I was appreciating my quiet life. I hoped Andrea wouldn't wake anyone so we'd have a little while longer to talk. When the boys were in the same room with her, they ran roughshod over Andrea's needs for attention. Ever the middle child, she ceded her space willingly and never complained. When she was in grade school, I would sometimes just spontaneously show up and sign her out for the day so she and I could share some uninterrupted time together. I missed that. I hoped she did too.

The sun was sinking low and our chairs were in full shadow. I was grateful again when Andrea returned alone with a steaming mug for each of us. I took mine and allowed her to settle before I asked: "Andrea, do you remember the time—I guess you were about 12—when I showed up to take you out of school early and we went shopping just for you?"

Andrea raised her legs to hook her heels on the rim of the low chair and brought her knees to her chest. She smiled and blew the steam from the top of her mug before taking a sip. "Yes, I do. You did that often, Chris. It always made me feel so happy—it made the other stuff easier."

"What other stuff?" I asked.

Andrea lay her head against the back of the chair and said, "Do you remember Trey playing that song 'Your Mama's on the Crack Rock' over and over?"

I did indeed remember. I never would have expected Trey to like hip-hop when he was 13, but he did. Oh God, did he ever. He played that song until I thought I would scream. 'Bitch Better Have My Money' was another of his favorites. Still, the kids loved it when they'd catch me dancing to hip-hop in the kitchen, awkwardly trying to re-create the moves I'd seen on BET and MTV. In answer to Andrea's question I sang the refrain in the song's same falsetto, "*Not my mama!*"

Andrea giggled but looked away from me and up at the darkening sky. "Kids at school used to sing at me, 'Yo mama's got a cock, doc!' Sometimes it was all I could do to keep from crying. But I never did. I just ignored them and walked away."

I let that lie in the lengthening shadows as Andrea took another sip of her coffee. I wrapped my hands around my cup to warm them. Finally I said, "Please know I wish you'd been spared all that, Andrea. But I never regret one moment I had with you kids. When I hear stories like that, I wish your father had made wiser choices for you."

Quick as a cat, Andrea spat, "He's a selfish prick and always has been."

I didn't respond; there was no need.

"I have a right to my anger, Chris."

I never bought into all of Andrea's psychobabble, but she was as entitled to it as she was to her anger—she'd earned the degrees. I had no doubt she was an exceptional therapist—certainly she had a deep well of issues to draw her empathy from—so no matter how corroding I thought her constant return to that well, I rarely called her on it. Still, I thought, the greatest gift I could give her on Christmas was some hard-earned wisdom. "Yes, Andrea, you do have a right to every ounce of anger you have for your father, and, I suspect, for me. But don't hold onto it so tightly you come to treasure it more than your other feelings. It's corrosive and eventually it'll eat away at everything you love."

"Please don't condescend to me, Chris," she said coolly.

"I wouldn't presume to do that. If you don't consider anything else I have to say, just please consider the respect I have for you as an adult."

That brought a sharp glance and a challenging reply. "I hope I've earned your respect."

I sighed deeply. I never wanted this stolen moment to turn into a fight. "As I hope I've earned yours."

The dying light betrayed a trickle of tears from the corner of Andrea's eyes. I'd have given anything at that moment to have understood if her tears were hormonal or grief-born. Fundamentally and always, I could never understand her. If men were from Mars and women from Venus, I was from an unknown star in neither orbit. My sensitivity, as finely honed a skill as I possessed, still lacked a working edge with my Andrea. I only wished she hadn't spent so much time in hurting, anger, and tears.

She sought my hand and squeezed it. I returned the pressure and we watched the last of Christmas day sink into deep twilight. I hoped that little bit of connection was enough.

Schooner appeared on the deck and plopped himself down in front of us. Cautiously he handed me a small, neat present, expertly wrapped. "This is from Frank," he said.

"Who's Frank," Andrea demanded.

I looked to Schooner for his reply.

"My boyfriend," he replied openly.

"At last!" Andrea answered dryly. Without another word, she took my coffee cup and went inside the house.

When she'd closed the door, I looked down at Schooner. He sat hunched over and cross-legged Indian-style before me with a happy grin on his face. "Boy, you sure got off easy," I said.

"Andrea found a stash of *Freshmen* magazines in my room years ago."

"You had a stash of those magazines and you never shared?" I teased.

"Mom, you are so gross sometimes. Shut up and open your present."

I carefully pulled away the paper to find a box from Diptych that held a very pricey candle labeled "Feu de Bois."

"Smell it and tell me what you think it is," Schooner said.

I inhaled the candle's scent deeply and was richly rewarded with the smell of a warm burning fireplace. I recalled telling Frank the only thing I didn't like about the gas logs in my fireplace was their lack of scent. I told him I missed the smell of wood smoke in the house. "He remembered," I said fondly.

Schooner patted my foot and said, "Frank's the best."

"I like your Frank a lot, Schooner. I really do."

"That's good, because I'm bringing him back on New Year's to take down the tree."

"Don't you guys have something better to do on New Year's than spend it with your old mom on a deserted beach?"

Schooner stood and reached for the candle. As I handed it to him, he said, "We talked about it. We want to spend it with you. It's nice to be able to be ourselves here."

"That's cool, baby. Come back down. I'll look forward to it. Besides, I was wondering how I was going to con you into coming back to take down that tree. Problem solved." As he turned to go back inside the house, I said, "Schooner, will you tell me something?"

"Depends."

"Okay, fair enough. How long have you and Frank been seeing each other?"

"Well, we've been *seeing* each other since sophomore year. We've got the same major. But we only hooked up right before Thanksgiving."

That certainly explained his preoccupation and his rush to get gone then.

"But look, Mom. It's like this: Neither one of us is *out* out, you know what I mean? My roommates don't really know—not that they'd give a fuck, considering some of the shit I've caught them in. But...it's all kinda new between me and Frank. You see what I'm saying?"

"I see what you're saying. I probably shouldn't make a great big deal out of this...is what I'm hearing."

He gave me a curt nod in reply and struck his chest with the side of his fist. "I'm going to stash this candle in your room, okay?"

"I'm feeling you," I said.

"Don't even try, Mom. Street slang, it doesn't sound good on you."

"Thanks for reminding me I watch way too much BET. Could you send Trey out if he's awake," I said as he loped away. "...And get him to bring me some more..."—the door closed harder than it should have—"coffee?"

I shrugged and dug into the pouch of my hoodie for my cigarettes and lighter. The best I could hope for was Trey anticipating my need for another cup of coffee. The twilight had deepened into darkness and chill, but it wasn't unpleasant. I was enjoying having some time alone with each of my kids on the deck. I lit a cigarette and waited for Trey to appear. Resting my head against the back of the Adirondack chair, I stretched my legs and sighed. It had turned out to be a wonderful Christmas Day.

Habits and traditions are grand for a while, but they can become a prison. Looking back on past Christmases, I was very relieved that I no longer had to face all the de-decorating and de–house trimming that was a consequence of living in Historic Oakwood. There were pedestrian and car Christmas tours through the neighborhood each year. Christmas revelers, done with the day's festivities or simply bored, came from the cookie-cutter suburbs and drove wistfully through our old neighborhood during the season. From all I read and heard, they really enjoyed looking at the large old homes decorated and on display for the holidays.

From inside our turn-of-the-century Italianate home, I watched them standing out on the sidewalk or peering from their car windows. I always wondered what they were looking for. Did they imagine life in the old homes was like a life they dreamed of and didn't have? Did they think the traces of fading graciousness and entitlement that emanated from the aging plaster and hardwood floors endowed the current occupants with lives that were more meaningful than their own?

The reality of the neighborhood was quite different from the imaginings of wistful tourists. Our neighbors struggled with house payments, dreamed of better things, quietly drank, and loudly fought just like folks did in Cary, North Raleigh, and Garner. Perched on the edge of the ghetto, the old houses were wired with ugly burglary systems installed to keep the real world from intruding on the myth.

I bought into that myth, and tried to live the life of an upwardly mobile mommy with three perfect kids, a handsome and affluent husband, and a properly genteel giant of a hunting dog. I hung baskets of geraniums between the porch posts in the summer. I perched pumpkins on the steps to the front door in the fall. And, yes, at Christmas I festooned the house with swags of clear white lights, real magnolia leaves, and fresh evergreen wreaths that I suspended from maroon ribbons in every high, narrow window.

It was all artifice. I flicked my cigarette off the deck and onto the sand below, stuck my chilled hands into my hoodie's pouch, and was quietly happy to leave the myth. That was all behind me. What was *really* behind me at that moment—across 14 feet of Trex deck—was my new house, securely set on pilings above the currents of the past. My new house sheltered the only true treasures that remained from my 22-year-old illusions. Those children were more my children than the woman's who ran from them in death. My children sat in my warm house and ate my food. My children followed me after their father had jerked us all from the old dream, revealing his love and the myth were a sham. And I was very, very grateful for that fact.

"I brought you some coffee." Susan, not Trey, stirred me from my reverie.

"Thanks," I said, taking my coffee with one hand and patting the chair next to me with the other. "Sit with me awhile, dear heart."

Susan settled in the chair next to me and sighed. "It's really not that cold out here is it?" she said.

"No, not at all. I'm enjoying watching the night come down."

"I thought we had all run you out of your own house, you sitting alone out here."

"Not at all. It's actually a trick of mine so I can spend some time alone with each of you rather than fighting for your attention inside."

Susan smiled and crossed her legs. "It's a pretty neat trick, Chris."

"How are you? I miss chatting with you like we did back in Raleigh. The job is going well?"

"Same ol', same ol'. Too much work, not enough staff to get it done. Every day's a challenge, but it's still exciting. I'm enjoying it."

"You seem tired," I said.

"Do I?"

"Well, perhaps not quite yourself. I chalked it up to you finally learning not to even try to keep up with all the Ronan holiday drinking."

Susan looked at me and gave me a quiet smile. "Actually..."

"Actually, what?"

Susan lay her head back and looked up at the brightening stars. The Adirondack chairs seemed to encourage that pose—that recumbent search for the inner thought in the expansive sky. "It's a secret," she said.

"I won't tell."

"Trey and I have been trying to get pregnant. My visitor is a week past due. I'm not making a big deal of it. It's *wa-a-ay* too soon to even speculate. But, Chris, I'm so ready for a baby, I'm not going to drink like a fish at Christmas and jinx it."

"Have you told Trey?"

"Oh hell no. A week late could just be excitement over the holiday. No need to trigger his expectations just yet." Susan giggled like a girl. "I need his trigger for trying until I'm sure."

I sat up and leaned toward her conspiratorially. "You know how happy your baby would make me, don't you? I mean, I know that has absolutely nothing to do with it. That's all between you and Trey, but I'm genuinely looking forward to being a grand...a grand..."

"A grandmom? Schooner has you brainwashed with that mommy stuff doesn't he? Well, you can say it. I'll be happy for my baby to have you as a doting grandmom. My mother has eight grandchildren already. As much as I'm sure she'll be excited, she's already told me she's been there and done that. You know what she said?"

"What?"

"She told me to tell you this one was all yours and you're welcome to it."

I laughed and leaned back, relaxing into my chair. "I love your mother. You tell her for me that I appreciate it."

Susan reached for my hand and gave it a quick squeeze. "My God, Chris. When she found out you and Zack had split up and you were moving to the beach, all she could do was bitch about losing a fellow grandparent to relieve her of the sitter chores."

I laughed and Susan let go of my hand and patted it. "You can expect to have a tiny visitor every other weekend."

"Oh darlin' don't be so sure about that." I said.

"Why?"

"When that baby comes, you're not going to want to let it out of your sight. Your whole world will change. When I walked into my prepackaged family, I took one look at Schooner and thought there was no way I could deal with diapers and an infant peeing and puking and crying. Then I held him and I lost my heart. Same thing with Trey and Andrea."

"Chris, some people are natural parents—you're the best example of that I know of—but for me, I'm not so sure. I want a baby badly, but I'm so into my career and my own world, I'm scared I'll just be having a fashion-accessory child."

I looked across the space between us. Her face was illuminated by the glow of light from the French doors behind us—she was beautiful. I took her hand and squeezed it reassuringly. "Don't let that worry you any, girl. No matter how you work it out, your little fellow will be totally blessed to have you as a mom."

Susan leaned over and gave me a quick peck on the cheek.

Behind us the door opened and Trey said, "What are you two plotting out here?"

He strode onto the deck, leaving the door open behind him. "Christ, it's hot in that house. I don't have to worry about you freezing to death."

Trey leaned against the deck rail in front of Susan and me. Washed with the glow of the light from the house, he was also beautiful to me. I quietly imagined what a lovely baby the two of them would make. Aloud I said, "So what do you think of our house now that it's done and moved into? I think it's wonderful."

"Chris, I have to admit I was a little frightened at how much money you spent finishing it out, but now that I see what you've done, I think you did a great job. Let me ask you something."

"Shoot."

"Do you remember a few years back when I was helping you wash dishes and I asked you why you had to have All-Clad pots and pans?"

"Yes. You said the pot you were drying weighed more than Beau."

"Well, you quite rightly answered that you'd never need to replace them. You told me if you bought cheap shit you'd just have to buy more cheap shit over and over."

"That I did."

"Well, that struck me as making a great deal of sense. I think you've done well here. This place ought to last a lifetime."

"So says my banker, baby. Now, what do you think of it as a home?"

"Well, Chris. Look at your watch. You notice none of us want to leave and I know for a fact Susan, David, and I all have to be back at work tomorrow."

"Thanks for reminding me," Susan said as she stood. "I'd better go in and start rounding up the troops."

"Give me a minute or two alone out here with Chris, will you hon?" Trey said.

"Sure thing." Susan gave my shoulder a squeeze, went back into the house, and closed the door behind her.

Trey took her vacated seat and sighed, as he rubbed his eyes.

"You're rubbing your eyes a lot these days, baby," I said. "Are you just tired or do you need to see the eye doctor?"

Trey laughed and said, "My eyes are fine, *Mom*. It's my head that's giving me hell. It's the fucking champagne. It does it to me every time."

"Did you find some aspirin?"

"Yep, right where you always kept it. It's kicking in. I quit drinking hours ago so I could drive back. I figured since David drove us up here with no sleep, the least I could do was give him a break on the way home."

"Good man," I said.

Trey half stood and moved his chair so he could look at me. "Chris, we have to talk finances."

I sighed, took a sip of my coffee, and summoned my patience

for the lecture I'd been expecting all day. "I know I have to get a job. I promise to start looking next week. It's going to be difficult, I'm sure, so I'm not limiting my choices."

"Well, that's good to hear. But don't sell yourself short. It is going to be difficult to explain your lack of experience and a résumé without going into a huge amount of personal detail. I just want you to know that Carteret County probably isn't as progressive as the Triangle when it comes to understanding or accepting the lifestyle stuff, okay?"

"Gotcha," I said. "I'm going to avoid the particulars if I can possibly help it."

Trey leaned forward and put his forearms on his legs, striking a confidential pose. I sat my coffee down and mimicked the pose to let him know I was aware he'd come down to talking cold, hard facts.

"Chris, I've got your money set up and put away like we've discussed. I've left you a $5,000 cushion in savings and a couple thousand more in your checking account. You've only got an American Express card, right?"

I nodded.

"Do *not* accept any credit card offers that come in the mail and let me tell you, they're going to start pouring in. Stick with the card you have to pay off every month and you won't get into trouble, okay?"

Like an obedient child, I nodded once more.

"With nothing but a light bill, cable bill, and a phone bill, you should be okay for a month, maybe two, on the money in your checking account if you live close to the bone. But it's very important you get some money coming in and fast. As much as I'd like to help you out a little every month, I'm just not in a position to…"

I waved off the suggestion like a worrisome fly. "Plus, it's not fair to you and Susan," I said. "Please know I understand that, Trey."

He reached over and patted my leg reassuringly. "I've got your new computer set up. You need to read the *Dummies* book we gave you, okay?"

"No probs. I played around some on your dad's. I know how to get on the Internet, do e-mail and stuff, but I do need to figure out more about the programs."

"Excellent. I wrote all of our e-mail addresses down for you inside the cover of the *Dummies* book, okay?"

"You kids spent way too much money on that computer setup for a Christmas present."

"No big deal, Chris. It's going to be easier to stay in touch with all of us over the Net. Just promise me something."

"What?"

"Please don't forward me a bunch of jokes and crap. Please, I'm pleading with you."

"I swear I won't."

Trey sighed and leaned back into his chair. Regarding me with a regal gaze, he smiled. "You're going to do great, Chris. I'm very proud of you."

"I'm already doing great," I said.

"Looks like it. Dr. Heath is a good-looking man."

I smiled and shook my head. "That's no big deal, Trey. Believe me. We're both just enjoying each other's company."

"So Andrea reports. It's good to hear you're not rushing into anything. I think you'll do a lot better by yourself rather than getting tangled up in a new domestic situation."

"I agree with you. It's the last thing I want or need right now."

Trey nodded, then with a solid shift of gears, he continued. "I understand Schooner has decided to date another boy for a while. What's that all about?"

"I've met him," I said. "His name is Frank and he's a good kid. Schooner seems happy."

Trey nodded. "Whatever. It's Andrea I'm concerned about."

"Really. Why?"

"She needs to get over her issues crap and get on with her life. Did you know she wouldn't let David put up a tree or anything? She's driving him nuts."

"I pretty much figured she was and it'd be a shame if she drove David away. I happen to think he's the best thing for her."

"David's a good man. I wish you'd have a talk with Andrea, Mom."

I noted his slip, but I didn't remark on it. He was sitting so large and responsible in his seat as head of the family, I didn't want to do a thing to make him feel small. "I had a nice chat with her a little while ago, Trey. I hope she heard it. In any event, I'll try to create some more time with her and keep an eye on the situation, okay?"

Trey nodded, then leaned forward conspiratorially again. "Want to hear something good?"

I leaned toward him again. "Tell me."

"I think Dad is one miserable son of a bitch," he said mischievously.

"Well, we knew that," I replied.

"No, really, Chris." He said, quickly becoming serious again. "I think he's really unhappy with Alicia already. I mean he puts on a good show, cooing all over the new baby and stuff, but he looks tired. He just looks really tired."

"So, there's no fountain of youth in a baby's diapers, huh?"

Trey nodded solemnly, then got a look of pure glee in his eyes. "Unless Schooner's in them."

We laughed until everyone, including Schooner, came out on the deck to see what was so damned funny.

CHAPTER FOUR,
WINTER

✦

By the first of February, I'd begun to think that e-mail was not much different from having a particularly demanding pet. I was all caught up in checking to see if I had any new messages and answering them immediately. E-mail was taking over my life. Sure, it was convenient and cheaper than the telephone, but it was also time-consuming, disappointing, and frustrating as hell. I enjoyed getting e-mails from the kids. I *really* enjoyed getting e-mails from Wade Lee, though his constant exhortations that I should go to this or that gay Web site and embark on a wild online affair got on my nerves. The worst thing was waiting for an e-mail reply and not getting one, especially an e-mail in response to a job query. I was having no luck at all on that front.

Twice a week, when the local paper came out, I pored over the meager help-wanted classifieds like the Holy Scripture. The few listings were often just as apocryphal and considerably less inspiring. The jobs I felt I could even try for were all minimum-wage positions, and I had to face it: Minimum wage wasn't even going to support my book habit, much less support the life I'd set up for myself.

Reading was my favorite escape from the dreariness of the job hunt, the unrelenting gray weather, and my own sense of isolation and frustration. I had long since devoured all the books I was interested in at the Pine Knoll Shores branch of the county library. I discovered Amazon.com for new books and Alibris.com for stuff that my earlier reading had steered me toward, like the *Regeneration* trilogy by Pat Barker, and all the early stuff by John McGahern and Colm Toibin. Before I knew it, I was ordering out-of-print books by Siegfried Sassoon and Colin Wilson.

I was becoming decidedly bookish and I hoped for a job in a bookstore or library, but most of the bookstores were closed for the winter or open on only off-season hours. The libraries had more retired volunteers than they had work for. So much for my fantasies of days spent contentedly shelving stock, making coffee, and talking highbrow trash with total strangers. I was looking more seriously at the listings for jobs as kitchen staff or working part-time at McDonald's when I finally decided to go take a look at Steve Willis's pups. E-mail and books were certainly diverting, but I was beginning to need flesh-and-blood company.

I explained all this to Heath, who continued to provide good conversation and occasional sex as the weeks after the holidays grew long in the low winter light. The pier had closed until Easter, so Heath stopped by for breakfast a couple of mornings a week, or stayed on if he'd happened to sleep over.

"I swear, I knew it was going to be tough to get a job this time of year, but I had no idea how tough," I said to him one morning.

Heath poured himself another cup of coffee and looked back at me from the kitchen, "Are you really hurting financially?" he asked.

"No, not yet. But I've got about four more weeks before I have to start dipping into my savings. I don't want to touch that in case the Expedition goes to hell or, God forbid, something breaks down here in the house."

Heath left the kitchen and returned to the table. "I wish I had a line on where to send you, but I don't know anyone who's looking for help right now. Everyone is hunkered down for the winter. If you can make it through March, everything will be opening back up again."

"That's comforting, at least," I said with a sigh.

"When you live here year-round it's something you prepare for and get used to. You should see my receipts. They suck."

"Well, at least Trey can't bitch at me for not trying."

"Is he giving you a hard time?"

"No, but he's rapidly growing into that head-of-the-family role. He's becoming a little unbearable. Sometimes he makes me feel like a complete ditz who has to be looked after or I'll wander off and drown or something. I know one thing: I'm never going to let him know if I get sick, God forbid. He'll have me in a fucking nursing home, and I'm still two years shy of 50."

Heath laughed and lit a cigarette. "I think you need to get your mind off yourself. I ran into Steve Willis the other day. He told me he's got a few puppies for you to choose from. They're six weeks old now. You should swing by his place and take a look."

"You know, that's a great idea. When do you think I could catch him at home?"

"How about tomorrow afternoon? Didn't you say you had an appointment with your priest tomorrow? You could go by on the way home."

I thought about it. Puppies were very expensive to start with, and then there was the cost of a new dog crate and shots, flea and tick treatments, heartworm pills. The list was near endless, and I said as much to Heath.

He ground out his cigarette, drained his coffee cup, and stood. "Look—I'm actually glad to hear you're going to crate-train the dog. It'll make it feel more secure to have its own space, and it won't drive you crazy chewing up all this pricey furniture of yours. I have a crate big enough for a grown Chessie I'll just give you. You'll need to hose it down, maybe give it a new coat of spray paint. That's all it needs. I've just given all Steve's pups their six-week shots and dewormed them, so you won't have to worry about that again until they're at 10 weeks. If I were you, I'd think pretty hard about getting it either spayed or neutered. There aren't any other breeders around here, so that's out of the question. In any event, by the time you have to worry about *that* bill, hopefully you'll have a job or a better chance to get one. How's that sound?

I stood up and kissed him. "That sounds great," I said.

Heath endured the kiss, which he didn't usually tolerate outside the bedroom. "Okay, I get it, you're grateful. No need to mush up all over me. Get me something to write directions on, and I'll give him a call and tell him you're coming when I get into the clinic."

After Heath left, I washed the breakfast dishes by hand and contemplated puppy names. I always got male dogs, so I thought about the short list: Siegfried, Rhett—I'd just had a Beau—Tonka. Siegfried was excellent, but I was scared it would turn into Siggy.

Rhett sounded too much like Red. Tonka was pretty cool; it made me think of Trey and Schooner's bright yellow truck toys. Chessies were stout, big-chested louts. I thought Tonka sounded pretty good; it would work for either a girl or a boy dog.

That settled, I poured myself another cup of coffee and returned to the table to contemplate my other errand for the following day. After Mass the preceding Sunday, I stopped to shake Father Fintan's hand. He was an older middle-aged man. He looked to be nearing 60, maybe as much as 62. Surprisingly, rather than just shaking my hand, nodding, and reaching for the next parishioner's extended paw, he held me fast in a strong grip and asked if I was free to stop by his office one day the following week. I said sure. With traces of his brogue intact, he told me to call him the next day at the rectory to schedule a time and day. Then, with a nod, he was on to the waiting parishioner behind me.

I was frankly puzzled as to why he'd want to meet with me. I had only just returned a card from the pew in front of me asking to become a member of the parish, though I'd been going to Mass there since early December. I was scared somehow he'd talked to our priest back in Raleigh—a forbidding but tolerant man—and would tell me I wasn't welcome in his parish.

Being Catholic and queer, I had an abiding fear that eventually I'd have a pastor who was down on homosexuals and simply wouldn't tolerate them in his parish. I didn't really ask much from my church—only not to be beat up from the pulpit. In our parish back home, I'd always kept as low a profile as I could, considering I was raising three children in the church. Toleration was easy to achieve, I thought, as long as you never directly challenged the church any more than you had to.

Not that this Father Fintan gave any hints of being intolerant. His homilies were quite folksy and charming, and he never was arrogant or condemning. In fact, the parishioners seemed to reserve a great affection for him that I felt all around me. Even seated alone, very near the back of the church, I never got the sense that he lead a cowering flock.

So, with only mild trepidation, I called Father Fintan, as he asked, on Monday afternoon. He was very pleasant as we compared schedules for the coming week and finally settled on that

Thursday. He graciously rang off after we'd agreed we'd meet at the church at 1 sharp.

Sitting with my coffee that morning, I wondered again what on earth the man wanted to talk with me about. My keeping the Catholic faith of my childhood was nothing I could justify to anyone on any grounds except that it made me happy and it made sense to me. In the past I'd had some spirited conversations with people who were not Catholic (or Catholic no longer) about the Church's intolerance on several major social issues—not the least was its alienation of its gay members. I told these cynics that as a queer mother figure running a traumatized family that I'd reconstructed out of loss, need, and a lot of love, I knew my effort wasn't disingenuous, campy, or half-assed. It was *real*.

What's more, it was art: It magnified and glorified a greater reality than my small life. I was rearing three beautiful children and giving love to a man who was often maddeningly complex in his demands and difficulties. I didn't give a damn that the Church thought my life's work was "wrong." It was nothing short of salvation for that man and his three little children. And, it was also my salvation. Armed with that knowledge, and thoroughly convinced that God lived somewhere above his own Church, I had no problems living on the edge of a community of faith built by fallible, human hands. What concerned me was being told I couldn't cling even to outside edges of my faith—being told that even the third-to-the-last pew in the back of the church was too good for me.

That old childhood fear of having it all taken away from me dogged me right up to Father Fintan's office door the next day. After the church secretary greeted me pleasantly, she buzzed Father Fintan to let him know I had arrived. He didn't keep me waiting a minute before he opened the door to the reception area, extended his hand, and encouraged me to follow him to his office.

His office was bright and cluttered and lined with overflowing bookshelves that reminded me of my own. As I sat, I noticed a broad range of topics—many I never would have thought to find in a pastor's office. I was encouraged to see both Bill Moyers and the Episcopal Bishop John Spong among the authors represented.

"I'm impressed with all your books, Father," I said. I was fishing tentatively but hopefully.

Father Fintan waved his hand dismissively at the shelves as he sat. "Some I've read, some I haven't had a chance to get to. I'm just so busy—I don't have time to keep up with my reading the way I want to."

"Still," I said, "I've always believed a full bookshelf is a pretty clear indicator of a vibrant, intelligent mind."

"Well, I hope you're right," he laughed. "You must be wondering why I've asked you in to visit."

Nothing like getting to the point, I thought. I said, "I am. I was wondering if you'd spoken with Monsignor DeMarco at my old parish in Raleigh."

"No, I haven't spoken with him. Is there any reason why I should?"

I was a bit thrown by his response. "No, I don't suppose there is. It's just that, becoming a new parishioner in a small town, I didn't know if you ever call to ask about people..."

Father Fintan smiled sympathetically. I felt my carefully streaked hair, my age and lack of a gut, my clothes—everything about me screamed *Gay.* I felt I stood out, starkly alone, in a church full of families. I braced myself for his response. "No, I don't do that," he replied. "We pastors don't check references. I'm just happy to have you as a new parishioner. As large as this church is, I still like to have a chance to meet everyone and learn how I might best meet their needs as their pastor."

My relief must have been apparent.

"Does this surprise you?" he asked.

"No, Father," I said. "As a matter of fact, I really appreciate it. I'm just not sure how to begin."

The kind man smiled. "First, I'd like you to know I'm not here to judge you. I hope that will help you consider me a friend as well as your priest."

I wanted desperately to believe him—to accept the warm connection he was offering. I looked at his waiting face, made my decision, and decided to risk it.

As I spoke, Father Fintan leaned back in his chair and put his feet up on his desk. He nodded encouragingly as I went through the story of my life. Glancing at the clock behind him, I was amazed to realize I'd been talking for a half an hour when I concluded with:

"So I'm here to start a new life. I'm not really bitter about how things turned out, or I try not to be. I just want to make the most of the chance I've been given to begin again. And I want you to know I'm not a big activist. I didn't come here to cause discord in your parish. I just simply want a place to come and worship. Do you understand?"

Father Fintan smiled, took his feet off his desk, and leaned forward on his forearms to look at me earnestly. "I do understand. I think it's remarkable that you've come through such a disturbing experience as your separation and divorce, as you say, without being bitter. I believe you have a pretty healthy spiritual life, and that's what I'm concerned with. Considering what I hear every day, yours isn't a unique story at all. What I don't want to see is you distancing yourself from the Sacraments, especially Holy Communion."

I was stunned and very grateful. "Father, thank you," I said. "You can imagine how scared I was to come to see you. I was really afraid you'd refuse to give me Communion. I was scared you'd never accept me in the parish."

"Chris, I wouldn't be doing my job if I drove you away from the Church."

"That's a very enlightened attitude, Father. There are many people out there who don't share it."

"That's true," he said. "But, the Church sometimes acts hysterically in reaction to social change. But it makes *me* incredibly aware of other's difficulties. I think of how hard it must be for gay Catholics to live their lives under constant scrutiny and condemnation."

I nodded and looked away. There was so much more I could have said, but exploring that topic could have taken the afternoon, the day, the week. It was enough that Father Fintan was both perceptive and intelligent in a way few other priests had been in my experience. I could have taken up the man's entire afternoon talking.

"Chris, I do welcome you into our parish, and I want to see you at Mass. I've been a priest for nearly 30 years. You've not told me anything I haven't heard before, though I have to say I've met very few people, gay or straight, who could've managing to rear three children under such difficult and peculiar circumstances."

"Thank you for that, Father. Up to this point it's been my life's work to the exclusion of everything else. Now I'm paying the price for that."

"Yes, you said you were having trouble finding a job. Let me ask you, can you type?"

Immediately alert, I answered in the affirmative.

"A parishioner who has a small clinical psychiatric practice is looking for someone discreet to do transcription and to work in the office five days a week as a receptionist. I think you'd be ideal. If you're interested, I could pass along your name and have him give you a call."

"Absolutely!" I said. I was beginning to believe the man was a saint, and I told him so.

"No, I'm hardly a saint," he replied. "I'm just trying to do my job."

"Father, for what it's worth coming from me, I think you're doing great."

'Well, I thank you. But now I must be a priest and ask something of you."

I was wary, but the man had just accepted me into his parish and helped in my job hunt, so I was open to hearing what he had to ask. "Shoot," I said happily.

Father Fintan stood, indicating our time was finished. "I'm having some trouble finding people willing to spend an hour with the Blessed Sacrament during the times we have set up for Adoration. If you'd consider coming for an hour of prayer in the chapel once a week, I'd really appreciate it."

"I could do that," I said. "I mean I've never done it before, but—"

"It's not at all formal. You'll just come and sit for an hour. You can meditate, say the Rosary, or just have a conversation in your mind with our Lord."

That sounded pretty good to me. "When would be a good time? When do you have need of someone? Right now, I have plenty of time."

Father Fintan chuckled at my eagerness. "Let's wait to see what you and Dr. Rivera work out. I intend to give you a very good recommendation." He gestured toward the door. "That's his name by the way. Rivera, Tony Rivera."

As he opened the door for me, I reached for his hand. Taking it and holding it in a firm handshake, I said, "Father, thanks so much for the warm welcome. You've gone out of your way to make me feel at home here."

Father Fintan shook my hand in return and said, "No, thank you. I'm looking forward to having you as a parishioner. Will you call me to let me know you and Tony have talked?"

"Certainly, Father," I said. "And I'll let you know about the Adoration time as well."

I walked back to my car in an unexpected shower of snowflakes and with a surprising sense of optimism. I slowed my pace and marveled at how quickly things could turn on a dime. All my angst about the Church had dissolved. My fear of being judged and found unworthy was gone. And there was the possibility of a job! Not just a job frying burgers or bagging groceries, but a job that was appropriate for someone my age and, perhaps, a job that would give me a chance to stretch my mind some.

Happily I drove away from the church in a flurry of snowflakes and happy possibilities. As I crossed the large bridge spanning Bogue Sound, I suddenly remembered the coming weekend was the first anniversary of Zack's leaving. In a year, my entire life had changed. And it wasn't a desolate anniversary at all. As I reached the top of the long bridge's high hump over the water, I glimpsed the ocean beyond the narrow strip of beach. Surrounded by a riot of snowflakes, I felt incredibly lucky to live at the beach year-round. It was an altogether beautiful place, and I sincerely believed I belonged to it now.

I still had another happy errand to run: I had a puppy to meet. After the bridge deposited me on the island, I turned right onto the beach road and tried to remember what Steve Willis looked like. "Who knows," I said aloud over the car radio's chatter. "I might just find out if Steve Willis still *likes* me." I laughed at how quickly I could segue from spiritual matters to my carnal ones. It didn't seem such a big deal right then—my life was all of a piece. One happy thing called to and ran toward another. "Who knows," I said. "I might just fall in love."

I consulted Heath's handwritten directions to Steve Willis's place in Salter Path. Turning off the beach road onto an unpaved road leading back to Bogue Sound, I drove through the helter-skelter assortment of small bungalows that lodged the original inhabitants of the island. Salter Path had been settled by squatters on the Roosevelt heir Alice Hoffman's land. Many robber baron families had acquired whole islands off the coasts of the southern states. Almost all of Bogue Banks had belonged to Alice Hoffman at one time.

When two particularly devastating hurricanes had finally driven the inhabitants of Cape Lookout to the mainland and Harker's Island, some had settled in Salter Path. They lived there for generations until Alice Hoffman grew weary of paying their taxes. She offered title to the land to the families who had lived there for a generation or more and insisted in return that they pay the taxes on the tracts they occupied. Fiercely independent and contrarian, the squatters resented the gift and the obligation. The settlement of fishermen and their families remained unincorporated to this day.

I wondered how Steve Willis ended up there. Willis was a local name, but I clearly recalled Heath saying his family had moved there when he was 12 or so. It seemed unlikely that someone from off-island could settle easily among the clannish squatters.

I found the house easily. It sat at the end of the oyster shell road, next to the water's edge. It was a simple white clapboard house with black trim and shutters. It was perched on stubby pilings that gave it a five-foot lift, above what I took to be some past storm's high-water mark. From its back deck a pier extended over the water to a dock. A trim white day shrimper was tied up there. In the yard, crab traps sat in stacks in various states of rust and repair. I saw no kennels, but I did see Steve's truck. The entire yard seemed to be both drive and parking lot, so I simply pulled up next to Steve's truck and cut the Expedition's engine.

As I got out, I heard a Chessie's unmistakable baying and I peered through the snow to see Steve on his front porch. He was pulling a thermal undershirt over his bare, lean, long-waisted, torso. He commanded the dog to sit, and waited for me to walk through the snow and up the steps to the porch.

"I guess I'm bringing the snow with me," I said.

"Snow got here way ahead of you." Steve offered his hand, and I took it. The large male Chesapeake Bay retriever on the porch sniffed me anxiously. With a grasp that returned and held my initial squeeze, he tugged me up the last few steps to the porch.

"Who's this then?" I asked. I extended the back my other hand toward the dog's head. The dog jerked his head back warily despite my deliberately unthreatening gesture. He sniffed at my hand and gave a low growl.

Without letting go of my hand, Steve nudged the big dog with his knee, knocking him away from me. "Get on away then, ya ill-natured son of a bitch." The dog sat on his back haunches, unperturbed by Steve's roughness. "His name's Petey."

Aware the man was still holding my hand, I looked up at him and smiled. "Like in *The Little Rascals*?"

Steve gave me a blank but still interested look.

"The dog in *The Little Rascals*? The old movies—they still show them on television sometimes. His name was Petey."

Steve let go of my hand and stuck his hands in his pockets, suddenly seeming shy and defensive. "Don't know about all that. I don't watch much TV, wasn't ever one for wasting time that way. This dog here's name is Parson's Peter the Great, Eye-Vee on his papers. AKC-registered. That's kind of a mouthful when you just want to call the bastard for his supper. I just call him Petey."

Still sitting, Petey nudged my hand for a head rub. I turned away from Steve's odd-looking eyes. His stare was disconcerting as much for its frankly appraising glare as for his eyes' riveting color: The irises a navy-blue rim that paled to nearly gray at the black pupils. I bent toward the dog and ruffled his ears. "Is he the puppy's daddy?"

"Yep. He's the sire. C'mon in and you can meet the mama and the puppies." With that, Steve broke his stare and opened the front door.

Once inside, I looked around. The place was painted white and sparsely furnished—two navy-blanket-covered white sofas and a grass cloth rug covering the floor. A fire crackled behind the hearth's wire grate. The teak end tables were like ones I'd seen in Gardeners Eden. Small stereo components were set up on the mantel along with a large photograph of a shirtless, grinning Steve next to a tail-hung black marlin on the scales at the Morehead

City docks. All in all, it was totally not what I expected. It had the look of someone who had an eye for design—not the digs of a brusque outdoorsman. "Cool place," I offered.

Steve closed the door and stepped from behind me. Truculently he asked, "What did you expect? A raggedy-assed recliner, a Bud Light neon sign and pine paneling?"

"No...that's not what I meant at all," I replied.

"Heath told me he thought you'd be amazed."

"Then Heath was being an asshole."

Steve laughed and turned toward a doorway off the living room. "You might as well come on then and drag your jaw along with you. The puppies and their mama are out on the porch behind the kitchen."

I followed along through the door that lead to a trim, neat kitchen. It held a heavy table with wheat-twist-turned legs and four Windsor chairs. It looked as if Martha Stewart had just left it. "*Nice* kitchen too," I said to be irritating.

Ahead of me by four steps, Steve just shook his head before he stepped through another doorway. Following along behind him, I entered an enclosed porch with windows on three sides. The porch looked directly out over the pier and the dock. The room was suffused with the snowy light reflected off the gray choppy sound. I didn't bother to examine the furnishings, because as soon as I entered the room, I was set up by a swarm of puppies. The mama dog padded along after them to sniff me and look up appealingly at Steve.

I couldn't help myself. I sat right down on the floor and surrendered to the sniffs, lickings, and frantic welcome of all the pups. I could barely contain my laughter as they tickled me with their wriggling bodies and wagging tails. They all gave out short, sharp barks of delight at their visitor. All but one. Alone at the other end of the room, a single pup sat alert but aloof from the fray all around me. "Hey baby," I said encouragingly. "Hey, come see me."

The puppy looked at me warily. I crawled a few feet toward him and settled back on my shins. "What's the matter baby? Come see me. I won't hurt you." I looked up at Steve, who leaned against the wall with his hands in his pockets, just watching. The puppy took a couple of halting bounds toward me then stopped again. Not thinking, or caring, what I looked like, I moved forward to rest on my forearms with my ass in the air. In the dog books I remembered, this was called a "bow-play" stance. Thinking like a dog, and not like a middle-aged man, I was rewarded when the puppy stood, took two steps toward me, and responded with the same bow-play stance.

"That's my baby, wanna play? Come see me. Come see me!"

The puppy ran to me and licked my face. Laughing, I lifted the chubby little pup up and checked. It was a female. I crossed my legs Indian fashion and set the puppy inside them. Contentedly, she rested her chin on my thigh and looked up at me with a pair of pale-blue eyes. She was a gorgeous little Chesapeake. "Aren't you a shy girl?" I looked up at Steve and grinned. "What a doll-baby. Which one do you have picked out for me?"

"Looks like you've been picked out. Want a beer?"

"Sure, but what do you mean?"

"I don't pick out no dogs for nobody. I wait and see who takes to who. She's yours if you'll have her." Before I could answer, he stepped into the kitchen.

I looked down at the puppy. She sighed and closed her eyes contentedly, her chin still on my thigh. I rubbed her small head gently with the back of my fingers. "I've not ever had a girl dog before," I said quietly.

Steve strode gently through the little swarm of puppies and extended a bottle of Corona. As I took it from him, I realized I was exactly eye level with his crotch and he was about a foot and a half closer than he needed to be to hand me a beer. "Girl dogs are good," he said. "They're not as prone to run off and they're protective as hell. She'll stand her ground and let somebody know right quick whether or not they're welcome."

With that, he sank down to the floor next to me and tied a bit of yellow yarn around the pup's neck.

"What's that for?" I asked.

Steve stood again. Unless I intended to carry on further conversation with his crotch, I decided I ought to stand as well. He looked down at me and, half smiling, offered his hand. I took it and helped me get to my feet.

"I got some other people coming to look at pups this weekend," he said. "I want to make sure they know this one's taken."

"Oh, I see." Again he held me in his unsettling gaze. It seemed a direct challenge for me to answer a seductive question he hadn't asked. I was getting a little sick of it. I decided to address his overt but unspoken sexual challenge. "By the way, nice package, too."

"That surprise you as much as the interior design?"

"Not really. I sort of expected it," I said.

Steve nodded and tried not to let slip a grin. He managed to suppress it. "You can come get her in a couple of weeks. I like to keep them until they're eight weeks old, let 'em get weaned good."

I took a hit off my Corona and looked at him. He was older than I recalled, but he still couldn't have been more than 30. The sun had etched a few lines in the corners of his eyes. His coarse, dark hairline was still well forward. He had at least a day's worth of dark stubble, and none of it betrayed any white. I reached into my jeans jacket's inner pocket and pulled out my cigarettes and lighter, then looked at him questioningly.

"Let's go out on the deck, I could use a cigarette myself," he said.

I followed him out the sunroom's door onto the deck's worn, gray boards. I offered him a cigarette, but he had already pulled a pack from his back pocket and was holding out his lighter with cupped hands toward me. I accepted his light and watched him get his own lit against the wind. The snow was whirling around us, but the house knocked off most of the wind. "I thought we'd be blown off our feet out here, but it's not so bad," I said.

Steve nodded. "Wind and snow's coming in from the southeast. This snow could go on awhile. The front's coming in off the ocean and meeting up with a lot of wet air."

"The view from here is incredible," I offered hesitantly.

Steve regarded me a bit more gently. "I didn't mean to give you a hard time in there, you know, about the house."

"No problem," I said.

"I was expecting some pissy queen until you got down, right in there, with the dogs. You're all right, Chris."

I drank my beer and smoked in silence for a while, wanting to ask, but trying to figure out the best way. Finally, I just said: "So, exactly what did our mutual friend Dr. Heath say about me? Did he tell you I was this precious prissy princess? I didn't think I came off that way."

Steve gave me a frankly appraising look up and down before he replied. "Naw, he didn't say nothing much like that. He told me you had some pricey furniture I'd get a kick out of, but he never said you were stuck up."

I ambled down the pier over the marsh grass to the dock. My beer was half gone and my cigarette nearly finished, but I didn't want to leave. Belatedly I asked, "Can I take a look at your boat?"

"Looks like you're heading that way," Steve said pointedly, and flicked his cigarette out into the snow. I did the same, and in two strides he was next to me. We walked in silence until we got to the dock. "She ain't a beauty, but she's reliable as the day is long."

I looked over the boat's clean lines. It had a flaring upsweep at the prow—boat people called it a Carolina Flair. It was meant to keep the spray and waves off the fishermen when the waters in the sound turned rough. "It's a day boat isn't it?" I asked.

"Yeah, that's what she's for—shrimping or crabbing."

"You still go out much?"

"Enough to get by, in the right times of year. It was my dad's. I keep it up and use it."

"What happened to your folks?" I asked.

Steve looked at me sharply, then turned his attention back out over the water. "They're gone. Dead a few years now."

"I'm sorry to hear it."

"Why?" he said. "You didn't know them."

Now I was pissed. The man switched from hot to cold so fast I couldn't keep up. He was impossible. "You know something?" I said. "You're a tough son of a bitch to have a conversation with." With that, I turned to head back down the pier toward the house.

Steve caught me by the upper arm and pulled me back. Taking the opportunity of the spin to catch me unawares, he kissed me, right on the mouth. As I pushed him away he said, "That's what I need to talk about with you."

"Fuck that," I replied. "What did you think? I was coming over here to pick out a puppy and get laid? I don't need this shit off of you."

"Okay. Don't stomp off all mad. I was getting your signals

crossed myself. Of course, you were on my floor with your pretty little ass all stuck up in the air and eyeing my crotch like you'd seen Christmas."

"Are the pickings so bad down here in the wintertime you can't even *ask* if someone wants to sleep with you?" I asked angrily.

"You tell me. If I know Heath, he's about done tapping that ass and already's got one foot out the door. I thought...forget it. Let's go." He grabbed me by the hand and started pulling me along the pier toward the house.

I snatched my hand away and said, "Would you quit grabbing me and pulling me places like I was five years old?"

Steve stopped and laughed, "Okay, *Little Bit*. I guess you can get back to your house under your own steam."

"*Little bit*? What the hell? I'm not so little. Goddamn, you're infuriating." Big as he was, I wanted to punch him in the head.

Steve laughed again, put his hands in his pockets, and took off. There was nothing to do but follow along behind him. Angrily, I threw my beer bottle off into the wind and started walking.

Over his shoulder Steve yelled something back that the wind snatched and carried away. Quickening my pace, I said, "What? I couldn't hear you."

Steve mounted the steps to the deck and waited for me with a disarming grin on his face.

"I said—what did you say? I couldn't hear you back there." I stood my ground on the pier below him, as if I had any choice other than to climb the stairs to the deck and go through the house to leave.

"What I said is: Can we start this over?" He looked down at me, still grinning. "How about we do start this over? You aren't a lot of things I thought you might be, so..."

"So what?" I said in reply to that maddening grin.

"So, would you like to start over?"

I stood and looked at him without saying anything.

"You know you've either got to swim or get past me to leave don't you?"

"Oh hell, yeah. I know that. Do you always trap your guests like this?"

Steve laughed happily. "Only the ones I don't want to get away."

"You do realize I'm 48 years old, right?"

"So what? I'm 38."

"You can't be that old."

"Hey, neither can you—you look about my age. Anyway, I couldn't care less how old you are. Do you want to pretend we're 20? 18?"

"No, that's not what I meant at all."

"Okay," he said.

"Okay then. But I'm not promising I'll end up sleeping with you."

"Fair enough. Since I got a do-over, I'll play nice from here on out. Now come on and take another look at your puppy before you leave."

I started up the steps, and he just watched me. He didn't get out of the way until I was standing a foot away from him on the step's edge. "You're an asshole, Steve Willis."

He looked at me without his normal hateful stare and said, "No I'm not. I'm actually a pretty nice guy—just remember: Pickings are slim in the wintertime."

"I'll think about that," I replied.

He stepped out of my way with a grin and said, "I think you and me are going to be real good friends, Chris Thayer." He stood waiting for my response.

I thought for a moment. Here was trouble with a capital T. But I'd gotten myself in trouble before and came out okay. "Maybe so, Steve Willis."

"I'll surprise you," he promised.

"No doubt."

When I got home, covered in puppy slobber and alternately infuriated and excited by Steve Willis, I had two messages waiting for me on voice mail. The first was from Trey. He wanted to know if he and Susan could come down and spend the night on Saturday. The next was from Dr. Rivera. He sounded frankly impressed when he said he had spoken with Father Fintan. Apologizing for the lack of notice, he wanted to know if I could come in at 8:30 the following morning for an interview. He asked if I would please call back to confirm the time.

Looking at my watch, I noticed it was nearly 4:30. I returned the call and spoke to a pleasant woman who explained the doctor was in a session, but said she'd be happy to pass along my message. She offered directions and waited while I scrambled for something to write them down on. We ended the conversation on a nice note when she explained she was the doctor's wife and she looked forward to meeting me as well.

Barely able to contain my excitement, I returned Trey's call next. After the usual hiatus of canned music, I heard him answer: "Trey Ronan."

"Well, hello Trey Ronan! Is it snowing in Raleigh?"

"Hey, Chris!" He sounded unusually happy to hear from me. "What do you mean, is it snowing?"

"We're in the midst of a wonderful snowstorm here," I said. "I haven't heard if it's going up mid state."

"Well, that's interesting. I haven't paid attention to the weather. In any event, that's not why I called earlier. It is okay if Susan and I drive down for the evening on Saturday, isn't it?"

"I'd be thrilled to have you guys. I'll cook you something you'd like. What sounds good?"

Trey hesitated a minute, then said, "Let's don't do that. We'd like to take you out for dinner, okay?"

"Sounds fine. Maybe I'll cook you a nice Sunday lunch then."

"Chris, don't go to any bother. We'll need to leave early afternoon on Sunday and I'll get sleepy driving if I'm stuffed from a big lunch."

"Okay, then." I was a little disappointed to be robbed of an opportunity to mother him, but what he said made sense.

"We'll see you about 3 o'clock Saturday afternoon."

"Okay, Trey. I'll see you then. Drive safely, okay?"

"Okay!"

And, he was gone. I was a little disappointed he didn't ask about my job search. For once, I had something exciting to tell him. Then I decided it was just as well. Who knew? This time tomorrow morning I might be in the same boat I was in today: jobless but happy.

I *was* happy. I made myself a rare drink. Heath's pointed questions over the holidays had made me self-conscious about the level of bourbon in the Jim Beam bottle. It could become very easy to drown my boredom in a mellow drunken haze as easily as I could go shopping on the Internet and spend what was left of my monthly allowance on books or DVDs or other stuff. I told myself the drink was to celebrate the snow and the rather exciting day I'd had.

I turned on my fireplace, but forewent sitting in the living room to sit on the sun porch instead. I curled up on the generous sofa and sat with my drink in the twilight without turning on a lamp. I wanted to watch the sky deepen with the snowy light and follow the flakes as they raced in off the beach. The windward sides of the houses up the street were bare of any accumulation, as was my deck. But under the scrubby live oaks, the snow accumulated in tiny drifts that gleamed in the silvery-blue light.

The wind was picking up, but I was warm in my house and warmed by my drink and excited by my first winter storm on the island. Contentedly, I let my mind go blank as I listened to the wind's faint howl, and the thoughts of the day became scoured out by a gentle kind of happiness. I did wonder at Steve Willis's bizarre behavior, but I was willing to give him some latitude. I supposed he was used to putting the moves on someone and having them fall into bed or onto the floor with him.

In any case, it was just a series of crossed signals between Steve and me. I would be seeing him again in two weeks to pick up my puppy. I was looking forward to it, as a matter of fact, but if he thought he'd be "tapping that ass" right from the get-go, he'd best be thinking about saving his time for something else. While I seriously doubted Heath gave a damn who I slept with, I did. The thought of doing Steve Willis had a lot of appeal, I had to admit. But, that would happen when I decided to let the wolf-eyed bastard break him off a piece, not before.

With the slip and slide the bourbon provided, my thoughts jumped then to Father Fintan. Who would have thought I'd discover such an intelligent, broad-minded priest in this back corner of the world? On a whole other level, of course, I was as excited to get to know him as I was Steve Willis. While I was hardly a social butterfly, I'd had more opportunities for intelligent conversation in Raleigh than I'd had here on the beach. I was looking forward to hearing what Father Fintan had to say on many other topics.

Night settled on the beach, with the snow still falling and the wind keeping me company. Reluctantly, I stood and went into the darkened house to look for something to wear for a job interview. The next day was certain to be as interesting as this one had been.

Dr. Anthony Rivera's practice occupied the second floor of a surf shop on the Atlantic Beach causeway. It seemed an incongruous pairing from the parking lot, but I thought the view of the marinas that flanked the building both in front and behind would be stunning. From one side at least, that proved to be a good assumption—I entered the patient's waiting room and stood looking out over the causeway and boats beyond. The early morning was filled with a cold, brittle light, intensified by the refracting waters of the sound. In the chill left by the winter storm, the snowy scene seemed almost unreal with its highly sharpened edges. I decided I wanted to work in this place—and badly.

After a few moments, the office door opened to reveal a lovely blonde woman who looked no older than 25. She had the fresh good looks of a beach girl, blanched pale and cool by the winter morning's light.

"Chris?" she asked.

"That's me," I said and extended my hand.

She strode into the waiting room and took my hand. "I'm Cathy Rivera. Tony has been delayed. Unfortunately, he had a patient admitted to the hospital last night. He's checking up on her before he comes in. Would you like some coffee?"

"Cathy, I'm afraid I'm a little coffee'd out. I was up early and walked on the beach this morning. It took nearly a full pot to warm me up, and now I've got the jitters."

"That's perfectly understandable. How about some decaf tea?" she asked.

"That sounds great."

Smiling, she indicated I should sit. "I hate to keep you in the waiting room, but with the new HIPAA laws, I can't ask you into my office, where all the records are. And, I prefer to let Tony invite you into his office. Would you care for sugar? The blue stuff?"

"The blue stuff is fine. What's HIPAA?"

She smiled. "HIPAA stands for the Health Insurance Portability and Accountability Act. It's also a massive pain in the you-know-what. But, I can explain all that eventually. I'll be right back."

I liked her. She seemed very intelligent and self-assured. More than that, she seemed very gracious as well. The thought suddenly occurred to me that I might have sounded like an idiot, asking what the HIPAA deal was. I hoped Father Fintan had explained my inexperience.

Cathy returned with two mugs of tea and sat carefully in the seat across a low coffee table from me. She extended my mug of tea, and I took it from her and sipped at it cautiously. When she was satisfied my tea was okay, she said, "You're very dressed up. I should have told you we're more concerned with being comfortable here than we are with business wear."

I smiled. "That's good to hear, because to be honest, this is my only suit. I don't have much of a business wardrobe."

Cathy returned my smile. "Let me explain to you what we need here and find out if you're still interested."

I sat my tea mug carefully on the low table between the copies of *People, Time,* and *Ladies' Home Journal,* then settled back in my seat expectantly.

Cathy leaned into the curve of her seat as well and began. "As I told you, Tony is my husband. We have a daughter—four years old—and now we're expecting again."

"Congratulations," I interrupted. "You certainly don't look old enough to have a four-year-old."

Cathy accepted the congratulations and compliment with a serene nod of her head, then continued. "As you might imagine, there's a lot of paperwork involved with a medical practice. Insurance alone is a full-time job. What we're hoping to find is someone who can transcribe Steve's session notes—he records them into a small pocket tape recorder after each appointment. We type the taped notes into hard copy to keep in the patient's permanent files. I hate doing that. I don't mind the insurance work—in fact, I enjoy it. But I don't like trying to juggle the phones, the transcription, *and* the insurance work. We hope you might be interested in working about 30 hours a week, handling the phones and the transcription."

It seemed like an excellent opportunity. "I'm very interested," I said. "But, in all honesty, I have to tell you: My typing skills are very rusty. I've not typed more than an e-mail in years."

Cathy nodded. "That's no big deal. You'd get better with practice. We're more concerned with finding someone who'd be a good fit with our work environment. We are so small right now—just Tony and me. We would really like to hire someone we feel we could work with. Do you like children?"

My face must have lit up. "I have three of my own," I said. "I don't know if Father Fintan told you or not, but I've just spent 22 years as a househusband. I was the kids' primary caregiver—I like children a great deal."

Cathy allowed a genuine smile to spread across her sunny face. "That's good to hear for several reasons. I sometimes bring our daughter to the office. She's very well behaved, but she's a child, nonetheless. When this baby is born, it'll also be coming to work with me as long as I'm breast feeding. Also, we have quite a few children and teenagers as patients. While you won't be interacting with them a great deal, it's a help to have someone who understands kids' peculiarities in addition to their personal difficulties. Some of our kids are quite antisocial, and some are very manipulative. The fine art in being our receptionist lies in learning to distinguish between a genuine emergency and a temper tantrum."

I nodded. "I understand. I don't think that'll be a problem. Could I ask what the position will pay?"

Cathy sighed. "Unfortunately, not what we think it's worth. But we're willing to be flexible about your work schedule, the stress level here is really low, and I think you'll like the people you'd encounter. We can offer you $500 a week. That translates to $24,000 a year for a 30-hour-a-week job."

I winced. It seemed like a small amount of money, considering my expenses.

Cathy acknowledged my reluctance but countered it with an explanation. "Chris, I know that sounds low. I said it wasn't what we think the job is worth, but you have to consider it's really in line with what people really make in Carteret County. Compared to Raleigh, it's a poor area. The median income is only $12,000 a year down here. Of course, that affects what we can charge our clients. So, you see…"

I nodded and smiled for her. The jobs I had called about in my job search actually paid a lot less. Minimum wage seemed the going rate, even for more demanding jobs.

Cathy returned my smile with an encouraging one of her own. Brightly, she said, "We also can offer you participation in our health coverage. It's not bad, considering...and, you'll be given some consideration for sick time and a week's paid vacation after the first year."

Considering my prospects, which were discouraging at best, it was not a bad deal. I decided to take the opportunity and run with it. "When can I start?"

Cathy laughed. "Are you really so eager? Isn't there anything you'd like to ask me?"

I thought a moment. She had answered all my questions, and she'd been generous about my lack of skills and inexperience. There was only one thing more I was concerned about. "May I see where I'll be working?"

Cathy gave me a puzzled look and said, "Certainly." She stood and motioned for me to follow her beyond the reception area's door. As I walked through the door, I looked to my left and saw the receptionist's work space. As I suspected, it had a large window that shared the same view as the reception area—looking out over the causeway and across to the marina. I was delighted.

"I think I would be very lucky and happy to work here," I said earnestly. "I like you very much and I think the job would be challenging and good for me in many ways. If you're willing to take a risk on someone so inexperienced, I would love to come to work for you."

Cathy smiled, then laughed. "I like you, Chris Thayer. You're forthright and honest. Are you sure you don't want to meet Tony before you sign on to work in this lunatic asylum? It gets pretty busy, believe it or not. And Tony has his own little ways about him."

I returned her smile and gave her a chuckle of my own.. "Cathy, believe it or not, I was married to someone with a lot of little ways for 22 years. I think I can handle that and the busyness."

Cathy nodded. "I thought as much. Our hours are from 9 to 5, but yours would be from 9 to 3, five days a week. We stop seeing patients after 3 so Tony can make rounds or get caught up on paperwork. Can you begin Monday?"

With little to do but wait for Trey and Susan on Saturday morning, I called the church office to leave Father Fintan a message to let him know how well my job interview had gone. Surprisingly, he picked up the phone himself.

"Hello Father, it's Chris Thayer," I said. "I was just going to leave a message."

"Yes, Chris. Well, I'm here doing me paperwork. 'Tis a never-ending job, the priest business. I take it you went to see the Riveras."

"I did, and it went very well. I start on Monday."

"I thought Cathy would like you. She's the real boss of himself, the doctor."

"I figured as much," I said. "I think she's charming. I really believe I'll be very happy working for her."

"I'm pleased you two got on. She's been looking for the right person for a while."

"I'd like to thank you so much for sending me over there. I was getting desperate to find a job."

Father Fintan laughed. "It was nothing. I'm glad to have helped."

I hesitated a moment, not wanting to tie the poor man up on the phone, then asked: "Father, where are you from in Ireland?"

"Ah, 30 years in this country and I'm still Irish is it? Well, I can't seem to lose me accent—nor do I want to—mind you. But it does seem to be sort of stereotypical—being the Irish priest in town. I'm from Kinsale, on the south coast, just below Cork."

"I know the town. I've stayed in the postmaster's residence—it's a bed-and-breakfast now."

"Have you now? I know it well, next door to the new post office on one side and the grocery on the other. What took you to Ireland, then?"

"Nuala O'Faolain, John McGahern, and Edna O'Brien. I'm a big Irish reader. The writers drew me to the place."

"You can't do better than those. My God, O'Brien! Oh, the magnificent anger and talent of the woman. I'm a fan meself. So, you've been to Dublin and the west of Ireland as well?"

"Yes! I've had coffee at Bewley's and I walked to 8 o'clock Mass at Saint Theresa's in Dublin. It's a wonderful place, a beautiful church."

"And where were you staying in Dublin to walk to Saint Theresa's for Mass?"

"I stayed at The Merrion."

"Ach! Not for the likes of us working people. I'll look forward to talking more about your travels and your reading. I need to go now. Unfortunately, I have a funeral this morning. But I thank you for calling."

"Wait, Father," I said. "One quick thing. I've thought about it, I was wondering if I could sign up for Adoration of the Blessed Sacrament for, say, 3:30 to 4:30 on Tuesdays? I'll be getting off work at 3, and that should give me plenty of time to get to the church."

"Hold a minute, let me look at the book," he said.

He put the phone down noisily and I waited for a moment before he returned. I had thought about this commitment—even going so far as to find my old rosary in a box I'd yet to unpack, in Schooner's loft. I thought of the luck and blessings I'd ended up with after a long, rough year and decided I could offer a little commitment to prayer in my new life.

"Chris, there's exactly the same time open on Thursdays. Could you be persuaded to make it then?"

"Absolutely, Father. Thursdays are fine."

"Well that's done. There's a sign-in book just as you come through the door to the chapel. If you would, please just sign it to help me keep tabs on you."

I laughed. "I'll do that. Thanks again, Father, *Dia duit*."

"*Dia es Muirre duit*. Listen to you, with the Gaelic. You're a surprising man. See you, then, Chris."

I hung up the phone with a smile. I was looking forward to talking more with Father Fintan. I had found another reader—that in itself was a treasure.

I looked over my rows of books and spotted the lines of titles Andrea called "The Irish Collection." She found the Irish writers collectively depressive. Zack just rolled his eyes at my absorption, and the boys simply couldn't be bothered. I thought it was a total abrogation of their heritage on their part. Having no discernable family history of my own—other than generations of shift work or tobacco fields—I eagerly assumed the responsibility of learning more about the heritage of my husband and kids. I was more Irish than they were, intellectually at least. If I couldn't become a Ronan by marriage, I certainly became one through literary osmosis. Zack laughed and told me I was Irish by injection. Which, come to think of it, I still considered pretty funny.

In a lot of little ways, I missed Zack a great deal. We shared many jokes where the punch line could be conveyed by a sort of verbal shorthand. There were grand times, like the trip to Ireland we'd taken the year before he'd given himself over to other dreams. And there were all the shared experiences of raising a family together.

I hadn't heard from Zack since Christmas. At times I had to practically sit on my hands to keep from calling him to share something funny I'd seen that I knew he'd see the humor in too. A conversation with one of the kids would spark a concern that I'd want to field with him. There were a thousand ways I sorely missed open communication with someone I'd shared a long life with. But, I resisted the urge to call.

On one level, I felt he didn't deserve to keep the emotional intimacy we'd shared any longer. It was Zack, after all, that had thrown it away. On another level, I didn't want to appear as if I were clinging to a past that was surely irrelevant now. Besides, I wouldn't interlope into concern or involvement with Zack's new life. It was none of my business, and the life I was working to build was none of his.

So I decided ruminating on Zack was a waste of my time. I left the bookcase and started toward the guest room to give it a final look when I heard a loud, heavy vehicle in my drive. I walked to the French doors that gave out onto the deck and saw Steve Willis's truck there. In a moment, the man himself stepped from the cab and walked to the back of his truck.

I opened the door, walked out on the deck, and called down to him. He looked up from the tailgate, where he was pulling a large red kennel from the truck's bed. "Hello, Chris. I have a present for you."

"I see that," I replied.

He lifted the heavy cage from the back of the truck and disappeared under the house. In a moment, I heard his heavy tread coming up my steps to the deck. I watched the cage appear first, followed by Steve. "Where do you want this? It ain't exactly light."

"The bedroom, I guess. C'mon."

Steve waited while I got both French doors opened and followed me through the house to my bedroom.

"Nice house," he muttered.

"Thanks, why don't you put the cage right over there." I pointed to an empty corner across from the bed.

Steve sat the kennel down easily, took off his baseball cap, and wiped his forehead with his forearm. "Looks like I got the paint color just about right."

"How did you know my bed was lacquer-red?" I asked.

"Heath. He told me."

"Good for Heath. He's got a sharp eye for color."

Steve gave a shake of his head. "No he don't, smart ass. Since you declined to visit my bedroom a couple of days ago, you wouldn't know I got a bed just like that, would you?"

"No I wouldn't. Where did you find a bed like this one?"

"I didn't find one, I built one. I copied the design out of one I saw in Met Home. I had it painted over at the body shop. That's where I got your kennel painted too."

"Well, I appreciate that, Steve. But—"

"Ain't you got any coffee to offer a man who's gone out of his way to do something nice for you?"

I fought back a grin. The man was nothing if not presumptuous. "How about I make you some fresh?" I offered.

Steve nodded and followed me to the front of the house. Once we got to the great room, I motioned for him to have a seat at the dining room table. I watched while he took the seat at the head of the table where I usually sat. Sighing with satisfaction, he pulled his cigarettes and lighter from his coat pocket and laid them on the table. *Proprietary bastard,* I thought as I got busy making a pot of fresh coffee. Task handled, I left the kitchen and pulled out a chair and sat next to Steve.

He looked at me and raised his eyebrows questioningly.

"So, what do you think?" I asked.

"Think about what?"

"Think about my house."

"I told you it was nice."

"Well, thanks. But I want to know your opinion. It's pretty obvious you have a great eye. Hell, anybody who can re-create an Italian-designed bed obviously has more talent and good sense than I do."

Steve shrugged and said, "Nah, I just have less money and more time. I like your house, but it's more than I could live with. I mean, it's nice and everything, but it's not right for my needs."

"That makes sense," I said. "Now can we get over the design-class warfare thing?"

"It's a deal. When you want someplace to kick back and walk around wet from the beach, come on over to my place. You could drag in a ton of sand there and never see it again."

I laughed and said, "Okay, and when you want a place to come and kick back, read, and…" I ran out of words. I didn't know what Steve Willis would do other than what he did, but I didn't want to give him the impression I had him pegged as some sort of low-class redneck. He'd gone out of his way to make me see he was anything but that.

"…and how about roll around naked on that big Oriental rug with your new puppy?" he asked.

I laughed. "It could happen—eventually," I said evenly.

Steve snickered, shook his head, pulled a cigarette from his pack, and lit it. There wasn't any need to ask if he could: There was a dirty ashtray on the table right in front of him. But I knew for certain he wouldn't have asked even if there weren't. Like Trey, he was a little king someone had reared to be head of a household. "Aren't you going to ask how I came to be bringing you a fresh-painted dog kennel to match your interior design?"

The coffee maker sighed and spat the last of the water into the basket with a hissing of steam. "Yes," I said. "But first, I want to ask how you knew I'd keep her in the bedroom."

Steve exhaled a long stream of smoke and settled back into the chair. "I saw you with that puppy, remember? You're tenderhearted. You know as good as I do that puppy'll cry a lot less spending her first nights in a crate if she's in the same room as you."

I stood to get our coffee and gave him a smile. "You have me pegged, for sure. That's dead-on. How do you want your coffee?"

"Light and sweet," he said, looking up at me, blue-eyed and earnest, "like somebody I know."

"You're a real charmer, Steve," I said skeptically. I walked into the kitchen and reached for two mugs. "So, I appreciate the cage from Heath and the paint job from you. But why so soon?"

I saw him flick his cigarette and rub his eyes tiredly. "There's been a change of plans on my part. I'm going to have to give you the puppy a week earlier than we planned on. A guy I've crewed for has his boat in Antigua right now and he wants me to fly down and work for him for a few weeks. It's good money and I can use it. I'm heading down there a week from Monday."

I stirred the coffee in both mugs, walked back to the table under the full glare of Steve's blue high beams, and sat down. He took his mug and continued to watch me. "What about the other puppies?" I asked. "And Petey, and their mama?"

Steve smiled. "All questions about the dogs? No more questions about me?"

"Sure, when are you coming back?"

"End of March or early April—it depends on how it goes. But I'll be back with more money than a motherfucker and horny as hell."

I looked at him and smiled. "As pushy as you are, I doubt you'll be all that horny."

Steve looked down at his mug of coffee and took a sip. "You don't know me." He put out his cigarette, took another out of his pack, and looked at me without any guile. "You don't know me at all."

I lit a cigarette of my own, then lit his. So much smoking carried the weight of a lot of unspoken words. "I don't know you, but I'm enjoying learning more about you," I replied.

"Most of the puppies are going to be picked up next Saturday. I'm only keeping two to gun-train. Heath'll look after all my dogs. He always has."

I nodded. "Are you and Heath still…"

"Knocking boots? Hell no. But we're still good friends. And right now, I'm wishing my friend hadn't gotten to you first."

I smiled and took his free hand. "It's like this, Steve. I think you were absolutely right when I was at your house and you said you thought Heath probably had one foot out the door. I've been thinking the same thing for a while now. It wasn't ever meant to be any big deal, both of us agreed on that. Okay?"

Steve turned his hand under mine so he was holding my hand, not the other way around. "I might seem pushy, but I'm not a big horndog. I want you to know that. I'm pretty particular."

I smiled. "I am too. I can count on two fingers the men I've had sex with in the past 23 years. You ought to know I'm not in a big hurry to put a name on the other ones."

Steve put his cigarette in the ashtray and turned my hand palm up. He took my ring finger and fiddled in his jacket pocket for something. Pulling out a ballpoint pen, he clicked it and took the tip gently to my fingertip. After a second or two of ticklish business, he let go of my hand. I held my fingertip up and saw he'd written "Steve" there in black ink. I shivered.

"Keep that one reserved for me, okay?" he said.

Disturbed, I asked, "Steve, do you have any tattoos?"

He looked at me searchingly before he replied. "No," he said. "Not a one. Why? Do you have a thing for them?"

I laughed. "Nope, I don't. I can take them or leave them."

Steve looked at me, then at my hand, and jerked his head. "Just remember what's on that finger when it washes off. I'm serious about wanting to know you better, man."

"I'll remember it. When do you want me to come get my puppy?"

"How about late Friday afternoon? About 5 o'clock. Saturday's going to be a bitch and Sunday's going to be worse with me leaving on Monday. Friday suit you?"

"Friday's fine."

"What are you going to name her? I need to get her papers ready for AKC. I thought I'd add your name in with the proper one."

I was at a loss. After I'd met the little girl puppy, "Tonka" sounded ridiculous. She'd been so shy at first, then she'd taken to my affection—as if she'd found a home, as if in the wrangle of puppies she'd become somebody. A trigger got pulled. I looked at Steve and laughed. "Nuala," I said.

"What?"

"Nuala. It's an Irish name."

"What the fuck kind of name is that for a dog? Nooh-lah, like moolah? Damn."

"It fits her. She's *somebody*."

Again, Steve fished in his pocket. This time he pulled out a small wire-bound pad. He turned the sheets to an empty page, picked up his pen, and asked me to spell the name.

"N-U-A-L-A," I said.

"Nuala. It looks better than it sounds."

I just smiled.

He looked at me questioningly once more. I nodded and, with a shrug, he folded the pen and pad back into the pocket of his jacket. Without knowing it, he'd written two names on my heart.

After a few more longing looks and unrewarded innuendos, Steve left and I took off to the grocery store. I decided if Susan and Trey couldn't stay for a proper Sunday meal, they could certainly have a large Sunday brunch. Besides, I had Puppy Chow, dog biscuits, and chew toys to buy. As long as Nuala couldn't outrun me, there was no need for a new collar or leash. Beau's old collar and leash still hung on a hook by the kitchen door. I had already decided to retire them in his honor. Now, with a little girl dog, I could buy something bright and new when the time came.

The grocery store errand filled what was left of my morning and early afternoon. With time still to kill before Susan's and Trey's arrival, I struck out for the beach, thinking a long walk would do me a world of good. I had much still swirling in my head. Though Thursday's snow was long gone, my thoughts were still as disorganized as that improbable, chaotic flurry.

The beach was cold, but with the wind calm, it was only just brisk. I was the only one out in the wintry sun. The ocean was as still as a bathtub. Only the shore break reared and receded with its unique susurrus. I let Steve Willis leave my mind first. For all that it might be frustrating him, I was enjoying putting off the inevitable. I was far too attracted to him not to surrender eventually, but I wasn't ready to contemplate what would come after the first rush of pleasure.

He was an odd man. Steve was isolated and alone here, but obviously he was also very much of the place. I wasn't of this place entirely—I was still a newcomer and I wanted to enjoy my time alone while I learned my place in the scheme of things. And, quite frankly, I was scared of Steve Willis. I was the marrying kind, but I wasn't ready to get married again quite yet. I wanted to belong to me for a while. And that brought another man into my thinking.

It was time to cut Heath loose. I did enjoy his company. He was the first friend I'd made here, and I didn't want to lose that, but I just didn't want to sleep with him anymore. As reluctant as I was to admit Steve Willis into my bed, I knew that's where he'd end up. I simply didn't have the mental or emotional capacity to carry on sexual relationships with more than one man at a time. I thought of how ludicrous that might sound to the rest of the gay world, but the gay world wasn't one I'd lived in for many years. I was who I was. In that regard, I didn't need to defend myself to anyone. I couldn't wait to tell Wade Lee. He'd have a fit.

I shuddered to think of the mental gymnastics it'd take to carry on two simultaneous affairs. I'd end up a patient of Dr. Rivera's, not just an employee. With that thought in mind, I allowed myself to get excited again about my new job. I strolled all the way to the pier feeling quite satisfied with myself. I knew the job would be more difficult than I'd imagined. It had to be more than sitting by the window in the receptionist's office, dressed in flip-flops, shorts, and a T-shirt and gazing out at the view. I wasn't stupid enough to believe that's all it'd be. If it was, I'd be bored to death.

I reached the pier with a happy mood settling around me. I turned around and headed back home with the sun on my face. I couldn't wait to have my new puppy along for the walk. She'd be too small at first to make it the whole way to the pier and back, but she'd grow fast, they always did. I recalled it seemed as if Beau had turned from a squirmy, pissing puppy into a big, bounding adolescent in a matter of days. Ol' Nuala would be a real joy.

So would this new baby of Trey and Susan's. After my chat with Susan on Christmas Day, I was certain that's why they were coming down. Already, in my heart, I knew Susan was pregnant. Trey's voice had betrayed so much happiness in our phone call, and his sudden need for a visit couldn't have been triggered by something as mundane as my finances. There was going be another baby Ronan for me to love—I was going to be a *grandmama*. The thought of it filled me with joyous laughter.

I recalled hearing Nuala O'Faolain in an NPR interview. She

said when she got old she wanted to live in a small place where she could walk to the pub each evening and sit to nurse a drink. She said she was looking forward to the time when she'd be sitting alone and someone would come into the pub and say, "Oh look—there's old Nuala. Let's buy her a drink." To me—having spent a small amount of time in such pubs along the southern and western coasts of Ireland—it did seem like a fine way to live out one's last days. But I wasn't in my last days—not yet. I still had much happiness to enjoy and many memories to make.

Up ahead I could see two figures walking toward me. They were close together, gently bumping each other, as best I could tell. Ah, yes. They were much too close together to be two men. Not on this beach, not at this time. That thought didn't bother me. I was prepared to live out my days alone, even if there were a world of possibilities in Steve Willis's blue-eyed stare. I'd have my Nuala for 12, maybe even 14 years to come. After that, I'd still only be on the working side of 60. There'd be time for another puppy again perhaps. And with a baby Ronan, there'd be a need for me even longer after that.

I wanted to hug the sky. I wanted to sing on the cold, sunny beach where I'd come to live out my life. I wanted to do more than just smile and put one foot in front of the other.

The couple in the distance grew more distinct the closer they came toward me. When they raised their arms to wave, I waved back. It had to be Susan and Trey. I wanted to run toward them, waving and crying out, but I didn't. The indignity of it be damned. I was mindful of the renewed hunger for Marlboro Lights in my lungs and the unforeseen fragility of a weakened spot on an artery, hiding itself away for another day. Instead, I smiled as big as I could, hoping to let them know how happy I was to see them, until I reached them and could tell them so myself.

CHAPTER FIVE, SPRING

✦

Late in the afternoon, on the Thursday before Holy Week, I looked out my window over the causeway and the marina and noted the steady stream of traffic heading in off the bridge from the mainland. The people with cottages were returning early to open up their places after a long winter's dream of warmth, sand, and summer. I fleetingly wished I could send them all home. Cathy told me Easter Weekend was the real start of the season; it was one of the busiest weekends of the year. None of us looked forward to the traffic or the crowds.

Cathy was gone to pick her daughter Sierra from day care. Tony was in session with a "client" as I'd been taught to say, and no one was due in for the rest of the day. I took off my earphone now that I'd caught up with yesterday's transcriptions. I'd found the task simple and interesting once I'd caught the hang of it. The best way to handle the transcription chore I discovered, was never to let it get ahead of me. Immediately on arriving at the office, I'd make myself some coffee and get to work. Sometimes, if the phones rang constantly, I'd fall behind during the day, but I wouldn't leave the office that afternoon until I'd completed the transcripts of all the sessions from the day before.

So far I was pleased with the Riveras, and they seemed pleased with me. Sierra was a doll baby. Though she was rarely at the office, she did come on the days that pre-K and day care were closed, or if she had a bug. Her mother was more than right: she was very well behaved.

I often brought Nuala to work with me. In fact, I brought Nuala to work with me every day but Thursdays, when I had

Adoration after work. I didn't know who was happier to see whom—Nuala and Sierra loved each other. I thought it was good for the puppy and the child to play together, and Cathy agreed. She said she was able to dodge Sierra's requests for a puppy by telling her she already had an office puppy.

It was really a laid-back place to work. Cathy was very personable, but most of the day she was bound to her desk, taking care of all the insurance work. The good doctor had quite a few patients for a relatively new practice, and he was happy with me as long as I had the right file ready for him before he greeted each patient at the waiting room door. I had some secret fears about internecine warfare between the husband-and-wife team, but they never were anything but affectionate and courteous to each other.

I once remarked to Cathy how happy their relationship seemed. She just laughed. "You should hear us at home sometimes. It'd freak you out. But in the office we have an agreement to treat each other as colleagues and business partners, not as husband and wife. We keep the irritating shit at home." They did a great job of it. I never once heard them say a cross word to each other.

With a bit of play in me, I pushed off hard from my computer desk and rolled my chair to the counter under the glass window where I welcomed clients and took their co-pay checks. By 10 of 3, I had the office's bank deposit ticket filled out and paper-clipped to the day's checks. With that done, the reception desk was neat as a pin and ready for me the next morning. I had nothing to do now but wait for Cathy to return from picking up her daughter from pre-K and take any stray calls that might come in.

On the wall under the reception window I had taped a row of postcards from the Caribbean. All of them had one- or two-line greetings from Steve on the back. Most recently, I'd gotten a stiff mailer envelope from St. Lucia that contained a color picture of Steve standing, lean and tanned, with a record marlin. Judging from the tick marks painted in foot increments on the uprights holding the crossbeam that held the hanging fish, Steve stood just past six feet (if you measured upside down); the fish came in at nearly nine feet from its tail to the end of its bill. On the back of the photo Steve had written, "I'm sick of white water and killing decent marlin for asshole rich people. Home April 11. Is my name still on that finger?" Either way I measured when I looked at that picture, I'd come to see both the man and the fish were prize catches.

On the night nearly six weeks ago when I'd gone to Steve's to get Nuala, we'd sat in the living room by his fire and talked over a bottle of red wine. I learned he was half Italian. His father was from Salter Path, but he'd joined the navy. When he was stationed at the navy yard in Boston he'd met Steve's mother, and that was all she wrote. She was a Gagliardo from Brookline. He was a Willis from Bogue Banks. It was an improbable combination, but it resulted in a happy marriage and Steve's long-waisted body, olive coloring, and dramatic eyes.

From his father he'd learned to be a waterman and he had no desire to be anything else, despite an undeniable intelligence and an artistic eye. It was his mother who encouraged that part of him. The three of them had been quite happy in that small house by the sound, but an accident claimed his father when Steve was 20, and cancer his mother not long after that. Except for a smattering of aunts, uncles and cousins, throughout Salter Path and far away places where different, sometimes better, lives had taken them, Steve was alone.

Learning this, I was able to get a better sense of his nature. He was no pushier than other guys probably were, but he did have the added impetuses of missing a loving home, and an Italian mother. Her son was a little prince who grew up to have no kingdom. Steve had tried and mostly failed over the years to connect with anyone special. I wasn't quite sure why he thought he might see that possibility in me.

I said as much to Heath when I told him—gently—we wouldn't be sleeping together anymore. He laughed and asked if Steve had finally staked his claim. Narrowing my eyes, I told him we hadn't slept together, if that's what he meant.

"Oh, hell," he said. "That'll be the end of it for sure. Once he gets you in bed, I'd give a hundred bucks to be a fly on the wall. You two were meant for each other. I can honestly tell you that because I've slept with both of you. You'll eat each other alive."

I didn't bother asking him to elaborate; I figured as much. In any case, Steve was on his way home, and I was ready, if he'd still have me.

"Hello, Chris!" I heard Sierra's happy greeting no sooner than her mom had cracked open the waiting room door.

"There's my Sierra girl," I said, opening the glass window to wave. "Come in here and give me a hug."

She ran to open the inner door to the office and then scampered to my lap. "Where's Nuala?" she asked.

She was a happy, loving child and it was hard not to spoil her. "Ol' Nuala's back at our house. Today's Thursday, remember?"

"She does love that dog," Cathy said. "Any calls, Chris?" She was now visibly pregnant and winced in pain as she braced her back with both hands.

"No, not a one. Why don't you tell Dr. Tony you've had enough for today and go home to take a nap? You've been hurting with that back all day."

Cathy smiled and shook her head. "That would be nice, but your rule about getting all your work done before you go home has rubbed off on me. I have a few more things to do and then I'll get out of here. Promise."

I nodded and turned my attention back to Sierra. "So, did you do any artwork today?"

"No," she said. "Pre-K has art on Friday. Today Miss Sharice did reading and arithmetic."

"Okay! Then you should like what I have for you in my knapsack. Bring it to me, okay?"

Excitedly, the little girl slid from my lap and walked across the office. She retrieved my knapsack from under my computer desk and brought it to me. I took it from her gently and fished around in it to find the Little Golden Book I had stashed there. I had discovered a trove of them for 10 cents each at a yard sale and bought the lot. Every week since, I had presented one to Sierra. I handed the book to the little girl and she hugged it to her chest and spun with it in her arms.

"What do you say to Chris, Sierra," her mother prompted.

Sierra reached out with both arms and I leaned down for a wet kiss on the cheek. "Thank you, Chris," she said.

"You spoil her terribly," Cathy said. "What are you going to do when you run out of those books?"

I gave Cathy a smile. "Well, I'll have to go to another yard sale, won't I? If she loves to read, she should have all the books she wants. It's a friend she'll keep the rest of her life."

"Go home, Chris. You're a trip."

"Promise me you'll do the same pretty quickly?"

Cathy nodded in reply, then lifted her chin and shifted her eyes to show me I should look to my right. Sierra was curled up and reading contentedly in the dog bed I kept for Nuala under the window. Having made both the child and her mother happy, I shouldered my knapsack and left the office.

Making a left turn against the incoming traffic was annoying, but I made it across and onto the bridge and got to the church quickly. I parked in the near-empty parking lot and made the short walk to the chapel, enjoying the spring warmth and the pleasant slap of my new leather flip-flops. Pulling open the heavy wooden door, I left the bright, slanting afternoon light for the semidarkness of the chapel. After placing the tip of my middle finger into the font and making the sign of the cross, I signed in for my hour of Adoration before the Blessed Sacrament. That done to please Father Fintan, I walked up the aisle to my favorite spot: a pew near the back, opposite a stained glass window picturing the Blessed Mother and Mary Magdalene meeting Christ on his way to Golgotha.

In the aisle at the edge of my pew, I knelt, crossed myself, and bowed low, remaining in my obeisance as I recited, "Oh Sacrament most holy / Oh Sacrament Divine / All praise and all thanksgiving / Be forever thine." I rose, made my way down the pew to sit near the window, kneeled again, and pulled my rosary from my pocket. I held it lightly, made the sign of the cross, and began my informal conversation with God.

Satisfied that God had heard my rambling and disjointed litany of requests, I crossed myself and began reciting the decades of the rosary. My special intentions were not complex. I prayed on behalf of my little family—soon to be expanded by one—my community, and the world. That finished, I simply sat and enjoyed being bathed in the light from the stained glass window at my side. It colored my world in pure primary colors, as I hoped my raw prayers would bathe myself and my world in a kind of benediction I believed in.

Then I stood, made my way to the end of the pew, made my obeisance once more to my God, and left to return to my world. I truly believed it would be a better place for my prayers.

Stepping from the dimness of the chapel into the sunshine outside, I thought of how easy it was to step back into the mundane from the divine. I laughed, struck by the two aspects of my nature and of the mystery of faith, and headed back over the bridge to the grocery store and home.

When I got back to my house, Steve was asleep in one of the Adirondack chairs on my deck, his feet propped on his duffel bag, I put my two handfuls of heavy plastic grocery bags by the door and walked quietly up behind him. His hair had grown from a dark bristly crew cut into sun-bleached curls. I gently ran my fingers through them until he stirred awake, looked up drowsily, and smiled. "You're early," I said.

He nodded, leaned forward from my touch, and rubbed his eyes. "I caught a ride in from the airport with a guy I crewed with." He yawned mightily and stretched. "He was heading to Morehead City and I had him drop me off here."

"I wondered where your truck was. Would you like some coffee?"

Steve stood and turned to face me. "What I want is a hot shower. I smell like bait, a dock shower, and three different airplanes." He smiled at me. "Mind if I get the shower first and the coffee after?"

"How about dinner after that?"

"Sounds good, as long as it's not fish, sandwiches, or limp salads. I've eaten enough of that onboard crap to last me awhile," he said.

"I had planned on cooking you dinner tomorrow night anyway. I just bought two steaks and I can have baked potatoes done in the microwave by the time the steaks are ready."

Steve grinned. "Then I'll carry your groceries in for you."

"Why don't you grab your duffel bag instead?"

"It's full of dirty clothes—you might like me better if it stayed outside."

"I got a washing machine and a dryer."

"I don't want you doing my dirty laundry."

"Oh shut up, Steve," I said amicably. "Just go get a shower, okay?"

I opened the door to Nuala's sharp barks. She'd been in her crate all day and was ready for a walk, dinner, and company, in pretty short order. I put the groceries on the counter and was stowing the things that needed to go in the refrigerator when she appeared in the kitchen, a toy in her mouth and Steve just behind her.

"I let her out," Steve said. "Do you want me to take her outside?"

"No, she'll keep a minute more until I can get some coffee started. You get in the shower, you look beat. There's clean towels in the bathroom closet."

Steve gave me a grateful look and headed back down the hall. My old ability to manage several things simultaneously came back to me from years gone by. I played a quick game of toss and fetch with Nuala while I got coffee started, set out a couple of mugs with two spoons by the coffee machine, and made the sugar bowl apparent. Then I got Nuala leashed and took off toward the beach.

The street from my house to the beach was still relatively quiet. Throughout the winter, I'd been the only full-time resident. I met my neighbors in the house at the end of the street over Christmas and asked their permission to cross the side of their lot to go straight to the beach. They were very gracious—they even gave me their home phone number in Kinston so I could call them if I noticed anything awry with their house or property. Since then I'd been vigilant about keeping an eye out for leaking or burst pipes and hints of vandalism or burglary. Thankfully, I'd never needed to call them. I was grateful for the right of passage, which kept me from having to walk two blocks away to the public beach access point.

Nuala was grateful too; she could never get to the beach fast enough. Now 4 months old, she was getting to the more difficult parts of her training, including coming when she was called and staying when she was told to stay. That was difficult with all the distractions of the shore. Like most hunting dogs, she was absolutely entranced by the wealth of scents on the beach, particularly those gruesome things that either had died there or washed ashore dead. I asked her to sit and unclicked her leash. As badly as I wanted to run through her essentials quickly, I still needed to dispense with the full gamut of training I'd started her on. Consistency was the key. If I was going to allow her off the leash on the beach, she had to be thoroughly trained.

Nuala was a happy but reserved dog. While she wasn't likely to run up to strangers and maul them with friendliness, she did have a lot of curiosity. There was little human activity to claim her attention—the beach was still as deserted as my street. Even the late-afternoon troops of retired beachcombers were few and far between. Nuala did her training paces with great enthusiasm, then just as determinedly let me know she was ready to go home. She knew dinner was waiting, and I chose to believe she knew Steve was waiting as well.

Dogs have a sense for people, just as some people have a sense for dogs. Steve was the first human she'd ever known. When he'd gone into my room to let her out of her kennel, she didn't bark. When he'd followed her into the kitchen, she just milled around and circled his legs with her ears and tail perched happily high and alert. It was as if she thought, *Okay—so you're back! Great!*

Many years before, I'd asked my vet back in Raleigh if Beau missed me when I dropped him off for boarding. The dog always seemed so happy to see me when I came to pick him up that I had guilty visions of him moping for the duration of his stay. The vet laughed and said, "He misses you for about 10 minutes, then he checks out his kennel. Dogs are great survivors. They aren't as sentimental as people suppose. Once you're out of sight, he's more concerned with making sure he can look after himself in a new place."

I'd not wanted to believe that, but I did see the great sense in it. In many ways, I'd reacted the same way over the past year and more since Zack had left. Then I thought of the weeks I'd just spent waiting for Steve to come back. I'd survived just fine, but Steve's actual return brought new kinds of excitement and reservation. I wondered just how well he'd done on his own while he was away. We'd not talked in depth about our sexual histories, and the de rigueur chat about our respective HIV exposure hadn't taken place yet.

One frightened visit to the health clinic at the start of my relationship with Zack had proven me negative, and him as well. In any case, Zack had a predisposition to urethritis, so he always wore a condom. With Heath, there was no discussion. He came with his own and he used them as a matter of course. With Steve naked in my shower back home and no clean clothes to put on—not to mention my own eagerness that was telling me I'd waited long enough—I knew the discussion was bound to come up pretty soon. I wasn't sure how to handle it. Steve had come on strong from the very first time we were together. If that was his real style—despite his telling me I didn't really know him at all—I was planning on erring on the side of caution. Like I told Andrea over Christmas, I had no intention of risking my future on a hot fuck.

Nuala strained at the leash the closer we got to the house. I looked up and saw Steve waiting at the corner of my deck, coffee cup in hand, dressed in boxer shorts I recognized as a particularly loud pair Schooner had left behind. He'd certainly made himself at home: Those boxers were in my underwear drawer. My irritation was quickly displaced by the thought that he was watching for us—waiting for *me*. I unclicked Nuala's leash and she took off, bounding toward Steve and home.

I kept my pace, watching Nuala as she made straight for the stairs and then for Steve, who danced round in circles as she circled with him, barking with delight to have found him once again. I climbed the stairs to the sounds of her claws clicking on the wood above then racing to the top of the stairs to noisily let me know who she'd found.

"Looks like this Nuala dog has taken up well with you," Steve said.

"I think she recognizes you."

"Probably. I hope you don't let a lot of guys leave their drawers at your house."

"They're my son's," I said. "They got mixed in with the laundry when he was here last."

"He must be a big boy. I couldn't even get a leg in your little ol' boxers."

I refused to become exasperated. For some reason, Steve liked to refer to me as something child-size. At 5 foot 9 and 138, I wasn't exactly vertically challenged or exceptionally small. It was teasing, I was sure, but underlying it all was a not so subtle domination play—not unlike dogs placing their neck over the neck of another dog. Seeing it for what it was, I figured it was no big deal to play along. "No-o-o, I'm not a big ol' mack daddy like you, for sure."

Steve grinned.

"Nuala's wanting her supper," I said. "Are you hungry too?"

"Not as hungry as I'm going to be later, or as tired either." His grin was definitely more than friendly.

"Then let me get the dog fed at least. Mind if I have some coffee first?"

Steve opened the door and scratched his head, striving to be endearingly ingratiating. "Well okay, I guess."

He succeeded. Walking past him, I pinched his ass hard. When he and Nuala followed me in, Steve closed the door and looked around. "Do you keep any music in the house?"

I walked into the kitchen and pointed to the CD player radio in the bookcase. "The CDs are on the shelves."

He whistled: "A Bose Wave. Are these things really as good as the magazine ads say they are?"

"Try it out and you tell me. It seemed like a good value, rather than spend a fortune on stereo components."

"Ah, here's something good."

"What did you find?" He didn't answer, so I made my coffee and waited to hear what he chose. In a moment, Steely Dan's *Aja* began to fill the space from the living room to the kitchen. I picked up my coffee and walked into the living room. Steve was stretched out on the sofa with his hands behind his head. Only two small ovoid stretches of skin under his arms weren't tanned. His chest was wide and flat, tanned, and smooth, tapering to a waist that belied his age. I sat on the floor by his chest between the sofa and the coffee table. "Nice choice."

Steve reached out and smoothed back my hair. "It's a little mellow, a little cynical, with a hard-nosed bite, like someone I know."

"So I'm not light and sweet anymore, right?"

"Jesus, do you remember everything I say?"

I nestled my cheek into his palm, resting for a moment, then moved away to light a cigarette. "I've had a few weeks to keep only a little bit of knowing you in my mind."

"Let me have one of those, will ya? Mine are in the pocket of my jeans on the floor in your bathroom."

I handed him my lit cigarette, then lit another one for myself.

Steve took a long drag and exhaled. "Did you get my postcards?"

Nuala finished her dinner, noisily banging her stainless steel bowl against the kickboard of the kitchen cabinets. After a moment, I heard her scratch at the prayer rug by the kitchen table and not so much lie as fall prone on her side with a long satisfied sigh. "If there were six, I have every one of them *and* your picture with the big marlin taped on the wall over my desk at work."

Steve turned to his side, bunched a cushion behind his head, and reached for the ashtray. "Then I guess you noticed I was thinking about you a lot."

"I did, Steve. It made me very happy and I'd be lying if I told you I wasn't thinking about you the whole time you were gone. But…"

"But what," he said, gently.

"I just have to wonder why you're so attracted to me so quickly. And worse, why I'm so attracted to you just as suddenly."

Steve took a last hit off his cigarette, stubbed it out in the ashtray, then lightly took the back of my neck in his broad palm and kneaded it gently. "Chris, I talk a lot of shit just to get a rise out of people…guys I meet, usually just to scare them away. I came on so strong to you because I thought you were cute. Like I always do, I thought I'd just run you off and then I wouldn't be disappointed. Just cut to the end, you know? Then you came back to pick up your puppy and we talked…hell, I don't know. I just think you might be somebody who might stick around. I don't want to run you off—believe me. If I'm still coming on too strong, I'm sorry. It's just my nature, see?"

I did see. Steve might be gay, but he was too much himself to want to change his life very much just for someone superficial who couldn't accept him as he was. I said, "You must have either been hurt a great deal over and over, or just really bad once."

Steve was quiet for a minute, but he kept stroking my neck. "I don't talk much about stuff like this," he said, "but I think you got me down cold. I guess what I'm asking you is…well, what kind of guy are you? I'm laying here on a $5,000 sofa, listening to a $500 boom box, and I'm wondering if I'm just a piece of trade, just some dirty dream, you're going to fuck around with until some big-shot lawyer or doctor comes around to hold your attention. That's the question you need to answer for me."

I took the last drag off my cigarette and stubbed it out. Shifting to rise and rest on my knees to face him, I put one arm over his waist and held him gently with my palm flat against his side. "Here's the kind of guy I am: You're laying on a *seven* thousand dollar sofa and listening to a such-and-such boom box because the man I lived with and loved for 22 years took our life, balled it up, and threw it in the trash. I got paid off and I took the money and spent it on things that made me happy for the two minutes I spent waiting for the charge to go through. I moved down here to start my life over, burned and bummed because something I thought was going to see me through to the end of my life turned out to be nothing more than a pretty dream."

"But—" Steve started, shifting himself into a sitting position.

"But nothing," I interrupted. "I'm the marrying kind Steve. To be honest with you, as bad as I hate to admit it, that's what I am. I spent nearly half my life raising another man's kids and running his house and washing his fucking dirty clothes. It's what I've always done. Now I'm learning to live a new kind of life, and there's a hell of a lot of room in it for you, if you want to be in it. But I'm not looking to dump somebody for a better model, like that asshole Zack did to me! Don't you, for one goddamn minute, think I'm some high-class whore looking around for a better offer—"

"Hold on—" Steve said sharply.

"Wait a minute, let me finish. I started out my life living in the fucking projects. I put all my trust in one man and you know what? He fucked up bad. Now, do I think every man is a bastard? No, I don't. And I don't think you're a bastard either. But Steve, I can't give up everything I'm starting to build a new life on and I don't want to trust anybody but me not to fuck it up. I'm my responsibility now. I want to be with you, Steve. And I ain't going nowhere, for nobody else. But if you want me to tell you I'll give my life up for you, I won't. But I'm loyal, and I'm kind and I'm a good friend, in or out of bed. You see what I'm saying?"

"You're hurting me, let go," he demanded.

"What? *What?*" I asked sharp as a razor and mad as hell.

Gently Steve took my hand at his side and squirmed away from it. I had gotten him in a death grasp. There was a dark red imprint on his tanned side that would surely turn into a bruise. With my wrist still in his grasp he said, "C'mere." He tugged me up to sit beside him on the couch's edge.

"Don't pull at me," I said, but my own vehemence was spent, and I didn't snatch away.

As best he could, sitting beside me, he wrapped his arms around me and rocked me a little. "I guess you just got hurt real bad one time, huh?"

"No, twice...but the first time was too far back to count."

Steve sighed. "They all count, Chris. Every one of them."

I rested my head against his shoulder. I was tired. I had no idea I had so much anger held back inside. "So what kind of guy are you, Steve?"

He dropped his arms but left one around my waist, keeping me close. "I'm the kind of guy who quit trying a long time ago, Chris. Heath was four years back. I quit after him. I ain't been with anybody since. But I've been thinking a lot about trying again. Are you up for that?"

I moved from the shelter of his chest and shoulder to look him in the eye. He returned my gaze without guile. "I think I want to start trying again, right now."

Steve grinned. "Me too."

Nuala raised her head and looked at us. Satisfied we were both fine, she laid her head down again with an annoyed sigh. Steve put his face in my hair and sniffed me deeply. With the hand around my waist he pulled me closer. The other searched for the hem of my T-shirt and, finding it, wound its way over the bare skin underneath to find the rise of my nipple.

"Steve, one thing..." I said.

He mumbled into my hair.

I stilled his hand on my chest by placing my palm over it, on top of the thin fabric. "Steve..." I said.

"Yep?" he asked, and let his hand slip from under my shirt.

"Health...I mean...have you been tested?"

Steve nodded. He took a deep breath, looked up at the ceiling, and then down at me. "Chris, I keep papers on my dogs and I keep papers on me. My last test was in December. I'm negative. If you got one big enough, I don't mind putting a piece of latex on my dick this one time, but once I prove to you that I'm negative, don't think it'll happen again. I'll show you the paper right now if you want to take me home and get it. I guess I don't have to worry about you, right?"

I stood and looked down at him. For once, I wasn't in a position to be pulled or tugged at. "No. You don't have to worry about me, I'm negative."

Steve reached up and took my hand. I pulled his arm until he stood up. "I guess it all starts with trust, right?" he said. He stepped past me toward the bedroom and stopped. "That's the kind of guy I am."

He waited until I joined him, then together we began to make our way toward the bedroom. At the bookcase I pulled away from him long enough to start the CD over. I wanted every minute of it to play.

In the bedroom I let him undress me. He pulled my T-shirt over my head and knelt in front of me to undo my shorts and pull them down. He left my boxer shorts untouched as he buried his face in my belly and reached upward, stroking my torso with flattened hands that found the rise of my breast and held me there, my nipples under his palms. He traced the rim of my navel with his tongue, darting it inside, filling me first there.

He slid his hands down my sides, turning me so that my back was to him. He put his mouth against the small of my back and, rising, slid his tongue the length of my spine until he reached my neck. Holding me by the waist, he pulled me against him; the slight swell of his taut belly fit inside the sway of my back before the fullness of my ass rolled and I felt him attempt to push himself between my legs. Kissing my neck and the top of my head, he ran his hands up my sides and over my chest, then down my belly and under the elastic of my boxers. He rested his palms against my thighs and stroked under my scrotum with his thumbs until I moaned. Only then did he slide away my boxers and let them fall.

Now naked, I turned to face him. My eyes were level with the hollow of his throat, and it was there I filled him first. I placed my hands where his neck joined his shoulders and I caressed the cords there. Then I ran my hands up into the hair at the back of his head, which I urged him to put down so I could reach his sweet, full lips and taste his tongue. Kissing him, I ran my hands over those broad shoulders once more then down his upper arms, squeezing the density of muscle, trying to get it all in my grasp. My hands finally found his, and my lips never lost his mouth.

I let go of Steve's hands and grasped his waist, caressing the face of it with my thumbs until, having waited long enough, I ran my hands down flat under the elastic of his boxer shorts and pulled them far enough away to ensure they'd fall straight away and reveal the man of him I'd only glimpsed behind layers of cotton and denim.

He was wide and thick, and the head of it was nearly square, flaring at its firm chin with a ridge that promised a deeper sort of pleasure. I reached to hold the heaviness that hung below and took the measure of the heft and weight there, the dimension of its swing. I looked up to meet Steve's eyes, expecting to see the pride and gentle mockery there, the challenge. But he looked at me sweetly, as if to say that nothing else needed to be said.

With the weight of his scrotum in my hand I knelt and guided him to my mouth. I took him inside, lightly, teasingly enclosing the broad-headed beginning of him between my lips, and pulled until he cried out and grasped my head in his hands. I felt him fight the urge to push deeper, but he held off instead. He knelt in front of me, hiding his treasure away, and found my mouth with his own. Then he eased me back onto the bed until the center of me stood up as my own offering, which he took deep within his own mouth, swallowing me until I gasped and gripped his curls to pull him away.

Steve grabbed my legs behind the knees, lifting and spreading them. He moved between them on his knees. Then, too soon and only spit-slicked, he pushed himself against me.

"Look at me," he whispered. "Look at me and don't look away."

And I didn't. He pushed hard and went inside me while I strained against torn tears to see his face as he claimed me and fucked me. He fucked me well, moving his hips while his chest stayed still. He fucked me like his ass had its own universal joint that left his dick to punish me and pleasure me with a repetition that was deep and hard, going on and on long after the music had faded from the living room.

He fucked me until, finally, I was spent like a thirsty drunk's last dime. Then he fucked me harder until he pulled out and came like a breached dam, all silver showers and thundering flood, over my chest and shoulders.

Done and wet, he cradled me with my head on his shoulder and my arm on his chest. He held me to him with the length of his arm down the line of my spine.

We slid toward the sleep of the bought and paid-for—one act so easily answering questions and sewing together two long-torn seams. We murmured together soft sounds that were only approximations of words and thoughts, but sufficed as final, finer stitching. Then we slept. Nuala eventually stole into the room and onto the bed to turn twice and sink contentedly at our feet.

"Dr. Rivera's office," I said.

"Hello Chris! I won't keep you long, I know you have phones to answer."

"Hey Andrea. Is everything still on for next weekend?"

"Sure. But I wanted to let you know David and I will be staying at the Pepper Tree. One of his buddies has a time-share there. He can't make it for Easter, so he offered it to David and me. Since you're going to have a full house, we took him up on it."

"Oh Andrea," I said, "that's very thoughtful of you. Susan and David will be in the guest room and Schooner and his friend Frank will have the loft. That *is* a full house, but I'll miss having you and David with everyone under one roof."

"We won't miss the bathroom situation," Andrea said frankly.

"I understand completely."

"Mom—"

"Oh, so it's *Mom* now is it? What's wrong?"

'Well, I just thought someone should warn you. Dad, Alicia, and the baby will be down as well. They've bought one of those new pastel Key West–type places on the way to Fort Macon."

"My God, your father's going to go broke keeping his wives in beach houses."

"Is that all you're concerned about?"

I glanced down the hall toward Cathy's office; she was now off the phone, and this conversation with my daughter was promising to get longer. I lowered my voice and said, "Andrea, I don't have time to get into this right now. Your father is completely free to buy a house wherever he wants one. It's none of my business."

"Mom, what about Mass? What are we all going to do—sit across two whole pews, one big unhappy dysfunctional family? It's such a mockery."

"Andrea, there is no problem unless you decide to make one. There will certainly be more than one Mass on Sunday. And besides, I had no idea Alicia was Catholic. I assumed she worshipped handling her relatives, the snakes. Even if she is Catholic, it's none of my business and it's none of yours either."

"Mom, it's my family. It is my business. Alicia converted, by the way."

I held my breath and counted to 10. "Andrea, I understand, but I also take it you've gotten to a point where you've started talking to your father again with some degree of civility. After all, you obviously know his Easter plans."

It was Andrea's turn to be silent. Finally she said, "Damn you're good. Yes, I've been having dinner with Dad fairly regularly. He's been making a meaningful effort to reach out."

"That's very good to hear Andrea. I'm proud of both of you. Since you've reached some sort of détente with him, maybe I should call to invite him and Alicia to Easter dinner."

"Chris, don't you dare!" Andrea hissed.

"So, I'm Chris again now," I laughed. "Andrea, you can't have it both ways unless you're enjoying the drama. Now, I have to go."

"Promise me you won't invite them over!"

"Whatever...now, Andrea I have to go or I'm going to get in trouble. You work in a psychiatrist's office don't you? It's very unprofessional for staff to drag their family woes into work."

"Chris, I love you, but you drive me crazy, you know that?" she said.

"That's a short drive, Andrea. Love you, hon. Call me when you get here. Bye." I hung up the phone. Cathy was leaning on the half wall that separated my area from the hall and she raised her eyebrows at me questioningly. "Was I loud?" I asked. "I apologize for disturbing you."

"No, you weren't loud, I was just interested. I take it that was your daughter."

I sighed. "Yes, my little drama queen. I told you she was an LCSW, right?"

"Yes, I believe you did," she said.

"Well, she seems to be somewhat immune to her own training when it comes to her father's and my breakup. But she's getting adjusted, slowly but surely."

Cathy nodded, and smiled. "Give her some time. I think you're handling her very well."

"Well, thanks for that. She's been mine since she was three years old, so I know how she works. She's not an easy adapter, but eventually she finds her feet and moves on."

Cathy left the wall to come into my area and sat on the spare chair near the copier. "Your daughter's not what I came in to talk about," she said.

For a moment I panicked. I was scared she was going to give me hell because I'd gotten to the office a little late that morning. It had everything to do with not wanting to get out of bed with Steve. His 5 A.M. round two had been more lingering and erotic than the first round the night before. Then I'd insisted on making him steak and eggs. By the time we were showered and dressed and out the door, I was late. It was nothing too bad, just under an hour, and I had called Cathy on her cell phone to let her know. "I'm sorry about this morning..." I began.

Cathy gave a dismissive flick of her hand and grinned. "So tell me, I want all the details!"

"What?" I said, confused.

"Don't *what* me! I drove past your house on the way home last night, and there he was"—she said, pointing at Steve's photo—"standing in a pair of boxer shorts and nothing else up on your deck. The car behind me almost slammed into my back end, I braked so hard to get a look."

Relieved, I leaned back in a long stretch as far as my office chair would carry me. I lifted my feet off the floor, extended my legs until my toes pointed, and touched the wall behind me with my back-stretched arms. I held the stretch until I shuddered and then sat back upright, giving Cathy the Cheshire cat's grin.

Cathy giggled, low from the back of her throat. "That good, huh?" she said.

Just then, Tony appeared with his departing client and asked for the next client's file. I straightened up as best I could and told him he'd had a cancellation. He lingered while I got busy scheduling the departing client's next appointment, bantering with her personally, consulting the calendar for a date two months hence, and filling out her appointment card. After she said her good-byes and left through the reception area, Tony waited for the outside door to close and asked, "What's got you two out here giggling?"

"Let's just say Chris's serotonin and dopamine levels are exaggerated this morning," Cathy replied.

"Yeah, what she said," I added.

Tony looked at me and grinned. "Oh! So that's why you were late this morning. Good for you. There's nothing like a little intimacy first thing in the A.M. to keep you firing on all cylinders. I take it your marlin-killer is back in port."

I smiled ruefully. "So you've seen the photo. Did you read what's on the back?"

Tony shook his head. "There are limits—you never shared the *back* of the photo."

I took Steve's photo from the wall and handed it to Tony so he could read Steve's regret over killing the great fish for sport.

He read the back and handed it to Cathy. "Is it killing the marlin he regrets, or just killing the marlin for 'asshole rich people,' that's what I don't get."

I explained that Steve preferred to release the fish back into the ocean unless the marlin had to be returned to dock in order to qualify for prize consideration in a tournament. Or if the guy paying for the boat demanded a trophy for his den. Though it paid well, Steve still considered commercial sportfishing a brutal, sorry business, all in all.

"I guess he's a true hunter, then," Tony said. "I've not met a good one that didn't have a great deal of respect—even affection—for what he 'took,' as they say. Still, it's not something I could do with any pride."

"If it helps any, Tony, I feel the same way," I said. "But he is who he is and I love him."

Cathy looked at me and her mouth opened. She glanced at Tony and returned her open-mouth gaze to me. "What did I just hear you say?" she asked.

My own mouth dropped open as what I said hit me. "I guess I just said I loved him. Oh my God."

" 'Goddamn' is more likely," Tony said. "You two are getting too Lifetime Television for me. Do you have my 2 o'clock file for me? I'm going back into my safe, manly-but-trophyless office."

Cathy laughed as I took the file off the top of the waiting pile on my desk, checked the name against the appointment calendar, and handed it to Tony.

He shook his head and walked away. When he was out of earshot, Cathy looked down at the photo of Steve once more and handed it back to me. "Was it really that good?"

I carefully stuck Steve's photo back to the wall. I thought, *I better get a frame for it now.* "It was epic...hypnotic..." I sighed contentedly. "Druglike."

Cathy upped the ante. "Two Valium and a glass of scotch after a long day–good?"

I looked anxiously down the hall toward the Tony's inner sanctum and said sotto voce: "An 'OxyContin, laying in the sun, and sipping a bottle of Prosecco through a straw' good."

Cathy stood, placed a hand to her aching back, and stretched her outsize belly. " 'Love' hell. Chris, you're done for...gone. Why don't you take off the rest of the day and go get you another hit off that beautiful beast of a man." She put both hands under the swell of her pregnancy. "Enjoy it for me."

"I can't, girl. He's got stuff to do. Besides, I'm going to his place for dinner tonight. He's got Nuala, who's visiting with her mama and daddy dog and a few random brothers he's still got. He's making me dinner. Homemade, real Italian."

"Let me get this straight," Cathy said. "He's Italian, he's a dog lover, and he cooks too?"

"Well, he's half Italian, but it's all—every inch—right where it counts."

"I hate you, bitch. Get back to work." With that, she gave me a wink and went back into her office.

In my growing awareness of light, I felt Steve stir and tense around me, then half-rise off me. Nuala barked and, in her rush off the bed, she scratched my ankle with her claws. I was trying to remember where I was. The night had started at Steve's but ended—drunkenly and in a fog of pleasure—in my own bed.

"Hey Mom!" Schooner yelled from the front of the house.

"What the fuck?" Steve growled. He swung off the bed and stood naked, half awake and ready for a fight.

"It's my son," I groaned and pulled my own naked self out of bed and looked for something to put on. Steve's boxers, which were still in his board shorts, were on my side of the bed. I plucked them out and tossed the bathing suit to him. "Hang on a minute Schooner!" I yelled. I pulled Steve's boxers on and gave him a smile. "He's got a key. I didn't know he was coming. You can either come on out and meet him or go back to sleep. It's only just after 6."

Steve looked at me, shook his head, then laughed. "Is this boxer shorts boy?"

"Yep. He's my baby and he's a trip, I warn you."

"Mom, where's this dog's food?" Schooner yelled from the front of the house.

"*Mom?*" Steve asked as he stepped into his bathing suit.

"I've had him since he was only a few months old," I said. "I'm the only mom he's ever known. I can't break him of the habit of calling me that. I know it's weird, but just try to deal with it, okay?"

Steve laced the front of his board shorts and gave me a happy grin. "C'mon then, Mom. We might as well face the music. I have to leave pretty soon to get my dogs fed."

I met him at the bedroom door and gave him a quick kiss. Together we walked down the hall and found Schooner in the kitchen giving an ecstatic Nuala a belly rub. Confronted with two sets of legs, Schooner stood and regarded Steve warily. "Who the hell are you?"

Steve stuck out his hand. "I'm Steve Willis, Chris's boyfriend. Nice to meet you."

Speechless for once, Schooner ignored Steve's hand, all the while looking from Steve back to me.

"That'll teach you to call first, buster," I said. "Steve, this is my son Schooner."

"Yeah, right," Schooner said grudgingly. He took Steve's hand and pumped it in a perfunctory shake. "Mom, goddamn." To Steve he said, "I'm sorry. I didn't mean to be rude, but he's my...he's mine."

· "Don't worry about it, it's no problem," Steve said. He gave Schooner an amused look and took his hand back. "I'm just going to slip out and take Nuala for a quick walk. I'll be right back." With that, Steve took Nuala's leash off the hook by the kitchen door, clicked it on her collar, and left.

Schooner walked to the kitchen door's window and watched Steve walk down the stairs from the deck. He looked back to me and gave me a look like he'd never done before, as if he were seeing me for the first time.

"What?" I asked impatiently. "Did you think I'd just never see anyone ever again?"

"No...it's not that." Schooner swallowed visibly. "It's just, it's just...you're hot-looking! And he's hot. I never thought of you that way...you should put some clothes on. Are those his drawers you're walking around in?"

"Well, I couldn't find mine when you just busted in here like that." I crossed my arms over my chest and gave him a stern look.

Schooner averted his gaze and shook his head. "You look like a whore," he said.

"I do not look like a whore. Watch your mouth."

When he could look back at me, he said, "I need a drink."

"At 6 o'clock in the morning?"

"Well goddamn, Chris. I didn't know I was going to walk into a Falcon video starring my mom and some redneck stud."

I laughed, long and well. Only in this improbable, ridiculous situation had I finally gotten Schooner to call me Chris. I turned to the pantry and pulled out a bottle of vodka, handed it to him, and walked to the refrigerator to get him some orange juice. When I turned around to get him a glass, he already had the cap off and was taking a long pull directly from the bottle.

Genuinely annoyed with him, I said "Give me that, right now" in my best Mom voice. After he handed me the bottle, I said, "Act like you've got some sense. Go sit down at the table." I waited and watched him until he had jerked out a chair next to where he knew I sat and flung himself into it angrily. He fumbled with the pack of cigarettes Steve had left on the table with his change, keys, and wallet and managed to get one lit. Then he gave me a hard glare and looked away.

I turned back to the counter; made him a stiff screwdriver with plenty of ice and took it to him without a word. Then I returned to the kitchen and got the coffee started. Without looking back at him, I was aware he was watching me the whole time. I was unembarrassed to have him see me dressed only in Steve's boxers—I figured it was a difficult lesson, but one we needed to get over and done with.

When I finished with the coffee, Schooner looked at me disgustedly and said, "You really should get cleaned up and put some clothes on."

"Oh for God's sake, Schooner. Grow up." I added, "It isn't as if you've never seen me in a bathing suit. You might as well start seeing me as an adult."

"It's very disturbing, Chris. You've lost a lot of weight and you're tanned. Now you're parading around like you're trying to be some Abercrombie and Fitch boy whore. You're freaking me out. You're definitely not the mom I know."

Resentfully I said, "Look, I'm not the mom you knew. My life has changed, and for the better. I love all of my kids, and you're a huge part of my life, but you'd each better get used to who I am now. I will always be your *mom,* but I am also every bit Chris. If I'm embarrassing you, it's your problem. And don't you ever call me a whore again, got it?"

Schooner just shook his head, turned his chair away from my direct line of sight, and stared out across the living room.

When the coffee was finished, I checked out the window to see if Steve was in sight. Evidently he had taken the opportunity to give Nuala a nice long stretch on the beach. Neither he nor the dog was in sight. I made my coffee the way I liked it and I made Schooner's as well. I carried the mugs to the table and sat at my place at the head of the table.

"I am so sorry," Schooner said as he turned his chair around. "Please don't be mad."

I found my own cigarettes in the mound of Steve's things and thought about how guys always leave something to mark the area they want to claim for themselves. Men were as bad as dogs pissing on trees to mark their territory. Schooner had just encountered somebody who could piss higher than he could. I was really tired of feeling like the tree that got pissed on, but I sighed and forged ahead to try to make several different points to my beloved youngest son.

"Schooner, we need to talk—" I began.

"I won't call you Mom anymore, I swear…"

Exasperated, I just lit my cigarette and shook my head. "Schooner, it's not about you calling me Mom, or knowing I *am* your mom or any of that. You can call me Mom the rest of my life and I'll take it as a sign of love and respect from you. But you've got to start facing the fact that I'm an adult, separate and apart from all that. You've got to start respecting some personal boundaries. I've been there for you all your life, and I'm not going to stop, do you understand me? I love you, but please treat me like I've always treated you. Barging in this house like you owned it first thing on a Saturday morning is not about being my child, it's about not respecting my space."

Schooner slammed his hand down on the table. He was so furious he was near tears. "What about you, sitting there with a streak of that guy's dried come on your neck! You're not respecting me."

I refused to be embarrassed. "Schooner," I said, "I'm not trying to disrespect you. You just caught me unawares—"

"There's a message on your goddamn voice mail right now, Mom." He started to cry. "Were you so…were you so eager to fuck that guy you couldn't even check your stupid goddamn voice mail? I did so respect you. I did so call." With that, he put his tear-stained face in his hands.

Dirty as I was, I made no effort to hug him. As old as he was, he shouldn't have needed hugging, in any event. I realized then, Zack had been right: I had spoiled Schooner badly. At 22 years of age, just about to graduate college, he'd just run smack into the realization that my entire world didn't revolve around him. I got up from the table and fetched a clean dish towel. I anxiously looked out to see if Steve and Nuala were on the approach. Luckily, they were not.

I sat back down at the table and handed Schooner the dish towel. "Wipe and blow, baby," I said gently. Obediently, he did as

I instructed. "First, I owe you an apology for not checking my messages so I'd know you were coming. But I still think you owe me a little latitude there. I haven't heard from you in three weeks. You can't believe I'm just sitting around waiting for your call can you?"

Schooner shook his head for "no," took a drag off his cigarette, and put it out.

"Okay," I said. "We got that straight. Now, I've somehow done you a great disservice by keeping you from this aspect of my life. I'm not trying to flaunt my sexuality in your face, but as I recall, you had no problem noisily fucking *your* boyfriend in my guest room, even if you did shower afterwards, am I right?"

Schooner chuckled, then took a thirsty gulp of his screwdriver. "Yeah, you're right," he admitted.

"Okay. You understand that my developing a relationship with a man outside of our family has nothing to do with you, and doesn't affect you, and isn't going to do any harm to you. You do understand that, right?"

Schooner wiped his eyes with his shoulders and gave me the start of a grin. "Right."

I took a long drag off my cigarette, looked him dead in the eye, and exhaled. "Now, *that guy*'s name is Steve—Steve Willis. He's a great guy and he's not somebody I'm just screwing around with, get me? He's someone I believe is going to stay pretty important to me."

"He better be or I'll fucking kill him," Schooner said. "He better be good to you."

I rolled my eyes. "He is good to me and he's good for me too, Schooner. You will be nice to him and you will not fucking kill him, or anybody, for my sake. I'm grown and I can fight my own battles. If I need your help, I'll ask for it. But the only help I need from you is to give the guy a chance to be a friend. He's worth it. You gotta give me that."

Schooner reluctantly nodded.

I heard Nuala's barking from down the street. "Okay, now be my big man and go wash your face. Steve'll be back with the dog any second and I want to start this all over."

Schooner drained his screwdriver to pulp and ice, then stood. "I'll be your *big man*, but you go wash your neck," he said.

"Deal," I replied.

Schooner tried to grin. He was not very convincing. Still, I was grateful for the effort.

I stood and walked to the kitchen to wet a paper towel and scrub my neck. From the kitchen window I saw Steve trotting toward the porch behind a fairly bounding Nuala. He was smiling. My dog was happy, my man was happy, and my son was—well, at least mollified. I grinned too as I got my neck cleaned up and checked for any other telltale signs of sex that would rub off.

Steve came in the kitchen door with Nuala, who raced off to find Schooner as soon as she was off her leash. Steve looked at me questioningly. I gave him the "okay" sign and steered him to the seat opposite the one Schooner had chosen. He was used to taking the seat at the head of the table, but he couldn't have it—not this morning. When he sat, I kissed the top of his head and asked, "You ready for some coffee?"

He rolled his eyes and said, "Sure, but you don't have to wait on me. I'll get it."

"No problem." I turned to get his coffee as Schooner came back into the dining area and took his seat. I heard him clear his throat and say, "Let's start over, Steve. I apologize if I was rude to you when I came in. And I apologize for just barging on in the house without knocking. I didn't mean to be an asshole."

Score one for my big man, I thought.

"No need to apologize, Schooner," Steve said. "I understand this place must be your home since Chris moved here. I'm a little embarrassed I had to meet you so unexpectedly. It would have been more respectful to you...you know, better if we met over a beer and dinner at the Crab Shack, right?"

Score two for Steve, I thought as I brought his coffee to the table and sat down.

"You know the Crab Shack?" Schooner said. "Their food's the best on the beach."

"I hope so, they get some of it from me," Steve said.

"No shit? So you're a fisherman, then."

"Not just a fisherman," I interjected, "Steve's also a hunting guide and crews a boat in marlin tournaments. And he's also the breeder where I got Nuala."

"Nuala's a great dog, Mom," Schooner replied offhandedly. "But Steve, can you tell me about crewing on a marlin boat? That must be awesome."

I sipped my cooling coffee. It had grown cold, in fact, but I drank it anyway. I didn't want to disturb the moment. I wanted it to knit itself into a morning's worth of moments until I was sure everything was going to be just fine.

Shortly before 8 A.M. Mass on Easter Sunday morning, I walked into church at the head of a line of Ronans. I stood aside and watched my children and their loved ones genuflect, take their seats, then kneel. Then I genuflected myself and joined them on the kneeler. I was proud of my gaggle of ducklings, wondering how I'd managed to rear and feed a family and proudly see my children in full force at Mass on such a fine morning.

On the row in front of us, Zack and Alicia sat with their little boy, not quite 7 months old. I had to admit he was a cute, chubby little fellow, dressed for Mass on an Easter morning like a little prince in a line of Ronan royalty. Despite Andrea's anxiety, all went well. It wasn't hard to shake both Zack's and Alicia's hands and wish them peace when the time came. I was serene and happy. All it would have taken to make my happiness complete was to have Steve there, but he was off on a boat. Easter tournaments were money in the bank, and that's how he made his living.

When the Mass had ended and we were blessed and bidden to go in peace, I took the opportunity to invite Zack and Alicia by for brunch and champagne. Andrea's jaw was clenched, but she did smile. The boys and their spouses made encouraging noises to their father and his wife. Graciously they declined. They had plans elsewhere.

As I turned to leave Zack touched my shoulder and said, "Chris—a word?"

I waited in the aisle while Alicia and baby Zack, then my entire brood, filed past as I waited behind with their father. When the last of the parishioners were ahead of us, I ignored Zack, genuflected, crossed myself, and waited while he made a perfunctory effort at the same gesture of piety. Then I waited to hear what the man had to say.

"Chris," he began, "I was wondering if I could stop by your place this afternoon, after the kids leave."

"I hope it won't be too late, Zack. I have plans this evening."

Zack raised an eyebrow and said, "Plans with a 38-year-old, from what I hear."

"Not in church, Zack," I said dismissively. "This isn't the time or the place."

"Oh for God's sake, Chris. Lighten up. I'm not trying to give you a hard time. You used to have a sense of humor."

I relaxed and gave him a small smile. "What time?" I asked.

"Is about 4 convenient?"

"Four's good. You know the address and how to get there?"

"I hope to hell I should. I've driven past it enough. Surprised?"

"Let's just do this at 4. You and Alicia have brunch reservations at the Coral Reef Club you need to get to."

"Yes, we do. Four then?"

I nodded and we walked together out into the bright sunshine with smiles for the families, his and ours. The morning proceeded smoothly after that. I'd made another ham—it was a holiday tradition, after all, and I had successfully raised a set of traditional-minded children. Once Frank relaxed around Schooner's siblings and in-laws, he turned out to be elfin, engaging, and thoroughly endearing to all of them. Susan had started to show, and her pregnancy was an endless source of conversation. Due in late August, she was feeling well and enjoyed being the center of attention.

I could tell Andrea was feeling a little left-out. She was used to being the sole embodiment of femininity in the crowd of Ronans, and I definitely heard her biological clock ticking loudly in competition. I pulled David aside and told him to start taking a lot of vitamins—and maybe even to try some boxers if he wore briefs. He rolled his eyes and told me she already had him working on a schedule, as a matter of fact. He endured both a quick kiss from me and my telling him I thought he was a saint for putting up with her.

By 3:30, they were all gone. I put Nuala into her kennel, took a quick shower, put on my new board shorts, and donned one of Steve's T-shirts that advertised a marina in Eleuthera. It was too big, but my men all seemed to have a thing for me dressing in their clothes. Just as Zack had liked to see me in his old reindeer sweater,

Schooner never left my house without "forgetting" something he knew I'd wear, and it had made Steve smile to see me walking around, my much smaller frame swimming in something of his. It was possession by apparel, and it made me happy to be so possessed.

I got a bottle of water and my cigarettes and went out on the deck to wait for Zack. I dragged an Adirondack chair into the sun and sat, enjoying the ocean breeze and letting my mind wander. Steve had told me he'd be by around 7. He said that would give him time to get home, feed the dogs and let them run, shower, and be back for something to eat.

Thinking back on it, I realized it had been one of the happiest weeks of my entire life. I could count the nights I'd spent with Steve in only double digits, but I felt like I could go on counting forever. I knew the heat of this passion would have to burn down eventually; otherwise my knee joints would melt and my hips would turn to jelly. The relationship would have to move along to someplace more adult, seasoned with a little more give-and-take. But for now, the spring sun was warming my skin and Steve was stoking my ass and my heart for the long climb up the hill that was sure to come. I knew better than to believe we'd always be like this.

I couldn't see any problems ahead we couldn't solve. I had no intention of asking Steve to be anyone different other than who he was. In turn, Steve regarded my family with a mixture of awe and amusement. He didn't begrudge my relationship with three kids, and their significant others, nor did he take issue with their foibles and their frank assessment of him over dinner the previous night.

Liberally greased with drinks at my house, Steve met them all on his own turf. His house in Salter Path was not far from the Crab Shack, where we were going for dinner. My brood all o-o-ohed and a-a-ahed appropriately over his home, his view, and his boat. They played with the dogs and slipped by me, one by one, to tell me they really liked Steve.

Only Schooner had remained somewhat distant, but I couldn't fault him for being anything other than friendly or polite. Something larger was gnawing at my baby—something I couldn't quite put my finger on. He and Frank seemed to be fine, teasingly still infatuated with each other. It was Schooner's first admission of his sexuality, at least with a living, breathing human being at his side, whom his brother and sister could either take to or not. I was very happy they had taken to Frank very well; of course, Frank had gone out of his way to be amiable and endearing. I thought the poor kid must be exhausted by now. I hoped Schooner would let him sleep on the way back to Greenville. The whole Ronan family in full holiday mode was a pretty intense experience.

Only once had Schooner sidled near me, wordlessly seeking the sort of comfort only physical proximity to his mom seemed to satisfy. I asked him if he was okay, and he gave me a weak smile. I sensed he was definitely *not* okay and I told him so. He muttered something about exams coming up and then graduation after that. He ended by asking me to call him sometime the following week. I took him so seriously, I walked him over to the church calendar I had taped to the side of my refrigerator and we agreed on a day and time right then and there. Tomorrow morning at 10 A.M.; I reminded myself of it once again as I drowsed in the sun and waited for Zack to show up.

I didn't have to wait long. He pulled into my drive behind the wheel of the same car he'd left me in. It sounded like it did then, smooth and purring with the slush of money and success. I hated that goddamn car—the freaking Nazimobile. I didn't get up to greet him. I just said hello casually as Zack shut the car's door with its smug *whumph*.

"I'm up here on the deck, Zack."

"I know," he said climbing the steps, "that's what you get for buying a house on a corner by the beach road. Everyone can see exactly where you are on this deck."

When he arrived at the top of the stairs, I was amazed at how old and tired he looked. I stood and motioned for him to take a seat in the shade. "Would you like a drink?" I asked.

Zack nodded gratefully but remained standing. "May I come in and see the house?"

"Certainly, but I warn you, it's not at its best. The kids only left a little while ago."

Zack just looked at me and shrugged. Following me inside, he stood at the counter separating the kitchen from the dining area and surveyed the living room and the sunroom beyond. "It's very nice, Chris. You and Wade Lee did a great job. I hope you're very happy here."

"I am, Zack," I said. "It surprises me, but it feels like home, even after only a few months."

"It looks like you. The books, the artwork—it looks like the place I had imagined us retiring to."

I quietly accepted the compliments and made him a gin and tonic. I knew Zack's seasonal liquor preferences had ticked toward that particular beverage after a winter's worth of scotch, switching that very morning. Deciding I could use one myself, I made two.

As I handed him his drink, I said, "Why don't we sit out on the deck? It's the most pleasant time of day between now and dark."

Zack nodded and followed me outside. I stood until he had settled into an Adirondack chair under the awning and nudged a footrest within reach of his feet. Then I settled into my own chair opposite him.

He put his sneakered feet on the footrest and sighed. "You look wonderful, Chris," he said.

"Thank Dr. Atkins and Dr. Hauschka. It's all diet and moisturizer." I took a sip of my drink and looked at Zack.

Zack laughed. "No, it's more than that. I know you, Chris. You really do seem happy and well."

"I have been walking a lot. And my liquor intake is down by...well, it's way down. I think that has a lot to do with it."

"Whatever you're doing, keep it up," he said.

Zack gave me a diffident smile, but I knew he was a master at handling difficult clients in difficult situations. "Thanks for all the good words, Zack," I said. "I know you're being sincere, but I can't help wondering what you're doing here and what you want to talk about."

He was quiet for a few seconds, then he said, "I've driven by here several times, but I didn't want to intrude. I just wanted to come by and see how you're doing. Hell, Chris, we shared a half a lifetime. I thought we might still be friends, at least."

I sighed. "I understand," I said. "There've been a few times when it was all I could do not to pick up the phone to tell you something funny or talk to you about something that was giving me some concern about the kids."

"You should have, Chris," he said.

I smiled and shook my head. "Cold turkey, Zack. No need to drag it all out like that. You were right when you told me we had grown apart. I respect what we had together for so long, but what we're doing now seems right for both of us, don't you think?"

"Still, Chris. You didn't have to just disappear from my life," he said. "There are three very real people who are going to keep us tied together for the rest of our lives."

"That's true. But over the past year I needed to get my life started over, Zack. I didn't really need your input or opinion on that."

"No, I suppose not." Zack looked around him and took another sip of his drink. "I'm being honest when I tell you it looks as if you've done a pretty good job of it."

"Well, I thank you for that, Zack. I don't think I've done too badly."

"You're enjoying your new job?" he asked.

"Yes, the people I work for are very nice. It's casual and it pays well for the area."

"Trey says you used your money wisely. You have been able to keep a healthy amount for your annuity…"

I laughed. "Only because Trey kept me to a budget. How did we make such a little banker, you and I? He sure didn't get it from me."

Zack allowed himself to laugh in reply, then his face darkened a bit. "He tells me he and Susan are going to break tradition and not keep the name running if their baby is a boy."

Cautiously I said, "Well, Zack, I'm really not trying to be a bitch, but Alicia sort of co-opted the name, didn't she? How many little Zacks can there be running around the family? You have two sons named after you. If they name the baby Zack, he'll have a grandfather and two uncles with the same name. My God, can you imagine explaining that to the little fellow? He's a handsome little boy, I meant to tell you."

Zack sighed, apparently willing to let me steer the conversation away from that minefield. "I have to tell you, it's been a long time since I was around babies," he said. "Handsome or not, he still screams like all hell at 2 in the morning." Zack sighed. "I understand Trey and Susan are making you their baby's godfather, and that—either girl or boy—they're going to call the baby Chris. Have they told you?"

I was stunned. They hadn't told me. It was so kind, it almost made me want to cry. I said nothing, in order to hide my feelings in front of this great love of my life. This bastard.

"Oh? No? Well, I apologize for ruining the surprise for you," he said. "Nonetheless, I suppose you…that news must make you very happy. It's very touching, I think."

I mastered my assorted feelings of happiness, anger, and the urge to stick an ice pick in him and set them aside. "It *is* touching. But in the first rush of joy in getting pregnant, they might have made decisions they'll want to change in nine months. If they do name the baby after me, I will be very pleased and proud. If they don't, I'll be just as happy for them. In any case, I'm looking forward to being a grandmom."

Zack harrumphed and shifted in his seat. "Really, Chris. Isn't this 'Mom' business a little much? I mean it was cute when Schooner was a baby, but he's keeping it up into adulthood. You should really think about putting a stop to it now. It seems a bit— well, silly, don't you agree?"

I was becoming angry, but I really didn't want this little visit to morph into a grudge match. I simply said, "That's certainly something to think about, Zack."

Zack took another sip of his drink. It looked as if his measured intake of alcohol was carefully timed to very specific points he wanted to address. I girded myself for whatever he was going to spring on me next.

"So," he began, "I hear you've become involved with someone. A professional fisherman, or dog breeder or something? I suppose you needed to find someone a little rough around the edges to fit in down here. I hope that works out for you, but is it really something you think is going to last long-term?"

I very carefully sat my gin and tonic on the generous arm of my chair, and got up to fetch my cigarettes and lighter from the deck railing near where I'd been sitting before Zack arrived for this lit- tle "torment Chris" episode. I didn't answer until I got one lit and stood a few feet from Zack to keep from slapping the shit out of him. I wanted to tell him I didn't care how long it lasted, but for however long it did, it was the best fucking I'd ever had in my life. However, long experience had taught me not to give Zack any reason to pull out the "white trash" knife to slash me with. Regaining my composure, I said, "I don't have a crystal ball, Zack. I have no idea how long it will last. What I'm concerned with is keeping *myself* responsible *for* myself. I don't have any years left to invest in dreams that are going to end up tossed in the trash. I've made the last of my unwise investments in that regard."

I noted his jaw muscles clench with no small amount of control. "Well, I'm glad to hear such a mature attitude, especially coming from you," Zack responded coldly.

"Thank you, Zack. But I think this conversation has gotten a little off track. Let's stick to talking about the kids, shall we? I understand David and Andrea are trying to get pregnant. I think that could be a very pleasant chore."

Zack looked away from me and off toward the beach. After a moment, his lips thinned into a small smile. "It might not be such a chore if Andrea hadn't been on the pill since she was 15," he said evenly. "She tells me that's most likely the cause of her difficulty getting pregnant."

Again, he had caught me off balance. Andrea had never mentioned any of this to me. I said, "I'm happy you and Andrea have gotten around her problems with our going our separate ways enough for her to confide in you."

Despite his attempt at a small smile, his eyes were hard. "She told me she didn't want to tell you," he said. "She was afraid you might shoulder some blame for getting her on birth control so early."

I gritted my teeth and flicked my cigarette's ash into the wind. I could see Andrea's hand in this quite clearly, the little bitch. She knew exactly how to stir the shit, just to make it stink.

Zack leaned forward in his chair and pointed his forefinger at me. "I don't think that was the wisest decision on your part, Chris. After all, it was you who dragged her to the gynecologist and got her started on the damn things."

Very calmly I took a long hit off my cigarette and thumped it into the yard below. I exhaled, fighting for calm, and casually returned to my seat and my drink across from Zack. "It was the best decision I could make at the time, Zack. She was so moody, she was unbearable before, during, and after her periods, and I knew she was sexually active. Since I had no real experience with the actual plumbing, I thought sending her to a woman gynecologist—someone she could confide in—was the right thing to do."

"Well that's all well and good, Chris. But now she's paying the price for it," Zack concluded triumphantly.

I took a sip of my drink. It was getting watery, and I needed it to be strong and clear and biting. "I am genuinely sorry for that, Zack. But I did the best I could with what I knew at the time. I regret it if you and Andrea have a problem with it all these many years later. But understand something, she never had to endure the trauma of an abortion, and her violent mood swings were put under control. There are many things I'm glad she didn't have to go through then, even if she's going through some difficulties now."

Zack drained his drink and rattled his ice in his glass expectantly. From sheer force of habit, I stood, took his glass, and went inside to make him another drink; when I had the gin bottle in my hand, it hit me what I was doing. It was all I could do not to spit in his glass—but I didn't. I simply made him another drink and carried it to him. He took it without a word of thanks and said, "Well, enough about Andrea. I have to give you credit—you did try your best. Andrea was not the easiest child at times. But it's not Andrea I've come to talk about, it's Schooner."

I walked to the railing for another cigarette.

"Would you please bring that goddamn pack of cigarettes and your lighter over here and sit down?" Zack said irritably. "You're not going to like what I have to tell you, but you might as well sit down and listen. Wandering around the deck smoking isn't going to get you or him out of this."

I lit my cigarette, leaned against the deck's railing, and crossed my feet at the ankles. There was no way I was going to obey the bastard. I hated it when people jerked and pulled and snatched at me. "I can hear you perfectly well from here Zack. Go ahead."

"Have it your way." Zack leaned back in his chair and crossed one leg over the other with an ankle braced on his knee. He was enjoying every minute of this. "As of his graduation day, Schooner is a free agent. I'm cutting him off financially. You have succeeded in creating a complete spoiled brat. He needs to learn to stand on his own two feet and pay his own bills. He's not going to see another dime from me."

I nodded and looked at Zack coldly. Clearly he wanted to make Schooner financially dependent on me. Schooner would need help until he could find a job. Though his truck was paid for, there was its insurance to keep up, a roof over his head to consider, and food to fill his seemingly bottomless stomach. Now I knew why Schooner had had such a hangdog sad look about him all weekend and why he needed to talk to me so badly.

"Okay, Zack," I said. "Whatever you think is best."

"I'm pleased you can be so sanguine. Schooner is a very expensive proposition. I can't imagine you're doing well enough to support him, and neither his brother nor his sister is in any position to help. The big baby is going to have to sink or swim on his own."

Zack finished his little pronouncement and, lifting his glass, tilted its bottom in a small, petty salute to me before he took a rather big swallow. Then he sat the glass on the arm of his chair and waited for me to respond. There was no way I was going to make his victory sweet.

"I understand, Zack," I said. "But like you've told me many times, you gave me these children a long time ago, and my responsibility for them hasn't ended. As long as I have a roof over my head, any of them—especially Schooner—has a home and help."

"Chris, there's no way you can afford—"

"Hold up, you son of a bitch," I said, finally allowing some of my anger to show. "I can afford whatever I please and if I please to make sure my baby boy gets every chance to find a decent job and get on with his life, then he'll get it. Do you understand me?"

Zack swatted at an early fly, catching it expertly in his hand. He shook his fist, then let the fly free. He was clearly amused by the tiny creature's disoriented, drunken attempt to fly away. "I thought you might say something along those lines. You're not going to be doing the boy any favors. In fact, you'll both probably end up being even more codependent, if that's humanly possible."

I empathized with the poor fly Zack was tormenting just for fun. I tried to remain calm, but my patience was nearly gone. "I don't know who you're trying to hurt here—me or Schooner—but neither one of us deserves this shit out of you."

Zack laughed. "Chris, this isn't about trying to hurt either of you—especially you. I don't give a damn how foolishly you spend your resources. And I'm certainly not trying to do Schooner any harm. I'm just sick of his constant wants and needs."

I hated him at that moment, and I wanted to strike back at him. I wasn't the kind to torment flies, and I got no pleasure out of what I knew I was going to say next, but I was going to say it, by God. "Zack you were sick of his constant wants and needs by the time he was 6 months old. You never did like your youngest child. In fact, I'd go so far as to say you've hated him since his mother took her life after he was born. Maybe before."

My arrow hit the mark, and Zack's arrogance fell away to reveal the true bastard underneath.

"That's completely unfair of you, Chris. When have I ever deprived that boy of one thing? When have I *not* gone out of my way to make sure he was taken care of? Now he's become a little faggot with a worthless degree in parks and recreation. What the hell is he going to do with that? That's what I resent—all my hard-earned money spent on four years of play theory and lawn mainte-nance training? And don't you ever drag his mother into this ever again. What the hell do you know about it?"

"I know enough to say what I think. Do you think I'm blind and deaf? You showed you resented him when you hung a name on him that would manage to renew and encourage your resentment of him every time you said it," I said and crossed my arms over my chest. Allowing myself a cold smile, I said, "And, as for his being gay, I'm really the one who knows you better than that, you've got no room to talk. Or is that why you resent him so bad, because he's young and not saddled with a wife and kids? You've finally found a way to get rid of all that resentment haven't you? Just cut him off now. Why wait? Why wait and watch him become what you wanted to be and then screwed up so bad when you started out."

Zack came half out of his chair, his fists balled and his face on fire. "Shut up! You petty, judgmental little faggot. How dare you say such things to me? Without my children you don't even have a reason to exist and you never did. You're a worthless little piece of shit."

I took two steps toward him and got right in his face. This time I had the advantage. He wasn't even out of his chair and I towered over him for once. "I'm worthless? Well, you know something?

You're goddamn good at making babies, but you damn sure aren't very good at anything to do with them afterwards."

"That may be true," he sneered. "But at least I'm a man and I took care of the things a man takes care of. *I* paid the bills and *I* made life grand for all of you. And what did you do, you little freak? Nothing a man would do, you just played at being a *mom,* for God's sake. Without me, you'd be living under a fucking bridge somewhere or dead from AIDS. You latched onto my kids like you'd found a cushy job for life. You're a pathetic, worthless loser."

"You're right! If I'm worth anything at all, if I ever did anything right at all with my life, it was for bringing up those kids for you. They'd despise you if it wasn't for me. Well, Trey and Andrea may be grown and out of your wallet and you may be done with Schooner, but I'm not. And let me tell you something, asshole, you aren't as great at being a man as you think. I've had much better, and recently, as a matter of fact."

"Oh, I have no doubt about that, you've always traded your ass for the good things in life," he spat at me. "What's this guy giving you? Free fish? You've found your level haven't you? You're right back in with the redneck, white trash you came out of. I bet you're happy as a bitch in heat."

"Fuck you, Zack."

The sound of thick truck tires in my drive drowned out his reply. We just glared at each other while a noisy engine shut down and a door slammed. "Chris?" Steve called.

"Up here, Steve," I said. "Come on up and meet my ex. He was just leaving."

After a few seconds of solid thumping on the wooden tread of the stairs, Steve appeared on the deck—shirtless, sweaty, and barefoot. Without missing a step, he walked straight over to Zack and thrust out his hand. Zack flinched a little, but he stood and took Steve's hand. "I'm Steve Willis. It's good to meet you," Steve said. "Now I've met all of Chris's family in one weekend."

"Zack Ronan. Nice to meet you," Zack replied. They appraised one another for a moment until Zack took back his hand. "Well, Chris was right. I was just leaving. I need to get back to my wife and baby."

Steve stepped back, but Zack still had to step sideways to get past him. Once he had, Steve moved to my side, draped one arm over my shoulders, and kissed the top of my head. "I'm a little early," he said.

"Nope. You're right on time," I replied. I smiled up at him and then nodded to Zack, who'd made it to the edge of the steps. "Zack, take care," I said evenly, "nice to get caught up."

"Will I see you at Schooner's graduation in a couple of weeks?" he asked.

"My baby's college graduation? I wouldn't miss starting him off on a new life for anything in the world."

Zack started to say something, then just nodded and took off down the stairs. Steve turned and watched him until he got in his car, started up its purring engine, and pulled out of the drive.

"You have the timing of a superhero," I said, finally turning to watch Zack drive off down the beach road.

"I don't know about all that, Chris," he said. All the adrenaline in the anger I had not completely vented on Zack was making me shake. Steve hugged me a little tighter. "Then again," he said, "maybe I do."

CHAPTER SIX
SUMMER

✦

Since the beginning of summer I had taken to spending most of my nights at Steve's house. I was rarely home with Schooner and Frank. Whether I came home very early in the morning or late in the afternoon, I never caught the house dirty. It was never draped in soggy towels or festooned with empty Corona bottles. Dirty dishes never were waiting for me in the sink, nor did I ever detect the ripe-boy stench I'd come to know over the years lingering in the bedrooms, the baths, and stealing out into the rest of the house where dirty sneakers, socks, or stinking T-shirts could usually be caught grinning and guilty. Schooner and Frank scrupulously kept their promises made when I offered to let them stay with me for the summer while they job-hunted.

Nuala found her full water bowl in the kitchen and began to lap at it in earnest. I had time to register the low hum of the clothes dryer before Frank appeared in the hall, striding toward me in a pair of old-fashioned gym shorts he must have had since middle school. He was taller than me, but not by much. A half summer's worth of sun had turned his cornflakes-and-cream complexion into something more mango-colored all over. At least where I cared to see.

"Good morning, Chris," he said, "can I get you some coffee?"

"No, son. I'm all coffee'd out. I've been up since 5:30. Steve likes a 'fisherman's breakfast' as he calls it. He wants the full works before he goes out to pull crab traps all day. I don't want coffee or food again for the rest of the day."

"There's real orange juice in the fridge," Frank offered.

"What's the vodka level?" I asked.

"I bought an el-cheapo half gallon yesterday."

"Good boy," I said. "Are you ready to lie in the sun and be fucked-up before 10?"

"I've been looking forward to it all week," he replied with a grin.

"Well, put a towel on my lounge chair, I'll be out in a minute."

"Would you like Nuala in or out?"

"I think ol' Nuala's wanting her morning nap." I whistled sharply, and Nuala bounded past us, heading straight for her kennel. "I'll be right out, I just need to get changed."

"I'll have you a screwdriver waiting," Frank said.

I gave him a quick head rub, enjoying the feel of his ruddy crew cut under my hand as I followed Nuala to my bedroom. Frank didn't have every Saturday off, but when he did I enjoyed lying in the sun on the deck with him, each of us in his own lounge chair. He was good company in a harmless way. Even if I hadn't been so thoroughly sexually satisfied by Steve, I never would have been turned-on by his near naked form stretched out near me.

In my room, I closed my door and looked longingly at my bed. The room was chilly from the air-conditioning and the blinds were still closed against the morning light. I wanted to lie down in the cool dimness and put off the day a while longer. I was feeling my age in the aftermath of Steve's continued hunger for my body in his late-ending nights and early-starting days. Over the long days and weeks of summer, my body had grown brown from the sun and taut under the ministrations of Steve's work-hardened hands, but it hummed always as if the string were drawn too tight. I wasn't complaining by any means—I just looked at my bed, nearly identical to the one I'd risen from three hours before—knowing it'd be all the more welcoming when I did find it again in the early afternoon, drunk more from the sun than the series of screwdrivers longer on juice than on vodka.

I stripped and found a pair of Steve's boxers to wear in lieu of a bathing suit. I'd bought him several new pairs from a cool store I'd found on a visit to Wade Lee in Norfolk. The shopping had been more successful than the visit. Wade Lee had liked the idea of Steve much more than the reality of him. Steve, in turn, had been bewildered and put off by Wade's high-fag world of fine china, antiques, and Old South manners. Neither of them could relax enough to match worn sailcloth to silk brocade. It was regrettable, but not unexpected.

Nuala licked my fingers as I settled the latch of her kennel and turned to sink into a morning nap with a contented sigh. She enjoyed the company of her family when I took her with me to Steve's, but— true to the nature she'd displayed the first time I saw her—she much preferred to be the only dog in my house and she liked her time alone. I left her to her dreams and stepped into my bathroom.

I slathered on lotion with sunscreen, enjoying the texture of my skin. I saw its slight crepe when I rubbed it this way or that. There was no denying I was a few days from my 49th birthday. Because I was staying trim and lean, I saw no seriously sagging places in my mirror, but I still caught glimpses of my mother as I'd remembered her as a child. When she was my age, I was only seven years old. I'd loved to kiss the creases at the edges of her eyes, when she had allowed me to be so affectionate. Now those creases showed on my own face. My brow had begun to slacken and rest more heavily over my eyes. The color of my lashes and eyebrows had been lightened by the sun to fair-frost, but there was a silvery quality there that betrayed the 48 summers I'd seen.

I found a hint of a bruise on the base of my neck where Steve had lingered too long and too hard in quenching his thirst for me. There were shadowy smudges under my tan where he'd gripped my shoulders in joining me from behind before he turned me so he could read on my face the pleasure of his filling me. That was what he always wanted, near the climax: to witness. I wondered what he read there. I wondered what he saw in me when he was driving all thought of anything but his body from my mind.

I had never seen anything remarkable in my own face. These days, I saw only a map of all the terrain that had gone past it. There were mysterious aspects—a stranger's expression in my own eyes— that must have come from a father I'd never seen, not once. There was nothing beautiful about me, as far as I was concerned, but I had been told I was beautiful, both casually and intimately. All I saw was a pair of eyes set in a face gently etched by memory.

Others—Steve especially—saw love looking back at them from my eyes, I hoped. Older now, and aging well, hopefully, I was still nothing special. Love was the one thing I had to give from a rather unremarkable and aging package.

Slathering a last bit of lotion over my right shin and foot, I looked up to the mirror quickly to try to catch the thing that others might see in me—what Steve, especially, might see in me. All I found was me—as ever—nothing special to look at. I straightened up, enjoying the smell of coconut oil and the promise of warmth in the sun. I still felt energized and totally alive. There was nothing I could do but laugh in amazement at how I'd found myself at this moment, in this place. Improbably, I had a great lover, grown children, and a mother lode of second chances. Snapping the elastic band of Steve's boxer shorts, I shook my head and went outside to join Frank on the deck.

When I got outside, Frank had his boom box playing an old Elvis Costello CD from about 1983. "My God, baby, that song is older than you are," I said.

Frank turned from his belly and raised the back of his lounge chair to sit upright. "My mom used to play a tape of this album when I was little. Somehow, it makes me think of being on the beach back home. I love 'Everyday I Write the Book.' "

"Your mom is a very cool lady," I said. "Have you spoken with her recently?"

Frank nodded and reached over his head to grasp the back of his lounge chair, exposing the pale underside of his arms. "There's a job coming open with the parks and recreation department in Mount Pleasant."

"That's just across the river from Charleston, isn't it? Are you going to apply?"

Frank closed his eyes and stretched his chin up toward the morning sun. "Schooner and I both are going to apply. It's the best thing we've heard about since we got out of school."

"But only one of you might get the job. What's the other going to do?"

Frank shrugged. "We've decided that we'll worry about that if we have to. The great thing about both of us applying for the same job is, it doubles our chances to be together. We don't want to get separated. Either way, no matter what job one of us gets, we'll adjust."

I thought about this and took a sip of the screwdriver Frank had made for me. I struggled to decide if I was pleased at their devotion to each other or disturbed that Schooner might end up working a less desirable job just to be with Frank. I'd agreed to let them live at my house over the summer so they could have an idyllic time together—Frank was working as a floating-shift lifeguard, and Schooner had gotten a job doing golf course maintenance on the mainland. But I had made it very clear to Schooner that his main job over the summer was to find a permanent, full-time job.

"We're thinking seriously about driving up to Massachusetts to get married," Frank said casually. "We have two days off together in July. If we leave after we get off work on Sunday, and drive straight through, we'll get there in time to get married Monday afternoon. We'll have to push it, but we can drive back in time to be back at work again on Wednesday."

I was stunned. I reminded Frank my birthday coincided with one of the days they had off.

"Schooner and I both think that it would be cool to have our wedding anniversary on your birthday," Frank replied apologetically. "You know how much he loves you. You've been so good to me, and I love you too. I hope you know that, Chris."

"Thanks, Frank. I love you back," I said distractedly.

"Don't you think it's so excellent that we can actually get married?" he said. "I mean, *legally*? We know that there's no reciprocity right now in either North or South Carolina, but that can't last forever."

Many thoughts fought for dominance in my mind. All around me the landscape receded sharply, as the sun-weathered beach houses and storm-tested scrub oaks and holly all vanished in the white hot summer morning's hazy light. All I could really focus on was my baby getting married. Whether it was to Frank or to anybody else was immaterial.

"I mean, it's such a cynical play to the radical religious right in an election year. The whole Bush team is holding up the gay marriage thing like something shiny to distract the American people," Frank burbled along happily. "They're all going like: 'Look, shiny, shiny. Gay people getting married! Don't look at the war, don't look at us raping the environment, don't look at the Patriot Act fucking the Bill of Rights. Gay people want to get *married*...ooh, scary!' I mean really, do you think the American people—"

"Frank, sugar," I said, "would you please shut up a minute?"

Frank stopped his political rant and gave me a hurt look.

"I'm sorry, Frank. It's just I'm kind of in shock a little. You said you and Schooner are going to get married, didn't you?"

Frank gave me a happy look. "Yes! I love him and he loves me. After this summer, here with you, I don't ever want to be apart from him. I don't care where either of us gets a job—I'm going to be with Schooner. He feels the same way about me. It's what we want."

Frank seemed so impossibly young just then. He seemed so fresh and fearless. And I flashed on the memory of my baby, determinedly looking at me across a stretch of hardwood floor, making a brave decision, and taking off toward my waiting arms.

When I had heard this announcement twice before, I'd had been all smiles and easy laughter and congratulations. But those times I was sending a young man and a young woman into a world geared for their success. This time, I saw a baby I loved, toddling off into a world that was going to greet him with bared teeth and brutal disdain.

"Please tell me you're happy for us, Chris," Frank said. "What you think means a great deal to me."

I looked at the boy stretched out beside me squinting in the harsh July morning sun. In some ways, I knew this boy better than my own son.

The house was always clean—and because Frank cleaned it. My son always had clean underwear because Frank did the laundry—I'd found him folding Schooner's clothes on more than one occasion. My son had a casual, possessive grin on his face in this freckled sprite's presence because Frank gave him unfettered access to his mind, body, and soul. Yes, I knew Frank very well. I knew him as well as I knew the cares that had bitten lines, after a lifetime of love, deep into the edges of my own eyes.

"Frank," I said, "it's because I do love you that I have to ask you something."

He shifted in his lounge chair to face me. I knew the hot gray wood of the deck was burning the soles of his feet. I saw the trickle of sweat that collected in the hollow of his neck and slid between the square planes of his chest. Oh I knew this boy all right.

"Ask me anything, Chris," he said. His earnest face shone in the sunlight.

"If you love Schooner—if you love him enough to marry him—

will you still be okay if he ever walks away from you?"

Frank looked at me wide-eyed. "I can't ever imagine that, Chris. I can't even imagine living without him."

I sighed. How could I break his heart and tell him life threw you curves and you goddamn better well be ready to swerve? Would I have believed that at his age? Could I have imagined Zack turning into the bitter stranger who now filled every space he'd once occupied with such easy, loving familiarity? I reached for my drink and took a long swallow, welcoming the cold, sour certainty of it. "Frank, what I have to say, I'm going to tell you because you're like me. You love too deep and you love a Ronan man."

Frank said nothing, and watched my face warily, fearful I might know some fact he didn't. I did, but it wasn't the kind of information that worried him. I knew of no other love in Schooner's life, no hidden girlfriend, no dirty secrets that could wound or destroy trust. I only knew what was possible.

"Frank, I want you to keep some love back for yourself. My baby is a good man. I raised him to be everything you see in him that you love. But the world and time has a way of changing people. You'll change, he'll change. But there's one thing in you that I know like I know the back of my own hand. You love him without any reservations. I'm pleased my baby has found someone like that. But...because I love you like I love myself...I want you to know life's a bitch sometimes and I want you to never stop staying strong for you. Okay?"

Frank looked confused, and I couldn't blame him. What I knew now was informed by experience and ingrained by pure instinct. "So, it's okay?" he asked.

"Yes, it's okay. Oh my baby—I'm so happy for you both. There's no one in this world I'd rather see my Schooner with than you."

I watched Frank's beautiful grin light up his face and bring the landscape of the summer morning back into focus. A loud radio played down the street, a car door slammed, and on the beach children cried out to each other with glee. Time and life moved on, and I took my place in its tide. Sighing once again, I closed my eyes against the harsh sun and the harsher world they both were walking into.

During Mass, I was keenly aware of Schooner's every movement as he sat, knelt, and rose next to me. It was just my baby and me—the other people who mattered to me at that moment weren't there. Steve was on a boat pulling crab traps and Frank was in a lifeguard stand ready and watching for trouble. Sitting next to me, Schooner exuded happiness even the strangers around us seemed to notice and respond to. The psalm reading was the 69th. We read:

> *I pray to you, O Lord*
> *For the time of your great favor, O God!*
> *In your great kindness answer me*
> *With your constant help*
> *Answer me, O Lord, for bounteous is your kindness*
> *In your great mercy turn toward me.*

Schooner looked at me and smiled happily. He and Frank would be leaving at 6 that evening for the drive to Raleigh, where they'd catch a flight to Boston the next day. I'd broken down and paid for two plane tickets. The purchase put a sizable dent in my savings, but I couldn't have them driving nearly 2,000 miles in two days.

I still had secret misgivings and fears about this momentous step for him. At the consecration of the host, I bowed my head at the sound of the bells and struck my breast as I'd been taught in the old liturgy. *Oh God,* I prayed, *if any fault of mine put this strong child of my heart in your hands in this way, please God, forgive me.* At the consecration of the wine, I bowed my head and struck my breast again and prayed, *Oh God, forgive your Church as it withholds its blessing from my child and his Frank. Forgive its faults. Forgive its most grievous faults.*

I walked behind Schooner's broad back and received Communion after he did. Kneeling again, I looked at Christ on the cross and prayed for my baby's safety—to Boston and back and into the years that stretched ahead. I had prayed the same prayer at the nuptial Masses for Trey and Susan and Andrea and David. I'd had no prayers for myself when I walked into Zack's house and took his children into my heart and put my future into his hands. I'd never had the benefit of the piece of paper Schooner and Frank would get in Boston. But I had been blessed nonetheless. I prayed as hard as I had in my life. Despite my faith, all I knew was everything about love that could pass away with time.

Oh God, I prayed, *look after my baby. Help him. Bless him and keep him. I did my best. Lord Jesus, please believe I did my best to try and show him how to do things right. Oh God, only you can take him from here. Please God, bless him and Frank. God, I'm begging you to do it now and for always.*

The last bowl holding the host was emptied and wiped clean. The deacon handed the bowl of remaining hosts to Father Fintan. He returned it to the tabernacle and closed the door. All the Communion servers and Father Fintan genuflected. I crossed myself and took my seat in the pew. Schooner gave me a questioning look that asked me if I was okay. I gave him a nod and the best smile I could manage. I knew I was going to be fine, and so was he. We were bound in love and blessed every step of the way.

The rest of the day was subdued. I couldn't find the words to communicate what I wanted to say to Schooner, so I said nothing. I just stayed close to him. I made him his favorite meal for lunch. I washed and folded his and Frank's clothes and talked and joked with him while he packed for them both. Schooner scolded me now and then for being so solicitous, but there was no meanness in his chidings.

Frank came home sun-scorched and tired from a long day in the sun. Schooner nearly pushed him into the shower, he was so anxious to get on the road—and probably, I thought, away from me. When Frank ambled into the living room after his shower, I asked both of them to sit down at the dining room table.

"We've really got to go, Mom," Schooner pleaded. "I want to get to Trey's and Susan's as soon as we can so we can get some sleep. Our flight is at 7, which means we need to be at RDU around 5."

"This won't take but a second, okay?" I promised.

I saw Frank give Schooner a look that told him to sit down and shut up. Once they were settled, I took my seat at the head of the table. "Have you two got rings?" I asked.

Schooner sagged in his chair and looked up at the ceiling. "Oh fuck!" he exclaimed.

"It's okay, Schooner," Frank said soothingly. "We'll get rings later. It's no big deal."

"I thought as much," I said as I reached in my pocket and retrieved what I'd stashed there. I lay Zack's wedding band on the table in front of me. He'd taken it off and put it in our underwear drawer when I'd first moved in. After that, he never wore any jewelry but his college class ring.

When we'd been together for 10 years, Zack surprised me by telling me I could have a wedding band if I wanted one. I'd mentioned that to him as a possible anniversary present. He told me the name of a jewelry store I could go to and pick out whatever I wanted. He'd already called and given the store's manager his American Express card number. Both Zack and the store manager were surprised when I selected a simple gold band. Nothing too fancy or too expensive for me—I had only wanted what the ring meant, not what it was worth to anyone else. I remembered it had cost less than $200.

Frank and Schooner watched as I pulled that ring off my finger and put it on the table next to the other one. "Schooner, this is the ring your mother gave your father on their wedding day. Frank, this is the ring Schooner's father let me buy when we'd been together for 10 years. I don't know if they'll fit you, or even if you want them, considering they've not proven to be the most successful charms in the past. Maybe you two will turn their luck. It would make me very happy if you will both accept them as my blessing and with my good wishes."

The boys looked at each other and then each reached for a ring. Zack's fit Schooner's finger loosely; mine, Frank's perfectly.

"Mom, I..." Schooner began. He twisted his father's ring on his finger and got up and walked into the living room with his back to me. Frank stood, walked around the table to me, and waited for me to stand. When I did, he wrapped his arms around me in a great, unreserved hug. Near his ear I whispered, "Don't you forget what I told you, okay?"

He let me go and nodded. "I love you," he said. "Thank you."

I had to walk over to Schooner, who turned from me when I reached him and wiped at his eyes with his shoulders. He never did like to let me see him cry. I just put my hand on the back of his neck and squeezed it gently. "Go get married, baby. I trust your Frank to look after you from here on out. He's a good kid. Your daddy gave you to me a long time ago, and now I'm sure you're going to be looked after, I can let you go."

Schooner turned and wrapped me in a hug that nearly crushed my poor ribs. "Thank you Mom," he said. "Thank you for everything."

I surrendered to his hug as long as I could stand, my heart breaking a little. This day came in different ways for every parent. It was never easy and never without some regret. I reached up, grasped his upper arms, and pushed him away. "Go on, baby. Drive safe. I'll see you on Wednesday."

Schooner nodded, smiled, and let me go.

Steve's back shone with sweat in the sunshine that was left in the day as he swung off the boat and onto his dock. I stood and watched as he stepped into a swirl of dogs. Petey, Nuala, Mama-dog, and the two remaining pups Steve had named Buster and Re-pete all barked and strove to be patted and stroked before trotting up and down the pier or jumping in the boat. Finally, he had a second's worth of attention to spare for me. "Hey, I didn't expect you out here waiting for me when I put in."

"I know, I just decided I'd wait for you. Me and the dogs are ready for you to get home by this time of day."

Steve tied the boat up secure against the change in tide for the night and gave me a smile. "I'm *hongry*. You got me some dinner cooked?"

"Yep. I know *hongry* is much more worser than just hungry," I teased.

Steve laughed. "My stomach has been emptier than my lunch bag since about 3 o'clock. What have you got for supper?"

"After the kids left, I just had time to feed the dogs and stew some pork chops and cook a pot of rice for you. There's that and some fresh sliced tomatoes—that's pretty much it. I need to go to the grocery store."

Without a word, Steve reached in his pocket and pulled out a fat wad of 20s. He counted off seven and handed them to me.

I whistled. "Somebody had full traps and a good buyer."

Steve took off his baseball cap, wiped his forehead with the back of his arm, and then wedged his cap back on his head. "It was a good day," he said. "Buy me a carton of cigarettes when you go. You got any on you?"

I reached back into the waistband of my board shorts and handed him the pack. "The lighter's inside."

Steve got one lit and handed the pack back to me, then turned on the hose and began to wash the muck and slime off the sides and deck of his boat. Seeing the hose come out, all the dogs retreated to lie along the pier, well out of reach of the hose's dreaded spray. I watched him make short work of cleaning the boat, handing him the broom and taking the hose without being asked. The day's-end routine had become familiar. When he'd finished and climbed back onto the pier, I reached in the small six-pack cooler I'd brought out and handed him a beer and cracked one open for myself.

I watched his throat move thirstily and waited for him to sit beside me on the bench. One beer gone, he sat and I handed him another.

"Best part of the day, sitting here like this," he said.

"That's a big compliment from a hongry man," I said.

He grinned at me then looked off in the west over the sound. The sun was still an orange ball, bearable to look at through the late afternoon's haze and the wide water's humidity. "My daddy used to say this time of day was pure-dee purty."

"Your daddy was right," I said. "I bet you miss the old man, don't you."

Steve nodded, gave Mama-dog and Nuala an affectionate ear-shaking, and gave me a grin and an amiable nudge in the side. "Not so much anymore. Not Mama so much anymore either, now I got me somebody who loves my dogs, and knows how to stew pork chops and cook a pot of rice."

"Not hard to do for a man who puts out the kind of loving you do," I said.

"I'll wear your little butt out every chance I can get."

"Listen at you. You're getting me hard just talking about it."

"I'd fuck you right now if we weren't sitting out here in front of all the Assembly of God and United Methodist worshippers in Salter Path."

"I'd let you if we weren't."

I lit a cigarette and offered Steve another one. We smoked

awhile in silence as the dogs drowsed on the sun-warmed boards. We watched the sky turn to riot and revel, showing off for the coming midsummer night.

"Schooner and Frank head out then?" Steve asked.

"Yeah. Right on time."

He sighed. "Would you marry me if I asked you to?"

"Yeah, I would. I wouldn't hesitate one second saying yes to you, Steve Willis."

"But you know I won't ask, don't you," Steve asked, rubbing Repete's belly with one bare foot. "I mean, I'm not interested in going off somewhere and getting a piece of paper to say we're married."

"Ask me a hard one, Steve. I know you wouldn't, for the same reason I wouldn't ask you to. We're not that kind of people. It's not how we were raised."

Steve looked ashore and gestured with his beer can toward a house not too far from his. "You know I got a cousin that lives in that house right?"

I nodded.

"Motherfucker asked me the other day if I was still queering off with the tourist in the Expedition. I told him hell yeah. Then I asked him if his goddamn feelings were hurt."

"What did he say?"

"Not a fucking thing when everybody else on the dock busted up laughing." Steve snorted, crunched his beer can, and tossed it in the trash barrel across the dock. "They all know. None of them really care, but they have to let you know they know. They don't never miss a chance to say something. I've lived around these sons-a-bitches all my life. I screwed around with some of them back when we were kids. They all went on and did what they thought was the right thing. I didn't never get in line that way."

"I'm the one who's glad you didn't, Steve," I said. "But it must have been difficult for you." Mama-dog came up to me with a stick in her mouth; very carefully, I tossed it down the length of the dock, not into the water. If I had, she'd have been in after it in a flash. "I sometimes wonder if I'm making things difficult for you now."

Steve laughed softly. "Naw, we can pretty much get by without any trouble. But I'm a local. I pull my traps and take care of my business same as they do and I let them all know they can go to hell if they don't like it. They can respect that. They won't fuck with me, and they won't fuck with you, neither. But it's not ever going to be all easy and open, not like with Frank and Schooner. You know that don't you?"

"I know it. I've lived my whole life like that, Steve."

"Can you live like that still, Chris?"

"I can. And believe me when I tell you: I don't want it any other way, Steve."

"Well, you got to believe me when I tell you I love you," he said. "There. You got me to say it and mean it. I hope that's good enough, because there ain't going to be no other way for me to show it other than treating you right, fucking you cross-eyed, and buying the groceries."

"Just don't forget to say you love me on a regular basis. You do that and show me you mean it like you just said and I can keep you in suppers and loving you back the best way I know how."

"I do love you, Little Bit," he said.

"And I love you, Big Man."

Steve stood. "Then there ain't nothing left to be said other than *Get my food on my plate.* I'm going to get me a shower, eat me some supper, and then give that pretty little ass of yours a right proper pounding. Sound good to you?"

I stood up and stretched. "Sounds good to me," I said.

Steve grinned. The setting sun burnished his broad shoulders and gave him a hazy gold nimbus around his curly-haired head. "Well all right," he said. In Banker brogue it came out sounding like *Wall awl roight.*

"Wall awl roight," I answered, mimicking him. He grabbed me by the nape of the neck and shook me gently. Then we headed up the pier to the house, trailed by dogs happily escorting us. No march down any church's aisle, no giddy flights to Boston or San Francisco for us. We were just together, plain and simple. The very last of the sun blessed us, the summer's cicadas sang a chirring recessional, and a few gulls dived and called congratulations. I was as happy as I'd ever hoped to be.

I woke to the sound of National Weather Service radio. Steve had the local station's marine forecast tuned in and playing loud in the kitchen. I smelled coffee and looked at the clock by the side of the bed. It was nearly 5:30—he'd let me sleep. By now, he was usually walking down the pier to his boat, lunch bag in hand and a full day on the water ahead of him. I felt bad. I usually tried to get up with him; we weren't morning talkers, but I wanted every moment I could get with him before the day began and we went our separate ways.

I got out of bed and searched in the early-dawn light for my underwear by the side of the bed. Finding my own for once, I slipped it on over my legs and stood to pull it to my waist, ignoring the sweet soreness in my muscles and on my beard-scraped skin that was the by-product of the night before's lovemaking. Still half asleep, I made my way into the kitchen, hoping to find Steve there, finishing his breakfast.

There was no one in the kitchen but the metallic voice of the National Weather Service announcer. Figuring Steve was out feeding the dogs on the deck, I made myself a cup of coffee. As I was pouring the cream, I felt him slip up behind me, put his arms around me, and bend at the knees to grind the thick width of his dick into my backside. Pinned to the kitchen counter, I lay my head back against his chest and sighed. It was a pleasant greeting for a Monday morning.

"Happy birthday, Little Bit. I got two presents for you. Which one do you want first, the one that goes here"—I felt an insistence at my backside—"or the one that goes here?" With that, I felt his hands gently encircle my neck and his thumbs stroke just under my ears.

I reached behind him and took his bare ass in my hands. I squeezed it and laughed. "I've had this present before and not too long ago." Letting go of his ass, I raised my hands to grasp his at my neck. "Can I have this one first?"

"Sure thing, but you can't see that one until I give you the other one."

"Okay." I began to turn, but he pressed me harder against the counter's edge. "Ow!" I said.

Steve whispered, "Shhh. Stay still and close your eyes." He waited two beats, then asked, "Are they closed?"

"Yep," I replied.

With that, he took his hands away from my neck and a moment

later I felt something heavy and cold encircle it. He tugged at it gently and it closed tighter around my throat, then it slid down to rest just above the hollow. It was pleasantly tight, like a choker, but with more suppleness and less resistance. "What is it?" I asked.

Steve shushed me softly again, put his hands inside my shorts, and cupped my hardening dick in his rough palm. With the other hand, he pulled down my shorts and bent his cock to fit between my legs. I shifted to hold him tightly there. He began to stroke me between my legs, his dick rubbing the hard ridge under my scrotum, while he gently tugged at my dick, rolling the head of it between his spit-slicked thumb and forefinger.

Guided by his hand, I wet my own fingers in my hot coffee and reached between my legs, found the head of his dick, and gently tugged at it in return. We rocked and traded moans until I couldn't hold it any longer. I came, and in coming, I gave up the wet he needed to climax too. We stood shuddering at the forbidden novelty of doing that thing that way. Sticky with each other, I turned around and held him tightly, my dick near screaming with tenderness under his scrotum with him pressed and rubbing against my belly.

Looking up at him, I grew shy and looked down. He kissed the top of my head and whispered, "I've always wanted to do it that way with you. I've daydreamed about it and nearly had to beat off out on the boat. There's a thousand ways to pleasure you I haven't even come up with yet. Will you let me do you like I dream about? Will you keep on letting me love you like I want to?"

"Will you never stop dreaming like that?" I said. "I won't stop if you won't."

Steve gently pushed me away, wet hands on my shoulders, and stooped to lick and kiss my nipples, each in turn. Then he licked up my neck and caught and held the choker in his teeth and pulled away from my throat. Dropping the choker, he looked in my eyes and said, "You want to see your other present now?"

I smiled and nodded at him, disgustingly wide-eyed for someone my age. I was now 49 years old, and Steve was opening me up to new experiences and making sex new and pleasantly dirty all over again. Whatever was around my neck was sure to be okay, but what he'd just done to me made me feel 14 again, and that was magical.

"C'mon then, my dirty little boy," he said. "Come see your birthday present." With that, Steve took my sticky hand in his own and pulled me toward the bathroom. For once I didn't mind being tugged and pulled along.

In the tiny bathroom I looked into the old mirror as Steve stood behind me with his dick pressing into the small of my back, his hands on my shoulders, and a lopsided grin on his face. The chain was made of solid rectangular links that looked to be a little less than an eighth of an inch thick and a quarter inch long. They linked to each other in their corners, which made the choker flexible but gave the impression of a nearly unbroken line draped around my neck. The weight and color suggested they were the real thing, not cheap gold plate.

"It's a baht chain," Steve said. "It's how the people in Thailand measure gold's weight and value. This one is 22-carat gold. I forget how many baht that translates to, but you're worth every ounce of it, Chris."

"Steve, it's wonderful. Where did you get it?"

Steve put his hands on my waist and turned me to him gently. "My father bought it for my mother when he was in the service. Besides her engagement and wedding rings, it was the only piece of jewelry he was ever able to give her. It may be the only piece of jewelry I'm ever able to give you. I hope you'll accept it knowing what it means to me. It's the best I can do for you. I hope you'll take it as a promise and I hope you'll keep it as one to me."

"Steve," I whispered. "I don't deserve this. I don't know how you can trust me with something so precious."

Steve pulled me closer and put his chin on top of my head. If his eyes were open, I knew he was looking at his own reflection when he said, "I make promises for the long haul, Little Bit. I'm counting on you to do the same."

I moved my head from under his chin and reached for his stubbled face. I cupped him in my palms and rubbed my thumbs over his cheek bones as I looked in his eyes. Their blueness dissolved to almost clear at the pupils in the light coming from the bathroom window. Dawn was gone and the sun was up now, hot in the pale sky outside. There was a whole universe under his black lashes. I bent his head down as far as I could and strained upward onto the balls of my feet to kiss each darkly limned lid in turn.

Done, I looked at him and said, "Big Man. You great big-hearted man, where did you come from to sew up my heart and make me believe in love again? I ain't got nothing to give you but myself. I am stunned you would want me this way, that you'd treasure me this way and give me anything at all. Nobody has ever kept their promises to me, but I believe in you, Steve. You can't out-give me. I promise you that. Whatever you give me, I'll try my damnedest to give you back twice as hard. I promise you that. I swear to God."

Steve smiled. "That's good enough for me. Now unless you want me to fuck you again, you better quit and get in the shower."

"I want you to fuck me again," I said. "It's my birthday."

"*We gon' party like it's your birthday.* Is that what you want? You want to party like it's your birthday?" Steve laughed as he picked up the tune and sang the lyrics of the 50 Cent and Beyoncé song. "C'mon back to bed then, *we gon' party like it's your birthday,* you little bitch. I'm gon' fuck you *like it's your birthday.*"

He slapped my ass. I grabbed him by his stiffening dick and we made it back to bed with the National Weather Service announcer predicting a very fine day on the beach.

Cathy was very pregnant now. I could hear her discomfort and impatience through the open door to the waiting room. Her temper had grown shorter with the people she had to deal with over the phone in the past week, and someone was on the receiving end of her ire as I walked in the office just after 10. Dr. Tony was short with me because I got in late, and gave me a shortish sermon on responsibility.

My mood was so great, I took the dressing-down cheerfully but showed the proper amount of remorse. "I'm so sorry," I said. "But I had a lot of trouble getting to work this morning. Today's my birthday, and I had two calls from my kids in Raleigh. They both wanted to make sure I started the day off right. And my marlin-killer gave me my present this morning. I am sorry—please believe me. I hope you'll be patient with me this once."

He seemed a little taken aback when I apologized so profusely. Mumbling something about how it was really okay and how he understood, Tony made an embarrassed escape. As I settled into my desk and checked the few phone messages from the weekend, both he and Cathy appeared at the half wall separating my area from the hall.

"Chris, forgive us—" Tony began.

"I had the day marked on my calendar," Cathy interjected, "but I put it under September instead of July. We would have given you something besides a chewing-out when you came in."

"Happy birthday, Chris," Tony said. "We just want you to know how fond we are of you and what a great job we think you're doing."

Big tears spilled from Cathy's eyes and over her cheeks. "Oh Chris, I'm so sorry for being so irritable. Birthdays are a big deal in our family, and you're like a part of the family now."

I stood and walked to the wall between us, and gave each of them a gentle pat on the hand. "I want you two not to beat yourselves up like this. You're both on your last good nerve with this baby so close to coming, and it's no big deal. I didn't tell you guys my birthday was today, and to tell you the truth, I should have been more considerate knowing the stress you both are under right now. Okay?"

When I finished, I handed Cathy a tissue and gave them each a great big grin.

They looked at each other and said, almost simultaneously, "God, I miss sex."

I laughed until they did.

"How does my appointment calendar look?" Tony asked.

I walked back to my desk and checked it. "You have clients from 10:30 straight through until noon, as usual. Then, you're clear of clients, but you have a meeting at the hospital from 1:30 until 4."

"That's not enough time to go out to lunch," Tony said.

"Let's order in! I could fucking murder a pepperoni pizza with hot peppers all by myself," Cathy announced.

"Okay, but just get a small one for yourself," Tony said. "There's not enough Zantac in the world to get me through the afternoon's meeting if I eat that. What do you like on your pizza, Chris? Is pizza good for you?"

"Absolutely. I can't think of anything I'd rather have, come to think of it. How about just plain cheese? We'll split one."

"Excellent!" Tony said. "Pizza for all my people!" He pulled two 20s out of his wallet and handed them to me. "Can you handle ordering it so they'll be here no later than 12:15?"

"Of course Chris can handle it, Tony. For God's sake."

"Down, Cathy! Down! I just meant I'll need to eat and run, I'm not attacking his competency. Sheesh."

Cathy gave her husband a pat on his ass and walked back toward her office as the outside waiting room door opened. "Sorry my pet," she said to Tony. "The evil bitch Cathy is coming out more frequently. I'm going to go vent on Aetna now."

I handed the doctor his first client folder and smiled at him. "Thanks, boss," I said. "Now, that should be Mr. Ellison." With that, I slid the open glass window to reveal Mr. Ellison himself. "Well good morning sir, we were just getting ready for you. How are you on a Monday?"

Mr. Ellison began a mumbled lithium litany of sorrow and wrote out his co-pay check. Tony walked the two steps to the reception door, opened it, and invited the client back to his office.

With Tony busy and Cathy on the phone, I turned my chair, put my elbow on my desk, and rested my head in my hand. I stared out the window, feeling the happy weight of gold and new promises around my neck. I felt at once very tired and very elated. I hadn't smoked pot in over 20 years, but the languor that overtook me at that moment felt not unlike being high. I knew—thoroughly fucked and very much in love—I could waste the entire day at my desk, staring out the window. For once I didn't care: That was exactly what I intended to do.

Thursday after work, Steve looked at me and shook his head disgustedly. Standing in the street in front of my house, it looked worse than it really was. Still, it was ugly—all vehement black paint, hurriedly sprayed and left to run in thick drips down the front of the pilings facing the street and writ large on the set of French doors on the deck. "You'd think the fucker would learn how to spell. Doesn't *faggot* have two *g*'s?"

I had to laugh. I didn't think proper spelling was the vandal's point. His anger and my humiliation was the point.

"It's not as bad as it looks, Chris. The paint'll sand off the pilings pretty quick with my belt sander and it'll scrape off the glass with a razor blade. The bitch of fixing it back will be painting the muntins on the doors and even that ain't no big deal. I can get it all done tomorrow."

"I'm tempted to just leave it," I said.

"C'mon Chris. Don't take it to heart," Steve said dismissively. "If it had to happen, this is shit that is easily fixable. It would be a lot worse if they'd gotten in the house, or wrote all over the cars."

"They didn't have enough guts," I said. "Frank and Schooner were inside asleep. The policeman that came this morning said it was probably some kids. Tourists, most likely. But I can't figure out how a tourist would know a house full of faggots lived here."

Steve reached in his back pocket and pulled out his pack of cigarettes. He offered me one and I took it. After he got them both lit, he gave me a squint-eyed look through the smoke and matter-of-factly reminded me of what I already knew. "Schooner and Frank ain't exactly discreet sitting up on that deck. They ain't flying no rainbow flag, but they can't seem to keep their hands off each other, and this ain't that kind of beach, you know what I mean?"

"Yeah, I hear you. Fly to Boston and get married on Monday, fly home all moonish on Tuesday, vandalized on Wednesday night, take off Thursday for job interviews on Friday. They're having an interesting week."

"Oh man, you got that right," he said. "I'm sure glad I ain't 22 no more."

I laughed.

"What cop did you say called you this afternoon to let you know he'd found the kids who did it?" Steve asked.

"He gave me his card this morning, but it's up in the house. I think he said his name was Eric something."

Steve nodded. "That'll be Eric Preston. He's a good guy. From off-island, came down here and married a local girl while he was stationed at Camp Lejeune. When he got out of the Marines, he stuck around."

"Damn, it sure is a small town," I said. "He asked me if I was your *friend*. I told him yeah. He was really nice, not an asshole at all."

"Well, like I said, Eric's a nice-enough guy. He sure put in some quick time finding the punks who did this. And I think he's about to drive up right now."

I looked toward the beach road in time to see an Emerald Isle police cruiser turn onto my street, closely followed by a GMC Envoy. Both cars pulled up and stopped in front of my house. Eric got out of the car first and opened the back door of the cruiser. With his assistance, a tall, scrawny kid of about 15 emerged, followed by a younger boy about 12. Both boys were dressed in board shorts and wifebeaters, and both were in handcuffs. Eric marched them to the end of my drive and nodded. "Chris, Steve," he said. We shook hands and waited while a man Steve's age and his wife climbed out of their SUV and came to stand at the foot of the drive with the boys and the cop.

The man shook his head and shot his wife a look of pure disgust. She held her head up, but she wouldn't meet his eyes. Instead, she just looked at the two boys worriedly.

"Chris, these two boys have been identified by your neighbors down the street as the kids who vandalized your house last night," Eric said. "When I confronted them with everything I had on them, including the paint on their hands, they confessed."

The man stepped around Eric and the boys and offered his hand. I took it and shook. "I'm Arnold Holscomb, this is my wife, Janet." The sunburned woman ducked her head nervously and tried out a weak smile. "I'd like to tell you I'm very sad and sorry for my boys' behavior. I hope we can work something out."

Eric ignored the man, woman, and the boys and addressed himself to Steve. "How much do you figure it'll cost to get this stupid mess scraped off and cleaned up?"

Steve turned around, gave the house a long look, turned back, and thumped his cigarette off into the street. "Well, if you're asking me if the dollars makes the difference between misdemeanor and felony vandalism, I suppose that depends on what Chris's homeowner's insurance has to say."

"Mr. Thayer, I'm hoping we can settle this without a lot of fuss," Arnold said. "I'll be perfectly happy to write you a check to cover any cost of repairs. My boys owe you an apology, and I guarantee you they'll be punished, but I'm asking you please, if we can keep this out of the courts. My boys acted stupid, but they're not bad kids, I promise you."

Eric scratched his head and gave me a long look. "Chris, it's up to you. I've got no problem booking them. But Mr. Holscomb's got a point. If you'll be lenient with the two little...with the two boys, I'm willing to settle it here."

I looked at the boys' father. He had the pompadour of a preacher. Then I looked at the two boys, heads hung low and hands cuffed behind their backs. From them I turned to their mother. She was clearly fearful for her sons. It radiated out of her like waves of pain. I sighed. "Boys, what are your names?"

The youngest one looked at me guiltily and said his name was Dewayne. The older one defiantly looked at his father.

"The man asked you a question, son," Arnold said.

The boy hung his head and mumbled, "Brandon."

Everyone's eyes were on me; everyone was watching and waiting to hear what I had to say. "Brandon, Dewayne, please look at me," I said. The little fellow started to cry, but he looked at me. The older one threw me a blazingly defiant stare. "You know, one time I had a friend. He was walking to his car out of the grocery store one night and four guys jumped him. They called him a faggot and a queer and a peter-puffer. They called him a whole lot worse, but the bad thing was, all the while they were calling him those names, they were beating him and kicking him. One of the boys beat his glasses into his eyes so bad he almost went blind. You know the worst part of it? Nobody helped him. Nobody in that parking lot made one move to keep those kids from beating him half to death."

The little boy was sobbing now. The teenager looked away. "Look at me, boys," I said more forcefully. I waited until I had their attention once more. "I just want to ask you, how far do you think it is from spraying the word *faggot* all over one person's house to kicking someone to death one night in a Food Lion parking lot?"

"Ah, man," Brandon said. "We didn't mean nothing like that by it."

"Son, do you know where the word *faggot* comes from?" I asked.

"No," he sneered. "We don't go to school to learn about faggots."

"Brandon, shut your mouth and listen to what the man has to

say. Right now!" The mother was clearly out of patience with her son and was willing to listen to whatever I had to say to get him out of trouble. But I could tell Brandon didn't care and he didn't really want to hear it either.

"Brandon, a faggot is a bundle of sticks tied together. It's what the church used to stack around gay people's feet when they burned them at the stake. Nice picture isn't it? That's why they call gay people faggots—because they burn so good. A harmless word doesn't mean nothing, does it, kid?" The boy tried to stare me down, but he couldn't.

Then I looked at Arnold. He couldn't meet my eyes either. "Sir?" He looked back at me miserably. "Please give some serious thought to the difference between what you're teaching them and what your boys are hearing."

I looked at Eric. "Let them go, officer. Send them home with their mama and daddy. There isn't anything more to be done here. Nothing I can do, anyway."

"You sure, Chris?" Steve said. "I think the ignorant little bastards ought to at least apologize." His words cut through the air like the real flashes of anger on all sides that remained unspoken.

"Boys, this man is doing you a tremendous good turn," Janet Holscomb said. "I want you to act like you've got some sense and some decent raising. Tell him you're sorry for what you did. Now!" Her voice carried far more sincerity and weight than her husband's had.

The little fellow looked up through tears and snot, and apologized sincerely.

"Thank you, Dewayne. Apology accepted." The little boy looked at his mother, who nodded at him gravely. He looked back at me and tried to smile. I gave him a smile in return for his efforts. There was goodness in this kid, I figured.

I looked at the teenager and met defiance in full bloom. He'd outgrow it—they all did—but he'd pay for a lot of harder lessons to get past it than I could give him. "You're forgiven too, kid," I said, "whether you want it or not." I turned my back on him and addressed Eric. "Officer, thank you for all your help." I stuck out my hand and Eric grasped it in a firm shake.

"No problem, Chris," he said. "Call on us anytime. That's what

we're here for. I think these boys don't realize how serious this is."
I watched him uncuff the kids, and I started to walk away.

"Mr. Thayer," the boy's mother said, "thank you. I really
appreciate this."

"Ma'am, you probably won't believe this, but I've raised three
kids of my own. Every day ain't easy, but every day you've got with
them is a blessing and another chance to get it right."

Without a word, Arnold Holscomb offered his hand as well. I
shook it firmly and gave him a smile. Tiredly, I knew smiles and
forgiveness were free, and if you worked them right, they got easier as the years went by.

Steve and I watched Eric drive off in the cruiser as the
Holscombs returned to their car. Mr. Holscomb was holding the
door as Brandon got in, and Steve called out, "Hey kid!"

The father and his elder son stopped and looked back. "You
better watch yourself if you ever come back here. Not everybody
who lives down here is as forgiving as this. I'll beat you and your
daddy's punk ass if you even think about pulling any more shit like
this on my beach."

Arnold pushed his son in the car, slammed the door, and got
himself behind the steering wheel. He had a little bit of a redneck
side himself, Arnold Holscomb did. He nearly squalled his tires getting back on the beach road and heading back to wherever he came
from.

Steve laughed. "Well, boyfriend, you got any razor blades?
Ain't no reason why we can't get started on the glass before we get
done with daylight."

"No, I probably don't have any in the whole house. Besides, I'm
hongry. Let's go get something to eat."

Steve grinned and gave me a look I liked. "Well get in the truck
then, bitch."

"Wow! Redneck foreplay," I said as I walked around to the passenger side of his truck.

"I tell you what, I always know just what to say, don't I,
Little Bit?"

I remembered the look on Brandon's and Arnold Holscomb's
faces and laughed. "Oh hell yeah, Big Man. You're a magician with
the words, *awl roight*."

David was surf casting, but not having that much luck catching anything. I got the feeling that didn't really matter to him. All he wanted to do was to stand on the sand shirtless and occasionally stride out into the water following his hook and bait when there was a tug on his line. Somehow he could distinguish between the water's pull and that of a bluefish. I always thought David was a cute-enough fellow—proportioned well from shoulders to hip— but he was getting sunburned, and he wouldn't be so cute then. I could look at him and tell he was getting fried.

"Your husband is going to be blistered if you don't go put some suntan lotion on him," I told Andrea.

She rolled her eyes at me, but rose from her lounge chair and pulled her bottle of Hawaiian Tropic from her tote bag. "Fine, Chris. But you just watch."

With that, she strode down to him and poured some lotion onto her hand and began to stroke it across his shoulders. David responded by winding his reel and stubbornly walking closer to the water's edge. Andrea followed him, all the while rubbing the lotion into his red shoulders. When he stopped, knee-high in the water, he leaned back awkwardly to kiss her, and she leaned forward to meet him. Then, he began to walk backward, out of the water, tightening his line and forcing her to retreat. She said something to him I couldn't hear over the breeze and the surf, and he laughed.

Shaking her head, she loped back to her lounge chair next to mine and said, "David is a stubborn fool. 'I don't burn,' he says, 'don't put that stinky crap all over me.' He smells like sweat and old bait and he thinks coconut oil stinks? Why do all men stink?"

Luckily, she couldn't see my eyes rolling behind my sunglasses. Unperturbed, I said, "They don't stink, they just smell like men. Would you want a man who smelled like Chanel No. 5? Besides, you women aren't always delicate flowers your own selves."

Andrea dropped her suntan oil into her bag and fished out her watch. "It's been 30 minutes. Time to turn over, Chris."

I lowered the back of my lounge chair and rolled over, resting my cheek against the terry-cloth towel I used to cover the plastic headrest. Andrea knelt on one knee, then stretched and lowered herself onto her stomach. For a moment I saw her breasts sway and swing inside her top. There was no doubt she was becoming fuller somehow. Her belly had a definite curve and firm rounded swing to it as she lay, before she was completely prone. She turned her face toward me, then rested her cheek on her towel and smiled.

I smiled back, enjoying the moment before I asked, "Andrea, are you pregnant?"

She met and held my gaze and gave me a sly wink. "I was wondering when you were going to ask me."

"Does David know yet?"

"Shhh, I kinda like the lovemaking routine we set up."

I snickered. "So when were you planning on telling us all?"

Andrea sighed happily. "I found out I was at three months this past week. I think it was just about the time Schooner and Frank were getting married. Sorry little twerp. I didn't want him to steal my thunder. An ordinary pregnant sister is nothing compared to the brave new world of gay marriage. I swear, he has some kind of psychic sense that lets him know when to upstage me."

"Oh Andrea. Nobody could ever upstage you. Do you know how happy I am for you? I love you so much."

Andrea smiled sweetly with the half of her face I could see. "Will you rub some lotion on my shoulders, Chris?"

I stood and found the lotion in her bag, squatted by her chair, and rubbed the lotion into her shoulders and upper back with gentle strokes. Then I put more lotion on her back below the line of her top.

"When we were little and came here," she said, "I used to be asleep on my towel and you'd wake me doing that. I'd be drowsy and sleepy, but I felt so safe because I knew you wouldn't let me get burned. You just let me sleep and never made a big deal of it."

I screwed the cap back onto the bottle of lotion and rubbed the residue on my palms on my shoulders before I lay back down and faced her. "I'd never have let anything happen to you. You were my only little girl."

She smiled and closed her eyes.

"Andrea, I'm sorry if you ever think in hindsight that I did anything to harm you," I said. "Please know I tried my best."

Andrea opened her eyes and lifted her head. "What are you talking about Chris?"

I propped myself on my elbows and looked at her. "At Easter, your father told me you were having trouble getting pregnant and that you figured it was because you'd been on birth control pills since you were 15. He was definitely not pleased with me. He told me the trouble you were having conceiving was partly my fault. I've thought about that a lot since then."

Andrea raised herself onto her elbows, mirroring my position. "He should never have told you that."

"Well, he did. Your father, for some reason, knows you kids are a convenient stick to hit me with these days. Please understand, Andrea—he'll use anything you tell him to strike at me. It's just where we are right now, and we'll probably be here for a while."

"I didn't know you two were as contentious as all that."

"Well, I'll tell you this and then I don't want to talk about your father anymore. I think part of him is very disappointed that I'm not miserable and broke. I don't think he *really* wants to see me that way, believe me. It's just your father had many, many years to get used to us all being dependent on him. A lot of his self-image is invested in that vision of himself as father and protector. Now we're all on our own and doing well. It's got to give him some pause, you know what I mean?"

Andrea nodded. "I think that's a very astute observation, Chris. If you were a colleague, I'd give you four gold stars. As it is, I don't think I've ever told you how much I admire you for handling him and the whole situation the way you have."

I dropped my head and rubbed my eyes, which were growing weary of the sun's sting and the salt breeze. "You know, everyone keeps telling me that. But what else was I going to do, become a complete and total bitch—or worse, fuck up what's left of my life as some sort of revenge? That wouldn't hurt your father. You know that. He's really good at walking away a winner, no matter what situation he gets himself into." I sighed. "I don't want to talk about him anymore. I wish him well, and I wish he'd stay well away from me. Do you feel me, girlfriend?"

Andrea hung her head and rubbed her temples. "He's not happy, Chris. He's gained a lot of weight and he's drinking like a fish."

"It gives me no pleasure to hear that, Andrea. But it's not any of my business anymore."

"Do you really feel that way, Chris?"

"Yes, I do. Your father made his choices and they've not served him well. But that has nothing to do with me. Please, can we talk about something else?"

Andrea giggled. "Okay, let's talk about your boy toy."

"Oh for God's sake Andrea. You can't be serious. You've met the man. There's nothing *boy* about him."

"You're 10 years older than he is—don't forget."

"Thanks for reminding me, bitch."

"I bet he's a beast in bed," she said with a gleam in her eyes.

"Oh, *hell* no. You aren't going to get me to go there. I'll tell you the gory details and you'll go running back to your father with it. He already never misses an opportunity to tell me I'm redneck white trash as it is. His ego is way too fragile to hear how well I'm taken care of in that regard."

"Oh really? I thought we weren't going to talk about Dad anymore."

"We're not. Let me just put it to you this way: You could take 22 years off my age and you'd be just about in the neighborhood of how Steve makes me feel—in bed or out."

"Damn! That good, huh?"

"You have no idea," I said, dropping my voice to a low growl.

"So are you two going to be jetting up to Boston like my little brother and that boyfriend of his?"

"No way. All that's all fine, well, and good for other people, but that's not who we are. Besides, I did that kind of marriage thing already. You should know—you lived it with me." I paused a moment, feeling the conviction creeping into my voice. "I'm enjoying being right where I am with myself and with Steve. We don't need any big pronouncements."

Andrea grew quiet for a while and I laid my head back down. She watched me for a minute and gave me a smile. I returned it and closed my eyes. The sun was making me sleepy, and I was definitely tired. I was too old to be having sex twice in one night, but while I was getting it, I wasn't going to say no. All around us the beach was alive with its familiar Sunday morning sounds: kids shrieking, radios playing, gulls' wheeling cries, and always the march and retreat of the waves. It was a summer lullaby. I wanted to allow it to billow my own thoughts until I fell asleep, happy as a teenager with a date later on, and still heavy and full as a successful matron with kids grown and gone.

"Mom?"

I rarely heard that word come from Andrea. I gave up on sleeping and raised back up on my elbows. "What is it, baby girl?"

"Do you think I'll be a good mother?"

I reached across the sandy space between us and put my hand gently on her warm shoulder. She stared off into the distance, toward the row of cottages on the oceanfront. I decided to try to tease her out of her sudden somber mood. "You had an excellent teacher, as far as I'm concerned."

"Shouldn't I be telling you that?" she replied.

"Andrea, so much of it comes from instinct and pure love. Only a little bit comes from example. You go with your heart first, instinct second, and if you have any other questions, call me. I think you'll be an excellent mother. Don't be afraid." I glanced back over my shoulder and caught sight of David, standing staunchly in the sun and patiently eyeing a nearly invisible filament line. "You have a good man to help you. David is a prize and a treasure."

Andrea looked at me with tears in her eyes. "Do you really think we'll do all right?"

I smiled at her. "Oh baby girl, I think you'll do just fine. So, let's see. If you're at three months, and it's mid July, seventh month of the year, plus six months, that puts you due in mid January, right?"

"Right around there."

"Do they know yet if it's a boy or girl?"

"The sonogram wasn't clear enough. I really don't care. Neither does David. I just want it to be a nice, healthy, skinny baby who'll slide right out like a letter through a mail slot."

I laughed until I choked.

"Well, you can laugh. You got all your children after someone else did all the hurting part. I am definitely not looking forward to all that."

"You're right about how I got my kids," I said. "It's easy to laugh when you don't have to carry them around inside for all that time and then give birth to them. You should talk to your sister-in-law. She'll set your mind at ease."

"Susan? Susan's big as a house and happy as a doodlebug. She'll give birth to a baby horse and be back at work the next day, if I know her."

"Have you talked to her lately?"

"Oh yeah. She's fine and Trey's walking around like the lord of the manor. Have you noticed how patriarchal he's gotten? It's amazing. He does everything but call us into his study to kiss his hand, like some kind of Irish Michael Corleone. I want to slap the shit out of him."

I laughed again; Andrea on a bitch jag could be hilarious if the sharpness of it wasn't aimed at you. "Yes, I've noticed. But Andrea, he's been a tremendous help to me. I have to give him the credit he's due."

Andrea sighed, then snorted softly and shook her head. "My whole family is just a damn trip. My daddy is on his second wife and round of kids. My gay mommy has turned into a reborn beach boy with an Italian stud boyfriend. My big brother is more proper than Boston Brahmin. My baby brother is one of the first people in the country to be in a real, legal gay marriage, and me? I'm just big ol' fat pregnant Andrea, dum-de-dum-de-dum."

"Oh come on girl, give me a break. Name me one person you know whose family isn't as bizarre as ours?"

Andrea stared off into space for a minute and looked back at me with a grin. "How about David Sedaris?"

CHAPTER SEVEN,
FALL

✛

It was as if someone turned a tap, and the stream of traffic and people slowed to a slender drizzle after the colleges and schools started their fall semester. By the Tuesday after Labor Day, they had dwindled to mere drops. From my office window, I could look across the causeway to the marina beyond and lose count of the long intervals between the cars on the road. What was most striking was the noise: There wasn't any. Quiet came down over the island once more and it seemed to sigh with relief from the strain it had borne under the crowds all summer. I sighed along with it.

Schooner and Frank were among the first to leave. Frank got the job with the parks department in Mount Pleasant. No doubt, having a hometown advantage swung the decision in his favor. Schooner didn't seem at all disappointed. He followed Frank to South Carolina with every bit of optimism in the world that he'd find a job and that until he did, he and Frank could live off Frank's $23,000-a-year salary. I did and said nothing to dampen his enthusiasm. Love alone was riches enough at that age, and they had plenty of that between them. I kissed my baby good-bye and wished him well, knowing everybody had to start somewhere. I was genuinely happy he was starting his adult life with Frank.

From Cathy's office, I heard Carlos wake and start to cry. She'd given birth to a handsome little baby boy on the 10th of September and was back in the office with him on the 13th. I looked at the steady light of her extension on my phone. She was on a call, and Tony had a client in his office. I put the phones on hold and walked down the hall to pick the little fellow up.

Cathy looked at me gratefully when I came through the door. Little Carlos was kicking and swinging his arms with a tiny baby's scrunched-up face. I stooped to retrieve Cathy's diaper bag, then picked up the baby and carried him into my area to see if he needed changing. I ran my finger down the inside of the front of his diaper and gave him a good sniff. He was wet but (thankfully) he wasn't stinky.

I cooed at him, laid him gently on the table next to the copier, and changed him efficiently without any fuss. Between the disposable diapers and the handy pop-up wipes, it was an easy business. Clean and dry and held close against my shoulder, the baby slowly traded crying for soft whimpers and mewing. He was hungry, but there wasn't anything I could do about that. Still, he felt good in my arms, all clean-smelling and black-haired. He was a little doll baby, and it had been a long time since I'd held a baby. I just kept him and rocked him while his mama finished her call.

"You know you don't have to do that, don't you Chris?" Cathy asked as she came in and took Carlos. "Don't get me wrong—I think you're an absolute angel for doing it—but you don't have to. We don't pay you enough to be a nanny."

"It's no big deal, Cathy. I've had a lot of practice, but it was awhile ago. It's good to be around a baby again, you know?"

Cathy settled into the spare seat in my area and unbuttoned her blouse. She drew a small soft blanket over the baby's head, covering him and her, preserving her modesty. With one hand under the blanket she helped him find her breast. It had taken some getting used to, but her breast feeding now was so matter-of-fact I hardly noticed anymore. "When is your daughter-in-law due?" she asked.

"Any day now. Trey tells me she's ready to go. The doctor says it's up to the baby at this point. I could get a call any minute."

Cathy nodded. "You know, if you want to head up there when he calls, just take off. This one is your first. Tony and I understand completely."

I remembered to take the phones off hold and quickly checked for any messages. Luckily, there weren't any. I gave Cathy a smile. "No, hon. I'm not going to go rushing up to Raleigh when that baby comes. Susan will need her mother a lot worse right then than she'll need me. I'll wait until the weekend after the baby comes and head up then. That'll give Susan and the baby time to get adjusted without another person breathing germs all over them."

Cathy stood and gave me a tired smile. "You're one of the best, most empathetic people I know Chris. Your daughter-in-law is very lucky to have you. I thought Tony's mother was going to take this one home with her in her purse. Sheesh, a *male* child. You'd have thought I was the infanta of Spain bringing the royal heir into the world."

I laughed. "There's an Irish version of that as well. Susan's is a boy. Trey e-mailed me a picture of his sonogram with a big red arrow pointing at the little thing's package."

"Have they decided on a name?"

I sighed. "My ex-bastard told me they were going to name it and call it Chris whether or not it was a boy or girl, but I don't know if he was just trying to be malicious in telling me or if that's really the truth of it. They haven't said and I won't ask. It's their decision, not mine."

Cathy just shook her head. "Have you talked to the ex lately? How's he dealing with becoming a grandfather?"

"I wouldn't know; we don't talk. His latest child is just now a toddler. I can't believe he'd let a grandchild affect him one way or another, other than to stoke his rather large ego."

"Won't you see him when you go up to see the new baby?"

"Oh God, I hope not. I'll take Steve with me, and that should scare him off."

"So, you think Steve will go with you?"

"Honestly, I doubt it. He's amused by my kids, but he's not a family kind of guy. He was an only child. Sometimes I think he wonders what all the fuss is about."

Cathy nodded and peeked under the blanket covering the baby and her breast. "He's asleep," she whispered. With that, she turned and went back into her office. And I got back to work.

When I woke up, the television was still on. Steve had brought one of his over from his house and installed it in my bedroom the night before. He was still in the same tense position he was sitting in when I went to sleep. The Weather Channel was showing the likely strike zones, and we were just inside the northernmost edge of the northernmost boundary of the red zone. Hurricane Joan was becoming a real threat after days of speculation and growing concern. Right then she was off the northern coast of South Carolina— a Category 3—and gaining strength as she rode north on the gulf stream.

I sat up and looked at the clock by my bed. It was nearly 4:30 in the morning. I wondered if Steve had done more than nap all night long under the soothing sounds of The Weather Channel expert's weary conjectures. "Are you ready for some coffee, Steve?" I asked.

He put his arm over my shoulder and kissed the side of my head distractedly. "You should go back to sleep," he said.

Nuala stirred at the foot of the bed, got up and stretched happily, and then came to lick my face. She had to climb over Steve to reach me.

"Get down, Nuala. Damn. Chris, why in the hell did we ever let this dog get used to sleeping on the bed?"

I got up and Nuala joined me. "C'mon girl, let's go make Steve some coffee."

"I'm sorry, Chris. I don't mean to be an asshole about the dog, okay?"

I walked around the bed and Nuala dashed past me, out the door, and down the hall. "I'll start the coffee and take her out for a minute. I'll bring you in some coffee when it's done, okay?"

Steve looked away from the television and gave me an appreciative look. "Did I ever tell you I like seeing you in my drawers first thing in the morning?"

I laughed. "Can't be as much as I like seeing you out of them."

Steve shook his head and threw back the covers from around his waist. He still wore the jeans he'd put on after his shower the night before. Nodding toward the TV, he said, "This one's got me worried, Chris. Come get me when the coffee's done. We need to have a talk about what we're going to do if this big bitch starts to turn."

I gave him a smile and took off down the hall after Nuala.

She was patient while I got the coffee started, but the minute I was done, she showed me her leash hanging by the kitchen door and whined. I took it down and clicked it onto her collar, then we took off out the door and down the stairs to the street.

So early in the morning, the stars were still out and full over my head. The sky was completely clear, and a slight onshore breeze stirred the trees and prompted the last soft chirring of the summer cicadas. It was a beautiful warm morning, and I followed behind Nuala as she sniffed and squatted happily.

I knew I should be more concerned about the storm, but I was actually sort of elated. This was my first hurricane—at least the first one I'd tracked with the real measure of concern a local knew. The year before I'd given up on the hype surrounding the arrival of Hurricane Isabel. Knowing the center of its eye was coming ashore at Cape Lookout was driving me crazy. My house was approaching the final stages of construction, and I knew if it were destroyed, I'd be in a world of hurt. I waited with shredded nerves until I got a call from my contractor letting me know all I'd lost was a few shingles. If Isabel had tracked in just a few ticks south, it could have been a whole different story.

Only a few years before, Hurricane Bertha had wreaked havoc on Emerald Isle. Between the high winds and micro tornadoes, the western end of Bogue Banks had caught hell as the storm came ashore near Wilmington. A few weeks after that, Floyd came in and flooded out all of eastern North Carolina, creating a disaster of epic proportions. Hurricanes weren't anything to feel elated over. But I couldn't deny the adrenaline rush and move with the wave of anxiety that played on TV 24 hours a day.

I stood and enjoyed the easy breeze on my face. It seemed nearly impossible to believe it could turn wide, vast, and furious, coming in anger to destroy things and places I knew and loved. Nuala nudged me with her nose. It was time for us to get back to the house, but I wanted to see the beach. I started up the street to my neighbor's house on the ocean front. It turned out they had identified the boys who vandalized my house. I stopped by and thanked them profusely. They'd waved off my thanks, telling me neighbors had to look out for each other. I made a mental note to find their phone number and ask if there was anything I could do to help secure their house for the coming storm.

Walking with Nuala up the rise of a dune, I looked out over the dark beach and sea. The moon had ridden at her highest and had retreated toward the end of the island. She was not quite full, but she was growing, which would make a great deal of difference with tides and storm surge when Joan came to call.

I listened to the sea. There was only a soft lap on the shore and the sound of distant waves farther out, all seeming to be calling to each other, spreading secrets and hints of what was coming that only their brothers down south and farther out knew for sure. I turned Nuala around gently, and we headed home.

Steve came into the kitchen while I was putting Nuala's food in her bowl. He watched me while I set her bowl down and as I made our coffee. He rubbed his chin and I heard the soft scrape of his beard in his fingers. When I handed him his mug he said, "Let's go on outside." Once we were there, he settled into an Adirondack chair and looked up at the sky before taking a sip of his coffee. He leaned forward and held the mug between his hands.

"Chris, I want you to go on up to Trey's and Susan's and meet the baby like you planned. I got a lot to do, and there's not a lot of it you can help me with. If this thing does like Isabel, I'll need every spare minute to get my place secure, triple-anchor my boat out in the sound, and hunker down. I'll help you get this place locked up today. After that, I want you to take off."

The coffee warmed my hands, and I held it there for a minute before I said anything. Nuala wandered out onto the deck and panted with her lips pulled back like she was grinning. Steve reached over and rubbed her neck behind her ears. She stretched happily and settled down near his feet. "What will you do with the dogs?" I asked.

"If it looks like it'll hit around here, I'll take Nuala and my dogs to Heath's. He knows to expect them—I've already talked to him. They'll be safer there than either here or my house. Heath's place is like a bunker."

I lit a cigarette and offered one to Steve. He took it and my lighter, then looked at me expectantly. "Well, what have you got to say?"

"I'm not leaving. I'm going to stay here with you."

"No hell, you ain't."

"Yes hell, I am. If I go up there it may be days before I can get back. I'm not going to do it. I'm staying my damn ass right here."

"Chris, act like you've got some sense. All those days you might be stuck in Raleigh, you'd be stuck here with no air-conditioning, no power, no nothing."

"I've got a gas range and extra ice and water already stored up.

The house has stormproofed, impact-resistant windows and doors, it's 10 feet above grade, and it's far enough back from the ocean that I'm not worried about storm surge."

"Chris don't be stupid. You might have all that figured out, but there ain't no house nowhere that can stand up to them baby tornadoes."

I sat my coffee mug on the arm of my chair and touched the baht chain around my neck while Steve got his cigarette lit. The gold was cooler than my skin in the early predawn damp outside. The coffee had warmed me, but my bare chest and shoulders were cool in the breeze. I shivered slightly. Steve gave me a squint-eyed look through his cigarette smoke. I tossed what was left of my cigarette off the deck onto the driveway below and looked him in the eye. "I'm not leaving you. It's that plain and simple. You better get used to the idea right now."

"You're a stubborn-ass fool. This ain't going to be no play party if it hits. Don't think it's going to be all dramatic and lovey-dovey. It ain't going to be nothing but screaming wind and scratchy weather radio. I'm going to be mean as a snake until it's over and I know all my shit is safe and sound. You're just going to be something else I have to worry about."

"Well, start worrying. Now, where do you want to stay, here or your house?"

"I can see my boat from my place and my house has ridden out a lot more storms than this one."

"Okay, fine. You just tell me what I have to do to help so I don't have to ask. Other than that, I'll stay out of your way."

"I ought to kick your little narrow ass across the bridge and onto Highway 70 heading west, you know that?"

"Oh shut up, Steve. Now tell me what you want me to do."

Steve drained his coffee mug, sighed, and stood up. "Well, the first thing I want you to do is make me some more coffee, then I want you to find me a pencil and some paper. I'm already pissed at you and I don't want to have to tell you things twice."

I stood as well and reached for his mug. He held it up and away from my grasp to tease me and laughed. "So Little Bit wants to be a O'er Banker. Can't even reach up to get my coffee cup and he's going to take on a hurricane."

I refused to jump for the cup or fall for the baiting. I'd made my mind up, period.

The phone rang as I was bringing the last chair off the deck and into the house. I wove my way through the bulky deck furniture that was never meant to be inside and caught the phone on its third ring.

"Hi Mom, isn't it high time you were heading out to Trey and Susan's?"

"Oh hello, Schooner. Are you and Frank ready in case it swings in at you?"

"We're going to be fine. We'll get a lot of rain, but no big deal. When was the last time you turned on the television?"

"I don't think the damn thing's been off for two days. I've been busy getting the house secure, why?"

"Damn, Mom. Get out of there. The thing has turned. You're dead in the middle of the strike zone."

"Schooner, it can wobble or turn again anytime it wants to. I'm getting sick and tired of panicking every time it sneezes out there."

"Mom, look, I know you're all about the beach now, but you need to get your ass in gear. I'm surprised Steve hasn't packed you off already. What is he thinking?"

"Schooner, settle down. Steve wanted me to leave hours ago, but I've made the decision to stay. If I go to Raleigh, it could take me days to get back, and I'm not going to sit up in Raleigh when my whole life's down here. Now, I'm not going to take any shit about it. Got that?"

I was met with dead silence on the other end of the phone. "Schooner?"

"Let me talk to Steve," he said.

"Schooner, Steve's not here, he's got a thousand things to do to get his own act together. I'm about to head over to his place to get all the dogs and take them to board at Heath's. They'll be safer there, and I don't want to ride this thing out with a bunch of whining dogs."

"There's a mandatory evacuation in effect, Mom."

"Yeah, yeah, yeah. I'll be with Steve, I'll be just fine."

"You two don't intend to stay at his place do you? He's not 50 feet off the water!"

"Schooner, his house has been there for over 60 years and it's not gone yet. Now look, I've got to go. Will you do me a favor and call your brother and sister for me?"

"Oh no, you're not putting that on me. Trey will have a fit and Andrea will freak out."

"That's exactly why I want you to call them. I've got enough to do without dealing with all that. Tell them I'll call them from my cell phone as soon as this thing is over and gone. Okay? Now tell me you love me and have a good hurricane. I got to go."

"Chris, I'll kill you the next time I see you for doing this to me."

"Hush baby, I'll be fine."

"You'll call me first?"

"Absolutely."

"I love you, you crazy-ass fool."

"I love you too, baby. You and Frank look out for each other. Bye."

I hung up the phone and immediately called the voice mail service to change my greeting. I punched in the right sequence of numbers and waited for the beep. Then I said: *Hello, this is Chris Thayer. It is 10:42 on Saturday morning. I'll be staying on the island for the hurricane. I'll be with Steve Willis in Salter Path. Please leave a message. I will return your call as soon as possible after the storm passes. Thanks and have a good day.*

I pressed the number for REPLAY GREETING. Satisfied that I sounded no-nonsense and practical, I hit the code for "save" and then APPLY RESPONSE. "That," I said aloud, "is that." The second I replaced the receiver in its cradle, the phone rang. I ignored it and went to the kitchen to get plastic garbage bags to securely wrap all my electronic stuff, just in case the water got in.

After I'd unplugged and double-bagged my computer components, my CD player, and all my other small appliances, I did the same with all my artwork and put it in the closet closest to the middle of the house. Also in that central closet were all my paper treasures—family photos and practical things like insurance policies, tax records, and bank stuff. All sealed in sturdy, waterproof plastic tubs. I looked around the house and sighed. I'd done all I could, and after all, they were just things. I considered how many times I might have to do this—again, and again, and again—as the years rolled along.

I had packed a few things in an L.L. Bean bag—just a change of clothes, a carton of cigarettes, and some toiletries. At the last moment I threw in a copy of a book I'd been meaning to get to. I hoped it would distract me and keep me from driving Steve crazy. That done, I let Nuala out of her kennel. She was whiney and hyper. Dogs and other animals knew way before humans that something awesome was impending. I nudged her toward the door and turned off the circuit breaker as I left. From here on out, the house was in God's hands, just like the rest of us left here on the island.

After I picked up the rest of the dogs at Steve's, I drove to Heath's with all five of them whimpering, panting and milling around the back of my Expedition. Together they were so heavy, they rocked the damn thing as I drove down the island. The wind began to pick up, as I herded them inside. For the first time, the paper work I always had to sign absolving the veterinary practice and kennel from responsibility in the event of an accident beyond their reasonable control gave me pause.

"Makes you think this time doesn't it," Heath said.

"Yeah, well...whatever." I signed the forms and pushed them across the counter to Heath. He tucked them all, including Nuala's, in a folder with Steve's name on it.

"Will they be okay? I mean, do they freak out?" I asked.

Heath gave me a smile and nodded his head. "Just a little. They howl some until it gets here, then they settle together like puppies in a pile to ride it out. I think they're actually better off here than with you."

"Why? I mean, Steve told me they were safer here, but—"

"Here they don't have to feel responsible for you, Chris. They're free to worry about themselves and each other. They'll be fine, I promise."

I nodded and turned to leave.

"Let me walk you out," Heath said. Once we were outside, he looked up at the sky and pointed: "Look."

Overhead, ragged clouds raced across the sky. They were moving faster than I'd ever seen clouds move. They looked like the tattered souls that flew over Dickens's London in the old movies of *A Christmas Carol*. Away to the south and east, the sky was growing darker and more ominous.

"It's going to be bad, isn't it?" I said.

Heath laughed. "Well, I heard Jim Cantore from The Weather Channel is setting up at the Holiday Inn. That can't be good news."

"Where will you be staying?"

"Here, with your dogs."

"Damn, Heath. I know how dedicated you are, but shouldn't you be at your place?"

"It's safer here than at my house. I rode out Bertha at my place. I won't do that again. Are you staying with Steve?"

"Yes. He says he's ridden out every storm since he was 12 in that house. He won't stay anywhere else."

Heath nodded. "You'll be fine. You might get your feet wet, but you'll be okay there." He looked up at the sky again and I followed his gaze into the wind. There were flashes of lightning far in the distance. "I'm very happy for you two. I told you at Christmas you'd be perfect for each other."

A huge gust of wind made the live oaks sway and sigh. With their limbs raised into their leafy tops, they looked like old women tossing their hair in wails. "What I recall you saying was, I needed to see a man about a dog," I replied.

"Well, that's what you did, isn't it? For what it's worth, Chris, I miss our breakfasts at the pier."

"Me too. You were a good friend to me when I first came down. You were a lifesaver, Heath. I thank you for sending me to see that man about the dog."

He gave me a wan smile. "You know what the young gay kids here call me?"

"No, I hope it's not unkind."

"No, it's funny. They call me the Welcome Wagon. Seems like I'm always the first one to get all the newcomers and the guys that are just coming out. Once I'm done with them, then I steer 'em toward somebody who'll take them off my hands."

"I don't think that's funny. I think it's mean."

Heath laughed. "It's only mean if it's not true. And I really rather enjoy it. I get to bust a lot of cherry that way. And I like the variety."

"You're a class act, Heath," I said with a smile.

He opened the driver's door to my SUV and waited for me to

get inside. "You take care of Steve. Me and your dogs will be waiting for you right here once Joan gets done with us."

I stepped into the truck and turned to face him. "Could you call and tell him I'm on the way back to my place? He's picking me up there."

"Sure," he said. "Leaving your car under your own house is smart. There's a lot less chance water will get in it there."

"You're scaring me now."

"You'd be a fool if you weren't scared. Just do what Steve tells you to and you'll be fine. Now get going. If I call right now, he'll probably get there ahead of you."

On the way home, the first strong rain band hit. For about two miles I had to slow to a crawl to keep from getting blown off the road or running off it blind. The rain passed quickly, but the wind was really picking up by the time I made it up my drive and under my house. I had just gotten out of the car when Steve drove up. He surprised me by turning off his truck's engine and getting out. He peeled off his shirt and stood grinning in the hard spatter of intermittent raindrops. "Pull your shirt off and c'mon!"

"Where are we going?"

"We're going to go walk on the beach. We might make it onto one of the TV stations. You know how they love to show the crazy rednecks who are out in the storm on television. Well, Little Bit, here's your chance."

"Why do I need to take my shirt off," I hollered back over a gust of wind.

"You want to walk around in a wet shirt, leave it on. Now let's go. There's a TV crew just up the beach. If it's Jim Cantore, I'm gonna kiss him right on his big bald head."

Laughing, I pulled my shirt over my head and I tossed it in Steve's truck. We took off down the street and over the dune beside my neighbor's place. When we crested the rise, a big blast of wind nearly knocked me off my feet. Steve reached back in time to catch me by my wrist and pull me forward and on down the ocean side of the dune.

"Damn, Steve, it's like getting sandblasted," I yelled as he let me go and trotted toward the water and dirty brown bits of sea foam being blown up the beach.

"Get down here near the water, it's not so bad here," Steve hollered.

He turned and faced into the wind with a big grin on his face. He whooped as a rush of shore break hit us and raced up our legs as I reached him. He took off and I followed him as best I could.

The ocean wasn't organized. The waves stacked on top of each other as if they were trying to beat each other down in their rush to run ahead of the wind. Between the blowing saltwater and rain, we were soaked within minutes. Steve pointed up ahead, and sure enough, there was a news reporter valiantly holding onto the railing of a set of steps leading down from the dune onto the beach. His cameraman crouched on the steps slightly above him, trying his best to hold his camera steady.

Steve looked at me and grinned. He took off in a trot, and I trotted along with him, both of us laughing. As we neared the camera crew, I watched the lens shift and track us in its sights. The reporter yelled something unintelligible and motioned us toward him.

"You wanna be on TV?" he yelled.

"Sure dude!" Steve yelled back. "C'mon Chris."

Pummeled by wind gusts, we made our way up the beach and joined the announcer at the foot of the steps.

"Get them to give us a video release," the cameraman said.

"I'm going to ask you to give me your full names and addresses on tape," the reporter said. "Then I'm going to ask you if you give your permission for CNN to use your image for broadcast, okay?"

"You're not going to put that part on television are you?" Steve demanded.

"No way—we just need it for legal if you get on the broadcast."

"Okay. Now?"

"Roll it, Eddie."

The reporter stuck his microphone at Steve and me in turn, and we recited our names and addresses and gave our permission.

"Okay! Now we're going for a take. Eddie?"

"Got it framed, give me a count."

"Five, four, three, two, one... As Hurricane Joan batters the southern coast of North Carolina on her way to make landfall near Ocracoke Island, we're here with Bogue Banks residents Steve and

Chris. Tell me, guys—do you really feel like you should be out on the beach just now with a Category 2 hurricane bearing down over your shoulders?"

"Well sir, it's like this," Steve said. "We've got everything tied down and locked up that can be, so we thought we'd get out for a minute before it got really bad. Beautiful storm, huh?"

"This is the first we've heard it was going in at Ocracoke and had gone down to a 2," I offered.

"You sound disappointed, Chris," the reporter said.

"Well, hell. You guys have had us hyped up for three days."

Steve laughed.

"What about you, Steve?"

"I'm just happy we're going to be on the weaker side of the storm, but I'm thinking about all the folks out on Ocracoke and up on the Northern Banks."

"Yeah, me too. I'm glad it's not going to be any worse than it is for all of us," I said.

"There you have it, folks; words of relief and concern from residents of North Carolina's southern Outer Banks. You guys get someplace safe okay? The worst part of this Hurricane Joan is still yet to come."

"Take it easy," Steve yelled over the wind. I just grinned like a fool.

"And cut. Good stuff, guys."

"How long before we're on CNN?" Steve asked.

"With the feed and the delay, you'll be on within 20 minutes if they decide to use you."

"C'mon, let's get going," Steve said to me.

We fought our way back up the beach and over the dune to my house once more. When Steve was satisfied everything there was as secure as it was going to get, we beat a rain band into the truck. Steve put it in gear and we took off to his house.

"Get us one of them beers out of the cooler under your feet," he said.

It was awkward getting my legs out of the way to lift the lid, but when I finally opened the cooler, I whistled. There must have been two 12-packs crammed in ice there. I opened a bottle of Corona and handed it to Steve and opened one for myself. He gave me a grin and wiped his mouth with the back of his hand.

"We can relax a little bit now knowing the eye's going in over Ocracoke or thereabouts. It's gone down to a Category 2 didn't the guy say?"

"Yeah, you wild ass," I said.

Steve laughed. "That's the best news I've had in three days."

"Is it still going to get worse?"

"Oh yeah, Little Bit. It'll get worse, but at least the worst part ain't coming in over the top of us. Do you think we'll make it on TV?"

By the time we got to Steve's the sound had already spilled into his yard and under his house. The water was ankle-deep and rising between the high ground Steve left his truck on and his front steps. When we got in the house, he headed straight for the television and selected CNN from the remote.

For the next little while, Steve drank beer and paced between the living room—where the television was on—and the back of the house—where he could watch his boat riding out the storm in the deeper water of the sound. I was in charge of monitoring the broadcast.

Steve was on his fourth beer and I was on my second when I hit the mute button on a set of commercials I'd seen about a thousand times, or so it seemed. I followed them, reciting the dialogue in my head, when the scene shifted to two guys getting blown around on a beach. They were laughing. "Oh shit! Steve! Get in here!" I un-hit the mute just as Steve stomped into the living room. Wordlessly we watched ourselves, just as dumb and happy as hell on a network that broadcast by satellite all over the world.

Steve whooped loud in the small room. "I did it! I finally did it! I finally got me on hurricane TV, Chris!" He was genuinely elated and as manic as going nearly two days without sleep could make him. Immediately his phone started to ring.

"Who do you want to bet that is?" he asked.

"Probably one of my kids."

Steve stomped over to the phone and picked it up, half drunk and dead tired. "Hello? Oh, yeah—that was us! No, it ain't all that bad, I'm looking after him... Okay, hold on, he's sitting right here, by the way, congratulations on that baby, Trey... Cool! I'll get him for you..."

Steve walked over, beaming, to hand me the phone.

I laughed out loud at his kidlike excitement and took the phone, "Hey son! How's the baby?"

"The baby is fine," Trey said, "or was until Susan screamed when you came on CNN. Chris, please tell me you aren't drunk."

"No, baby. I'm not drunk, just kinda tired. I've been up since 4:30 getting everything—"

"Chris, do you realize what you're doing to my nerves?"

"Oh Trey, settle down. I'm perfectly all right."

"Well, at least you're not caught on the highway in this mess. You know something Chris? Next time, if you want us to know you're all right you don't need to get on CNN. Just use the phone, okay?"

"I promise."

"You're having the time of your life, aren't you?"

I looked around the tiny living room and snuggled deeper into the overstuffed cushions of Steve's Pottery Barn sofa when a hard slap of wind and rain hit the window behind me. I had a beer beside me on the table and Steve gazing at me with a happy grin on his face. "Yes, Trey. I am."

"Dad called," he said after a pause.

"And?"

"He was livid. I think he's totally jealous, but he'd never say so. He just went off on how he resented financing your second childhood."

"So, he's watching CNN too, huh?"

"Oh no, he caught you on The Weather Channel."

"Hey Steve! We're on The Weather Channel too!" I said and laughed.

"Enjoy your hurricane, Chris. Call me when it's over, okay?"

"Sure thing, babe. My love to Susan and my grandson."

"Please get on up here as soon as you can, we're dying to see you."

"I will. Bye."

When I stood to carry Steve's cordless receiver back to its cradle, a sound like a bomb going off came from not too far away. Everything in the house went quiet and still.

"There went the power!" Steve yelled from the back porch. I walked through the kitchen and onto the back porch to stand beside him at the windows overlooking the sound. The view was a near uniform gray—with the water distinguishable from the driving rain only by its darker color and motion. Steve's boat, the Lina G, was riding along with the waves, still held fast by three separate anchors.

"Steve, I've never asked you, but why is the boat named the Lina G?"

"For my mother, Angelina Gagliardo." He looked out at her with pride. "She's doing all right out there."

"Why did you anchor her out in the sound?"

Steve never took his eyes off the boat. "So she wouldn't get beat up against the dock. If she breaks a line rope, or drags anchor, there's nothing for her to bash up on. Even out that far, the water's not real deep. It's only up to my chest where I put her." He sighed and looked down at me. "You look beat."

"You look worse," I said. "I don't think you've slept in two days."

The wind pushed so hard against the house that it creaked and moaned. Steve looked around and slapped the wall below the window. "Hold on, old girl. Keep your roof on." With that, he walked into the kitchen. All his manic elation at being on television had vanished. I heard the battery-operated radio come alive with the familiar voice of the announcer from the Morehead City NOAA station. The monotonous litany of latitudes and longitudes began, along with the marine warnings. Only a few miles south of Cape Lookout, the eye was passing us now without even coming ashore.

I walked into the living room to find Steve sitting on the end of the sofa, looking out the living room windows that gave a view of the front yard. I willed myself not to look out to see how deep the water had gotten. As if he were reading my mind, Steve said, "Once the eye passes, it'll be blowing the water away from us to the north. What's up in the yard now is what was pushed ahead of the storm. Don't worry—it won't get in the house."

I sat next to him on the sofa, and he patted his lap. Gratefully, I swung around to stretch out on the sofa and laid my head there. He tucked a hand possessively just inside the waistband of my shorts under my navel, looked down at me, and smoothed back my hair with the other hand. "You know, I think this is the first time my head has been between your legs without my having an ulterior motive," I said.

Steve rubbed his eyes and leaned his head back. "I'm so goddamn tired, I bet you couldn't get a rise in these Levi's for love or money."

"Can you sleep a little now that the worst is going by?"

Steve stroked my hair once more, then let his arm dangle down the side of the sofa. "Naw, but you can if you want. It's been a long day for you Little Bit. Go on and rest your eyes awhile."

From this angle Steve looked his age, if not older, from the fatigue. He had a two-day beard and the muscled weight of him seemed to droop with weariness. "I hope I wasn't in your way, Steve."

"No way. You did good. Besides, who else would go out on the beach with me in a hurricane to be on TV?"

"That was crazy, you know. But it was a hell of a lot of fun. You've been so dead serious the past couple of days, I had no idea you'd want to run into the teeth of it like that."

"I wouldn't have done it without you," he said. "You make me feel like a kid, Chris. Oh man! We've only just started having fun, you and me. I can promise you that."

"I love you Steve Willis."

"Not as much as I love you."

That said, I let him rest and keep watch. We listened to the wind howl and the old house moan. I felt like I was exactly where I needed to be.

The wind lay to near calm by twilight. Steve and I walked out to the dock under a sky full of stars that were struggling to show themselves over the remaining clouds racing overhead. Out in the sound, the Lina G rode calmly on the waves remaining in the sound. Near the dock, pieces of wood, shingles, and trash bumped up against the pilings; trash brought in from anywhere and nowhere, littering the water, souvenirs of the storm.

We retraced our steps along the pier, and Steve tensely checked out the sound side of his house. It looked fine. Wordlessly I followed him down the stairs from the back deck into the shin-high water running back to the sound. As we walked around the house, I could see his tense body loosen with relief. All that seemed to be wrong were some missing shingles on the many-times-patched roof.

"Looks okay, Little Bit. But I have to tell you, I could kill for a hot cup of coffee, a hot shower, and a shave."

"The power could be back on at my house. Even if it isn't, I can still make hot coffee. That's why I have a gas stove and hot water heater. If you want, we can go back over there for the night."

"You know, I'm getting tired of going back and forth between two houses, but for once, I'm glad we have your house to go to. Let's get your stuff and me something clean to change into and we'll head on over there."

I didn't know Steve was growing weary of our living between two houses—he'd never mentioned it before. I didn't have a clue about the man sometimes, but this wasn't the time to bring that subject up. We were both dead tired, and I knew our weariness wouldn't bring good discussion, just an argument. I was dead on my feet, more from tension than anything else. I didn't say anything, I just followed Steve into the house to collect my stuff.

We drove to my house without a word. It was dark once we got there, but there was enough light from the moon and the streetlight to see the house was mainly fine. Like Steve, I had lost a few shingles, but other than that, everything looked great. We climbed the stairs with leaden legs. Steve used his key to let us in and flicked the switch nearest the door, only to be rewarded with a responding darkness.

"Your streetlight's on," he said. "You ought to have power. What the hell?"

I pushed past him and headed for the breaker box. "I switched off the main circuit breaker before I left. Hold on."

"Why the hell did you do that?"

"It's a habit from living in an old house in Raleigh. Anytime we had a bad storm, I switched it off so when the power came back on it wouldn't overload the system. I heard somewhere that was a good idea." I found the main breaker and pushed it. Immediately we were welcomed by the hum of the house's white noise. The switch Steve had turned on flickered to life down the hall.

"Chris, that's the goddamnedest thing I ever heard." He walked toward me down the hall. "Start us some coffee, will you? And I could eat something, if you got anything easy."

"How about grilled cheese sandwiches and tomato soup?"

"By tomato soup, do you mean that canned bisque stuff? The kind you doctor up with...what is it? Wine? I could eat the hell out of that."

"It's sherry. I put sherry in the tomato bisque. If that's what you want, I can have it done in no time."

Steve sighed with happiness. "If you can get it done so quick, why don't you take your shower with me?"

I took him by the hand and led him to my bathroom. We stripped in silence and, running the water, I found it was still plenty hot. By instinct, we knew what we needed from each other was more tender ministration than sex. I lathered his chest and lingered over the slick heaviness of his bulky genitals, rewarded more by a friendly fullness than by stiffening demand. I washed him like a small child—even shampooing and conditioning his hair—before I turned his big body to be rinsed in the hot water. Clumsily but lovingly, he responded in kind.

Steaming in the rush of air-conditioned air from the bathroom's vents, we toweled off and I left him to shave nearly three days' worth of beard. I slipped on a loose, clean pair of his boxers that I retrieved from the dresser drawer that had become his by squatter's rights. I briefly recalled him saying he was tired of living between two houses; it was a frustration I hadn't seen coming. I filed it away for pondering later and went into the kitchen to make our supper and call my kids to let them know we were fine.

I didn't recognize the man standing on my deck. He looked to be in his early 60s, grizzled white and sweating in his gray long-sleeved working man's shirt, slacks, and wet, heavy boots. But I could smell smoke coming of him as he stood outside the kitchen door and asked for Steve. "Please tell him his Uncle Buddy needs to see him bad."

"Won't you come in? There's coffee." I stuck out my hand, feeling self-conscious and insubstantial standing before this genuine example of a Salter Path fisherman. "My name's Chris Thayer."

The man hesitantly took my hand and gave it a shake. "Mr. Thayer, I hate to come in, I've—"

"Chris, who the hell is it?" Steve yelled from the back of the house.

"Please call me Chris, and come on in. Please."

Steve's Uncle Buddy wiped his feet on a nonexisting mat, pulled off his cap, and stepped inside the door. He paused and looked around, and I couldn't tell what his eyes registered. They only swept the house, taking in all they could see.

I pulled a chair away from the dining room table and motioned for him to sit. He looked at the chair as if it might not hold him, but he sank into it easily and sighed as it accepted and held his weight.

Steve walked into the great room barefoot and dressed only in a pair of jeans. He came to the table and leaned across to reach for his uncle's hand. "Uncle Buddy, it's good to see you. You've met Chris?"

"Yeah, I did." He looked at me and smiled shyly. "Chris, I'll take a cup of that coffee, black, please, sir." He looked at Steve and his voice grew gentle. "Son, you better sit down. I've got some bad news for you."

Steve looked at his uncle anxiously and took a seat across the table from him. I hesitated and caught Steve's eyes before they went back to his uncle's face. "What is it? Nothing's wrong with my Aunt Peg, is there?"

Uncle Buddy spared me a glance. "No, son. Your Aunt Peg's fine. Your boat's right where you left it." I walked into the kitchen and pulled down three coffee mugs, filling one first with black coffee, then making Steve's the way he liked it, and carried them back to the table, sitting Uncle Buddy's before him first.

"Thank you," he said before he blew across the mug's rim and took a sip.

Steve ignored his. "Well, what is it then?" he asked.

"Son, there ain't no easy way to tell this, but it's your house. We managed to save it as best we could, but she's burned out over your mama and daddy's bedroom and all through the attic. Water damage is pretty bad inside. I'm so sorry."

The blood drained from Steve's face and he sat back in his chair. "What? How? When we left last night about dark, everything was just fine. Did somebody try to burn my house down? Who would do that? Who do I have to kill, Uncle Buddy?"

"Settle down, boy. Ain't nobody tried to burn your house down. Best the fire department can figure is the electrical feed outside your mama and daddy's bedroom window got damaged in the wind. When the power came back on about 4 A.M., it started arcing and tore off through the wiring in the attic. Your cousin Eddie saw the smoke and called the volunteer fire department, but we had a hell of a time getting a crew together so quick after the storm. The wind took out our radio tower, but they patched us through to the county's system. All of us got there as quick as we could, and we managed to save the deck and most of the house. But, son, you can't live there. It's that messed up."

Steve slammed his hand down on the table and stood up to stalk into the living room. "I gotta get over there. I got to see what I got left."

"I'll wait for you, Steve. I'll carry you over there," his Uncle Buddy said sympathetically. Then he drained his coffee mug.

Steve looked at me and raised a finger to point. "If I had been home, if I hadn't been over here, I might've done something. Oh shit!"

Uncle Buddy pushed back from the table and stood heavily. Commandingly he said, "That's enough of that, boy. If you'd have been home, I'd be waiting on a coroner right now, and that's the God's honest truth. You'd have been dead from the smoke before you even woke up. The way I see it, you owe your friend here your life. Now go get some clothes on and come on. You've heard the worst of it—you might as well let me take you on over."

Steve rubbed his face and nodded. He gave me an apologetic look and headed dejectedly toward the bedroom.

"Chris, could I trouble you for some more of that coffee?" Uncle Buddy said.

"Yes, sir." I said. I took his mug from his extended hand and walked back to the kitchen. I realized the man knew I'd been with Steve throughout the storm, and he knew exactly where to come to find him, to bring his bad news. He clearly carried the authority of the head of the family. Steve hadn't even protested when the man told him what to do or how to act. I filled the man's mug and brought it back to where he stood in the dining room.

Uncle Buddy accepted the coffee with a nod of thanks and stood sipping it. He look me over now as appraisingly as he had surveyed the house when he first walked in.

"Should I come too?" I asked quietly.

Uncle Buddy shook his head. "No, Chris, not this time. I'm pretty sure I know how Steve feels about you, but he won't welcome you being there right now. I helped his granddaddy build that house myself. His family'll be there for him. As soon as he's seen all there is to see, I'll bring him back to you. Family's good at a time like this, but there ain't but so much we can do. He's going to need you worse when he gets back. I hope you'll take care of him."

I looked at the man with genuine respect—the same he was trying to show me—and nodded. "I appreciate you being so understanding of how things are with—" I began.

The man raised his hand. "That's enough of that. There's some things that don't need to be said. I've known Steve since my brother brought him and his mama here to live 26 years ago. He was a fine boy then and he's grown to be a fine man. A man's business is his own business. And you seem like a pretty decent sort. In a place this small, folks don't miss much. We look out for family around here, you understand what I mean?"

There was both an earnest promise and an implicit threat in what he said—a callused fist in a velvet glove. I understood what he said, and I understood what didn't need saying. This was a world where actions spoke a lot louder than words. "What can I do to help?" I asked.

Uncle Buddy looked around the house once more and then back at me. "Just keep on doing what you're doing. Steve's no different than any other man. What he's always needed was a home. It looks like that's what you've got to offer."

Steve returned to the great room, dressed and ready to go. "Uncle Buddy?" he said.

"Chris, nice to meet you," Uncle Buddy said sincerely, then gave me a earnest look. "This ain't the best time to mention it, but we have a big family get-together coming up. There's a lot of people that would be very pleased to meet you, if Steve'll bring you."

Once again, I thrust out my hand for Uncle Buddy to accept. He took it in a firm grip. "I'll look forward to it, sir. And if Steve won't bring me, I'll come on my own."

Uncle Buddy stroked my knuckles with his thumb like an adult will do with a fond child, smiled, and nodded. "Come on then, Steve. Let's go get your Aunt Peg and see what we can save."

From the dock, the house looked fine viewed dead-on. It wasn't until your eyes wandered to the west end that things went awry. That gable end was burned and blackened from halfway up the side of the house to the charred, exposed rafters of the roof. There was no way Steve could live there.

We sat as the sun set over the water, and drank beer, with Steve staring at what was left of his house. He'd found the metal box that held his insurance papers, deed, and title to the long-paid-for house. His tax records and bank papers were damp but certainly salvageable. His Aunt Peg had taken the clothes that weren't irreparably smoke-damaged, washed them, and packed them neatly in cardboard boxes that we'd loaded in the back of the Expedition for the trip back home. The family photos were few, but they had been buried so deeply under other boxes in Steve's parents' room that they escaped both water and smoke. Except for the indestructible weather radio in the kitchen, just about everything else was gone. All the dishes had cracked from the heat and were shattered by the water from the fire hoses. The family Christmas ornaments in the attic were among the first to be consumed. The bits of his past that weren't blackened and ruined were smoke and ash on the wind.

For a little while, he let himself hold my hand and cry. Then he stood and carefully placed our empty beer bottles in the 55-gallon plastic garbage can on the end of the dock. He stood next to his boat and looked her over. One of his many cousins had swum out to bring her back in safely to dock. "You know, if it had to be one or the other," he said, "I'm glad it was the house and not the Lina G. As long as I have the boat I can earn a living and rebuild." He sounded as if he was finding relief at last.

"That old house was too small, anyways," he continued. "Between the insurance on the house and the value of the land, I can build me a house like I want. I got my pier and dock. It's going to be okay, Chris."

He turned around to face me and allowed himself a small grin. "I'm going to have to work hard for a few years, but I'll end up better off. Hell, the land with the pier and dock is worth a half million. By God, I'm lucky."

I whistled and looked at him wide-eyed. "I had no idea I was sleeping with a rich man," I said.

Steve chuckled. "Well, you better get used to it, because I don't intend for you to sleep with nobody else, Little Bit."

I remembered his Uncle Buddy's words from the day before. "I think nobody else around here does, either."

"What are you talking about?" he said.

I recounted the conversation I'd had with his uncle. "So, when you told me they all knew, you were right," I said. "I seemed to have passed some sort of test."

Steve snorted. "They all get *Oprah* and those kinds of shows down here just like the rest of the country. They know what's what. But I had no idea Uncle Buddy would say anything. Damn. He told you that?"

I nodded. "They love you, Steve."

"Yeah, that's all fine, well, and good. I guess they've grown some since my daddy brought my mama down here. She had a rough time of it at first."

"Why? Were they mean to her?"

Steve shrugged. "They weren't exactly mean, but...well, my mama didn't help any. She was a Yankee and a Catholic. As if that wasn't bad enough, she was a women's libber in their eyes and she also washed clothes on Sundays. It was just a culture clash. After a while, though, they all grew accustomed to each other."

"Why do you think Uncle Buddy and Aunt Peg are so nice to me, then? I mean I have the right accent, but I'm Catholic and I'm gay as a goose."

Steve stuck his hands in his pockets and slowly paced around the dock. "Well, you may be Catholic, but they know you go to church. And they're probably hoping you'll get me to start going back—that's two things you got going for you. We're at least the same religion, and my heathen ass needs to be sitting in a church somewheres come Sunday morning as far as they're concerned. The other thing is, they figure I'm less likely to be out getting some strange disease, if I've got somebody taking care of me at home. It fits their...para...para...para-thing."

"Paradigm," I said.

"Yeah, that. They think being an un-hitched male is the worse thing you can be—that's the women talking. The men, hell...*Uncle Buddy*? I don't know what he's thinking, but if he's saying it, you can best believe he's voicing the popular opinion."

I didn't respond. I'd never been around such a tight-knit, family-oriented bunch of people. I had no conception of it. My kids didn't have much extended family, and but for them, I'd be completely alone in the world.

"There's another thing, too," Steve said.

"What's that, Big Man."

Steve swung back down next to me on the bench at the end of the dock and lit a cigarette. "There's not a one of these families that hasn't lost a son or daughter to being gay. My Uncle Tommy and Aunt Pat—Aunt Pat and Aunt Peg are sisters by the way—they have a son my age named Chad. Chad could suck the chrome off a trailer hitch. Chad's *been* gone. He lives in Charlotte and ain't been home as long as I can remember. I got another cousin who's a dyke. She lives in Richmond. These folks all had gay kids that left and don't want to come back. The old folks are looking around and seeing it's getting to be just them. The way of life around here is dying, Chris. And I hate to see it. This is my home. I don't want to live nowhere else." Steve looked back at his burned-out house for a long time. "No sirree. I'm not going to live anywhere else."

There were three long tables set up on one end of the church hall. One held nothing but desserts: beautiful cakes crafted of coconut, chocolate, and browning bananas; pies proudly crowned with golden meringue or mahogany crusts of pecans; plates of brownies and pans of layered confections rich with cream cheese and nuts, or made with chocolate or pistachio pudding, nuts, and canned mandarin orange sections topped with shredded coconut and whipped crème.

The other two tables were laden with plates of deviled eggs and deviled crab; platters of fried chicken and fish filets; slices of roast beef; plates of sliced tomatoes and cucumbers swimming in vinegar; an odd platter of crudités; bowls of field peas cooked with okra; snap beans glistening with the shine of the fat of pot liquor; the seasoning of country ham tucked into biscuits homemade and so light they would have floated off the plates that held them were it not for the ham.

Everyone greeted us warmly along with all the other smiles of welcome and cries of *Come here and let me hug your neck, Bless your sweet heart,* and *Don't you look good!* A stranger, but not an alien, I pulled into the fold without reservation and held closely— not at arm's length.

Steve grinned and eyed the tables of food and endured more than one scolding for keeping me hid away and he grinned some more. I trailed him around the church hall from cousin to uncle to aunt to old family friend until my head spun with names and my faced ached from smiling. My ears fought to catch and hold a dis- tinctive accent that was broad in the vowels and left consonants behind in a blur of sweetness.

After a while Uncle Buddy called for quiet while the pastor led us all in returning thanks. As the amens were said, the din resumed, and the line formed for Chinet plates and plastic forks, I tugged at Steve's sleeve and told him I needed to go smoke a cigarette. In truth, I was overcome with so much feeling. I had expected to be received with the chilliness of the late October outside; instead, my heart was full of their warmth of the welcome. It was almost too much.

"Not until you meet somebody else," Steve said. "You have to pay your respects to Granny Effie."

I gave him a quizzing look in reply that held more than one question. He divined them all.

"You haven't met her. See that tiny little lady over at that table? She's my great-great aunt. She's 92 and sharp as a tack. She's real- ly the head of the clan. Are you ready?"

I nodded and let him steer me through the crowd and present me to the lady herself. In her presence his Banker brogue grew broader. It was almost as if she spoke a different, older language that he switched to when he introduced me as his friend.

"Sit down here by me, son," she said. "I can't see so good if you're too far."

Steve squatted before her; I sat in the metal folding chair next to her. She took and held my hand in hers. Liver-spotted and age- freckled, her tiny grasp was cool but firm. "So, you're the boy's come and got Steve finally settled some," she said.

"Yes ma'am. I hope so anyway."

"It's high time," she said. It sounded like *Uhts hoi toime.*

She gave Steve a disapproving look then turned back to me.

"Back when I was a young woman, there was only one kind of way to live. One kind of way to do things. Fish was fish and fowl was fowl. Nowadays, there's all kinds of ways to live that we couldn't imagine back in them old, hard days. But I have to ask you, son. Do you love the Lord?"

"Yes, ma'am," I said. "I go to my church twice a week and I try to do right."

"But do you love the Lord?"

"Yes ma'am. I do. I can tell you that honestly."

"Well, I know you do, or you wouldn't have the courage to be here today. All good things come from the Lord, and I believe the Lord sent you to our Steve. Ever since he come back down here with his mama and daddy, I knew he was trying to do right and take his place in this herd of mine. But he wasn't ever going to be married."

"Grannie—" Steve began, but hung his head.

With a smile, she continued, "No, son. I knew that." Then she looked back to me. "There's just some God makes that way," She paused, and a sly grin spread across her face. "But he's still pretty. His mama's from way off somewhere, and that's how come he's so dark and light all at the same time. Pretty mama, pretty son."

She looked at me and pulled my hand to make me lean in closer. "He needs somebody to love him and look after him. These men that pulls their living out of the water, it makes them hard men. Hard to live with, bad for drinking. I tell you what—I know. You hear me?"

"Yes ma'am. I hear you," I replied.

"Now, I'm too old to give a durn what any of them that's here thinks. But they seem to put a lot of care into what I think, so I tell 'em. If you'll take care of my pretty baby right here—love him and look after him—I'll not have one bad word to say, and none of them better not neither, or they'll answer to me. You hear me, son?"

She tightened her grasp on my hand. I rubbed my thumb gently over her bony knuckles. "I promise you, Granny Effie, I'll do my best."

"All right, then," she said. "Now one more thing. You got to get him going back to church like his mama worked hard and raised him to. You have to promise me that. His mama had that old kind of religion, and she kept it up down here, so far away from her own people. I don't know nothing about Catholics, but I knew his mama, and she was a good woman. If you love the Lord like you say you do, you get Steve back to his mama's church, now."

I lifted her hands and kissed them. Very gently, she let my hand go and touched my cheek. "Steve?" she said.

"Yes, ma'am?"

"You do right, you hear me? You look after this man, because the Lord sent him here to you. I'm watching you."

"I will, I swear," he said.

"Don't you swear nothing, standing in the Lord's house. Now go get this man something to eat. He ain't bigger than a minute, and you're a lot of work."

Stuffed to the point of bursting—with food and goodwill and the kind of pride I never thought I'd find in such a place—Steve and I finally took our leave. The day had dwindled to late afternoon when we'd said our rounds of good-byes and headed out into the church's parking lot. I was heading for the Expedition when Steve caught me by the hand and swung me around. "C'mon, Little Bit, there's somebody I need to talk to."

I almost groaned. I felt as if I'd just met and spoken with every person Steve knew or was related to in all of Carteret County. He let go of my hand as we reached a young couple with a toddler, just getting into their own Expedition. Everyone at this family gathering was driving a truck, a dual-ly, or an SUV. Even the younger kids and newlywed couples drove huge beast vehicles. In Raleigh my Expedition was a fashion statement; here, it was a way of life. I didn't think my truck had ever been in four-wheel-drive mode, and I didn't think any of the ones in the parking lot were ever out of it.

"Chris, this is Monte and Eileen, good friends of mine from over in Back Beaufort."

Monte stuck out his hand for a shake, and Eileen gave me an open, sunny smile. She had a little boy who looked to be about 3 on her hip. The little boy turned his head away from us and wouldn't look around. Monte shook my hand and said, "My son's name is Miles—Miles Standoffish."

Eileen rolled her eyes and looked at me. "He thinks that's the funniest joke. Miles Standoffish, Miles Standish, get it?"

I gave Monte a grin. "I think it's funny." Then, to the little boy, I said, "I don't think you're Standoffish. You're probably just sick of being around all these strange grown-ups, aren't you?"

The little boy turned around, gave me a bashful grin, then ducked his head into his mother's neck.

"I swear, I don't know why he's so shy," Eileen said. "Me and his daddy would talk to a stump, we're so social."

I laughed.

Steve said, "Chris, Monte is one of my hunting buddies. He's going to take the two boy puppies off our hands and train them."

"Monte, I can't thank you enough," I said. "I've got one of the puppies myself, and with Petey and Mama-dog, my house is just about full."

"No problem. I'll take two of Steve's dogs anytime I can get them," Monte replied.

Eileen nodded. "Hell, I've always got room for a couple more. We have 10 acres, so there's plenty of room to run them. I understand Steve's over at your place for the time being."

I nodded. "I've got enough room for him—I'm lucky to have him as a stray."

Monte looked at Steve and grinned. "You've got this one fooled into believing that?"

Eileen laughed. "Lord, you two are as good as married, now Granny Effie has blessed you. They don't really give a damn about a preacher in this family—it's Granny Effie that does the marrying. You're stuck with him now, Chris."

"You know she's right," Monte said as he wrapped me in a bear hug, lifted me off my feet, and swung me around. "Welcome to the family, Chris."

"Damn, Monte!" Eileen said. "Put him down or somebody'll think I'm in trouble."

"As if I'd ever leave you, my darling," Monte rejoined.

Steve shook his head. "My God, you all too noticed it too? I feel like I've just left my own wedding reception. Was it that obvious?"

"Oh hell yeah," Monte said. "You two were the most interesting thing about this whole shebang, weren't they Eileen."

Steve groaned.

"Come here and give me a hug, Chris," Eileen said, "Every one of us was wondering if Steve would ever find somebody. He's such a moody-ass loner. I hope you have a steady supply of Valium, you're gonna need it."

I hugged Eileen. When I did, Miles kissed my cheek.

"Oh hell, did you see that?" Monte said.

Eileen laughed. "I sure did, I told you."

"See what?" I asked, suddenly alarmed by the little boy's kiss.

"Eileen swears this one's going to grow up to be gay. He's the baby of four. Look over yonder."

Following his pointed hand, I saw three other little boys, stair-stepped in ages from about 8 down to about 5. Two of them were rolling in the dirt in the middle of a fight while the youngest kicked dirt on both of them.

"Those are my other three. Eileen's been *praying* Miles would be gay."

Eileen hoisted the little boy up on her hip and said, "Don't you want to go see Uncle Chris?" The little boy nodded and reached his arms out to me. "Take him, please. Maybe some will rub off on him."

I took the little fellow and put him on my nonexistent hip. "You want to come go home with me?" I asked.

Miles looked from his mother to his father and back to me. He looked at me with his big brown eyes and simply said: "Help?"

Steve, Eileen, and Monte all laughed uproariously. I looked back at his brothers rolling in the dirt and almost wished I could take him home with me. I looked at Miles and said, "You know something Miles?"

Once again the little boy turned an enormous set of beautiful brown eyes at me, and said, "Whut?"

"Your mama and daddy are pretty wonderful people did you know that?" I looked at Eileen and said, "Maybe you should bring him to visit one of these days, you know I have three grown ones of my own...well, not my own, but three I raised."

"Get out," she said.

"No *you* get out. You do not look old enough to have four children."

"Well, Monte loaded and pumped his first round of shot when I was 17."

"Oh man, listen to her," Monte snorted. "Like she was a deer I was hunting with lights."

Steve laughed. "Listen to the both of you. I've known you for a long time. You both had each other in the sights when we were freshmen in high school. Chris, if you ever want to see two people who were made for each other, you're looking at them."

I enjoyed the weight and heft of Miles in my arms and against my hip. On a day when a family of good country people from Carteret County, North Carolina, could meet a twink well past his expiration date and accept him with open hearts and arms, I almost wished I could have another child to raise. Anything was possible. I looked at Steve and smiled. If there was one man I felt like I was made for at this time in my life, I knew I was looking at him.

The breeze off the ocean was still warm, even this deep into October. Halloween was so close it was scaring me. I had baby Chris's christening in Raleigh the second weekend in November—time was moving far too fast for me to keep up anymore. I stuck my hands into my hoodie's pouch and stretched until my toes came into contact with a dog's back; it was too dark to tell which one. I looked over at Steve staring at the stars and reached over to take his hand. "It was a wonderful day, Big Man. Your family was wonderful."

Steve spared me a glance and smiled, then looked back into the stars overhead. He had been unusually quiet since we'd gotten home from the reunion. We'd walked on the beach to work off some of the big dinner, and I took his introspection as a consequence of being talked out. Even *I* was talked out and I was a far bigger talker than Steve. There was a lot for both of us to process from the day. I thought Steve was as taken aback by the open-hearted acceptance of our obvious coupledom as I was. It was a tender new thing and it was going to take some time to sink in, at least it did for me.

"Little Bit," he said. "I have something to ask you, and you don't have to answer right away, but it's something you need to think about."

I didn't look at him, but shifted my position to stare up into the same stars he had been studying. "Okay, ask away," I said.

"Back in the spring, the first time we got together, you told me you weren't willing to give up your life for me. I guess I need to know what you meant by that."

"I don't know Steve. I'm not sure how I should answer. In many ways, I *have* given up parts of my life for you—and gladly. I'm in love with you."

"I know that. You show me that in a hundred little ways and some big ones. Hell, I'm living in your house. And I trust you. I mean, I know you're not running around on me, sleeping with other guys—"

"Well, you sure as hell don't have to worry about that. My God, I couldn't be more satisfied in that regard. I couldn't even think about finding another lover like you, nor do I want to."

"Well, thanks. But that's not really what I mean."

"Well, I'm listening, go ahead."

"Back then, you said you were the marrying kind, but you weren't that person anymore. That you'd done that already. I guess what I'm asking you is: Do you still feel that way?"

I felt myself grow tense. Honestly, I didn't know how far I'd come from that person. I was hurt then, and Steve hadn't begun the healing he initiated and both carelessly and carefully tended in my heart. I didn't answer, but stayed quiet to see if he had more to say.

Steve turned in his chair to face me and reached out to touch my cheek. "What I got to know is: If I asked you, would you marry me? Would you share your life with me, for real and for good?"

I let out a long sigh. "Haven't I proven I would? I don't want to be three feet from you as it is. I don't understand what you're asking me."

Steve shifted uncomfortably. "I want us to live together in my house. In a house I'll build for us, together. Could you give up this place to help me do that?"

I got up and walked to the edge of my deck and looked out toward the ocean. The deck I was standing on was mine. It was something no one could take away from me. I flashed back to so many points of my life where I lived with no assurances that I couldn't be told to pack up and move out, to be thrown out like the garbage. One misstep, one thoughtless act might mean the world beneath my feet could crumble and I could fall away into the unknown. My mother was always worried about being fired or laid off. Zack grew tired of me and put me out. The house behind me was every bit of security I had in the world. But it was so much more in my psyche.

Steve could never live comfortably in my house. It was too much mine. There was no Steve to it except for an underwear drawer and a loft packed with the things that were salvaged from the fire. I had never told him—up to that moment, I don't think I'd really admitted to myself—that even giving up that tiny swath of turf was hard for me.

I simply hadn't yet let go the primal fear that a traitor's heart might beat in Steve's broad chest. I didn't know. That was the long and short of it. I was scared.

I turned back to him and said, "I want to live with you for the rest of my life, Steve Willis. I want to carry cakes and fried chicken to your family reunions and I want to sit next to you at Mass. I want to walk in rooms that smell of you while you're out in the Caribbean somewhere on a boat. But I'm scared of you too. I'm scared you'll wait until I'm 65 years old and you'll say, 'Hey, I'm only 55. I want to live a different life now! I don't want you anymore Little Bit, so off you go! Good bye and good luck! Now fuck off.' Will you do that to me? Or will you die on me? Will you fall off a boat and drown? Will you wrap your truck around a tree? Oh Jesus, Steve..."

There were too many emotions welling up inside me. The day had been too full of people and warmth and food and everything I never dared to expect and everything I wanted. My stomach revolted. I made it to the side of the deck and threw up. After I threw up I began to cry. I cried for the first time since I'd sat on the tailgate of my truck and let Beau slip away from me, and with him, every last vestige of the life I'd known.

Steve was behind me in a flash, holding me and wrapping his arms around my chest and pulling me back and away from the edge of my deck where every car on the bypass could see me puking and crying like a terrified little boy beat up again by bullies, just trying to get home. Just trying his damnedest to get somewhere safe.

I straightened up and wiped my mouth with the back of my hand. "Don't promise me and then take it back. Don't... Don't..."

I shrugged and twisted free of his arms and walked behind my chair, holding it between him and me like a cornered animal.

"I could kill that bastard for doing this to you," he said. "Don't push me away, Chris. I'm offering everything I am, everything I have in the world."

I sighed and nodded tiredly. I knew that's what he was offering. I released my death grip on the back of my chair and wiped my eyes on my sleeves. In a voice choked with snot, I said, "Don't you know how bad I want you? Don't you see how scared I am of losing you?"

Steve stepped tentatively back to his own chair and waited while I sat back down in mine. Once I'd sunk into it, he said, "Are you okay now? Can I get you some water?"

I nodded, and he walked into the house.

Part of me wanted to take off down the stairs and into the street, running for the beach and then to...then to where? I had nowhere to go. I was exactly where I wanted to be. And that place *still* scared the shit out of me.

Steve stepped back out onto the deck. "Here," he said as handed me a bottle of water.

I drank some thirstily and washed the stale taste of vomit from my mouth. "Thanks, Big Man. I'm sorry I freaked out on you like that."

Satisfied I was somewhat okay, Steve sat beside me and reached to take my hand. "It's not about the money, Chris. I have money. I can build the house, maybe not as nice as this one, but I can build us a place to live. You can keep this one and rent it out if you want to."

I looked at him, shook my head, and laughed. "No, no way. Out of respect for what you're asking me to do, I owe you a real commitment."

Steve leaned back in his chair and looked up at the stars again. "That's why I love you," he said. "Think about it—there's ain't no rush. I have no place to go. And Chris, there's no place I want to go. I don't know how to prove it to you other than day by day. But I want you as part of my world. God knows, it seems like my world wants you to be a part of it."

I laughed. "Well, if Granny Effie has blessed it..."

"Exactly."

I joined Steve looking at the stars. They were as inscrutable as ever. "I want to talk to Trey," I said. "Can you hold on for a couple of weeks for my final answer?"

"I've got the rest of my life to wait on you, Little Bit." He looked at me and waited for me to look back. Under the meager light of the beach's brightest stars, his eyes told me his mouth wasn't lying.

"I want a big-ass nice house," I said. "Not no bullshit prefab house."

"Okay," he said, acting serious but doing a poor job of hiding a smile.

"I want it to be big enough for my kids and my grandkids to visit."

"That goes without saying."

"Okay," I said.

"Okay."

But it wasn't okay. Not yet. The house wasn't all of it. What I really had to tussle with and chew over was a different kind of gristle altogether. I had a harder question I needed to answer for myself because it had only to do with me.

Part of me—a big part of me, I had to admit—had come to like who I was these days. I liked who I saw as I moved through my days. The fact that I liked who I saw in the mirror had more to do with self-respect than simple vanity.

These days, I saw myself as a man who lived his life well in all aspects: mentally, physically, intellectually, and spiritually. I saw myself as who I'd been working to become, for years, even before Zack left me. I didn't know how that fit in with me running back to belonging to another man, becoming a wife again. There was no other way to say it. I would be Steve's wife. I'd be *Little Bit,* just a piece of someone else's life. That's not how I wanted to live after Zack and I split up. I'd finally learned to see myself as an individual—a *me,* not part of a *we.*

"Are you getting about ready to go to bed? I'm beat," Steve said.

"Why don't you go on inside, Big Man. I need a minute or two more out here. All of a sudden you've given me a lot to think about, you know?"

"Chris, I didn't mean to upset you like I did. We can just forget about it for now. Come on in and let's go to bed."

"I'm okay, Steve. It's all good, I swear. I just need a few more minutes to calm down and then I'll bring the dogs in and come to bed."

"Okay, Little Bit, but don't make it too long. Sometimes you can think something to death. Plus, you know I won't be able to get to sleep as long as you're out here by yourself." With that, he stood and stretched. Unexpectedly, he bent down to kiss me. Steve wasn't ever demonstrative in any place he determined to be "all out in public."

Mama-dog and Nuala followed him into the house. Petey came and nudged my hand, urging me to get up and go inside with the rest of the pack. I took his big head between my hands and gave him a good rubbing under his ears. He shook his head happily when I was done, and sat next to me, watchful as a Marine Lance Corporal at attention and on guard.

Even the male dog sensed my place in the pack and behaved accordingly. The Willis clan had reacted to me in much the same way. The most convenient role to assign me was as a wife, a helpmeet, or a homemaker. If there was no precedent for someone like me, a wife's portion would suffice for them all. That was how they saw me, not ungenerously.

The question remained: Was that how I saw myself now? I didn't have the answer at hand. I thought I had grown into something new, someone that belonged more to myself.

In Steve's house, in Steve's world, I'd belong to Steve. There was no other paradigm for the community that had embraced me so willingly at the reunion. I'd be an extension of him. In the comings and goings of my day in Salter Path, I'd be observed and judged against the community's perceptions of marriage and a life well lived. I had to ask myself if that was what I wanted.

Could I stand on my own two feet and still honor what was truest to my nature: nurture and fidelity? I wasn't sure if I could have it both ways.

I stood, and Petey stood along with me. He waited, watching the world in the darkness, while I got my tired self across the deck and into the doorway. Once I was safely inside, he followed me in and waited for me to lock the door and turn out the lights. Together we walked down the hall and into the bedroom.

Steve was propped up on pillows, on top of the covers with his arms crossed behind his head, watching television. I paused in the doorway and took in the sight of him on my bed. I loved looking at his generous body. I inventoried the width of his shoulders, the brown nipples on his broad chest, and the tiny navel centered in the slight swell of his belly. Inside his shorts lay a generous, full dick on a pillow of heavy balls. His thighs were well muscled, and his legs, not as long as his stretch of torso, ended in broad feet built to hold and carry much.

He bore my admiring scrutiny without arrogance. His eyes betrayed no inclination toward the power he knew he could assert over my slighter body. There was simply no cruelty in him—there was only an open and easy generosity with everything he had to give. He patted the bed beside him and smiled.

I stripped down for sleep and climbed in, which satisfied the dogs who settled into the spots they'd claimed for the night. Their pack was all accounted for. Their long night's rhythm of dozing and dreaming and watching was ready to begin.

As I lay on the bed, Steve pulled me to him with one arm and turned off the lamp by the bed with the other. As I moved closer to his side, he sighed and shifted slightly to give me better access to the whole long length of him.

"Did you get it all worked out up there?" he asked.

"Yes, Big Man," I lied. There were still arguments in my own head that had to be fought and won. In my mind the debate was far from over, but as my body sought the solid comfort of the man next to me, I knew Steve had already won.

CHAPTER EIGHT,
CHRISTENING

✦

The sheer logistics of it were a bitch. Steve needed something as nearly resembling dress clothes as he could tolerate for the baby's christening that followed Saturday's Vigil Mass. And, to further complicate matters, Zack had politely insisted on meeting me somewhere alone so we could "talk." After a four-hour drive into Raleigh the Friday before the christening, I agreed to meet Zack at the School of Design at North Carolina State while Steve went shopping at Cameron Village a few blocks away.

I had Steve drive the maze of small streets between the campus and Cameron Village Shopping Center before he dropped me off on the steps of the School of Design's main building. He promised to be back to pick me up there in an hour and a half. Like everyone else in my family, Steve was unsettled by just the thought of Zack and me being anywhere near each other. But when I explained Zack wanted to bury the hatchet before our first grandchild's christening the following day, Steve had grumpily agreed to let me go.

Against all likelihood in my imagining, Zack had been invited to teach a graduate-level seminar in business management for creatives in the school's graphic arts program. His hourlong class ended promptly at 2, and he said we could use his classroom to meet and "clear the air."

In my view, there was nothing but empty sky between Zack and me, but he felt the need to talk, so I agreed.

Steve dropped me off with a vow to buy something "churchy," but he withheld any promise not to kick Zack's ass if he got me all upset. In turn, I promised to be waiting for him alone on the steps at the front of the building in exactly an hour and a half. With all that negotiated, I crossed the street and walked through the school's main doors to find Zack's classroom on the second floor in the original building's newer addition. I got there in time to hear him finish up with his students as I waited in the hall outside.

Zack sounded affable and seemingly well liked by his students as they said their good-byes. They spilled out into the hall in a rush of pierced, tattooed, and black-clad fashion attitude. Zack followed the last of them out and smiled when he found me waiting. Surprisingly, he opened his arms for a hug. I stepped into his embrace and inhaled his familiar scent. Pressed into the close, warm quarters of his chest, it was like returning to a long-unvisited room.

His embrace was fond, not perfunctory. He let me go and stepped back to look me over and nod approvingly. Zack liked all his accessories to complement him, his status, and his sense of self. I was oddly pleased to be found to be worthy, still. My pleasure faded quickly as I recalled how superficial Zack's standards were.

"Beautiful as ever, Chris," he said. "I suppose I should say 'handsome,' but I've always thought you were beautiful, rather than handsome."

Yeah, right, I thought. *If you had to think of me as handsome, you'd also have to think of me as an equal.* I only gave him a sincere smile and looked at him. He had lost most of his liquor bloat as well as the harried look he'd had when I'd last seen him. He certainly appeared handsome, and somewhat distinguished and professorial as well. I hoped his healthier appearance meant he had resolved some of his anger. I hadn't spoken to Andrea or the boys to get a read on his current matrimonial state, and they had given nothing away in that regard.

"Thanks Zack," I said. "You're looking pretty spiffy yourself. The academic sideline suits you. You look like you did 10 years ago."

Zack nodded to acknowledge the compliment and stepped away from the door. "I appreciate your agreeing to see me. Come on in."

I stepped inside. There were three tables arranged in a generous U-shaped configuration. From the location of his neatly organized notes, I guessed Zack sat at the end of one of the arms of the U rather than at its center. I walked past his spot to look out the window. It was a lovely afternoon. Across the street, Pullen Park was awash in fallen leaves from the old oaks. The chilly breeze blew them prettily in eddies of golden-brown. "What a lovely place this is," I said. "Since I've lived on the beach, I've forgotten how nice all the leaves from the big trees can be in the fall."

Zack closed the door, walked past his things, and took a seat near where I was standing. "I take it all for granted, I'm afraid."

With one last look out the window, I turned and sat a few chairs from Zack, but close enough for easy conversation. I looked at him expectantly.

"Did you and Steve have a nice drive in?" he asked.

"Yes. We stopped for lunch at Wilbur's Barbeque outside Goldsboro, then drove the rest of the way on up. It was good to be out in the middle of the day."

"And where is Steve?"

"I sent him over to Cameron Village to find something presentable to wear to the church tomorrow. No one really dresses up at the beach. Not even for Mass."

Zack nodded.

"Zack, I'm not quite sure why you wanted to see me."

"Ah, to the point of it then. Before we meet tomorrow at church, I believe I have some mea culpas to get out of the way. We haven't really talked since Easter, and that was not pleasant. I'm sorry about that. We haven't really spoken except in anger in nearly two years, and that's pretty much my fault. I wanted to apologize."

I looked at him to gauge whether he was softening me up for any bombshells. He'd been pleasant enough at Easter before he started in on me about Andrea and Schooner. Warily I said, "Well, I have to take credit for some of that too. Two people who've known each other as long as you and I have certainly know what words will wound the quickest and punch the hardest. I have to admit to playing quick-draw with your feelings as well."

Zack lifted his eyebrows and looked over my shoulder through the window and into the bare oak limbs beyond. "The whole business about Schooner…"

"Yes," I said cautiously.

Zack looked me in the eye. "What you said about my resenting him his entire life was dead on the money, Chris. Sometimes I have acted regrettably toward my own son, and that's one of the things I've tried to come to terms with since that day."

"Have you told Schooner that?"

Zack shook his head and sighed. "Twenty-three years of habit is difficult to break, Chris. But please believe me when I tell you, it's a problem I recognize and I'm resolved to work on it? I love Schooner. But—"

"Zack, don't beat yourself up about it. Schooner is spoiled in many ways and you were right to lay that at my feet. If it's any help for you, believe *me* when I tell you I don't think I was a perfect mo...ma...parent."

Zack smiled. "It's okay. You can say 'mother.' That's something else I have to own up to. I forced that role on you and reinforced it every way I knew how." Zack placed an elbow on the table and rubbed his forehead for a moment before finding my eyes again. "Unfair of me...I admit that now. But Chris, I was so scared back then. I felt so lucky to have you to count on for my children's sake."

"Oh God, Zack," I sighed. "Sometimes I wonder if we fucked it all up really badly, or if we did something so right it astounds me. I have to think God played a hand in it, bringing us together. It's molded my entire life, and it's something that I'm still dealing with on a day-to-day basis."

"What do you mean?"

"Well. It has nothing to do with you or the kids—it's just me figuring out who I am, walking out the other side of the forest."

Zack was quiet for a moment and looked down at his hands. Then he said, "You're a fine, generous, and loving man, Chris. I don't think you have to define yourself beyond that. At this point of your life...my life...I think recognizing we did the best we could—with what we had—that's the only thing we can do, isn't it?"

"I suppose so, Zack. There really isn't any other way to look at it that isn't either a pity party or World War III."

"Well, we've had a taste of both, haven't we?"

We shared a smile and a nod. It felt good. "You know something, Zack? We're both pretty lucky to have our second chances—

that's how I've come to see it. I'll admit you damn near killed me, walking out on me. But two years down the road, I think it was the right thing for both of us. That is…" I hesitated.

"That is, what?"

"That is, if you're happy," I said. "I know you probably won't believe me when I say this, but I worry about you sometimes. I swear Zack, I never once thought of you being unhappy with any sense of pleasure."

Zack smiled—not a happy smile but the smile of an adult familiar with the long road that had brought him to the place he found himself. "Chris, I believe what you're telling me. I wish I could set your mind at ease and tell you that I'm happy and satisfied with my life. Oh, it's not bad—don't get me wrong, Alicia and I are doing okay. My new boy fills me with a lot of optimism—just watching him learn all about the world around him is a joy. With the first bunch I was just too busy becoming a success to pay much attention to what I see now with this one. Like you said, he's my second chance to do it right. But do I regret the cost to you and my kids? Oh hell yes, Chris. *Hell* yes."

I returned his smile; I'd taken part of that road with him. "We came out just fine, Zack," I said. "I've long since stopped blaming you. I think the kids have made some peace with it too. They're caught up in the drama of their own lives now—you and I are just subplots at this point."

Zack nodded in agreement. All of this had been perfectly pleasant so far. I took a deep breath. "Zack, I need your opinion about something. You're the only person who can answer this question, but I'm scared to ask you."

"Why are you scared?"

"I'm scared because you know how to hurt me like no one else can, and this is a deeply personal matter."

Zack gently leaned toward me, reached across the table, and touched my hand. "I wish I could say you could trust me, but I'm the last person who should plead my credibility to you."

"Hearing you say that somehow makes me feel better, Zack."

We shared a laugh. It felt comfortable. It felt good.

"Steve has asked me to marry him," I said. "I don't mean flying off to God knows where to find a judge or justice of the peace or whoever is hooking gay people together these days. But you know what I'm talking about. Steve wants me to marry him."

Zack leaned back in his chair and looked at me with something akin to remorse in his eyes. For that unmasked expression of genuine regret alone I was grateful. "Steve would be a lucky man to have you, Chris. I know how lucky."

"I guess that's my question, Zack. Why would he be lucky? Is there something about me that just cries out, *Take me, make me your wife, your bitch...*"

"Chris, what would make you think that? I don't understand."

"I'm not trying to be an asshole, Zack, but one time you told me I was worthless without you and your kids to raise. I've thought a lot about that since."

"Chris, I was angry. You can't take that to heart."

"Well, in a way, I have. Tell me, Zack. Am I just half of a person? Do I need a man to make me whole? Or am I just a piece of ass that needs plugging to operate like a housekeeper and a mother? What am I, just a cunt of a man?"

I stood up and turned my back to him to stare out the window into the afternoon. I felt naked of my pretensions. I felt all of my hard-won assumptions of who I was laying like so many fallen leaves, caught and scattered around by a chill wind on a November afternoon. "That's what I'm thinking about before I tell Steve yes, Zack. That's what I'm trying to figure out."

Zack's chair scraped backward from the table. It was a sound I'd heard thousands of times as he pushed himself away from the table in our home after breakfast and lunch, after a dinner I'd made like a dutiful Donna Reed housewife. Was that me now?

Zack gently took my shoulders in his hands and rested his chin on top of my head. "Oh Jesus, Chris! I hate myself for putting you through 22 years of life that would ever make you even think those hateful things about yourself."

"Is that what I am, Zack?" I persisted. "Be honest with me—don't just pity me and lie. I couldn't take that, not now."

Zack turned me around to face him. "Do you know what I see when I look at you, Chris?" he asked. I looked up at him wondering what kind of pretty lie he could come up with on such short notice. "I see the best friend I ever had in my life. And I'm sorry I lost you through my selfishness, arrogance, and sheer stupidity."

I looked away from him and shook my head. "That's something pretty to say Zack, and I do appreciate you saying it. But it doesn't answer my question. You could say the same thing about a dog you forgot and left in the car on a hot day." I shrugged out of his grasp and sat back down. I gave him a small smile, just to show him I wasn't mad. "You still haven't answered my question."

Zack looked at me with what I recognized as longing. It was part sexual, and it was also a desire for something only I could give: a sense of home, of comfort, and pure acceptance. Those were the things you encountered in one person only once or twice in your life, if you were lucky. I had my answer—I knew who I was.

He resumed his seat and looked at me earnestly. It took him a full minute to gather his thoughts, then he spoke. "There were a thousand times in my life that you've done things no one else could do. You're perceptive in ways that other people just aren't. You know exactly what to do and say to make the best out of the worst. And, to put it bluntly, you're the best fuck I ever had because you made me feel, every time, that I was the best you ever had."

"Zack, wait—" I began.

"What are you looking for beyond that, Chris? That's what marriage is. That's all it is. You have a gift—for making men happy. What do you want me to say? That's the pure fact of it. If you want to beat yourself up wondering if you're some kind of Stepford Wife, then go for it. You're not. You're just a wonderful, loving man, Chris. Accept it. I think Steve is one lucky son of a bitch."

I nodded and let his words sink in. "Okay, Zack. I understand all that, and believe me, I thank you for every word you said. What I'm wondering is, what about the rest of me? I know I'm good at making love, and giving love. I'll even cop to admitting I enjoy the hell out of it. But what about my mind? My intelligence? What about my soul?"

Zack just started laughing.

"What's so funny?" I asked.

"You. You're so funny. You're such a serious person. Who the hell gives a fuck if you could get on PBS to talk about Nabokov with Azar Nafisi or trade inside jokes with what's his name... Anderson Cooper. I wouldn't kick Cooper out of bed and I wouldn't mind having Nafisi on my arm if I was going to a New York cocktail party. But I wouldn't want either one of them in my heart or raising my kids. Look at Steve and ask him the same question. All that intellectual bullshit is something just for you. That's *yours*. It's nothing but pretty wrapping paper for the men in your life."

"Really..." I had to admit, Zack surprised me.

"Oh yes, my beautiful, serious ex-wife. Really. To this day I'd rather call you my wife than call you my frickin' partner, for God's sake. You should be proud of *that,* if nothing else. What made me happiest was watching you walk around my house in my reindeer sweater, reading those books while you stirred the pots and answered the phone and yelled at the kids. My God, you were something else. Something wonderful, as a matter of fact."

I started to laugh.

"Chris, I used to hide whatever book you were reading while you brushed your teeth because I was scared you'd try to be reading while I fucked you."

"Oh come on, Zack. You were a better fuck than that."

Zack looked at me and grinned, then we both laughed.

"Oh Chris, this feels so good, running on again with you like this."

"It does, Zack. I've missed you. For everything that Steve is to me now, I haven't had—what is it now—24 years with him like I've had with you."

Zack smiled and nodded. "Can we please not fight anymore? If for nothing else, for the sake of our grandson? Baby Chris...who would have ever thought?"

"Zack, I'm so lucky to have you and those kids of ours. We had some damn good times."

"Yeah we did. Now we have a grandbaby. Jeez."

"Soon to be another."

"Oh hell. Don't even bring it up. I love my daughter, but who could ever imagine Andrea as a mother? The poor kid will be as intellectually overanalytical as you are and all the worse for Andrea's psychobabble. I shudder at the thought of it." Zack laughed glanced at his watch and stood up. "Steve's going to be waiting, and I sure don't want to piss him off. You're worth fighting over, Chris. I just don't want to fight *with* you anymore."

I stood and touched Zack's cheek. "Only people who love each other can fight like we did, Zack," I said.

"I'll never stop caring for you, you know that."

"I know, Granddaddy."

"Listen at you, Grandmom."

"Oh shut the hell up."

We walked down the stairs and on into the old building's rotunda. The front steps were in one direction and Zack's car was parked in the other. Once again, he opened his arms and I stepped into them. He kissed the top of my head and let me go. "So, I'll see you tomorrow at the church?" he asked.

"Yes, I'll be there for the Mass as well."

"I should hope so." He looked around the deserted space, then back down at me. "Chris, please tell that bruiser of yours that we're okay, will you? Seriously. I'm nearly 59 years old. The last thing I need is to get into some big confrontation—"

"It'll be okay, Zack. Make nice a little tomorrow, talk to him. I really haven't painted you as that big of a jerk, okay? But you said it yourself—I know how to make my men happy. I also make them protective as hell. I guess it comes from being so much shorter than all of them, our sons included."

"Short, maybe; in need of protecting? Never. I'd put you up against Stone Cold Steve Austin."

"Only because you think he'd be in my lap with me rocking him within the first round."

Zack laughed. "My best to Alicia, okay?" I said.

"She'll appreciate that. If you want to find someone who values your intellect, she's the one. I think you fascinate her."

"Why, do you suppose?"

"I'll make nice with Steve if you ask Alicia that question."

"Deal. See you tomorrow, dear heart."

That bought a smile from Zack that still dazzled me, then he strode away. I went out the double doors and looked for Steve. The Expedition wasn't in sight. I looked at my watch—he had 15 minutes before I told him I'd be waiting. I pulled my cigarettes out of my back pocket, lit, and sat on the white marble steps to smoke and enjoy the afternoon. And play the conversation with Zack over in my mind.

Zack had blinked hard when I told him Steve wanted me to marry him. In retrospect, I think what I saw in Zack's eyes wasn't regret. It was simple jealousy. I knew Alicia wasn't anything like me. She was a bright, ambitious business woman. I wasn't business-minded at all: In fact, I was most likely a tremendous slacker. I loved my job as a receptionist for Dr. Tony, but I took the damn job because it had a wonderful window and view I could look out on and daydream.

I thumped my cigarette into the street and blew a long stream of smoke before I started to crack up with laughter. It was probably a good thing I had a knack for making my men happy. On my own I wasn't exactly an airhead, but I was satisfied just to float along, reading and thinking. It wasn't that I projected myself as something frail or particularly feminine; it was simply they felt so protective over me because they were scared I'd wander into traffic with a book in my hands and my head full of dreams, not recipes. It was so fucked-up it was funny.

I left my thoughts to dance with the leaves across the park. What I wanted most now was to be with Steve. I loved the idea of being a lone wolf living in the house on stilts by the sea, but...I also deeply needed and wanted to be Steve's wife, knit into the community that had reached out to welcome me into their small world. Most of all, I needed to trust my heart again and quit living in my head. Alone.

I was just reaching for another cigarette when a car horn tooted. I looked toward the street to find Steve waiting. As I walked toward the car I realized there was something different about him. He'd gotten a haircut! His hair tended toward ringlets when it got too long. Now it was cut short from the nape and on the sides and brushed forward on top in a trendy upsweep at his brow. He looked dashing. I whistled.

"Hello, sailor. Got some time to kill?" I said as I climbed in.

"Like it?"

"It looks pretty hot, Big Man."

"It'll get all curly without the goop the son of a bitch put into it on top."

A car behind us honked, and Steve let off the brake and started to drive toward Western Boulevard. "Where's your new clothes?" I asked.

"In the backseat. Look, forget about that for a minute. Where the hell am I going now?"

"Pull over the next chance you get, and we'll switch places. I know exactly how to get there, so I'll drive."

Steve found an empty space in front of a row of dorms and just barely slid the Expedition into it. The cars behind us passed in a steady stream. We got out of the car and switched places. Once I was in the driver's seat, Steve reached behind him and pulled out a bag from an expensive men's store. Inside I saw a navy-blue blazer, a pair of khaki trousers, and a blue oxford cloth shirt. Tucked underneath was a brand-new belt. "Shoes?" I asked.

Steve grinned. "New Nikes. High-tops."

I laughed. "You're going to look like a million bucks in basketball shoes, baby."

Steve nodded. "I ought to, for what all this shit cost." He turned around to replace the bag in the backseat. "Chris? Are we anywhere near where you used to live? I'd like to see it."

I calculated the time of day against the traffic between Oakwood on the south side and North Raleigh, just outside the belt line where Trey and Susan lived. It would be a bitch, but I could make it happen if I didn't go back through downtown. "We won't be able to do more than drive past it, but I guess we can make it before the worst of rush hour, if you really want to go."

"I do, Chris. I want to see where you came from, before you met me."

I pulled into the flow of traffic headed for Western Boulevard and from there to Oakwood on the other side of downtown. I turned on the radio to entertain Steve so I wouldn't have to talk about the past or give him the guided tour. We would drive past much of my old life—including the pre-Zack days along the way. I had no intention of recalling the gay bars and the houses in Boylan Heights I'd tricked in for Steve's benefit. Those times were too long past. I didn't want to revisit any of those memories.

Steve took in the cityscape and didn't say much the whole way. At last, I pulled up in front of the large, old Italianate house with its tall, narrow windows I'd last left with Beau nearly a year before.

"This is it, Steve," I said.

He craned his neck to take it all in, then looked at me with a grin. "No wonder you said you wanted me to build you a big-ass house. I bet this place has five bedrooms."

"Yep. And a front parlor, a back parlor, a dining room, and a kitchen with a fireplace too."

Steve whistled appreciatively, then shook his head. "Do you ever miss it?"

"Never." Then I thought again. "Well, I miss who we were in that house. I miss the kids in it. I sometimes miss the Zack that lived there in the best days. But do I ever miss *myself*—the man I used to be there? No, Big Man, I'm happy with me now."

Steve turned to me. "Are you happy with me now?"

I looked at him and laughed. "More than you'll ever know."

"Chris, have you given any more thought to what we could build to live in together?"

"I've not stopped thinking about it since you brought it up, Steve."

"Well...and...? You've got me sitting on pins and needles here, Chris."

"Hold on a little bit longer, Steve. I need to talk to Trey."

"Goddamn it, what does Trey have to do with it?"

"Steve. Just hold tight. By the time we're on the road heading back home, we'll have a great deal to talk about concerning our new house. Trust me."

Steve's eyes lit up. "You said *our* new house. Does that mean you're saying yes? Does that mean you're going to marry me and live with me like we talked about?"

I smiled and pulled away from the curb in front of the Oakwood house I'd lived in for over 20 years. The road to the rest of my life was beneath the wheels of my car, and the man I most wanted as my traveling companion was sitting next to me. My mind was made up, my questions were answered.

"I think when we get back to the beach you can have the old house cleared away and get the lot ready," I said. "What I have to talk to Trey about is how we're going to swing paying for it. The hard way, or the easy way."

"I don't get it, Chris. What the hell are you talking about?"

"I'm going to marry you, Steve Willis."

Steve looked annoyed and a little let down. "Well, thank God that mystery's solved. But Chris, I still don't understand what the hell Trey has to do with anything about it."

I sighed. For all the talks Steve and I had about ourselves and our future, we'd never discussed our finances. I had only the roughest estimate of what he earned each year, and I'd never discussed my financial resources with him. It was far easier to have sex with somebody than it was to talk about money. Now Steve and I had come to that point. If he wanted to build a house for us to share, it was only reasonable for me to be honest about my expectations for a house and a home.

"Steve, I guess it's time we talked about money. I need to talk to Trey because he handles all my money. He's an investment banker, for godsakes. I trust him to take care of my finances so I have something to live off of when I get old, or at least to the point I can't work anymore. I'm 10 years older than you are. I have to consider those things a lot sooner than you do."

Steve nodded. Very soberly he asked, "How much money are we talking about?"

I hesitated. Driving across Raleigh during rush hour was not how I intended to have this discussion, but there was no way to postpone it now. "You just saw the house we all used to live in, right?"

"Yes."

"Well, the house was my settlement from Zack. When it sold, I used some of the money to buy the beach house outright. That didn't even take half the money. The rest is in an annuity."

Steve whistled softly. "That much, huh?"

"Well, it's not really that much when you look at how long I could live. With the beach house mine free and clear, I not only have a place to live, I also have another investment for the future."

"So what you and Trey have to decide is whether or not to risk your future by investing in me. Nice, Chris. I really appreciate being broken down to numbers like that."

I gave him a sharp look and said, "Don't get pissy on me now, Steve. That's not the issue at all. I've already decided to invest my life in you. What I need to know from Trey is what's the best way to use the beach house now. We need to figure out how we're going to pay for a house we both want to live in and we both can afford. Do you see what I'm saying?"

"Well, you're acting like I'm not going to put anything into it. The land under the house is mine and like I said, it's easily worth a half million. I got a hundred and eighteen for the house when the insurance company totaled it. I can get the money for us on my own."

"That's not the issue Steve. The issue is, how hard do you want to have to work to pay off a mortgage? To build us a house we both want to live in is going to cost way over three hundred grand. If we mortgage two hundred grand of that for 30 years, the payment is still going to be anywhere from eighteen hundred to twenty-five hundred a month when you consider taxes and insurance. Alone, I don't make that much. I have no idea what you make a month, but if I back you out of the equation altogether, like if I had to make the house payment every month by myself, I wouldn't be able to afford to live in my own home. Do you understand?"

"You're giving me a headache," Steve said wearily.

"Tell me about it. Do you think I haven't been thinking about all this shit since you and I first talked about this? We aren't 18 and just starting out, Steve. This is big-boy stuff."

"There ain't no need to talk to me like I'm a kid, Chris. I understand all that. What you don't know is how much I have in the bank."

"No, I don't. That's not what's important. Keep what you have in the bank for the future. What if we could pay cash for the new house? That would be like saving money for the next 30 years."

"Chris, I have enough money in the bank to pay cash for whatever kind of house you want and still have plenty left over."

I looked at him dumbfounded.

"Um, Chris. You better keep your mind on your driving right now, okay?"

I looked back at the road just in time to keep from running over the Geo in front of me. I had to brake so hard that Steve instinctively reached for the dashboard to brace himself. Then he started laughing.

"You should see the look on your face," he said. "You thought you were dating some hard-luck po' boy, didn't you? All like, 'I have an *annuity;* I have to talk to my personal *investment* banker' and shit." Steve hooted and drummed on the dash in time with the music from the radio.

"Okay, fair enough," I said. "You got me. Now, I showed you

mine, you show me yours. Put your cards out where I can see them."

"How about I tell you what's in my hand and you keep your eyes on the road, big shot?"

"Stop fucking with me, Steve."

"Okay, listen up. I had both my parents' life insurance money to start with, and let me tell you something: My daddy believed in life insurance like my mama believed in Jesus. *I* believed in the stock market for a long time, until it started getting scary good. I was out of it and into nice, safe T-bills four months before 9/11. My house was paid for before I was born, and you can't say I exactly live an extravagant lifestyle. I get my fill of traveling and nice, big toy boats crewing in the Caribbean during the tournament season. I've never had a boyfriend that stuck around or cared anything about me, much less what I might be worth. So the question was and is, Do you want me to build us a house to live in on my little piece of Salter Path? If you do, then don't worry about your precious little ol' beach house. Keep it or sell it—I couldn't care less. I don't need your money. I need you."

I followed the flow of traffic, making my way to Trey's and Susan's without saying anything. Steve settled back in his seat on the passenger side and moved only to punch the buttons on the radio in search of songs he could tolerate.

Nearing my son's house, I pulled into an empty corner of the parking lot at North Hills Mall, rolled down our windows, and shut off the car. Steve lit a cigarette and looked at me with a smirk on his face that I wanted to both slap and kiss. I lit my own cigarette and watched him look around.

"What store does Trey and Susan live in?" he asked.

"God, you're impossible sometimes. Can you at least credit me for trying to be mature and responsible with money?"

Steve flicked ash out his window. "I've always credited you with that, Chris. That's one reason why I'm asking you to tie yourself up with me. You never gave me any reason to believe you were money-hungry. I asked you about that shit the first time we slept together, remember? You just accepted the me I showed you and loved me like I was."

"True," I said. "But, Steve, I was never about the money. Do you understand that? What you've just told me only saves me from having an annoying conversation with Trey. I'm about the love, Steve. I've proven to myself I can be okay without it. I hope you know you have me for life, now you've got me believing that's what you want."

"Oh hell yeah, Little Bit. I know it. I figured that out way ahead of you."

"Then why didn't you say anything?"

"I tried, but you had to talk yourself into it. There wasn't anything I could say that was good enough."

"Well, I'm convinced."

"Good. I'm glad we finally got all that bullshit out of the way. Now, when do we get started figuring out what kind of house we want?"

Christian Timothy Ronan received the trickle of water across his soft brow and into his dark hair with his blue eyes open and a smile on his face. He cooed and gently kicked at the center of attention in a circle of family around the baptismal font. When Father Andrew was finished with that part of the rite, he handed Little Chris back to his mother and father, who passed him to me. I never wanted to let him go again.

For all I cared, everyone else could have disappeared among the canapés and glasses of champagne back at Trey's and Susan's, where we went after Little Chris's christening. I wouldn't have noticed. Susan sat me in the sunroom they had added on to the back of their early '70s ranch house in North Hills, then gave me my first grandchild to hold and feed with a bottle.

"What, no breast feeding?" I asked.

"To hell with that." Susan placed a burp towel over my shoulder and smoothed it down. "I tried and gave it up. He latched onto me like a snapping turtle. By the time he was done I felt like a bush woman in *National Geographic*. He's got my milk, but I'm keeping my tits away from him, thank you very much."

Little Chris looked up at me and smiled around the bottle's nipple in his mouth. "Well, he's got my sense of humor, at least," I said.

"Thank God for that. His father's losing a little more of his every day."

"C'mon, Susan, is he becoming that much of a banker?"

Susan gave me a happy laugh. "I married him for his di...um, his *looks,* not his sense of humor. That hasn't suffered from seriousness, so I'm good."

"Susan, you're a trip. If you don't watch out, you're going to be telling me you're pregnant again before this one gets out of diapers."

"I might be, Chris. I want to get the breeding part over with. We're thinking about having three more. Gotta keep those Catholics coming. If I'm going to have that many, I want to be done with popping them out before I'm 35."

"Do you really want four kids?" I asked. "Three damn near killed me, and I didn't have to do the hard part."

Susan smiled. "Oh yeah. I came from a big house full of kids. It's what makes a house seem like home, you know?"

Just as she finished speaking, Alicia hesitantly made her way into the room. She looked stunning. "May I come in?" she asked.

Susan looked at me to answer. "Please," I said. "Come sit by me and this gorgeous little present Susan and Trey have given me."

Susan laughed. "I hope you still feel that way when I give you a call to pick him and his diaper bag up at the Greyhound bus station in Morehead City."

Alicia gave Susan a frankly astounded look before she sat in the chair next to me and the baby.

"It's okay, Alicia," Susan said. "Chris gets me."

"Yes, I do, you crazy heifer. Go have as much champagne as you can get away with. I'll look after your little passenger here." The baby looked at me and gave me another big smile.

Susan nodded and left me with Alicia. I gave her a shy smile.

"Thanks for seeing me, Chris. I won't keep you. I just wanted to say hello."

"We should have talked long before now, Alicia. I apologize for that. It's only just...well, it's only recently that Zack and I could be civil to one another. There wasn't any need to subject you to any spillover from that unpleasantness."

Alicia crossed her long legs elegantly and assumed a model's posture of earnest attention. I had to assume her apparent sincerity was genuine—I really didn't know the woman. "I imagine you must despise me," she said. "I apologize for that if you do. I'm really not such a cunt."

My arm was going to sleep. I looked for a pillow and saw one behind her. "Hon, could you take that pillow behind you and tuck it under my elbow. He's heavy and my arm is going all numb."

"Certainly," she said. Very gently, she did as I'd asked and then waited expectantly for my reply.

"Alicia, I never really despised you. I didn't two years ago and I don't now. Zack is who he is, and he was certainly attracted to women before he met me. I've come to believe what broke us apart was something that would have happened sooner or later. In any event, you're a lovely woman, and Zack seems very happy. The only thing I ask is that you take care of him. He can cause many bumps in the road, but he doesn't ride over other people's bumps easily. You know what I'm saying, right?"

"Yes, I do, Chris." She looked at me through impossibly long lashes and let a small, intriguing smile pass across her lips. "I've found he's been spoiled terribly."

I laughed as gently as I could, but I still managed to dislodge the baby's bottle. He gave me a puzzled look, grinned, and let out a loud burp. I put the bottle back to his lips and he sighed happily. "I am bad for spoiling my men. Or so I've been told. This one is going to be rotten when I get done with him."

Alicia looked toward the living room beyond the opposite end of the sunroom. "Congratulations on the new one," she said. "My God, he's a charmer."

"Alicia?"

She looked at me curiously.

"One time is enough. If you try to get between me and this one, it'll just be you, me, and my ice pick."

She looked at me with alarm, but when I smiled, she laughed nervously. When I joined her, her laughter became less perfunctory and more genuine.

"Zack told me not to underestimate you or your mouth," she said.

"Well, he knows me."

Alicia nodded. "Friends, then?"

"I'd give you a hug right now, but my arms are kinda full."

"Can I take a rain check on that hug?"

"That one and a lifetime more. I'm counting on you to look

after Zack from here on out. You and I both know he's high-main-
tenance."

"I do love him, Chris. Please know that."

"Then he's a lucky man. Not only are you model-gorgeous,
you're also a very intelligent, successful business woman. Zack has
a thing for intelligent lovers. With you, he got the *Jeopardy!* Daily
Double."

"From what I understand, you're no slouch in the brains
department either, and you're certainly a good-looking man."

"I'm not so smart, Alicia. I'm just a great reader and maybe that
makes me an interesting person to talk to. As for being nice looking, well, let's just say I own up to every one of my 49 years."

"Chris, the bisexual thing about Zack does concern me. Let's
just say I know he has an appreciation for *all* nice-looking things."

I noted a bit of anxiety in her eyes, and I gave her a knowing
smile. "Alicia, don't worry so much about that. Many men are sit-
uationally homosexual. I think Zack is. In retrospect, I think even
he would tell you hooking up with a gay guy who was starved for
a family and a home was the best thing he could have done for his
kids. There never would have been a need for me in his life if his
first wife hadn't died."

"I've never really thought of it that way. I thought it had more
to do with raw sexual attraction."

"I won't lie to you and say that it didn't at first. But Zack knew
what he was looking for over the long haul. I think he was bank-
ing on the old kind of gay stereotype...I know that some people
might see me that way. But I don't believe my life was—or is—all
camp and calculated irony. I just happen to be good at being a wife
and mom."

"I don't see you in any other way, Chris. My God, I couldn't
have done what you did."

"Thanks. I don't like being seen as some sort of cartoon Zack saw
me as, someone who happened to fit his need for a mother and housekeeper. It sounds cold to say it that bluntly, but we had a perfect neu-
rotic mesh for many years. Now he's moved on and so have I."

"Thanks for helping me understand that, Chris. Zack's tried
telling me the same thing, but it's so much more comforting coming
from you." She was quiet for a moment as we both watched Little

Chris begin to drowse. "Could we sometimes talk, if you know—"

"Absolutely, Alicia. Feel free to give me a call when he starts to drive you nuts. One thing you can count on me for is the unvarnished truth."

She gave me a smile and stood. "So I see. I appreciate that, Chris."

"Hon, I'm playing grandmom and holding court in here, it seems. Could you send Andrea in to see me?"

Alicia gave me another smile and nodded before getting her long lovely legs moving. I looked down at my grandson. He was done with his bottle and fussily moving his head. I put the empty bottle on the side table and lifted him to rest on my shoulder. I gently rubbed and patted his back. Before long I was rewarded with both a burp and a fart. I held him out and away and laughed to try to make him laugh. Instead, he yawned deeply. I switched the pillow Alicia had given me to my other side along with the baby. He was asleep before Andrea came in.

She was showing now—carrying high and all up-front. "It looks like another boy is on the way," I said as she lowered herself into the chair Alicia had vacated.

"Actually, Mom, it's one of each."

"Oh God, are you serious?"

"As serious as twins can get. Two heartbeats, two little heads, two complete sets of arms and legs, one nice package, and one tiny little twat."

"When were you planning to share this information? When you called me to tell me they'd arrived?"

"Oh no, Mom. You get to be right there in the delivery room so I can crush your hand for helping me keep those eggs backed up since I was 15. I told David to go buy a catcher's mitt because I intend to shoot 'em out and be done with the birthing business."

"Are you happy?" I asked.

Andrea sighed, then giggled. "Actually I'm delighted. I think David is a bit overwhelmed, but he'll get over it. He told me I never did anything half-assed. Why have just one when I can double up and get it over with?"

"So you two aren't planning on any more?"

"Well, let me put it to you this way: David better sleep in a cup, because if these two are healthy and happy, it's going to be *snip*

snip for his boys. Even if I have to do it myself."

"Susan wants three more," I said.

"Oh...my...God. Well good luck to her. I'm thinking ba-da-bing and ba-da-boom here are going to do it for me and David."

I laughed. My girl was at the top of her form.

"You laugh now," she said. "You better put a nursery into that new house you and Steve are planning on building."

"How do you know about that?" I asked cautiously.

"Steve and Trey are in there having an economic summit," Andrea said. "God, Chris. You sure know how to pick 'em. Please tell me Steve is bisexual like Dad. Then I can believe there's some hope for the women of the world."

"Don't even think it, bitch," I said.

"Oh come on," Andrea said sarcastically, "you're great at breaking them in—admit it."

"Yeah, right, then I get paid off and shooed away. I'd kill this one if he did that to me."

Andrea got a conspiratorial look in here eyes and said, "I saw you and Alicia having a little *tête-à-tête*. What was that all about?"

"Just making nice. It's a new-millennium baby—divorce doesn't mean war."

"Yeah," she said, "especially if you get a consolation prize like Steve."

The baby grumped a bit and stretched in my arms. He was surprisingly strong for such a tiny fellow. In a moment he was settled and sleeping again.

"Enough smarty-pants banter, young lady. What are you doing for Christmas besides being miserable?"

"You know I won't be able to travel then, Mom. It'll be way too close to my due date. The larger question is: What are *you* planning to do this year?"

"Right now, nothing. Steve is part of that whole Salter Path world. Relatives out the ying-yang. Would you mind terribly if I just stayed with him at the beach?"

Andrea yawned and stood carefully. "Actually, Chris, I think it's time we let our mom have his life back. If you don't want to visit one of us here in Raleigh, that's okay. Schooner's the only one you have to worry about."

"Why should I be worried about Schooner?"

"God, I'm tired all of a sudden." My supposedly empathetic daughter was guardedly oblivious to my efforts at changing the subject. "I'm ready to go home. But what did I want to tell you? Oh! I do want my Christmas ornaments this year. I plan to do the house up big-time."

"Andrea, you can certainly have your Christmas ornaments, but you didn't answer my question. Should I be worried about Schooner?"

Andrea bent carefully to give me a hug and a kiss on the top of my head. "I'll send your baby in here on my way out. He can speak for himself. My only comment is: Do you see Frank anywhere? Love you Mom!"

"I love you too, girl-baby."

"I'm serious, Chris. Don't think you get off the hook from being with me in the delivery room. I'm due sometime around the first week of January. Be ready when we call, okay? I really need you with me. Please?"

"Okay, sweetheart. I figured I wouldn't be able to get out of that. You know I'll come as quickly as I can. Just call me, okay?"

Andrea gave me a sweet smile and left.

I waited for Schooner, but he never appeared. I didn't worry about him too long. My grandbaby stirred and wanted to fret. I adjusted his position in my arms and cooed down into his tiny, beautiful face. It really felt like he was looking at me—like he knew me already. From deep in my memory came the song I'd sung to Schooner when he was still an infant. I didn't know any lullabies back then. I still don't. I just reached into the store of songs in the back of my head and in my heart and came up with the one that made Schooner smile when he was a baby. Softly I sang to little Chris, "*To love you, child, my whole life long / Be it right, or be it wrong...*" I was no Chaka Khan, and I didn't know all the words to "Sweet Thing," but I knew enough to growl most of the song in a Marlboro monotone. My grandbaby smiled and searched my face to imprint the odd song with my image in his tiny mind.

After I got through what I could remember of the song he fell back to sleep. I only knew tears were running down my cheeks when I found I had to whisper the last of it. I couldn't sing anymore.

I was such an odd adjunct to this small family of Ronans. But somehow, I'd become an integral part of a larger lineage. The tiny boy I held in my arms would soon have to decide what to call me; there was no genuine title to fill the bill. He'd learn why he was called Chris—a gentle reminder each time someone spoke his name that a man came along when his father was only five years old to love him and take a lost mother's place.

I was so tremendously grateful to have shared his daddy's life. Now, I'd share this little boy's life. I'd watch him through the wonder of his childhood and the gangly-ness of his adolescence and along his sure-footed strides into adulthood, if I was lucky to live long enough. It was a great gift to know another human being that way. It was a wonder to be able to hold this tiny life in my arms now. Now, he smelled sweet and lay secure in my arms. And he made me a grandparent, and I fell in love for life.

When I looked up to see Susan and Trey standing in front of me, they caught me with tears lining my face like guilty secrets.

Susan reached for our baby and I lifted him to give him back to his mama. The day would come when he'd run to me to claim presents and ply me with secrets. But for right now, he had to get back to her.

"Don't cry, Chris. Please...I can't stand it," Trey said softly.

"Oh, my son. You've given me the whole world back for the little bit of loving I gave you. I got to be the one to cry with happiness and joy. That's my job. That's what I do in this family. You ought to know that by now."

"I know it, but you *can't* cry, please." He stretched out his hands to me.

I took them and kissed them. "Thank you, baby, for not cutting me out now. Thank you so much."

Trey crowded next to me on the love seat where I sat and put his arm over my shoulders. "Stop it, Chris," he pleaded. "You'll make me cry and I'm not supposed to. Not anymore. I'm the oldest one, remember? I have to look after the little ones. Big boys don't cry, right?"

"I'm sorry, son. It's just that, sometimes, I don't feel like I deserve for y'all to love me so much. I just did my best, Trey. Oh, Jesus, I just tried to do my best."

"Hush, Chris." Trey tightened his grip on my shoulders and sobbed. "Oh fuck! I can't do this. I won't cry. Now be serious."

"I'm so proud of you, boy. Thank you so much for keeping me in your life."

"Mama...how could I..."

"I love you so much," I said.

"I love you, Chris, please don't leave us, please don't leave us alone."

"I'll never leave you, my baby."

"Not never, please. Oh, Christ, I'm so scared sometimes, I don't know if this is right."

"You don't ever have to worry. You're my big man."

"I need your help, Mama. Help me get it right, please."

Susan turned and stood between us and the folks who had heard me weeping and wandered in to witness what must have been a maudlin sight. With a look Susan sent them away while Trey and I just held each other and cried. Me from gratitude and joy. Him from the awesome responsibility he was taking on. Our tears, our bond—this is what it meant for two people to intertwine their lives and promise to help each other over the next day, and the next. This was family, this was love.

The next morning, I got up early and left Steve sleeping so I could make the dawn Mass. No one else planned on going at all on Sunday; the Vigil Mass and Christening had been enough for them the night before. Sometimes, if you believe, there are no words for what compels you out of a warm bed and into the winter's chill to make your way to worship. It's just something you do. It's part of who you are. It was part of who I was that morning.

The church was nearly empty, so I was surprised when Schooner appeared at my pew, genuflected, and crossed himself quickly before sliding in next to me with a smile. We didn't talk until after the Mass was over and the priest and his attendants had made their way down the aisle past us. Once they were out the front door, Schooner and I genuflected and followed them out into the cold.

After shaking the priest's hand, I waited until we were on the way to the parking lot to give Schooner a quick hug. "Hey baby.

I'm happy to see you, but what are you doing here?"

Schooner gave me a half-wattage version of his normal grin. "I wanted to spend some time alone with you before I had to head back down home. I stayed with Andrea and David last night. I didn't want to interrupt you and Trey—it was something I couldn't get into, or I'd have started crying too."

"Why is that, baby?"

"It just made me realize how much I need you too right now."

"Why? What's up with my baby?"

"Aw, man...it's no big deal. Anyways, when I got to Trey and Susan's this morning, you were pulling out of the drive so I just followed you here. I guess I came on in for the good of my soul. Sheesh, Mass twice in 24 hours. My drive back should be blessed for sure."

I found his hand and squeezed it. "I haven't seen much of you since we got here. I've missed you."

"I've missed you too. The thing is—I've got to take off. I was wondering if I could come home for Thanksgiving?"

"Of course. What about Frank?"

"Um...I think Frank will be with his family."

"You *think*? What's going on, Schooner? Talk to me."

"Aw, Mom. It's cold out here, and I gotta dash."

"Get in the car, Schooner."

He gave me a disgusted look, but he climbed into the Expedition's passenger seat. "Look, Mom, I know you're going to drill me until I give it up, so I'm just going to spit it out. Frank and I are thinking of splitting up."

"No hell, you aren't," I told him firmly. "What was that piece of paper you got in Massachusetts all about?"

"That was probably a mistake," he said, and looked out his window away from me.

I sighed. "Schooner, if you don't have much time, you better give me the worst of it. Is one of you running around?"

"No, I'm not. And I don't think Frank is either. He's home all the damn time."

"Are you homesick?" I asked.

Schooner ducked his head and shrugged.

"Not good enough, Schooner."

"Well, I don't know if I'm homesick as much as I miss being…being…well, not having so many expectations on me all the time."

"What kind of expectations?"

"It's all the time like, 'Schooner, the light bill's due! Schooner, I'm not your *maid. Scho-o-oner,* if you drink all the milk, buy more.' It's just all that bullshit, all the goddamn time. I'm sick of it."

I pulled a pack of cigarettes out of my coat pocket and lit one.

"Can I have one of yours? I'm kinda broke," he said.

I tossed him the pack and then my lighter. I waited until he got one lit before I shook my head and gave him a long look. "Schooner, you're a spoiled brat."

"Oh yeah, I get that all the time too," he said.

I laughed—I couldn't help it. "No, baby. *I'm* saying it. You are a spoiled brat. That's my fault. I have spoiled you rotten because I've always loved you to damn death. Did you think Frank was going to just pick up where I left off and treat you like his baby? Frank wants a man, not a little boy."

Schooner's eyes got wide and he shook his head. "Damn, Mom. That's cold."

"No it's not. It's the truth. Well, you can get mad at me if you want and you can call me a bitch and everything else, but I want you to hear what I'm saying. You made the decision to marry Frank and you're going to stick with your obligation because that's how I raised you. If you don't spend the drive home thinking how Frank might be right sometimes, you're a fool. Frank's a great guy and if he's gotten that frustrated with you, it's probably because you gave him a good reason to be—"

"Wait, Mom. Hold up—"

"No! You hold up and listen to what I'm saying. If you don't take the next two weeks and spend some time thinking how to make your marriage work, don't come home. I'm telling you this for your own good and it hurts me to say it. God, you don't know how it hurts, but you can't come home to me ever again. We did that already. You're a grown man, with a grown man's responsibilities. If you can't handle it, go sell it to someone else. I ain't buying."

Schooner opened his car door and gave me a hard look back. "If that's the way you want it."

"No, Schooner, that's not how I want it. What I want is to see the man I love most in the world walk into my house with his partner and share my life as an adult. I don't have any more little boys—"

"Well, you sure had one in your arms last night, o-o-ohing and a-a-ahing over that baby like he was the last one on earth."

"Hey now—" I suddenly realized I'd walked into a minefield.

"What are you doing singing that kid *my* song? I went in to talk to you and I hear you growling 'Sweet Thing' to that kid. You should really quit smoking. You sounded like Chaka Khan on crack."

"I can't believe what I'm hearing. Are you jealous of an infant? Oh for God's sake, Schooner, please."

Schooner tried to grin, but he was having a hard time of it. "I didn't mean for that to come out that way, I swear. But that is my song."

I started laughing.

"Oh Mom, come on, get over it already."

I stopped laughing and wiped my eyes. I took another drag off my cigarette and flicked what was left of it into the church's parking lot. "I love you best, you know that don't you?" I said.

Schooner thumped his cigarette out into the lot with mine. "Yeah, I know. I'm your baby."

"Uh-huh. That's right, and that's why you've always gotten away with murder."

"Okay, so what's your point?"

"Frank isn't me, Schooner. Help him out a little bit. Pay attention to what he doesn't say, just like you should to what he does say."

Schooner shifted in his seat and leaned toward me. "Being married is hard, Mom."

"Schooner, did you ever think it was going to be easy?"

"You made it look easy," he said as he leaned back and looked away.

"Oh hell no. Don't you put this on me. I just did the best I could. That's all I'm asking you...no, that's all *Frank's* asking you to do."

"Were you serious that I can't come home for Thanksgiving without Frank?"

"Oh *hell* yeah. Married people spend holidays together. That's the nice thing about it. You always have plans."

"He wants to spend it with his family," Schooner said gloomily.

"Does his family welcome you?"

"Yeah, they're great, super, really. But you won't be there."

"Bad answer, Schooner."

"You know, you really piss me off sometimes, Mom."

"That's good to hear," I said with a deadpan look on my face. "I wouldn't be doing my job right if I didn't."

Schooner got out of my car and stared up at the sky. It looked like snow—I'd noticed that myself. The road had to be on his mind; it was on mine. "Look, Mom. I really got to go. I don't want to leave all mad. Can I call you if I get really frustrated?"

"Of course, baby. I never said you couldn't call me."

"Okay. Maybe I will go to Frank's old house for Thanksgiving. But it looks like Christmas is going to have to be in Charleston. We both have to work the day after."

"Maybe you two can come and get my tree up one weekend. We had a good time last year didn't we?"

"Would Steve care?"

"Steve and I have this deal, see. He doesn't bitch about my family and I don't bitch about his, and let me tell you: He's related to half of Carteret County."

"Can I take back my share of the ornaments?"

"Yes. You need them for your and Frank's first tree. That's how you do marriage, you keep finding ways to knit yourselves together."

"Knitting ourselves together has never been a problem, Mom," he said with a lewd grin.

"So I've heard for myself," I replied coolly.

Schooner snickered. "I gotta go. I love you."

"I love you too. Do you need some money for gas and cigarettes?"

"Well, some cigarette money would really be sweet."

I dug into my pocket and pulled out two 20s and handed them to him. "I don't want you on the road with no money."

Schooner grinned and stuffed the 20s in his jeans pocket.

"Schooner, where's your coat?" I asked, as I realized he only had on a flannel shirt against the icy breeze.

"There's nothing wrong with the truck's heater, Mom. What am I going to do, get pneumonia crossing the parking lot?"

I wanted to touch him, to hug him, but instead I just watched him walk across the parking lot and get into his truck. I watched him wave and drive out of sight before I switched on the Expedition, lit a cigarette, and headed back to Susan's and Trey's. A few snowflakes tumbled from the sky, and I was ready to get on back home.

From the bench at the end of the dock, it looked like the old house had never been there at all. Where its squat white frame had been, there was a tidy two-foot-high mound of dirt that stretched 50 feet wide along the sound and a hundred feet inland. By Steve's calculation, that was enough fill to keep the vehicles above of the high water in a storm the size of Joan. The house would rise on pilings above that. The old deck was where it had always been. For the moment, it ended blindly, waiting for steps that would hook it up to the house that would rise behind it.

"So, what you want is a great room that is all windows on three sides, like the old back porch was, right?"

"Right, Steve, just like the sketch plan shows. The only thing that'll separate the kitchen part from the great room is that long island, which means I can look over the great room and straight out to the sound, no matter where I am in the back of the house."

"And the upstairs porch is off our bedroom on the second floor. Right?"

"Yes."

"Well, where are the guests going to sit and watch the water?"

"Either from the great room or the deck. If they're lucky, we'll let them come outside and sit on our porch, but it's not like they don't have other places to sit."

"Well, you're the boss, but it seems kind of selfish to keep the upstairs porch just for ourselves."

"Steve, how many guests do you intend on having here at any given time? There's two guest rooms behind the kitchen and two upstairs. There's plenty of room for that many people on the deck."

"That ain't the point. Maybe I should ask you how many bookcases you intend to put on how many walls?"

"Books don't need a view, Steve."

Steve threw his head back and laughed. "So I guess the only place I get any real say is in my shop and storeroom under the house."

"No. You can't say that. I let you pick out all that British Classics crap from Ethan Allen for the bedroom and put a Jello television in there."

"Plasma screen TV, not Jello."

"Well, you know what I mean, anyway."

"Okay, okay. I surrender. We're on budget. The contractor says we'll be in by next fall. I'm happy."

"Are you really?"

"Yeah, I kinda am, actually. I'm not in love with the cedar shake siding, but I'll get over it."

"So we'll do the shiplap. I like either one." I flicked my cigarette into the water and tucked my hands into the pouch of my hoodie.

"I'm getting kinda cold out here, are you ready to head back to your little old house?"

"Yeah. Let's go," I said.

Steve whistled for the dogs, and they all jumped from the Lina G onto the dock, and we all strolled back toward land.

"Steve, do you know what I was doing a year ago tonight?"

"Naw. What were you up to?"

"I was packing the last of my stuff out of the house in Oakwood to move here. As of about 10:30 tonight, I've lived here for a year."

"Well, you know what we should do to celebrate your anniversary?"

"I got a good idea from that look in your eyes."

"You're looking a little too high up."

"So, you're planning on doing a little pile driving early huh?"

"I'm being serious," Steve said, trying hard to look serious.

"So am I," I said and grinned happily.

"Look in my hand, Chris, not between my legs. Damn, you got a one-track mind."

I looked in his hand and saw a largish black velvet box. Steve grinned and opened it. Inside were two wide gold bands, one larger than the other.

"Steve?" The man never ceased to surprise me.

"Well, you're on all the papers, I thought we should at least have the rings." He looked out over the water toward the sun, beginning its final blaze of orange in the clear, cold evening as it slipped into the sound. "Take the big one—easy...I don't want to have you drop it between the boards. It's too cold for me to have to go diving in to get it."

I took out the larger of the two gold bands. Steve took the smaller one, closed the box, and slipped it back into the pouch of his hoodie.

"Do you think we can manage doing this at the same time?" he asked.

I nodded and splayed out the fingers of my left hand. Steve stepped closer to me and did the same.

"Now, on the count of three, okay?" he said.

"Okay. One...two...three..."

The rings slid on with a snug certainty that defied any dissent.

"I love you, Chris Thayer."

"I love you, Steve Willis."

"Do you promise to keep on loving me like you do?"

"Yeah, more than that. Do you?"

"Yeah, more, too. More than you love me."

"Do you suppose we can risk a kiss?" I asked.

"Do you need one to seal the deal, Chris?"

"No. How about we shake hands for now and leave the kisses for when we can make them last for hours?"

"Deal." Steve took my right hand and held it firmly.

"Deal," I said and shook on it. Letting go of his hand, I crossed myself quickly over my heart. I was both surprised and very happy to see Steve do the same.

We started walking down the pier toward where the house would stand with the dogs running ahead of us.

"Chris?"

"Yeah?"

"About this church deal. I've decided I'll go with you during Advent, but I'm not making any promises after that, understand?"

"Steve, if you think I'm going to start bitching at you to go to church, I'm not. It means a lot to me, but it has to mean something to you. Otherwise it's just a waste of your Sunday mornings."

"Well, I want to go all during Christmas. After that, we'll see."

"Okay, cool."

"Do you feel married, Chris?"

"I have for a while, Steve. I think since you gave me your mama's baht chain."

"Well, I wanted to do it up right. That's why the rings. Is that good enough for you?"

We stepped up onto the solid dirt pad that would raise the house above storm waters. I stopped and looked back over the sound and watched as the sun surrendered the sky and sank below the horizon. Steve gave me a smile. The rings were wonderful, but I knew sharing sunsets like this one was the real stuff of living. I said, "It's more than enough, Steve. It's not about the rings—it's about living it. It's about getting up in the morning and going to bed at night, next to you, for all the years ahead. The rings are just a reminder of that promise."

"Well, all that's fine, but I've not ever been married before. I wanted rings."

"The rings are perfect."

"Little Bit, does it always feel this good?"

"Big Man, this is exactly how I intend to make it feel for the rest of your life."

CHAPTER NINE,
EPIPHANY

✥

The office had been too busy all day for me to do any transcription. Finally, I just gave up. The phones had rung off the hook, and the stream of old and new clients arrived every 10 or 15 minutes. I handed Dr. Tony his last file as Cathy scooted past him on her way in with Carlos in her arms and Sierra skipping along behind her.

"Shouldn't you be getting out of here, Chris?" Cathy asked. Sierra ran to me and climbed into my lap.

"Mommy said you had something for me. Did you know today is the day the wise men found the baby Jesus?"

I nodded to Sierra and said to Cathy, "I'll leave as soon as I give Carlos and Sierra their Three Kings Day presents."

Cathy shook her head. "You're terrible." Then she laughed. "Can I open the one you got for Carlos?"

Sierra had already slid off my lap and was timidly poking around in my knapsack. Expertly she lifted the two wrapped presents out and marched with them back to me. "Is the big one mine? Carlos is too small for the big one."

"Yes, sweetheart," I said. "The big present is for you. Can you guess what it is?

Sierra gave me a wide, happy smile. "A book." Then she looked at her mother.

"You can open it now," Cathy said.

Sierra eagerly tore the wrapping from a large illustrated storybook and held it up for her mother to see.

Cathy squinted to read the title from across the room. "*Five-Minute Bedtime Stories*. Chris, I feel like that's more of a gift for me. Thanks. Sierra?"

The little girl tugged on my arm, and I leaned down for a kiss. "Take your mommy the present for Carlos, okay?" I said.

Proud to have a mission, the child carried the smaller box across the room and handed it to her mother. Cathy switched the 4-month-old little boy to her other hip and tore at the gift wrap as expectantly as her daughter had. "*Baby Einstein*! Look Sierra, a new video! Chris..." she said conspiratorially, "I wish I could still g-e-t...h-i-g-h. These videos are perfect adult viewing if you're s-t-o-n-e-d."

I laughed. "Don't you just hate being the grown-up?"

"What does *stoned* mean Chris?" Sierra asked.

Cathy and I exchanged guilty glances. "No," she said. "What I hate is when you can't spell around them any more. I don't think I'll get to have another adult conversation until I'm 60."

"Oh, sweetheart, wait until they start speaking in code around you. It begins at about 12 and doesn't ever really stop after that." I picked up the shreds of wrapping from Sierra's gift and tossed them in the wastebasket. "Well, I guess I better scoot. It's going to be a long night."

"Is Steve going with you?" Cathy asked.

"Oh yeah. All of a sudden I'm senile and shouldn't be driving alone after dark."

"Is Andrea all right?"

I slipped on my jeans jacket and took my knapsack from Sierra, who had already fetched it for me from under my transcription desk. "Yes. She called again about a half hour ago to hurry me up. Evidently, she's putting off going to the hospital until she knows I've left the beach."

"Do you think she'll be able to hold out that long?"

"Oh yeah. Her water broke only about noon. She imagines they'll just be out of the chute and already walking within a few hours. The truth is, David says they're so big, the doctor will probably end up doing a C-section."

"Well, travel safely. I'll say a little prayer for Andrea and the twins."

"Don't forget one for me. That heifer is going to make me suffer right along with her."

Cathy gave me a smile and held up one of Carlos's arms to wave bye-bye. "Don't worry about rushing back. Take as long as you need," she said.

I thanked her and was heading out the door when Sierra called for me to wait. Cathy held the waiting room door open for her as she ran out carrying the book-size box that had arrived for me with the UPS man that day. "Don't forget *your* Three Kings Day gift. Will you tell me what it is when you open it?"

"That I will," I said. "Take care of your mommy and Carlos for me until I get back, okay?"

In the car on the way home, I didn't give the box much thought. I had too much of a list in my head to run down before Steve and I left for Raleigh. Steve told me he would take the dogs to Heath's to board, so that was one thing out of the way. But I still needed to call Father Fintan to let him know I wouldn't be at Adoration. I had clothes to pack—I knew better than to let Steve handle that. If he did the packing we'd be wearing the same thing for three days with only a change of underwear. If we took the bridge at the other end of the island, we could gas up the Expedition in Swansboro. That was still an item on the list to be checked off later.

Back at the house, I almost left the package in the car. My curiosity finally caught up with me, and I stopped halfway up the stairs to the deck and went back down to get it. After I let myself in the house, I left it on the dining room table and got busy with the packing. Finally, with everything packed—down to toothbrushes and vitamins—I hauled the suitcase back into the family room and left it by the French doors out onto the deck. I picked up the package and looked at the label. It wasn't anything I was expecting—I already had all my traditional Epiphany cards from the kids. Not one of them had forgotten to mail them.

Schooner's card had come first. For once, his message to the baby Jesus wasn't flippant. Neither was Trey's or Andrea's. Their faith had ripened as they moved into adulthood. I was impressed with the sincerity of their efforts, but I also missed the humor and childishness I'd read in those cards for so many years. But my babies were making babies and living lives that spun them in orbits farther from me. Life moved on. We all moved on.

I walked into my kitchen to rummage around in my junk drawer to find a razor to open the surprise package. After Steve and I had spent a couple of hours scraping the spray-painted FAGOT off my French doors, that's where I'd tossed the blades that were left. I rummaged through pieces of twine, owner's guides, paper clips, pens and pencils, corks, and abandoned pairs of reading glasses. I found a razor blade.

Deciding I could risk a drink, I put some ice in a glass and poured some Jim Beam over it. Steve would insist on driving to Raleigh. And to face Andrea's imminent births, I'd want a drink but I wouldn't be able to have one. I took a sip of my bourbon and looked out over the great room of my house.

The place I'd moved into brand-new now smelled like wet dogs and Steve. So soon it bore the scuffs and scrubbings of life and living. Compared to how I thought I'd keep it, the house looked like hell. But it was really beautiful because it looked like *home* with all its details knocked slightly askew and filmed over with the dust that sometimes settles on a life lived with the doors wide open.

With my drink in one hand, and the razor in the other, I settled at the dining room table and opened my box. Inside the spill of packing peanuts and bubble wrap was a card addressed to me in Trey's hand. I sat the card aside and unwrapped the bubble wrap from what felt like a slender, heavy book. With the bubble wrap out of the way and resting on the floor, I held a small, heavy set of boards. The top set was split down the middle from a high pointed crown, hinged on the sides, and closed with a small brass clasp. The edges were trimmed in molding bright with gilding. The two leaves of the boards joined at the seams under the clasp to form a gilt Orthodox cross on a field of mahogany-stained wood.

I carefully laid the treasure on the table and placed the box it came in out of the way on the floor beside me. I pushed open the small clasp and opened the two leaves from the center. Opened, they lay flat to reveal a beautiful icon of the Blessed Mother, who was holding the Christ child as a toddler before her. In his hands, he grasped a ball painted to look like the earth. Over their heads a naked putto held a banner with Cyrillic writing on it. On the panels flanking the image, two pairs of archangels turned toward the mother and child, but one angel looked away while the others faced the viewer with smiles. Around them was all gilt and enameled blue.

It was both enchanting and haunting. There was something about the images that seemed familiar, but also somehow not right, not what I'd expect in an icon. The faces seemed too contemporary, too...

I recognized Schooner first. He was the angel on the lower left side, grinning mischievously. Trey was above him, painfully serious. Across from them was a youthful picture of Zack—taken perhaps 20 years before—looking over his shoulder with a selfsatisfied grin. Below him was Andrea offering the shy smile she always gave to the camera. The putto was circumcised and looked to be baby Chris, beaming with an infant's happy smile.

Then I recognized the face under the Madonna's blue mantle and the pose of the infant before her and gasped.

I took a largish sip of my drink and closed my eyes. I remembered the picture. Trey had asked about it when we packed up the house after Thanksgiving. It had hung, along with so many other family photos, along the upstairs hall in the old house. I was only 27 when it was taken. Schooner couldn't have been more than a year old. As I recalled, the photo had been taken on the beach not far from where I was sitting at that very moment. I'd encouraged Schooner to take the ball away from his mouth, and just as Zack had taken the picture, he'd held the ball out for his father to see.

I opened my eyes and looked at the icon again. The audacity of the imagery shook me to my conservative Catholic core. And the love it bespoke broke my heart. There was no denying the thing was beautiful, but I seriously wondered if I could ever look at it as an object of prayer and a source of blessings.

I reached for the envelope that bore Trey's handwriting and opened it carefully. The front of the heavy card was embossed with an Orthodox cross. I knew Trey must have given a lot of thought to the words he would write on such a formal and expensive card.

Dear Chris (Mom),
If I know you, you are just getting over the shock of this skladen—that's what the Russians call this kind of icon. The icon painter is a recent immigrant from the Ukraine. He told me many people had their own faces and their loved ones painted as the characters in their icons. It is not sacrilegious; it is an honor. We hope you will take it as a message of love and esteem from all of your family

(we all chipped in—even Schooner). The Slavonic on the
banner reads: "One law I give you, Love one another."
You are that love for us. It has been blessed by both the
local Orthodox patriarch and our own Father Andrew.
God bless you on the Feast of Epiphany.
Your son, Trey

I folded the card carefully and slipped it back into its envelope to hold and treasure. I looked at the icon—the *skladen*—again. The gilt glowed warmly against the bright enameled cerulean of the sky and the Madonna's paler blue mantle. I looked at my own young face looking back at me and I closed my eyes.

When I thought of the Blessed Mother, as I said the rosary, or muttered a quick prayer, I didn't immediately picture her statue or her image on a stained glass window or a painting by Giotto, or Da Vinci. I saw my own mother's face first, before I strove to replace that image with one less personal, less secular, and more tradition-ally divine.

Still, I wondered—what was our first earthly understanding of the pure kind of love that the Madonna embodied? Wasn't it our mothers? Wasn't it their faces we turned to when we were too small, too hurt, or too overwhelmed by others' failures to bear us and heal us and carry us over?

When hurt and damaged in a thousand ways by the horror of the world, soldiers mortally wounded in combat, the meanest thug, the merciless lawyer, the beat-hardened cop will call for his mama in fear and panic and hurt. That's who we look to heaven to see for the kind of comfort we can need to feel.

I searched the faces of my family painted as angels. I looked at the grave face of my sturdy little Schooner as he held the world in his outstretched hands. I saw my own gently smiling face looking at the baby I'd taken into my heart to love and bring to manhood. If they held that picture of me in their minds, I must have done something right. And I must have been blessed.

I looked at the *skladen* again and smiled. I stood and propped it up in the middle of the table, where I could see it as I went into the kitchen and opened my junk drawer. After some rooting around, I found a clear glass votive holder and the bag of votive candles I usually burned on holy days. Then I carried the votive back to the table and placed it before the icon, crossed myself, and lit it.

I said a Hail Mary for the soul of my mother, and a Hail Holy Queen for my daughter-in-law Susan and the Memorare for my daughter Andrea as she prepared to take her place in the world of mothers of all kinds. Then I said a Glory Be for the great mystery of the will of God. I said an Oh My Jesus for my presumption and failings great and small. My devotion done, I crossed myself and whispered thanks.

With everything in my house squared away, I went outside to stand under the cold blue sky to wait for Steve. For everything I was, I was back where I started. I needed to get to my hurting, scared child and do exactly what I was meant to do with my life.